Irish ... C...mel ... from Co. Wexf... ... liv... with ... nd their rescue ... ...rge ...ailey. Her b...k h...e captured the hearts of readers worldwide a...d have been described by the *Daily Mail* as 'beautifully written, emotionally intelligent and moving in the extreme.' Her recent novels include *A Thousand Roads Home*, *The Woman at 72 Derry Lane* and the official ITV novel *Cold Feet: The Lost Years*, based on the hit TV show, *Cold Feet*. Carmel was shortlisted for an Irish Book Award in 2016 & 2017 and won Kindle Book of the Year and Romantic eBook of the Year in 2013.

Carmel is a regular panellist on Virgin Media's *Elaine* and is also a co-founder of *The Inspiration Project*, a coaching and writing retreat. Carmel's warmth and infectious humour make her a popular speaker at festivals, schools and libraries. She has given talks and been interviewed on TV and radio in Ireland, the UK and USA.

f www.facebook.com/happymrsh/
🐦 📷 @HappyMrsH
www.carmelharrington.com

Praise for Carmel Harrington:

'Warm, moving and life-affirming . . . Greta is a gorg...us character that you will fall ...

'Beautifully written, emotio... the extreme'

'Heartwarming humour, wit... ...ghter & friendship. Immensely enjoyable'   *Irish Times*

Also by Carmel Harrington

MY PEAR-SHAPED LIFE

CARMEL HARRINGTON

HarperCollins*Publishers*

HarperCollins*Publishers* Ltd
1 London Bridge Street,
London SE1 9GF

www.harpercollins.co.uk

HarperCollins*Publishers*
1st Floor, Watermarque Building, Ringsend Road
Dublin 4, Ireland

First published by HarperCollins*Publishers* 2020

This paperback edition 2021

3

ISBN: 978-0-00-827665-2

Set in Sabon LT Std by Palimpsest Book Production Limited,
Falkirk, Stirlingshire

Printed and bound in the UK by
CPI Group (UK) Ltd, Croydon CR0 4YY

MIX
Paper from
responsible sources
FSC™ C007454

For Evelyn Harrington, Adrienne Harrington, Evelyn Moher and Leah Harrington. When I married Roger we became family. But I'm so very grateful that we also became friends.

I am convinced that the only people worthy of consideration in this world are the unusual ones. For the common folks are like the leaves of a tree, and live and die unnoticed.

The Wonderful Wizard of Oz, L. Frank Baum

It isn't what we are, but what folks think we are,
that counts in this world.

The Road to Oz, L. Frank Baum

Part One

Chapter 1

Greta walked into the kitchen rubbing her eyes. She smiled her thanks to her mam, Emily, who placed a mug of dark brown tea in front of her. The Gales all drank their tea the same way – brewed or, as some might say, stewed.

'Sleep OK?' Emily asked.

'Like a baby,' Greta replied.

'You didn't take any more of those sleeping pills, did you?' Emily's forehead wrinkled in a frown.

'Give over, Mam. I only take the odd one when my insomnia gets out of hand. I keep telling you that,' Greta said. Her mother worried way too much. Greta had taken one the previous evening, as it happened, but there was no point worrying her mam admitting that. When it came to her parents, some things were better on a 'need to know' basis.

Greta opened her phone and flicked through Instagram. 'Oh Mam look—' Greta began, but was silenced with a shush and a wave at the TV screen. Eamonn Holmes, one of the anchors of her mam's favourite TV show *This Morning* was speaking. Emily always denied that she had a crush on him, but when he spoke her face softened, and she hung on his every word.

Only when Eamonn had finished talking did Emily answer, 'What's that love?'

Greta pointed to a photograph of Dr Greta Gale, her famous namesake.

In the photo, Dr Gale was sitting on a red-brick wall, with the backdrop of a green ocean behind her, smiling to the camera. 'Doesn't she look beautiful?'

'How does she get her hair to look like that?' Emily asked, smoothing down her own shoulder-length bob. 'Maybe I should grow mine out a bit.'

'She probably has a glam squad at her disposal twenty-four/seven,' Greta replied. 'What do you think she means by being the same personally as well as privately and publicly?'

Drgretagale Be the same person privately, publicly and – most importantly – personally. Can I get a hell yeah? #inspirationalquotes #drgretagale #inspire #mindfulness #strong #whatsinyourcupboard

---

Emily put her glasses on to read the post beneath the photograph. 'I don't know. Half the stuff she posts is a load of mumbo jumbo if you ask me.'

'Mam!' Greta loved Dr Gale and wouldn't have a word said against her. And that wasn't just because they shared the same name – although that was part of it. It was more because Dr Gale epitomized everything that Greta wished she could be herself. Dr Gale was successful, beautiful and loved. She was living her best life. She represented hope for Greta. Maybe one day she too could have everything that Dr Gale had. There wasn't a single Instagram post that Greta had not read. And with each new double tap of love, she felt her connection to her grow stronger.

Greta would lie in bed, late at night, knowing she should be at least making an attempt to sleep, but somehow unable to take her eyes off Dr Gale's Instafeed. She would lose hours googling books, food, art and restaurants that Dr Gale tagged in a photo. She followed accounts that Dr Gale followed. Last year she bought a green kaftan similar to the one that Dr Gale wore to a beach party, but that had not ended well. On Dr Gale the kaftan looked very boho chic. On Greta it looked as if she'd eaten all the pies.

More than how Dr Gale looked, lately her Instagram posts felt as if they were speaking directly to Greta. Every word seemed like a secret message just for her, as if Dr Gale had looked into Greta's mind and knew exactly what to say to help her, support her, advise her.

While her mam's back was turned, Greta picked up the remote control and hit the Netflix button, pressing play on the one-hour Dr Greta Gale Special, 'What's In Your Cupboard?'

'Not again,' Emily groaned.

'What?' Greta feigned innocence. 'You like her as much as me. And I love this bit. Look at that strut.'

9

They both watched Dr Gale sashaying onto a stage, the spotlight following her as she walked. 'Hello y'all.'

'Hello y'all,' Greta and Emily called back to the screen in their best copycat US accent.

'When I grew up in Kansas, on a little old bitty farm, I could never have dreamed that one day I'd be standing here in front of y'all. A *New York Times* bestseller, translated into thirty-three languages – so far – with my own TV special. I'm not sharing that to brag, but to illustrate how life is full of surprises. You never know what is around your corner for you. Am I right? Can I get a hell yeah!'

'Hell yeah!' Greta and Emily called back.

'I'd love to know where she got that dress. I've got your second cousin Breda's confirmation coming up in April. I'd take the sight out of their eyes if I walked into the church in that.'

'It's Diane von Fürstenberg. $1,800. Sorry, Mam. But guess what? Dr Greta has announced her first-ever live one-day seminar in Las Vegas. Wouldn't it be something else to go and see her there?' She felt a frisson of excitement at the very thought.

Emily muttered something about notions and outrageous airfares under her breath then went back to making a pot of porridge. A loud bang from upstairs ricocheted down the stairs into the kitchen. Emily and Greta raised their eyes upwards. The boys were up.

'Wait till I get hold of those . . . those two bowsies!' Emily said. Bowsie was Emily's favourite slang for her two sons whenever they were being unruly.

Greta slipped into actress mode and raised a perfectly

arched eyebrow in question, a move she had been practising for weeks. She had a big audition later today in
London and she planned to end her prepared monologue
with this facial expression. Emily sighed as only a mother
who had the full weight of her irresponsible boys on her
shoulders could. She pointed to the grill. 'It was left on
all night. We could have burned to a crisp, the whole
house up like a light.' She blessed herself quickly, muttering
thanks to St Anthony, her saint of choice for keeping them
safe.

Greta felt a shiver of *something* ripple through her.
Staring at the grill, she imagined flames bursting from its
dark cave, filling the kitchen, sneaking up the stairs to
the sleeping family.

'Did they wake you up with all their drunken shenanigans last night?' Emily asked.

'No. I slept like a log,' Greta replied, focusing on her
phone.

'Ah, good girl,' Emily said. 'Did you . . .'

Her question hung unasked because Aidan and Ciaran
bounced into the room, seconds apart. Greta marvelled
that she was related to them at all. She never bounced
anywhere. Unless you counted every evening when she
took her bra off . . .

Greta had been nine years old when Aidan had been
born, with Ciaran following on a mere ten months later.
Irish twins, as the saying went. She loved them and the
feeling was mutual. They would sit in their high chairs,
captivated by their big sister who sang and danced for
them both, making them squeal with delight.

'I'm starving, Mam!' Aidan said, throwing an arm

around his mother's shoulder. 'Any chance of a bacon sandwich?'

'Same. Make that two!' Ciaran said, pouring two mugs of tea.

'Sit down,' Emily said to them, smiling. 'I've already made your breakfast. The full Irish.'

'You da best,' Aidan said, a loud rumble escaping his stomach. 'Big G in da house.'

He took a seat opposite Greta at the table and saluted her. Aidan had given her the nickname 'G' when he was a toddler and couldn't get his tongue around Greta. And as is often the way with childhood nicknames, the name somehow stuck. Ciaran amended it to Big G a few years later. He said it made her sound like a rapper. That used to make Greta laugh. She would put a baseball cap on sideways, throw on a load of her mam's costume jewellery and do a mean Jay-Z impression. It always ended with all three of them collapsed into a big pile of giggling.

Big G in da house.

With the emphasis on the word big.

They watched Emily as she opened the grill and loaded two plates with an imaginary fry. Ciaran whispered to Greta, 'Is Mam all right?'

Greta looked away, unable to watch the drama about to unfold. Never mind the grill going on fire, her brothers were about to get roasted.

'There you go,' Emily said, as she placed an empty plate in front of Aidan, and then another in front of Ciaran. 'Enjoy that now.'

'But there's nothing there,' Ciaran said. 'Is there no fry then? What about a bacon sandwich?'

Emily sat down beside Greta. 'Sure how could I make you a sandwich when I've not got a single slice of bread left.'

'Ah Mam,' Aidan complained. 'You had me looking forward to a fry.'

'Don't you be ah Mam-ing me! It's a wonder we're not all dead the way you left this place last night.'

'What are you talking about?' Aidan asked.

'I'll tell you what I'm talking about. I'm talking about the fact that I got up this morning to the smell of smoke. Black fecking smoke, coming from the kitchen. The grill was left on, all night. What have you to say for yourselves?'

'Don't be looking at me,' Ciaran said. 'I went straight to bed when I got in.'

'So did I,' Aidan replied. 'I never even came into the kitchen! I got a spice bag in the chipper on the way home.'

'A likely story. Do you think I came down in the last shower?' Emily said. 'The butter left open. And the bread gone. Do you think I'm made of money or something? That's the drink for you. You're drowning all your brain cells in Guinness, you can't even remember when you are up to devilment.'

'We don't remember 'cos we didn't do anything. Who says it was us, anyhow? What about Dad or Big G?' Aidan's face flushed red with indignation.

'Don't be pulling your sister into this; sure she was up in bed fast asleep while you two were out carousing. As for your father, you know he doesn't eat white bread – he'd as soon cut off his arm.'

On cue, they heard the key in the front door, and their

13

father, Stephen, walked in, red and sweating. He looked at his Apple Watch and clicked a few buttons, nodding in satisfaction at the result. 'That's thirty-eight point three kilometres done so far this month. And it's only a few days into February!'

'Well done love,' Emily said.

'Dad, did you leave the grill on before you went out for your run?' Aidan asked.

'Indeed I did not. I haven't had any bread in months, as well you know. Except for my porridge loaf that I make myself.' He patted his flat stomach as he spoke, a habit he'd formed at the same time his keep fit passion had ignited.

'Well if it wasn't Dad and it wasn't Ciaran or me, who does that leave?' Aidan said, glaring at Greta.

'Well, bring out the Bible then, Mam,' Greta remarked, hoping to lighten the mood, making Ciaran snigger. When they were kids, one of them drew all over the kitchen door in crayon. Aidan, Ciaran and Greta denied the crime, despite Emily's best efforts to uncover the culprit. So her interrogation progressed to threatening them all with the wooden spoon – which failed – and escalated to the family Bible. Each of them was made to swear on their innocence, the threat of eternal damnation laid out before them. The Bible won and Ciaran sang like a canary. Now 'Bring out the Bible' was a tried-and-tested Gale catchphrase that was part of their family's folklore.

'Maybe I should,' Emily said, but the corners of her mouth began to twitch too and soon she was smiling herself.

Greta sloped out of the room, happy that she'd managed

to diffuse the tension as always. She hated seeing her family at odds with each other. Always had. Which was why it was Big G's role to make everyone laugh. The family joker, her Uncle Ray often said. But sometimes she wondered if they were laughing with her . . . or at her?

It was time she got ready for her trip to London anyhow. Her audition later today was for a part in a new drama series. It could be life changing for her. Ever since she had starred in a Christmas ad when she was little, she knew the bright lights of stardom beckoned for her. She showered and dressed, then packed her overnight bag, making sure she had everything. Actors' portfolio, make-up bag, deodorant, her tablets. Check! Satisfied that all was in order, she made her way to the kitchen to say goodbye to her folks. Aidan passed her on the stairs, but as he did, he gave her shoulder a hard shove.

'Hey! Watch it. What did I do?' she asked to his retreating back. That had been deliberate and it hurt.

His response was to glower at her and mutter something under his breath, before slamming the door to his bedroom.

'Charming!' she shouted after him.

Both her parents were eating porridge and drinking more tea when she went back into the kitchen. 'Want some, G?' Emily asked, pointing to the pot behind her.

Greta shook her head. 'I'll grab something to eat in the airport.'

'I've had a bowl of porridge every morning since I was a toddler,' Stephen said. He patted his nonexistent stomach again and continued, 'No cholesterol and my digestion is in prime condition. If you want my advice, G, you could do a lot worse than following the lead of your mother and me on this matter.'

'Sure, Dad. I'll get some later,' Greta replied. 'I need to get going, though. I don't want to be late for Uncle Ray, especially when he's kind enough to give me a lift.'

'I offered to take you to the airport,' Stephen said, a slight edge to his voice.

'I know you did. I appreciate it.'

'Sometimes I think you prefer him to me,' Stephen griped. And although Greta made the appropriate denial noises, there was an element of truth in his words.

Greta had a special bond with her Uncle Ray, her dad's brother, which she supposed was inevitable considering how he'd had to become a makeshift midwife to deliver her. Emily went into labour early at home. Stephen was on nights, so Ray was called to bring her to the hospital. They never made it there in the end. Ray had delivered Greta on the sitting-room floor, while they were waiting for the paramedics to arrive and he was trying not to pass out from the sight of blood. The story went that Greta had looked into Ray's eyes when she slipped into his hands and an unbreakable connection was made.

Emily looked up at the clock. 'You're way too early to go to the airport. Your flight isn't for hours. Tell you what, why don't you come with me to my slimming class? The ladies are such a nice bunch. They'd all love to meet you. And then I'll drop you to Ray's on the way back home.'

This suggestion was met with great enthusiasm from Stephen, who began to congratulate Emily on her ingenuity to think it up. Greta knew a set-up when she saw one.

'Maybe next time,' Greta said, knowing that hell would freeze over before she'd ever go to a slimming class with her mother. 'I need the extra time to practise my lines for the audition.'

Stephen exhaled a loud, disgruntled sigh of annoyance. Greta was used to this particular sound. In fact, if she had to equate one sound with her father when he was in her presence, it would be this one. 'When I was your age . . .' he began, which meant that another of his fun 'lose weight and keep fit' pep talks was about to start. Before another word flew out of his mouth, Greta ran out through the front door, shouting goodbyes over her shoulder.

As Greta pounded the footpath towards her Uncle Ray's house, pulling her cabin bag behind her, she fantasized about having enough money to move out. Her mam she could take, but her dad was relentless in his quest to make her thinner. She was exhausted from dodging his lectures. Greta slowed down at the end of their road, already out of breath, and took a seat on the edge of a garden wall. She pulled a bag of Maltesers from her handbag and threw a handful into her mouth. As the chocolate melted and the malty inside fizzed on her tongue, she sighed with contentment.

'Hey!' Greta squealed in shock when she felt something brush against her leg. She looked down, praying it wasn't a cat – she hated cats – and saw a dirty black scrappy dog staring up at her. The dog barked, then sat in front of her, eyes begging for a chocolate.

'No can do, little doggie. These are bad for you.' Then

Greta began to giggle as she realized what she was saying. 'I know, "pot kettle black" and all the rest. But I *need* these.' She threw another handful in her mouth. He nuzzled her ankle with his nose.

'I can't,' Greta said. 'Chocolate is bad for dogs, honestly.' She opened her bag and searched for something she could share with him. Bingo! She pulled out a half-eaten rice cake. 'It tastes like cardboard, just warning you.' The mutt didn't care and wolfed it down in one bite before he moved closer and gave her another nuzzle. Poor thing was hungry. Greta hadn't seen him before. Maybe the family who had moved into number 9 the previous month owned him.

'Go on home, boy,' she said. 'I've got to go now.' He ignored her and followed her as she turned the corner into Ray's road. Greta stopped once more and said firmly, 'You can't come with me, little man. You have to stay here. Go back to your owners.' He cocked his head to one side and she could have sworn she saw tears in his black eyes. She recognized something in that look. He was lost. Alone. Shrugging it off, she turned and walked away.

As Greta got close to her uncle's house, she spotted Ray wheeling in bins down neighbours' drives.

'What are you doing?' Greta shouted out.

'The bin man has been. And I'm not working today. So I thought I'd save some of the neighbours a job when they get home tonight. Nice to be nice. Speaking of which, you look lovely.'

She did a little curtsey, delighted with the compliment. She felt good in her new dress.

Greta told Ray about the dog she'd made friends with, worried that the little thing couldn't find his way home again, wherever that was.

'He could be a stray. Don't fret, I'll keep my eye open for him when I get back from the airport,' Ray said, kind as always.

And Greta felt herself relax, as she always did in his company.

'Why were you eating Maltesers for breakfast anyhow?' Ray asked when they had moved inside and gone into the kitchen. He was putting two slices of thick white bread into the toaster. He flicked the switch on the kettle, to make a pot of tea.

'Because dad wanted me to eat porridge.'

'Pushing that red button again,' Ray said, knowing his niece better than anyone. Greta had always been the same, ever since she had been a little girl. Tell her not to do something and you could be guaranteed she'd feel compelled to do that very thing.

'Guilty. But they make me so stressed sometimes. Mam was going on about her slimming class. You know what she's like when she starts talking about that.'

'I know. But Emily is looking great, though. Didn't she get her one-stone badge or something last week?'

'Yes she is and yes she did. But it's not in me to go to a slimming class with my mother. I couldn't bear it, Uncle Ray.'

'Kerrygold butter or the low-fat stuff?' Ray asked, when the toaster popped.

Greta had spent the previous two weeks eating next to nothing, in an effort to slim down for her audition.

19

'Hit me with the real stuff,' Greta decided. She'd not managed to lose anything despite her best efforts. So, she figured, what was the actual point?

Ray made no comment. He was used to her on/off dieting whims, so tended to have all options covered when Greta called in to see him.

'Your mam and dad only have your best interests at heart,' Ray said, as he smeared toast with butter and jam.

'I know. But there's something in my genetic make-up that makes me not listen to authority. Teachers, work, Mam, Dad . . . I'm a lost cause.' She looked at her slice of hot toast, which had melted the Kerrygold into a golden syrup that seeped into the crunchy bread. 'I swore to myself that me and butter were breaking up. But as soon as I did that, I started to have dreams about it. On spuds. On baguettes. On brown soda bread. On crackers with cheese. On toast.' She groaned as she took a bite.

'It's the "forbidden fruit tasting so much sweeter" scenario,' Uncle Ray said. 'So maybe, rather than denying yourself something altogether, you should eat the butter. But cut down the amount you have.'

'Maybe,' Greta replied, finishing her tea. 'Only problem with that is, I don't know when to stop! I have to be the only person who ever did the Atkins diet and *put* on weight when they cut out carbs. I was having butter on my cream, on my cheese, on my rib-eye steak.'

'Now you're making me hungry. We better make a move though. Can't have you missing this flight. Are you sure you've got everything? Passport, toothbrush, money.'

'Sir, yes, sir.' Greta saluted him.

Twenty minutes later, he pulled into a space in the drop-down area of Dublin Airport.

Greta glanced up at the entrance to Terminal Two, which was several hundred feet away. Uncle Ray always seemed to go out of his way to park as far away from his destination as possible. 'I think there's a space out in Swords village that might be closer,' Greta teased.

'This is grand. Sure it's not raining,' Ray replied, switching the engine off. Ray knew the value of a large parking spot when he saw one. He'd been listening to his family slag off his parking skills for decades. The joke was on them, though: he'd managed to get through over twenty years of driving without a single dint or dang.

'Thanks for the lift, Uncle Ray, you're the best.'

'My pleasure. Good luck with the audition. I've everything crossed for you. And don't waste the chance for a great adventure by staying cooped up in your hotel room. Go see the sights. Madame Tussauds or the London Eye – whatever it is that you young'uns are into these days.'

'The greatest adventure is what lies next on my Netflix list.' Greta spoke with great solemnity, making Ray laugh, as she intended.

'Don't waste the pretty, Greta.'

'Eh?' Greta asked.

'You're young and beautiful with the whole world at your feet. Don't let it pass you by. Don't waste the pretty.'

Greta mock-saluted him, but felt a lump in her throat all the same. Is that what she was doing? Ray kissed her on her forehead, the way he always did, waving her goodbye as she made her way inside the airport.

As she queued at security, Greta ran through her lines for the hundredth time. The role of Clara, the chubby best friend to the female lead in a new psychological thriller series, was one she wanted with every fibre of herself. If she got this role, she knew it would be the start of something new. Dr Gale often spoke about corners and how you never knew when it was your moment to turn a new one. This could be hers. She didn't think she could bear another season of playing multiple mind-numbing roles with the Murder Mystery Crew. She'd worked part time for the Murder Mystery Crew for two years; they staged various whodunnit plays for hen and stag parties, and performed at the odd corporate event. While they also did the occasional private gig, most of their shows were in Grayson Castle, Wexford, at weekends. One good thing about the job, though, was that she got to spend a couple of days each week in a hotel room, away from the madness of her family. It also paid the bills while she waited for her big break, and she got to spend time with Dylan, her best friend.

Talk of the devil . . . She grabbed her phone when it beeped.

Dylan: Good luck at the audition, Silver Lady. You've got this.

She smiled, thinking not for the first time how lucky she was to have Dylan in her corner. He was the stage manager with the Murder Mystery Crew and popular with all the cast as he owned a seven-seater, which drove the cast to their venue in Wexford. He also took the bookings, chased around after the talent, sorted the props, organized the hotel and kept the guests happy. She'd be lost without him.

She contemplated ringing him, but knew that he preferred messaging to phone chats. He had a stutter, and sometimes the words just wouldn't cooperate for him. Greta knew this bothered him, but she never really thought about it. It was just part of who Dylan was, how his brain was wired.

They had shared a moment a year or so ago, when their friendship could have taken a turn into something else. She'd just finished their show *Inspector Clueless*, where she played the main role of the hapless French detective. It was a fun part to play, getting laughs for every mispronunciation or mishap she made, whilst trying to solve the inevitable murder for the guests. After the final curtain, they went for a walk in the grounds, as was their habit. They were both movie buffs and loved to analyse scenes.

But this time, as they strolled, shoulder to shoulder, Greta felt something shift between them. It was one of those perfect nights, the air still and quiet, with a large white moon, full, throwing light and shadow into the garden. And Greta thought about every romantic comedy she'd watched, where the girl got the guy. Could she too? What would happen if she reached over to clasp Dylan's hand in hers? Or perhaps he would throw his arm around her shoulder, then pull her into his arms, his breath warm on her cheek. Greta longed to be part of something, a couple, a world, where someone cared about her and only her.

When they reached the entrance to the hotel, their cast mate Donna was watching them, a wave of cigarette smoke wafting into the air around her. She shouted over, jokingly, 'You two look very cosy. Something you want to tell us?' Greta flushed from head to toe. Had Donna somehow guessed what Greta had been fantasizing about? Was it written all over her face? She was about to tell Donna to feck off when she saw a look cross Dylan's face. He looked horrified at Donna's insinuation. The dream melted into the air, leaving Greta feeling silly for ever contemplating that she and Dylan should or could be anything but friends. She was happy on her own.

As Greta inched closer to the conveyor belt at security, another moment flashed into her head. A moment where she'd almost messed up her friendship with Dylan for ever, because she stupidly . . . she shook her head and forced herself to shove the memory back into a place deep inside her. Now was not the time to dwell on the past. She had to focus for her audition.

She typed a message back to Dylan, smiling through her pain, and did what she did best – when all else fails, make 'em laugh.

> **Greta:** I'd better not read the lines as Inspector Clueless by mistake! Can you imagine? Good moaning, this iz Clara. Do you 'ave a massage for me?
> **Dylan:** Never mind Inspector Clueless, all you need to do is put on your Ruby Mae costume and the job would be yours!
> **Greta:** Er, I told you what happened with that a few weeks back. Don't mention the war!

She'd played the part of Ruby Mae, a curvy, sexy saloon girl, until she'd had a wardrobe malfunction. Greta had stepped into her red and black cancan dress, but it wouldn't go up over her thighs. It had been getting tight for months, but she'd always been able to manoeuvre her way into it, once she was wearing her Spanx knickers and slip. She stepped out of the dress and decided to put it on over her shoulders, so that she could shimmy her way into it. Several shimmies later, she was standing in her room, with a dress wedged on her shoulders. Her face was scarlet and her hair, washed and curled only twenty minutes previously, was now half stuck to her head. With two arms above her head, she couldn't pull the damn thing either up or down.

Greta knew she was not going to extricate herself from this situation on her own. Dylan might be her closest friend, but there was no way she was showing him her lumps and bumps. So she had no choice but to call her cast mate, Donna, for help. Skinny Donna, who had two pert boobs that defied gravity, and an even perter personality. It was the worst ten minutes of Greta's life, as Donna squished Greta's boobs down as flat as possible, so that she could yank the dress up and off.

Then, when the mission was accomplished, Donna asked, 'Shall I play Ruby Mae, seeing as the costume doesn't fit?' She'd had her eye on the role for months and practically danced out of the room with it in her hands.

Dylan: I told you we can just buy another costume. It probably shrunk in the tumble dryer.
Greta: Maybe you should throw me into the dryer too the next time! This queue to security is horrendous. Distract me with another URG example.

This was one of their things. Dylan the hopeless romantic, Greta the cynic, discussing moments in cinematic history that were Ultimate Romantic Gestures, or URGs, as they nicknamed them.

Dylan: I need to bring out the big guns so. How's about *Bridget Jones's Diary*? The first one, though. When Mr Darcy buys Bridget a new diary so she can make a fresh start. URG central.
Greta: OK, that's creepy not romantic. I mean, the guy read her diary. Shootable offence.
Dylan: Noted. No reading of girls' diaries.
Greta: I'd have shoved his new diary where . . . well . . . somewhere painful!

Greta put her phone away and placed her luggage in the large square plastic box on the conveyor belt.

'You'll have to take those shoes off,' the security guard said, pointing to her boots.

She held onto the side of the conveyor belt and felt a shot of pain to her ribcage as she leaned down. The first time she'd experienced it, she thought she must have a serious illness. So she'd approached Doctor Google for help. And found two words that made her flush in shame and recognition. Apparently the pain was a fat cramp, caused by her lungs being flattened by her organs. By the time she managed to pull her shoes off and had placed them beside her iPad and handbag, a line of sweat had formed above her lips. She swiped it away with the back of her hand as she walked towards the security gate.

The alarm went off. The alarm always went off. Greta

moved to the left as indicated and looked upwards with embarrassment while the female security guard patted her down. She was mortified by the woman's touch, especially when her hands felt her back fat. And as always when she was embarrassed, Greta started to sweat like Donald Trump in a spelling bee. She could feel trickles of water snaking its way down her back, under her boobs, between her legs. And the shower she'd had only a few hours earlier began to feel like a distant memory. She couldn't turn up at her audition looking like a sweaty mess.

Greta took a steadying deep breath and willed the perspiration to disappear. She made her way to the ladies' bathroom, so that she could freshen up before it was time to board. A full-length mirror ran along the wall at the entrance which meant it was impossible to miss seeing her reflection.

Who was that woman staring back at her? A round face, shiny and patchy with sweat, looked back in horror. Greta walked closer to the reflection to study herself, something she didn't do very often. This morning when she'd dressed she had felt good about her appearance. Her midi print dress in navy and ochre, with three-quarter-length sleeves, felt like the perfect audition dress. It had skimmed over her wobbly bits; paired with her ankle boots, she felt hip and trendy. As the saying went, fake it till you make it.

Now all her eyes could see were the two dark stains that lay under her armpits. She pulled her shoulders forward and tried to hide them, mortified that she'd walked through the airport unaware that they were there. Then she noticed a pull in the buttons that strained over her breasts. Had her boobs grown since she'd left home an hour ago? Was that even possible? And the print that she thought hid her extra weight, now seemed to offer a neon-light invitation for all and sundry to look more closely at her imperfections.

Her body had let her down.

Which wasn't strictly true. It was *she* who was letting her body down. She had done this to herself.

Greta thought of her two brothers at home, fit and toned. And thin. She thought of her parents, now in their fifties, both managing to keep any middle-aged spread at bay. She stood out like a sore, angry thumb. The runt of the Gale litter. Except she was as far from little as you could be. What had the lads at the bus stop called her the other day? *Fat cow*.

Greta tugged at her dress. She had to get it off. What on earth had she been thinking? She felt something new and insidious begin to nip at her. Shame, she knew well. Anger; self-doubt too. But this pain in her stomach, the trouble catching her breath, it felt like . . . fear, panic. And it wasn't like her. She was the girl who just brushed herself off, dusted herself down when life threw a curve ball at her. But right now, Greta knew that if she didn't change her clothes, her audition would bomb. An irrational thought, but now that it was planted in her head it started to grow and blossom, until it took over everything.

Greta made her way into one of the cubicles and placed her case on the toilet. She pulled off the dress then mopped the sweat from her body with swabs of toilet tissue. They turned to pulp in seconds. She sat down on the toilet and closed her eyes for a moment, to let the fresh air from the air conditioning waft over her. When her body temperature regulated back to the normal zone, she doused herself in deodorant once more, then changed into her black trousers and her oversized black tunic. They were her staples, her wardrobe of choice and her planned clothes for tomorrow. As she smoothed down the tunic over her hips, she felt better instantly. Less conspicuous. *Less her.*

Greta stuffed the dress, alongside her hidden pain, into her small case with a stifled sob. She zipped it closed, took a deep breath and exited the cubicle. She walked to the mirror and reapplied another layer of translucent powder, erasing the shine of sweat from her face. She couldn't afford the luxury of feeling sorry for herself.

As she passed by WHSmith, a display of books stopped her in her tracks. A large cardboard poster hung from the ceiling at the front of the store, in bright red, saying DOCTOR GRETA GALE, THE NEW YORK TIMES BESTSELLER! Underneath it was a display of hardback books, dozens of them, piled high in stacks, side by side. Her book, *What's In Your Cupboard*, had been in the Irish bestseller charts for over a year and showed no signs of leaving it any time soon. There was a giant photograph of her namesake on the poster – a triumph of shining platinum-blonde hair, Hollywood smile and translucent, porcelain skin. Her familiar brown eyes twinkled and seemed to say,

Greta, you've got this!

'I know what I have to do. I'm gonna fake it till I make it,' she whispered to the poster, then forced a smile onto her face. And with every step Greta took as she made her way to the departure gate, her smile grew wider.

Chapter 2

By the time Greta inched her way down the aisle of the aeroplane towards her seat, she had successfully managed to bury her feelings about how she had looked in that mirror. Until she sat down and realized that her seatbelt would not clasp shut. She felt her body tense in shock and took several deep breaths to try and calm herself down, not quite believing the situation that was unfolding.

She checked to make sure her belt was not tangled. It wasn't.

She then pulled the lever to extend the belt to its full length, getting an extra millimetre by doing so. But no matter how hard she tugged and pulled, the two ends never met. A glob of acidic bile made its way into the back of her throat, as the enormity of this discovery hit her. The unimaginable had happened. She was too fat to fly.

In silent loathing, she went through her options. She

could call the attendant and ask for a seatbelt extender. This she eliminated immediately, because she couldn't bear the shame of saying the words out loud, feeling the judgemental side-eye of her fellow passengers as they took in the fat girl. There was only one other choice. Deception. Greta took her jacket off and placed it over her lap hiding her unclasped belt. With a bit of luck, the stewardess would only glance in her direction and not insist on double-checking that all was buckled under her jacket. Then her mind jumped to a movie she'd seen a few years ago. What was it? Not that it mattered. All that mattered was the fact that in the film an aeroplane took a sudden drop in altitude and a guy who'd undone his seatbelt had catapulted to the roof of the plane, where his head proceeded to split open. Touching her head, which she happened to like, Greta knew something for sure.

A scenario that included possible death was still preferable to admitting publicly that she was too fat to fly.

Greta glanced at the man who sat to her left. He had pushed himself closer to the window, as if touching her would contaminate him. She looked to her right at the woman who was reading a book, oblivious to her predicament. Maybe she was being polite, who knew? Greta closed her eyes for a moment and silently asked Dr Gale what would she do in this situation. She imagined her idol taking her hands between her own, saying, 'Honey child, there are a lot of problems in this world, but this sure as hell isn't one of them. Now you need to use your weight as your strength. Reclaim your power, be a grown-ass woman, and ask for that extender.'

Feck it. Taking a deep breath, Greta pushed the call

button, and when the stewardess walked over to her, with a big pearly-white smile, Greta mustered every bit of the kind of dignity and defiance she believed Dr Gale would adopt in the situation.

'My New Year's resolution was to lose twenty pounds. Only twenty-five to go . . .' Greta pointed to her tummy, smiling ruefully at the stewardess.

'Oh I hear you!' The stewardess smiled. 'The struggle is real.'

'For sure.' Greta lowered her voice a fraction and asked, 'Could I have a seatbelt extender, please?'

The stewardess smiled even more brightly and said, 'With pleasure, I often use one myself, it's far more comfortable.' Then she trotted away to fetch it.

The man in the suit had contempt written over every chiselled part of his face as Greta added the extra section to the seatbelt and tightened it. She had only needed an inch, but that was all it had taken to shame her. The woman on her right had sympathy written all over her face. And there was something else there too. Relief. She knew what she was thinking. She'd seen it reflected in the eyes of many other women too. While that woman might be carrying a few extra pounds, she wasn't as fat as Greta was.

Greta closed her mind to them all and concentrated on today's audition. This month alone she'd read parts for two adverts, a play in The Gaeity and a new character in *Fair City*, Ireland's longest-running soap opera. The odds should have been in her favour for at least one call-back. But each time she was told that while they'd enjoyed her audition, they'd decided to go in a different direction.

Greta wished someone would tell her what direction all these roles went in, so she could set it as a favourite in Google maps on her phone. The last time her agent Michelle had rung with bad news, Greta had joked, 'If at first, you don't succeed . . . it's probably never going to happen.' They'd both laughed for a moment, before awkwardly falling into silence.

But the audition today felt different. Even Michelle had said so when she'd emailed her the main characteristics of Clara: This role has your name on it! It could have been written for you. Clara, *in her thirties, fat, unattractive, funny, wisecracker.*

While Greta had long since given up on the dream of ever being cast as the good-looking lead, the fact that her agent had emphasized the words *fat* and *unattractive* still stung. Unfortunately she knew her agent was right: it did sound like a great part for her.

But Greta was a trouper and she shoved the hurt deep inside her and focused on the words *funny* and *wisecracker*. She'd been playing that role her whole life.

She arrived at the casting studio in London fifteen minutes early, which gave her plenty of time to freshen up before her audition. As she looked around the reception hall for the ladies, a woman marched over to her holding a clipboard.

'I'm Maria. You are?' Maria looked down at the page in front of her, while she waited for an answer.

'Greta Gale.'

Maria tilted her head to one side as she contemplated the puzzle that was in front of her.

'You mean like the real Dr Greta Gale?'

34

'Real as opposed to me, the fake one standing in front of you?' Greta said.

Maria smiled, 'You know I have a friend called Tony Hadley. He does a pretty good version of "Gold", as it happens. Right, follow me, we've had a cancellation, so you're up next.'

'If I could just have five minutes . . .' But before Greta could ask where the bathroom was, Maria had marched through a set of double doors, leaving her with no choice but to follow.

'Greta Gale auditioning for the part of Clara,' Maria called out, leading her into a studio.

Three sets of eyes looked up from their smartphones and scanned Greta up and down. Greta wheeled her luggage over to the side of the room, wishing that she'd had the foresight to put tissues in her trouser pocket. Could she ask for a moment to go to the ladies? Or would that go against her?

'Whenever you're ready,' Maria said. It appeared that no introductions were to be made.

Greta grabbed her résumé and headshot folder from her handbag and walked to the centre of the room. She stood in front of the panel, who were seated behind a long rectangular desk. Louise Cavendish, a casting director, sat at one end. Greta had auditioned for her a few times and she'd also taken one of her workshops. And while it was never promised outright, rumour had it that by attending a course taught by Louise you had a better chance at being picked for a role cast by her. It cost Greta a full month's wages to go to it, so she hoped the rumours were true.

Greta smiled in Louise's direction. She got nothing in

return. Not even a cursory nod of acknowledgement. So she turned her attention to the guy in the middle. He looked as though he was no more than sixteen years old and was more interested in his phone than in Greta. A little less brightly, Greta smiled at the last member of the panel, a woman who was wearing earrings the size of satellites. Earring lady just shook her head in response to her smile, then looked away.

Why didn't they say something? I should say something. This must be a test to see if I can channel Clara!

'Hey everyone.' It might not have been fierce, but at least it sounded more confident than she felt. She wiped a bead of sweat that had pooled above her lip with the back of her hand and willed her body to cool down. Her body ignored every plea she whispered, until her face was covered in a layer of sweat that dribbled down her double chin, landing in big plops onto her black tunic top. The panel began to whisper to each other, glancing back and forth towards her.

Louise was the first to speak. 'Would you like a napkin?' She waved a white tissue in her direction.

Greta nodded and bit her lip. She needed to pull herself together, fast. She walked over to Louise and took the tissue, which disintegrated into mush within seconds when she dabbed her face.

'We're going to need a bigger boat,' Greta joked in her best Sheriff Brody voice from *Jaws*.

Laughter. *Thank God.*

Louise handed her the full pack of tissues. Greta nodded her thanks, then walked at a snail's pace back to her mark, mopping her face as she went.

'Would you like a glass of water?' the man-child asked. His face had landed on a sneer.

Greta felt that she was in danger of losing them before she'd even started. She had to take control of the situation. So she straightened her back and said, 'No thank you. I'm excited to read for you. I have never felt more connected to a part before. I *am* Clara. Albeit a sweaty one right now. But that's real life for you. If Clara had been through my commute of a flight, the Gatwick Express, and then two Tube rides that frankly felt like an endurance test, then she'd be . . .' She motioned towards her soggy face.

'The Tube *was* like a sauna this morning,' Man-child agreed.

'Why do you think you're a good fit for Clara?' Earring lady asked.

'Well, to start with, I look like her. Or at least how you described her, and how I read her in the script. She's sassy. She's got style. I'm the same size as her – not Bridget Jones fat – which has to be a plus.'

'What do you mean by that?' Louise asked.

'Bridget Jones was meant to be overweight. But clearly in the movie she was just an average-sized woman. I mean if Bridget Jones is fat, what does that make me? Actually, don't answer that.'

Earring lady smiled. 'You know what bugs me every Christmas? The way everyone keeps referring to Natalie in *Love Actually* as chubby and plump! Martine McCutcheon has a lovely figure.'

'Yes! I felt sorry for Aurélia's sister in that movie. They described her as Miss Dunkin' Donut 2013. And pretty much said that she was too fat and ugly to get a man,' Greta said. 'Mind you, she was a bit weird the way she kissed Colin Firth.'

Heartened by their laughter, Greta continued, 'I want to assure you that most days I can pull this look off.' Greta laid her headshot and CV onto the table in front of them. She was proud of that photograph. She looked like herself, just the very best version possible.

They picked it up and passed it from one to the other.

'Actually, this *is* how I saw Clara in my mind's eye,' Earring lady said to Louise and the man-child.

Louise said to her panel, 'By the way, Greta played the part of that cute kid in the biscuit Christmas advert.'

'I love that advert!' Earring lady said.

This was Greta's only real claim to fame. Her one big TV moment. Twenty-five years earlier, she had been cast in a Christmas advert for biscuits. The advert in question was played for the first time just before *The Late Late Toy Show* began, one of Ireland's favourite Christmas TV shows on RTÉ One.

'You were so cute!' Earring lady enthused, clearly a fan.

And she wasn't the only one who thought so. The nation sighed a collective *aww* when the pigtailed little Greta, in her red plaid pyjamas, filled their TV screens. She walked into her living room, wiping her tired eyes with her little chubby hands, where she found a rosy-cheeked Santa eating biscuits she'd left for him earlier. 'I want one too, Santa!' she cried with a perfect pout, one hand held on her hip. Then she snatched a biscuit from Santa's white-gloved hand. He laughed a big ho, ho, ho, and the advert ended with the little girl winking at the camera. It was an instant Christmas hit, one of those adverts that never failed to make people yearn for yester-year and good old family values.

'Say the line!' Earring lady begged.

Greta put a hand on her hip, then said, 'I want one too, Santa!', then winked at them all. They all clapped and Greta took a bow. The biscuit advert that had haunted her for years was helping her out of a tight spot. 'Twenty-five years later and some things never change!'

'I like that! OK, let's hear your prepared piece,' Louise said, scribbling something into her notebook.

Greta straightened her back and began to recite her Clara monologue. As soon as the first word left her, she felt a familiar shift, as she morphed into Clara. She felt the energy in the room change too as the panel sat forward and listened to her words. This was it. The stars were finally aligning in her favour.

She finished her lines, ending with a perfectly arched raised eyebrow. Greta took a moment to compose herself, then looked over to the panel to check out their reaction. They loved it!

'Excellent work, Greta,' Louise said. 'I really enjoyed that, a truly believable performance.'

'Thank you!' Greta said and resisted the urge to do a victory dance. 'If you cast me, I promise I'll eat, sleep and dream Clara! I'll work so hard, I won't let you down.'

'I believe you!' Man-child said, grinning now too. It was an unadulterated smile-fest in the audition room now. 'Can we confirm that you are available in September for filming?'

She might not know his name, but right now Greta wanted to run across the room, take his baby face between her hands and kiss him. 'I know I should be all cool here and tell you that I need to check my diary. But honest to goodness, I'd cancel my own wedding to do this show if you cast me.'

'I told you she was funny,' Louise said, then turned to Greta. 'We'll be in touch. Now go and get a cold drink – you look like you need one.'

Greta grabbed her bags, adrenalin pumping through her body, and she Beyoncé'd her way out of the room, messaging Dylan as soon as she got to the lobby.

Greta: I nailed it! They asked me if I was free for filming later this year.

Dylan: I knew you would. You better not forget me when you get this part and leave Inspector Clueless behind.

Greta: How very dare you. I liv and breeve for ze murder in ze Castle.

Dylan: Ha! Go out and celebrate. I think you'd love Soho – there's loads of fringe theatres in the West End.

Greta: I'm gonna peel back this city's juicy layers and take a big old bite out of it. Promise. Chat later!

By the time she'd taken the two Tube rides to get to her hotel, her adrenalin had leaked a bit. It didn't help that the ten-minute walk to the hotel from the Tube turned into a twenty-minute hike because she turned right instead of left when she exited the station. Exhausted, she told herself that as everything was open so late in London, it made sense that she should take a short break to recharge.

She'd been up since the crack of dawn and her stomach growled, reminding her that she'd not eaten since her breakfast. She popped into a Sainsbury's Local on the way to the hotel to pick up some refreshments. With the audition going so well, surely she could treat herself to a celebration? Wine, cheese, crackers, chocolate and crisps. She threw in a bunch of grapes, an apple and a pear too, sorting her five a day. She'd snack, rest, then head to the West End early in the evening.

But when Greta got back to the hotel, the buzz of the audition had worn off replaced by all-too-familiar doubts creeping in. Greta sipped a glass of wine and munched on a bag of cheese and onion crisps, trying to switch off her brain to the constant buzz of the what-ifs. Would the sweating put them off? Or had she managed to turn the audition around with her reading? What were they whispering about when she delivered that final line? What if her five minutes of fame had happened when she was a child in that Christmas advert and that was it for her? This thought crippled her more than anything else. She simply could not imagine a world where she wasn't an actress. The feeling of transformation when she played a role – sharing a character's pain, happiness, fear or joy with an audience – was all consuming. Being someone else. Leaving Greta Gale behind. If she wasn't an actress, then who or what was she? Over and over, the thoughts continued, until her eyes stung and her head pounded. She couldn't ditch the feeling that time was running out for her. Her eyes stung with tiredness because she'd only managed a few hours' sleep the night before. But yet her mind would not switch off. On and on it continued, telling her she wasn't good enough. If she could just lose some weight, then maybe people would pay more attention to her? Maybe then she would be more than the fat girl with sweat patches under her arms. She disgusted herself, she couldn't really blame anyone else for feeling the same way.

When had her life gone so pear-shaped? Then she noticed the green pear she'd bought earlier. Lying toppled on its side, wobbling on a round body. And she started to sob, because she didn't want to be a pear any more.

Enough. Only one thing could ever silence her horrible, sad thoughts.

Greta opened her toiletry bag and pulled out her pack of sleeping tablets. She placed one onto her tongue, then washed it down with a glass of red. Then she broke a second one in half and popped that in too.

London could wait.

Chapter 3

Greta was disorientated at first. She couldn't remember where she was, and even though the room was pitch black, something about it felt wrong. Different. This wasn't home. Then her brain clicked into gear, and her memory came back. She was in a hotel. In London. The sound of housekeeping banging on her hotel room door startled her, alerting her to the fact that it was well after eleven a.m., her checkout time. She pulled herself up to a sitting position and looked around the room in alarm. Strewn across the floor were empty packets of crisps and chocolate. She'd eaten all of this? She closed her eyes and tried to piece together the events of the previous evening. The last thing she remembered was falling asleep at about four in the afternoon. Nearly twelve hours previously. And she'd only eaten one bag of crisps before that. She was sure of that fact.

Something was slipping inside her; her control on the

situation, on herself, on life. She was losing . . . she just wasn't sure what that was yet. It must be jet lag, from the early flight.

She pushed aside the fact that there was no time zone change between Ireland and the UK. Her hands itched to find her bottle of tablets again. Had she taken another tablet during the night? Her rule of an occasional tablet to help with her insomnia and anxiety had somehow drifted to one every night these past few months . . .

She took a quick shower, dressed, packed her case and made her way to the airport. She noticed she had dozens of missed calls and messages from her family. A flurry of messages had come in from various Gales throughout the morning. Including a new text message from Aidan.

Aidan: Why do you have to be such a bitch? Just let Mam and Dad know you are alive.

Talk about going over the top. She wasn't a seven-year-old. She was a grown woman!

Greta: Soz Mam and Dad. Did I nearly give you a heart attack with the worry? I'm such an eejit. I left my charger on the train yesterday and phone went dead. Had to buy a new one today. Hope you weren't too worried. London is so much fun! Love it here. G x

That should quieten them all down. And she would even be magnanimous with Aidan when he apologized for his unnecessary comment. After all, it was hardly her fault she had no charge for her phone.

That was the thing with lies, when you told enough of them, they became easier to believe.

After traipsing through security, and feeling ravenous because she'd missed breakfast, she headed to Burger King for a Chicken Sandwich meal. An hour later she boarded her flight. The meal she'd eaten made her feel sluggish. She wished she could click her heels and be at home in her warm bed. Once she was buckled into her seatbelt, with the help of the extender strap, she thought about the half tablet from the night before. She scooped it out and swallowed it dry.

Hands gripped her shoulders, shaking her, hard. It hurt and Greta shrugged them off. A voice shouted in her ear, 'Are you OK? Hello? Are you OK, miss?'

Greta opened her eyes and realized that her head was slumped against the aeroplane seat in front of her. She could feel the imprint of the table-top on her forehead. She looked around and saw that the plane was empty. They'd landed in Dublin and she couldn't even remember taking off in Gatwick. Greta wiped away a line of drool that was making its way down her chin. Her face flamed as she felt a flush rush over her body, top to toe. *Please don't let me have done anything stupid.*

'It looked like you weren't breathing there for a minute. I got quite a fright,' the stewardess said.

'What must you think of me? I'm so sorry. Honestly, I'm an eejit,' Greta replied. 'I didn't get much sleep last night; it must have caught up on me. Someone had a party in the room next door to me in my hotel. It kept me awake all night.'

'I thought you were dead.'

Greta put her two hands up and did her best zombie impression. 'I feel a bit like the walking dead, for sure.' Greta unclipped her belt. The stewardess looked unsure. Greta wanted to get off the plane and away from her probing eyes and questions. She'd been stupid to take a pill when on public transport. Rookie error. She needed to be more careful. And as Greta made her way through the arrivals hall, that new feeling joined the regular residents of shame and embarrassment that lived inside her these days. She was scared. But she didn't have time to analyse that because her mother was waiting for her, smiling, eyes bright with expectation. Emily opened her arms to welcome her daughter home.

'All OK, love?'

Greta could still feel the imprint of the hard seat on her forehead, where she'd slumped for the one-hour flight. But she pushed that away and gushed, 'Mam, London was amazeballs. Honestly, we have to go together soon! The view from the London Eye is incredible. It made me quite emotional, took my breath away.'

'You wouldn't get me up into one of those things! Look at you, all flushed with excitement from the trip!'

Greta thought about the too-small seatbelts, the sweating and the blackouts. 'It's been so much fun. And they loved me in the audition. Nailed it!'

'Course they loved you. That dress was beautiful on you. The nicest thing I've seen on you in years.'

'Thanks, Mam. I felt really good in it.'

'Did you take lots of photos?'

'I couldn't, Mam. No charge on my phone, remember? And I really am sorry about scaring you.'

'That's all right love. Once you are safe and happy, I'm happy. When will you hear about the part do you think?' Emily asked as she paid for the airport car park.

Greta shrugged. 'It's hard to know. Could be weeks. But they did ask me if I was free in September when they start shooting.'

'I'll start the novenas tonight then. No harm in asking for a bit of help from up there,' Emily said as she fed money into the car-park machine, and Greta wondered if the nine days of prayer might indeed make the difference between success and failure.

All of a sudden Greta felt the ground swoop up towards her. Her head swam and her eyes blurred as she grabbed onto the wall to steady herself.

Emily missed the whole thing. She chattered on, happily unaware of her daughter's light-headedness. As she was about to get into the driver's seat, her phone rang. 'Oh, it's your aunty Amanda!' She tossed the car keys to Greta and said, 'You'd better drive home. I haven't spoken to her since she got home from New York last week.'

Greta knew she should tell her mother that she didn't feel well enough to drive. She was out of sorts, woozy from her sleep on the flight. But her mother was oblivious to everything but the animated conversation she was already having with her sister. They were close and spoke every few days. Sometimes they drove each other mad, and her mother often called her Amazing Amanda behind her back, because her life was . . . well, amazing. But it was said in affection.

'What are you waiting for, G?' Emily said. 'We want to beat the M50 traffic before the evening rush.'

47

You should drive, Mam. I don't feel well. But the words in Greta's head refused to form. She couldn't cope with the inevitable questions that her admission would evoke. The looks she would be given, the unsaid accusations about her weight and the effect it was having on her health. So Greta shook herself both mentally and physically, then switched the engine on. She could do this drive in her sleep. Greta stifled a yawn. For someone who found it hard to sleep most of the time, right now she'd give anything to close her eyes.

The traffic was kind, and Greta was on the M50 in under five minutes. She stayed in the slow lane and turned the air con down to fifteen, its lowest setting. She needed the cold blast to keep awake.

'One-sec, Mand' . . .' Emily paused her conversation and fiddled with the air con. 'Are you trying to turn me to ice?! Honestly sometimes, G . . .'

As the temperature rose from ice cold to warm, Greta felt the weight of lead pushing her eyelids closed. Her feet felt numb. She felt her head loll down but jumped back up when her mother's voice exclaimed loudly, 'Go away! As big as that? Well, I never . . .'

Greta was surprised when she found herself turning into her road. She had driven the twenty-five-minute journey to Lucan on autopilot.

'Greta! In the name of God, what are you doing!' Emily shrieked suddenly.

Greta's eyes opened just in time to see their car moving towards the lawn outside Mrs Oaks's house, their next-door neighbour. She pushed down hard on the brakes, but it was too late to stop or swerve back onto the road.

She felt her mother's hand on her arm, and heard her screams. But the car continued through Mrs Oaks's rhododendron bushes, before hitting the side of her garage face on. The airbags exploded on impact and Greta blacked out for the third time in less than twenty-four hours.

When she came to, the first thing she noticed was the smell. Then she heard her mother whimpering beside her. *Mam!* She turned towards her and saw blood trickling down the side of Emily's face. *What had she done? What was that smell? Smoke. Was the car on fire? Mam. I'm sorry. I'm so so sorry, Mam.*

Emily got out of the car, staggering as she stood up. She walked around to the driver's side and pulled Greta out. 'Are you OK?'

Greta nodded, unable to speak, shocked by the blood on her mother's head. It made her feel ill, and she felt the contents of her stomach heave. She proceeded to vomit everything up onto the grass.

'That's the shock. It's OK. We're both OK. I'd better ring the guards. Do you need an ambulance? Are you hurt? What on earth will Mrs Oaks say when she sees the state of her garden?'

Greta felt herself sway again at her mother's words. 'If the guards come, they will want to know if I'm under the influence.'

Shock flashed across Emily's face.

'Have you been drinking?' Emily whispered.

'No.'

'Oh, thank goodness.'

'But I did take a sleeping pill on the flight.'

49

Now anger flashed across Emily's face. 'You stupid, stupid girl. How could you be so reckless?'

Greta couldn't look her in the eye. She hung her head low, 'I'm sorry, Mam. I'm so sorry.'

Emily ignored her, reaching into the car until she found her phone on the floor.

'What happened? I heard screams,' Amanda asked, when she rang her back.

'We crashed the car. But we are both fine. I just wanted to tell you that. But I've got to go now. I need to get hold of Stephen.'

His phone went to voicemail, so she left a message, then rang Ray who thankfully was at home and could come over straight away.

'Mam . . .' Greta reached over to touch her mother's arm. All she wanted was to feel her mam's embrace, telling her that it would be OK, everything would be fine.

'Don't!' Emily took a step back from her.

Greta blanched at the intensity of Emily's reaction.

'Just don't. I'll deal with you in a bit. For now, we need to clear your mess up.'

When Ray arrived, the first thing he noticed was that Emily and Greta were standing three feet apart. His sister-in-law had a trickle of red blood staining her white face. His niece was pale, shaking, with her two arms wrapped around her chest, as if she were giving herself a hug. Ray had a feeling that whatever pain was afflicting his niece, it was the kind that you couldn't see with the naked eye.

'What happened?' He walked around the car, surveying the damage.

'I was driving. I swerved to miss a cat and lost control of the car,' Emily said.

Ray watched the look that passed between his sister-in-law and his niece. Something didn't add up here. 'What am I missing here?'

Emily held eye contact with her brother-in-law and a silent communication passed between the two. The kind that only family who had shared history for decades could understand. They were the keeper of each other's secrets. He looked around to see if there were any twitching curtains. The road was deserted, with the neighbourhood all at work. A good guess was that if anyone had seen the accident they would be out here already, rubber-necking. That was the way with most folk.

'Is Mrs Oaks in?' Ray asked.

Emily shook her head. She wouldn't get home from work until after six at the earliest.

Ray squeezed into the driver's seat, pushing the deflated airbag away from him. The smell of smoke and powder tickled his nose, making his throat feel scratchy. He switched the engine on and was surprised to hear it turn over. He reversed it out slowly, then moved it into its rightful place, next door. He'd call a tow truck, later on, to take it away. He figured it was a write-off. Mrs Oaks's garage wall was unmarked, with not even a scratch on it. But there was considerable damage to the lawn and the flowerbeds. Ray felt his stomach flip as he contemplated how much worse this could be. If anything had happened to Emily or Greta. . . He saw Emily wipe another trickle of blood away and he took hold of her arm and led her towards the house. 'Let's go inside and have a cup of tea. I want to take a look at that cut.'

'I'd better ring Mrs Oaks to tell her what's happened,' Emily said.

Greta couldn't take her eyes off the squashed flowers. Muddy brown tyre marks ripped through the green lawn, telling tales of the reckless, stupid, unforgivable thing she'd done. She'd put her mother's life at risk. Her own, she didn't care about.

The weather was in sync with how she felt, because all at once it began to lash rain, the clouds grey and thunderous above them. She felt movement at her feet; when she looked down, the scrappy black dog was sitting beside her again. His coat was drenched, showing how thin and bedraggled he was. Poor little mite. His eyes met hers, and Greta recognized something of herself in him again.

'Inside,' Emily shouted, her voice shrill. 'Now!'

Greta followed her indoors, looking back one last time at the dog. And the fear that had been snaking its way around her body since she'd arrived at Dublin airport made its way to her neck and started to tighten, strangling her. She wasn't sure she was ever going to be able to untangle herself from its grasp ever again.

Chapter 4

Greta was aware of whispered conversations being held in the kitchen. When she went downstairs, Uncle Ray had already left and her parents were sitting side by side.

'Sit down.' Emily's voice made her jump. The tone was firm, and one that Greta knew well. It was the one Emily used throughout their childhood when she had reached her limit. It said enough was enough.

'I want you to get all of your tablets and bring them down to us,' Emily said.

Greta had not expected this and felt panic creeping its way through her body. Only a few weeks previously, Emily had voiced concerns about her over-reliance on taking tablets to help her sleep. Greta had been 'sleep walking', doing strange things, while under their influence. This was pure nonsense. She'd told her mam that, who was prone to drama at the best of times. But she'd also promised

53

her she'd only take a tablet in an emergency. That, of course, was a lie.

'It's time to knock them on the head,' Stephen added, firmly.

Thoughts began to race around Greta's mind, excuses that she could make, that would get her off the hook she was dangling on so precariously. She took a deep breath, sat up straight and tried to give the performance of a lifetime. 'Look, I'm really sorry about what happened yesterday. I will pay for the damage to the car and Mrs Oaks's garden.'

'That you will,' Stephen answered.

'And I'll help Uncle Ray sow the new flowers,' Greta threw in, feeling magnanimous. Everyone knew that she wasn't the outdoorsy type, never showing any interest in their garden at home – or, in fact, any garden. Greta didn't see the point of flowers, being more of a tree woman. She glanced at both their faces, expecting to see a softening, a sign that she was making ground with them.

But there was nothing but disappointment and anger there.

'You know I've suffered from insomnia for years. The pills were prescribed by Dr Hanrahan! And I've been thinking about what happened. It wasn't the pills. You see, I had the most terrible time in London. I didn't want to tell you, to worry you, but the hotel was awful. I think there was a party going on in the room beside me. I complained several times to reception. So you see, I'd not slept a wink all night, and I thought, I'll never manage the flight home unless I get a quick nap. I only took half a pill. Thinking about it now, I must have caught a virus on the flight. The air conditioning is notorious for doing that. The virus made me dizzy . . .' She stopped talking when she saw her mother's face.

'Liar.' Emily's voice, cold and hard, sliced through the air. 'No more excuses, I want those pills now.' When Greta didn't move, she continued, 'If necessary I'll go get them for you.'

'You've not been yourself for months now. And your weight is a disgrace. Every time I look at you, you've got bigger. I should have said something sooner,' Stephen chipped in. 'But enough already.'

'Jeez, Dad, you'd turn a girl's head with all those compliments.' Greta stood up and pulled her pyjamas down over her stomach and hips, feeling her father's eyes on her. His shame and disappointment with her was a poor match for her own feelings. She grabbed a pack of tablets from her bedside locker, then walked the green mile back to the kitchen.

'There.' She placed them on the kitchen table. They were small and white, inoffensive. They were also circles of destruction.

'Swear to us that you'll not take any more of these,' Emily said.

'Do I have to swear on the Bible?' Greta asked. For the first time in the history of that family joke, nobody laughed.

'Say it out loud so we can hear you,' Stephen said. 'Swear that you will never take another sleeping tablet.'

Greta didn't answer straight away. Because, to her horror, she realized that she didn't want to make that promise. In fact, if she were honest, she wanted to take one of her pills so that she could go to sleep and escape from this moment.

'I swear.'

'Good. We'll say no more about it,' Emily said.

Stephen cleared his throat to say something, but Emily silenced him with a shake of her head.

'We'll say no more,' Emily repeated. 'Have something to eat. Then get dressed and go next door to help your Uncle Ray out.'

'I'm not hungry. I'll go straight over to Ray.' She walked over and gave her mam a hug. 'Don't be worrying about me. I'm not an addict or anything. I'll show you. I was reckless. Honestly, it won't happen again.'

Back in her room, Greta turned to social media to help her forget the noise in her head. Though sometimes, if she were honest, seeing all the smiling, happy people she followed only increased the volume of that noise. Maybe it was because she wanted to be just like them.

There was a new post from Dr Gale, who had shared a black-and-white photo still from *The Wizard of Oz*. Dorothy was standing by a broken picket fence, with Toto the dog in her arms, as a tornado raced towards her.

Drgretagale There are days when I feel just like Dorothy here, about to be swept away in a tornado. We all have our 'Dorothy' moments, times when life rages around us, and all we can do is cling on and wait for the storm to pass. But remember this, my friends: maybe that nasty old storm will shake your cupboards and clear them out a little more . . .

#drgretagale #wizardofoz #dorothy #storm #inspire #inspirationalquotes #whatsinyourcupboard

---

Greta felt tears prick her eyes. How did Dr Gale do that? She always seemed to know what Greta was thinking. That was all she had to do. She had to cling on a little bit longer, then maybe the storm would pass.

Once Greta finished helping Uncle Ray, she retreated to her bedroom again, where she stayed for most of the day. But by four o'clock, the shock and the embarrassment of the past twenty-four hours caught up with her. Her head buzzed, while her stomach flipped. Greta put her hands over her ears and closed her eyes, but that didn't stop the torment inside of her. Her mind refused to switch off and as her body began to shake, she felt the walls of her bedroom begin to close around her. The need to get out of the house overwhelmed her. She didn't have a destination in mind, she just wanted to be anywhere else but here. So she ran out and made her way to the nearby Griffeen Valley Park, welcoming the soft rain that fell on her as she moved. It was only a short shower and by the time she arrived at the water's edge at the back of the park, it had stopped. She paused to watch the ducks swim. And for a moment, she wondered what it would be like to jump in. Was it possible to swim away from her life, the mess she'd gotten herself into? Because she realized that no matter how far Greta walked away from her bedroom, the storm came with her.

She looked up to the sky which was dark and ominous, reflecting her mood. But then, the sunshine made its presence felt and a bright rainbow appeared. Could it melt her troubles away like lemon drops? Greta walked back home, watching the rainbow move further from her with every step.

'That you, love?' Emily called out when she heard the key in the door.

'The one and only,' Greta said. She took a deep breath, then plastered a smile on her face.

'You're looking fierce tired today, G. Peaky, in fact. Now, don't get annoyed with me, but I read an article online earlier. And, to be honest with you, you fit the bill of an addict. To a T.'

'Ah Mam! I'm hardly shooting up drugs on the side of the street!'

'No, you're not doing that,' Emily agreed.

Please let this be the end of this discussion. The gods ignored Greta.

'But you've had blackouts quite a few times. You've driven a car and nearly killed both of us.' Emily blessed herself again. 'And you look wrecked.'

'I'll go to bed early tonight. You won't know me tomorrow.'

'Well, they do say that the best eraser in the world is a good night's sleep,' Emily said. 'Tell you what, I'll run you a bath. Nothing like a nice long relaxing soak to set you up for bed. Your dad will be home soon to make his curry. By the time you come down, dinner will be ready.'

'You know I hate baths. I don't like to lie in my own filth.'

'How dirty are you? Go away out of that!' Emily said. 'Follow me up in five minutes and I'll have it ready for you.'

Greta watched her mam walk out of the kitchen, then sank into one of the dining-room chairs. She was so tired. Every bone in her body cried out in protest. But once her mam got a bee in her bonnet, there was no stopping her. She'd have the bath and go straight to bed, skipping her dad's dinner. And, hopefully, her body would have no choice but to cooperate and sleep.

Her stomach flipped and fluttered as Greta's mind spiralled. She walked over to the larder press and stood on her tippy toes to reach the good tin, which her mam had hidden behind a double pack of kitchen towels. Greta opened the lid and pulled out a treat-size bar of Crunchie. She unwrapped it and stuffed it whole in her mouth, feeling the chocolate melt on her tongue, followed by a hit of the sugary fizz of the honeycomb centre. But it wasn't enough. So she grabbed a Cadbury's Caramel too. But no matter how much she stuffed into her mouth, her heart continued to pound and her belly ached. The caramel bar hadn't made life easy. The bunny was full of shit.

Chapter 5

'I've put the good stuff in.' Upstairs in the bathroom, Emily held up her Jo Malone birthday gift set to Greta. She had also put tea-light candles onto every available surface, which were few and far between in the small family bathroom. But they did look pretty as they flickered in the dusky evening, throwing shapes and shadows on the wall. There was a large glass of red wine for Greta, which sat on the ledge beside the bath. Emily was prepared to do anything to get her daughter to relax and fall asleep without the need for any tablets. How could she have let it go on for so long?

'I think I'll skip dinner, Mam. Once I get out of the bath I'll just go straight to bed,' Greta said.

'Are you not hungry?' Emily asked.

'I'm trying to cut down,' Greta said, trying not to think about the chocolate bars from the tin. There was a time when Greta and her mam had no secrets. Emily was always on her side. She used to say, 'Us women have to stick together! Stand united against your dad and the boys!' It had been a while since Greta had heard that or felt it either.

'Oh love, that's great. I think this is your time to shine, do you know that? Just try to forget about everything and relax in the bath. Have a total switch-off and let all your worries disappear. Tomorrow is another day.'

'To mess it all up again?' Greta joked, but it landed wrong and just made her mam frown.

'Ah no, love.'

'Ah yes, Mam.'

'You don't mean that?' Emily asked.

'Course I don't. I'm joking. Now scoot. Let me get the full benefit of your Jo Malone!'

Greta slipped out of her dressing gown and hung it on the back of the door. The mirror above the sink had clouded over with steam. She ran her hand across it and revealed her naked body. Her breasts were OK, she supposed. And her waist had always been small. But her stomach protruded so much that people thought she was pregnant. In fact, one day a guy had stood up to give her his seat on the bus. She had been too embarrassed to say she wasn't pregnant, so Greta had patted her tummy and smiled her thanks. She'd cried herself to sleep that night.

Now, she sank into the tub and felt the sting of the too-hot water as it covered her body. This was one of the main problems she had with baths. Greta was always bored by the time the water reached optimum temperature. She preferred showers; there was less pressure to relax. The other issue with baths was that no matter which way she manoeuvred her body in the tub, parts of her white, flabby flesh were exposed through the bubbles. It wasn't like this in the movie, where the heroine always looked so petite as she frolicked in a large bathtub. Mind you, the way her career was going right now, Greta would never have to worry about a bath scene in anything.

She looked up to the ceiling and became distracted by a crack. *How long had that been there?* The more she tried to relax, the more her body tensed. She should never have let her mam talk her into this. It was different when they were kids. They used to call it Splash Time. Her mam would squeeze the suds out of a yellow sponge, letting them run down Greta's back, while she sang nursery rhymes to her. Greta blinked away tears and gulped down a mouthful of the Cabernet Sauvignon.

A fly appeared out of nowhere. There weren't any open windows in the bathroom, yet somehow it had done a Houdini on it and was buzzing around like it owned the joint. It paused to take a rest and joined in Greta's fascination of the ceiling above her and its new crack.

Rest. If only. Her body and mind were stretched so taut that she could feel cracks splintering through her just like the one above her. She imagined the ceiling collapsing on top of her, splashing water onto the floor. Her mam would hate that. And she loved her mam, even if she bugged the life out of her sometimes. She closed her mind to the worried frown that had been etched across Emily's forehead as she closed the bathroom door a few minutes ago. And instead, she watched the fly, which watched the crack in the ceiling.

I'm cracking up. She grabbed her phone and saw a new

text message had come in from her agent Michelle. With a shaking hand she pressed open.

> **Michelle:** I've just heard from Louise. It was down to you and one other actress but unfortunately they went in a different direction for Clara. Give me a call and we'll arrange a time for you to call in. I think it's time we had a chat.

The disappointment was crushing. Greta was so tired of playing this game, but never winning. How was she supposed to tell her family that once again she was close but no cigar. She flicked through her feed, until she found her balm.

Dr Gale was looking directly into the camera, with tears in her eyes.

> **Drgretagale** We're all damaged, some of us are better at hiding it than others, that's all. Can I get a hell yeah? #timetoletgo #wellness #drgretagale #whatsinyourcupboard #mindfulness #inspire #drgretagale #positivethoughts #findyourtribe

Once again it was as if Dr Gale was speaking directly to Greta's pain. The pain of rejection, the pain of being 'Big G'. She put the phone back in her toiletry bag, her fingers brushing against a pack of cotton-wool pads.

Greta had another swig of wine as the fly landed with a tickle on her right shoulder. He was fearless. Or stupid.

'There was an old lady who swallowed a fly, I don't

know why she swallowed a fly, Perhaps she'll die,' Greta sang, remembering one of her childhood nursery rhymes. 'Run for your little life, fly, before this old lady goes in for the kill.'

She swiped him off her with a gentle pat. Now that the rhyme was in her head, it refused to leave, and over and over again she repeated each line until she wished the ceiling would collapse, if only to put an end to the blasted song.

Like a guilty kid reaching for the good biscuit tin, Greta watched the door in case her mam was hovering outside ready to pounce. She counted to ten, and when the handle didn't move, she reached inside her toiletry bag and took out the pack of cotton-wool pads. She removed a bundle of them until she saw what she was looking for. Her sleeping pills. She had kept an emergency stash hidden from her parents. And there was no doubt that this was a code red emergency.

'I'm sorry.' She apologized to her family. She'd made and broken promises to them and to herself. Then she swallowed a tablet with another gulp of red wine.

With great clarity, she realized that – because of the terrible week she had just been through – one more tablet couldn't hurt. In fact, she reasoned, as she shook the tablets out into her hand without really counting them, her taking a second tablet was for her mam's sake. Because when she got into bed and slept, Emily would think her bath had done the trick. She popped them into her mouth just to be safe . . .

Safe, that's all I want to be, safe and sound, asleep, away from all of this . . .

Safe, not sorry.

Minutes moved on, or at least she guessed they did. Greta began to feel the familiar, heavy, melting sensation snake its way through her arms and legs. She loved and craved it. Greta sank further into the tub, and the water felt as if it was giving her a warm hug; no longer shaming her, it was her friend. Her eyes were heavy, and she couldn't see the fly any more.

'There was an old woman who swallowed a fly . . .' Greta mumbled.

And as she finally felt that blessed relief of sleep, her last thought was: *Perhaps I'll die . . .*

Hands, rough, tried to grip Greta's body, but they kept slipping with the soapy water.

'Is she dead . . . Stephen, is she dead, please god, no, is she dead . . . my poor baby, is she dead?'

Who was Mam talking about? And why was Mam screaming like that? Ow! That hurt. Greta tried to open her eyes, but they felt so heavy, so she closed them again. She awoke feeling something cold and hard underneath her. The tiled floor. Glimpses of the drama unfolding slipped through the slits in her eyes. Her dad and Ciaran. Her mam, hysterical, kneeling beside her, sobbing. Greta was cold.

Someone placed a towel over her naked body. She trembled not just with the chill but with shame. It must be a nightmare. She willed herself to wake up, to make it stop. *I don't like this. Please. No more.*

'Oh love, what did you do, oh my love.' Emily was cradling Greta's head in her arms, stroking her hair and sobbing.

She tried to speak, but no words would come out. *Why was her dad so wet?* His two arms were stained with water, right up to the collar of his shirt. Ciaran was the same. Only his joggers were wet too. Had he jumped in water?

The bath. She had been taking a bath.

And now she was on the floor with a towel covering her, with her mother crying and her father and brother wet. Greta opened her eyes and saw the fly one more time. It paused for a moment before it escaped through the open bathroom door, past Aidan and Ciaran.

I'm dead and this is hell, with me naked on a cold floor.

But Greta wasn't dead. She was in the centre of a tornado, spinning so fast and fierce that she might never leave it.

No one has ever destroyed her before, so I naturally thought she would make slaves of you, as she has of the rest. But take care; for she is wicked and fierce, and may not allow you to destroy her.

The Wonderful Wizard of Oz, L. Frank Baum

Part Two

Chapter 6

Hope Crossing Addiction Treatment Centre,
Tipperary, Ireland

Greta went to the small ensuite bathroom and splashed water over her red puffy face. There was no mirror over the sink, or in fact anywhere in her new bedroom. Greta wondered if it was because people might be tempted to smash the glass and cut themselves. Not an hour in rehab and her mind had already gone to self-harm. By the time she'd finished her three-week stint here, she'd be a basket case.

Not that she cared about the mirror. She didn't need reminding of how she looked. She knew that her eyes, once one of her best features, were now dull and small, like pebbles lost in her round face. Her skin was blotchy and red.

At only six p.m. the rest of the evening loomed ahead

of her. She flicked through a bundle of leaflets that sat on the bedside locker. One was a schedule of group classes for the forthcoming week, counselling, meditation, yoga, meal times. Another outlined the treatment plan.

We holistically approach addiction, working with mind, body and spirit to come together in one healthy life.

Addiction. There was that bloody word again. Every time Greta heard it she wanted to jump in a shower and scrub herself clean. She felt like a fraud. Greta was not an addict and was most probably taking a bed from someone who genuinely needed it. Once again she asked herself how had this happened to her? And the sting in the tail was that she wasn't even famous. She was forever reading about A-listers in Hollywood disappearing to the Betty Ford for a reboot when life got too difficult for them. She'd even daydreamed about being that famous and needing rehab herself one day too.

But not like this. There were no celebrities here. It was most likely full of junkies and alcoholics, who'd been found huddled under a railway bridge, shooting up or sculling cans. Not ordinary people like her. OK, things may have got out of control lately, but she was handling it.

The fallout from her bathtub incident had been apocalyptic. Her mam had started to cry and said, 'You never sat still, not even for a moment, when you were a child. But now it's as if a tornado is tossing you around and around. I can't reach you to pull you out. And you can't get out yourself either. Let us help you, please G.'

So here she was, at Hope Crossing, feeling like Dorothy dropped into the Land of Oz. She looked down at her red Converse and clicked her heels to escape. Unfortunately this was real life, not a childhood fantasy.

Greta was still smarting from her first encounter with Caroline, the rehab nurse, who had searched Greta's bags the second she'd arrived.

'You can't do that surely!' She was indignant at the invasion of her privacy.

'You have nowhere to hide in this place. Learn that little lesson right up front, and it will be easier for you to settle in,' she replied, not unkindly. The first things to be confiscated were Greta's phone and iPad. 'We find that it's in the interest of patients to have time away from all outside distractions. Think of your time here as a digital detox. If you need to make a call, you come to find me, and we can discuss it.'

Caroline then rifled through Greta's make-up bag and took out her tweezers and nail clippers.

'Why are you taking those?' Greta ran her hand over her chin, already feeling the start of regrowth of a hair. 'What do you think I'll do with them? Pluck myself to death?'

'Never mind your tweezers, how will we call our daughter if she has no access to her phone? Or the family WhatsApp group!' Emily was stricken at the thought.

'Sorry, but there are no phone calls from family allowed until Greta's counsellor says it's OK for her to make or take them. Don't worry, we'll keep you informed of any issues that you need to know about,' Caroline replied.

And it was in that moment that it hit Greta that if they had her devices, she couldn't log on to Instagram. No Dr Gale. For three whole weeks. No lovely supportive messages from her Uncle Ray, who always seemed to know what to say to cheer her up.

She had to find a way to keep her iPhone and iPad. She looked at Caroline and decided she was probably more of a reader than a social media lover. She had that geeky look about her. It was time for a white lie. 'When I can't sleep, I like to read my Kindle app on that iPad.'

Caroline was unmoved.

So Greta ploughed on, 'I won't switch on the Wi-Fi, you have my word on that. I get that you don't want me to talk to the outside world. And, quite frankly, I'm ready for some solitude. I just want to read my books.' She tried to think of a title of a book to throw in, just to validate her argument. Her mind went blank. What was that book she did in school? She should have listened more. 'Dickens and the like.'

She could feel her mam and dad's eyes on stalks as they listened to her. OK, she may not have read much of the classics before, but she might do if she had her iPad.

Caroline shrugged and placed the devices with the rest of her contraband in a box, then she stuck a white label onto it with her name typed across it. 'All of these will be waiting for you when you leave. We've a pretty decent library in the TV room, so you'll have lots to choose from there. Not sure if we have any Dickens, but I'm sure we can find some if you let me know the exact title you prefer.'

Greta gave her the stink eye. Wagon.

'And now, all that's left to do is search you.'

'For what?' Greta took a step backwards. This was going from bad to horrific.

'You'd be surprised what people try to sneak into rehab.' Caroline said this in the same cheery voice that made Greta want to reach over, and punch her.

'My daughter wouldn't be that stupid.' Stephen said, backing his daughter's integrity in a statement that would come back to bite him in moments.

'You could at least buy me dinner first,' Greta laughed, trying to distract Caroline, who was relentless in her search as she patted her down. Her hands were everywhere.

And then, to Greta's horror, Caroline paused as she came to Greta's breasts. Without too much effort she had found her secret stash of pills, hidden in her bra. She could feel her parents' disappointment fill the air between them. Once again she had messed up. You'd think she would get used to that feeling, but it always took her by surprise.

'This . . .' Caroline pointed to the tablets, 'goes down the toilet. And, just so you know, if you are found with any contraband in the future, you will be asked to leave.' She didn't sound so cheery anymore.

Until her parents walked out the door, ignoring Greta's pleas to take her with them, she didn't quite believe that this was happening to her. She looked down at her hands which began to shake and tremble. The bedroom started to close in on her, the four walls pulsated as they moved nearer and nearer. If she didn't get out of this room, straight away, she knew that she would suffocate.

Sticking her hands in her pockets to try and stop the shaking, she made her way to the TV room. About a dozen people were sitting in front of the TV, with a few reading books. They looked up briefly as she entered, then lost interest and went back to whatever they were doing. That was fine with Greta. Because her plan was simple. She was going to avoid talking to any of her fellow . . . what should she call them?

Patients?

Addicts?

Inmates?

Yes, inmates. They were all prisoners.

'First day?' A voice said from behind her. 'First days are the worst.'

The voice belonged to a tall man, youngish, she guessed in his mid- to late twenties. He looked at Greta with interest. 'Come over and sit with me if you want.' He nodded towards a table at the back of the room. 'Oh, by the way, I'm Sam.'

Greta wasn't sure she wanted to sit with him or anyone else. She had no interest in adding a junkie friend at this stage in her life.

'Or don't. Suit yourself,' Sam said, then walked away.

On the other hand, Greta didn't fancy going back to her pulsating bedroom. Maybe Sam was her best bet for now. He had good taste in movies at least, wearing a *Jurassic Park* T-shirt, one of the originals, baggy and worn with age. She followed him over to a table in the corner of the room, where two men were playing a game of dominos and a woman was reading a battered copy of *Unravelling Oliver*. She knew the feeling; she was unravelling by the second here.

'Say hello to another newbie,' Sam said to the three people seated at the table. They gave Greta the once-over. 'That's Rory, Tim and Eileen.'

'Hey.'

'What are you in for?' Rory asked.

Greta wasn't prepared for that question. It made her sound like she'd committed a crime. And in truth, she didn't know how to answer it.

'Booze by the look of her, I'd say,' Tim piped in.

'Well I won't lie, I could do with a glass of red right now,' Greta said, which made them laugh.

'I'd say painkillers. Most of the under thirties are in for drugs of some kind,' Eileen said, then grinned triumphantly when she saw recognition flash in Greta's face. 'Knew it.' They all began high-fiving her.

'Excuse me, I don't take painkillers,' Greta said loudly just as the room went quiet. She felt eyes on her from all directions, looking to see what the hullabaloo was about.

'If it's not painkillers, it's definitely pills of some description. We're a nation under sedation,' Eileen said.

'Give the lady some space lads,' Sam said. 'She's just arrived. Here, take a load off.'

Greta sat down beside him and to her horror realized that she had to squeeze her hips between the two arms of the chair. Bulges of fat spilt out from under the wings on either side. If they noticed, they didn't say anything. But every part of her cringed in embarrassment.

'It can get boring in here. So we play the "Guess the Addiction" game to pass the time. No offence meant,' Sam said.

Greta couldn't help herself; she was now wondering what he was in for. And as if he pulled the thought from her brain, he said, 'Gambling.'

'Alcohol,' Rory said.

'Booze for me too,' Eileen added.

'Heroin,' Tim said.

'So what's the deal here? Do I have to make a big Hollywood dramatic reveal and say, I'm Greta Gale, I'm a drug addict?' Greta asked.

'It doesn't have to be Hollywood but it does have to happen,' Sam said.

'I blame my mother's addiction to soap operas. Irish, UK, American, Australian, she watches them all. And that's all very well when it doesn't affect my life. All they do is make her overactive imagination worse. And to make matters even more dire, she's riled up my dad and my brothers too. There's not a member of my family now who isn't convinced that I'm a druggie. When the truth of the matter is that I have gotten a little too reliant on sleeping pills. No big deal. So, for the purpose of accuracy, I'm Greta Gale, and my parents think I'm a drug addict.'

Sam, Rory, Eileen and Tim smiled knowingly, like they were privy to some private joke.

'Hey!' Eileen said, pointing at Greta. 'You're not the doctor who wrote all those books, are you? That Doctor Greta Gale who is always on TV!'

'Sorry to disappoint but I'm the messed-up Irish version who lives at home with her parents. And if I were that Greta, I'd demand a better room than the one I have.'

'It ain't the Shelbourne for sure,' Eileen agreed.

'Are there any celebs here, by the way?' Greta asked.

'No. But there is a guy who looks a lot like Donald Trump. He even has the weird hair,' Eileen answered.

'I saw him on the way in,' Greta shuddered. 'Not a good look.' She held her shaking hands out. 'And to add insult to being here – no offence – I think I've caught some kind of weird virus. I can't even Google it to see what it might be.'

Sam reached over and placed his hands over Greta's to quieten them, 'How long since you had any pills?'

Greta looked at him sharply, to see if he was taking the piss, but could only see concern on his face.

'The shakes are from detoxing,' Sam explained.

Greta chose to ignore his diagnosis. 'I need a coffee. Is there a Nespresso anywhere?'

'There's a tea and coffee station in most common areas.' Sam nodded in the direction of the kettle.

She stood up to investigate, taking the chair with her. She pulled her bum from its clutches and, with as much dignity as she could muster, walked over to make a drink. 'Anyone want one? This is all herbal teas and decaf. Where's the real deal?' She picked up a raspberry and fennel tea, sniffed it, then put it back.

'Caffeine is a stimulant. So it's banned,' Eileen shouted over. She looked almost gleeful at Greta's obvious annoyance.

'Sshh.' A wild-looking woman with wiry grey hair shouted, 'Some of us are trying to watch the TV.'

'You get used to the herbal stuff. Try a peppermint. Will help with your stomach,' Sam said.

'There's nothing wrong with my stomach.'

'Just wait,' Sam said.

Greta didn't care for the doom-and-gloom forewarnings. She was scared, and she felt rubbish. If she ran out the front door, she wondered if she could hitch a lift home to Dublin? Knowing her luck, she'd be picked up by a serial killer. Could she get a message to Uncle Ray? He'd get in the car and come and get her. She could hide in his house. But when her family had staged their intervention and insisted she come here he'd ignored her pleas for help and agreed with her parents. She was on her own. The loneliness floored her. She'd never lived away from home before. She wanted her mam. But most of all she wanted to go home.

'I think I'll give it a miss. Nice talking to you all,' Greta said, waving goodbye to them. She walked, half jogged back to her room, throwing herself onto the bed, panting. Then she sobbed until there was nothing left inside of her. She blew her nose and realized that she was alone, with only her thoughts for company. She wondered if Dylan had sent her any more messages. She hadn't told him where she was going, just that she was sick and wouldn't be in work for a while. He must be so annoyed with her. And she couldn't get the scrappy little dog that had been hanging around their street out of her head. She'd asked Ray to find his owners before she left. She hoped he was OK.

When Caroline brought her to this room earlier today, she'd given Greta a green journal. She explained that keeping a diary was compulsory. What could they do to her if she didn't comply? A vision of herself locked in a padded white room, in a straightjacket, sprang to mind. Could they do that? Bloody Caroline was certainly strong enough to put her in one.

Greta picked it up in desperation, hoping it might give her something to do to help pass the time. At the top of each blank page, there were prompts to fill in.

Hours slept.

How I felt.

My truth.

She hadn't the first clue as to what to write. Despite receiving lots of pink, secret diaries with padlocks over the years from Santa as a kid, she'd never written a word in them. She wasn't one of those reflective types who continuously needed to self-analyse. But things had changed a lot in the past twenty-four hours. She was in prison now – or as good as. Sighing, she realized that she could lie in bed for hours, staring at the ceiling with her eyes wide open. Or she could give this a go. With nothing else to do and the whole night to do it in, she picked up a pencil and wrote her first entry.

Chapter 7

'Pop on the scales, thanks Greta.' Earlier that morning, Caroline had called Greta to the medical office.

'No thank you,' Greta said. There was no way she was getting on scales for anybody. 'Why do you need to know my weight?'

Caroline said, 'It's compulsory, G. We have to monitor all your vitals, to make sure we keep you healthy while you're here. Your body is about to go through some traumatic changes as you withdraw from the tablets you have been taking.'

Greta had spent most of her adult life avoiding scales. And she'd never weighed herself in front of anyone else. Wiping back tears, Greta stepped onto the black scales and saw the red digits move up and down. Greta pulled in her stomach, in automatic response to the shame she felt. She closed her eyes to avoid the number. Caroline didn't pick up on social cues and called the number out loud as she wrote it down on her checklist.

'An even 250 pounds.' She made the number sound like it was an achievement. A nice neat and tidy number. Greta's first reaction was relief – at least her parents were not there to witness her shame. Then she wondered if perhaps she had misheard the woman. Maybe she said 'an even 150 pounds.'

Maybe not.

Caroline's eyes locked onto Greta's gut, which spilt over her too-tight leggings. And they judged Greta, who wanted to cry hot, angry tears of shame. But she pinched herself hard, to stem them. That number meant that she was twenty pounds heavier than she'd been less than a year ago when she joined a local gym. Back then, she'd been mortified when the scales read 230 pounds. But her personal trainer had smiled encouragingly and said with so much conviction that Greta had believed her, 'Don't worry, you'll never see that number again.'

She was right, of course, but not in the way she'd hoped.

Greta realized with horror that she had morphed into her childhood nickname.

Big G in da house.

Fatter than before.

Caroline said. 'It's just a number. Try not to think about it for now. Focus on the thought that today is the first day of the rest of your life.'

'How many people have you shovelled that pile of shit to?' Greta said.

'Don't be so quick to judge. In my experience, it's true for most.'

'And in my experience, I've found that something wonderful never happens for most of us.'

Caroline shrugged then handed a tissue to Greta, who was seconds from not just tears but a whole ugly cry. But there was no way she was going to give into them in front of Caroline. She took a deep breath, wiped her eyes and said, 'What's next?'

'It's time for group therapy.'

'If everyone starts singing folk songs, I'm out of here.'

'That happens after dinner,' Caroline said with a wink.

Greta followed her to the large hall where all group sessions took place. Rows of framed inspirational quotes lined the walls. Her eyes blurred as she read each one.

Stay Positive. Stay Focused. Stay Strong.

On and on they went, all with the same condescending and pretentious nonsense. This was Greta's idea of living hell.

'Sit anywhere you like,' Caroline said.

'Answer me truthfully. Am I dead? Is this my punishment and I'm really in the bad place?'

Caroline walked over and pinched her hard on the arm.

'Ow!'

'You felt that, you're not dead.' Caroline was actually laughing as she walked away.

Greta walked to the back of the room and took a seat nearest to the door.

'What a crock of shit,' she mumbled, reading the poster nearest to the seat she'd just taken. You never fail until you stop trying.

'Not a fan of the wall art?' Sam asked, sitting in beside her.

'How'd you guess?'

'The look of contempt on your face was kind of a giveaway.'

Greta would have to watch that. She made a note to take more care to cover how she felt in public. 'I just find them dishonest.'

'How so?' Sam asked.

'They're empty words spouted by people who are in the most case full of shit themselves.'

'I've always liked that one,' Sam said, pointing to his left.

F.L.Y.

First. Love. Yourself.

Others will come next.

Greta told him: 'You see when I see that, I feel obliged to redress the bullshit balance. It would be more honest if it said, "If you hate yourself, remember you are not alone. A lot of other people hate you too".'

As Sam burst into laughter, he added, 'You're funny. Do that one over there.'

A bright yellow poster said:

You will succeed.

Just keep going.

'That's too easy. If at first you don't succeed, then it's probably never going to happen.'

'I'd buy a T-shirt with that on it. And it pretty much sums up my life right now,' Sam laughed. 'Oh, oh, here we go.'

A tiny woman walked in and told them all to take a seat. She was so petite, she could have fitted into one of Greta's pockets. She had masses of blonde curls that looked like they belonged on an Irish dancer about to launch into Riverdance.

'That's Noreen,' Sam whispered. 'She's the main therapist here. She does the daily group sessions and also all the one-on-ones. She's great. You'll like her.'

Greta wasn't so sure about that.

'We have some new members today who joined us yesterday. I know it can be intimidating coming to group sessions, so for those who are feeling overwhelmed right now, try to relax. You can observe, take it all in until you find your feet,' Noreen said.

Greta slouched down lower into her seat, feeling eyes on her as the room checked out who the newbies were. She had a peek herself, trying to work out who the other one was but she couldn't tell. What she did note was the fact that everyone looked like they wanted to be anywhere but in this room.

'Today I'd like us to explore the rock-bottom moment you experienced as part of your addiction,' Noreen said. 'We all have one. And we can't hide from it. We have to face it, accept it and finally learn from it. Only then can we move on.'

No sooner had she finished this statement than Heather had her hand up.

Sam nudged Greta and whispered, 'That's Heather. She's a therapy junkie and a classic oversharer. Noreen can never shut her up.'

'I've had lots of rock-bottom moments,' Heather boasted. But before she could launch into a litany of them all, Noreen cut in and asked her to only share her worst one.

'It has to be the day my husband found out that I had sold my diamond engagement ring and replaced it with a cubic zirconia fake one that I bought on the shopping channel.' Heather paused for dramatic effect and looked around the room to make sure she had everyone's attention. In fairness, even Greta was eager to hear how this played out. It was like an episode of *Jeremy Kyle*.

When her husband had her ring evaluated for an insurance policy, the truth came out. 'He went ballistic. He accused them of swapping the diamond out. He even rang our local radio station to complain when they refused to own up to the scam,' Heather continued.

'That's bat-shit crazy,' Greta said, just as the room went deathly quiet. Everyone turned to look at her.

'Before you speak, remember to let your words pass through three gates,' Noreen said. 'Let's remind ourselves of them.'

Everyone began to chant, 'Is it true, is it necessary, is it kind?'

'What the actual?' Greta whispered.

'It's Rumi. We say it a lot around here,' Sam said.

'What's a Rumi?'

'He was a famous Persian poet.'

'Oh, I must have missed his stuff in school,' Greta said. Noreen looked at Greta expectantly.

'Say sorry,' Sam whispered.

'Sorry, Heather.' Greta apologized, but didn't really mean it. 'My words were not kind or necessary.' She paused, before adding, 'But they were true.'

The room giggled and even Noreen had a smile on her face. 'Go on, Heather. What happened next?'

'He threw me out. I ended up sleeping in my car, homeless.'

'And that was your rock-bottom moment?' Noreen asked gently.

Heather shook her head. 'No. I deserved that. In fact, I almost welcomed it. It was the look on his face when he realized what I'd done that nearly killed me. My betrayal. I'd told myself for years that my drinking was not affecting anyone but me. I had it under control. But at that moment, I saw what I had done to him, and I've never felt shame like it.'

'Excellent work, Heather. Thank you for sharing with the group.'

A chorus of 'well dones' and other platitudes of approval erupted around the room. Greta gulped down a lump that had appeared in her throat. She had felt amused by Heather's story right up to the moment she mentioned her shame. *That* she understood. And there was nothing funny about that feeling.

Noreen looked around the room, ready to hear someone else's story. Greta kept her head down low. She had no intention of getting involved in this conversation. She needn't have worried because it appeared that now Heather had got the ball rolling, the group were all ready to spill their particular brand of beans. They held their hands up in the air, one by one, eager to prove that sharing is caring.

Eileen admitted to waking up in bed with someone who wasn't her husband. Tim broke into his next-door neighbours' house, looking for painkillers in their bathroom cabinet. Sam admitted to gambling away his house and savings. Rory woke up in a jail cell in Wexford, with no clue how he ended up there.

'Many of us have done things when under the influence that we would never do with a clear head,' Noreen said.

A sea of yeses filled the room. Not from Greta, though. She'd never done anything like that. Once again she felt smug and removed from her counterparts here. She wasn't like them.

Liar, liar pants on fire. Greta pushed the thought down hard.

'Be honest with yourselves. There is no point hiding from this. I'd like everyone to ask themselves if you have ever done something that you were ashamed of while under the influence of your addiction?'

Greta felt Noreen's eyes rest on her. They seemed to be probing into her head, searching until they dislodged a memory, buried.

Dylan.

She'd avoided thinking about the incident she'd had with him six months ago. Despite Dylan's efforts to discuss it with her, she'd made it quite clear that she would never do so. Now Greta could think of nothing else as flashes of that weekend demanded attention.

The Murder Mystery Crew were a social gang. Plus, as they all stayed in the hotel each weekend, it was inevitable that a party happened in one of the rooms. Greta wasn't a big drinker, but she'd had more than her usual couple on this occasion. Seeing Donna play the part of Ruby Mae, wearing *her* costume, hurt. With every swish of that red saloon girl's costume, with every swing of her hip, Greta felt . . . less beautiful. Less funny. Less talented. Less loved. Less *her*. So she decided to drown her sorrows in red wine. It worked for a bit. She forgot that she didn't like herself very much and she partied hard with her cast mates. And when Donna decided it would be fun to tell everyone about Greta's wardrobe malfunction, oh how they all laughed. They clutched their sides and howled at their funny fat friend who could no longer fit into her costume. And Greta let them make *her body* the punch line. She gave them permission to laugh when she laughed the loudest at herself.

When she went back to her hotel room, she took a pill to help her sleep. Thinking about this now, she realized that was a bit weird in itself. There was a time that a few drinks would send her to the land of nod as soon as her head hit the pillow. When had it become normal to her to follow that with sleeping aids too? That's when things got weird. The next morning she awoke in bed, lying beside Dylan. She had no memory of how she got there or what they had done. Then Greta realized that she wasn't even in her own room, she was in his. In her underwear. Shocked and horrified, she dressed as quietly as she could, then sneaked out the door, leaving him asleep in the bed alone. What had she done? Dylan was her friend and she'd jeopardized that. And it was only when she was back in her own room that the full impact of her actions hit her. Dylan had seen her body. No Spanx slip to hold everything in. Just Greta in her bra and knickers with all her lumps and bumps, ugly dimpled cellulite and stretch marks. She couldn't laugh this one off.

She couldn't face it either. So she did a classic Greta move. She shoved the memory down deep inside her, to sit with all the other painful and sad ones.

Dylan had tried to talk to her about their sleepover, several times, but she'd refused to engage. 'If you value our friendship, you will never mention it again,' she'd said to him. And that was that.

But here, in this roomful of strangers, with raw pain intensifying as each person shared their lowest points, Greta couldn't shove the memory away. It tumbled around her mind, demanding her attention.

Noreen helped each person work through their rock-bottom moments, and she never showed shock or surprise, just gentle support and encouragement. And when she murmured the odd inspirational cliché, Greta found herself forgiving her. To her surprise, Greta found herself murmuring the odd word of encouragement to each person as they spoke.

Noreen raised an eyebrow in question to Greta to see if she would like to share anything. Greta shook her head vigorously. There was nothing she wanted to say. She just wanted to return to her room, lie down on her bed and find a way to fall asleep. It had been an intense morning and she was overwhelmed with it all. So much pain bouncing around this room.

Noreen said, 'As you can see, rock bottom is different for everyone. For one person it's the breakup of a relationship, for another it's the loss of their home. Everyone here is unique, but we share something, me included. We've done things and said things that we would never have believed possible before our addiction. Because addiction changes us.'

Have I changed? Greta thought about the past twelve months and realized she no longer recognized herself. Who was she now?

Noreen continued, 'But make no mistake. These moments you have shared here today were carried out by the addict in you. You have to own them. It's the only way to make sure that they no longer define who *you* are. Not unless you let them.' She looked around the room, making sure she made eye contact with every single one of them. 'I'm proud of you all. You have all taken steps today to seek recovery.'

Greta felt a bit like a fraud. All she'd done was listen, so she wasn't sure she deserved any praise. She remained in her chair as the others left the room and tried to work out what she should do next.

'You're shaking.'

Greta looked up in surprise. Noreen was standing beside her. 'It will get harder before it gets easier.'

Noreen was an addict too. She might understand Greta's inability to sleep. There must be something Noreen could give her, even half a tablet. Greta suggested as much to her. Noreen smiled and listened as Greta relayed her difficulty sleeping. The endless hours she had put in the night before. The shakes. Nausea. 'So you see, I thought it would make more sense if you could tell Caroline or whoever to fill a prescription for me. Just to help me wean off the pills. I'd take them here, under medical supervision of course. That way you all can be reassured that I'm safe.'

Greta felt smug again. She had been articulate and reasonable. Not desperate in the least. When would she learn that whenever she felt smug, it usually meant that things were about to go any which way but hers?

'No.'

'That doesn't make sense!' Greta was outraged, then shoved her hands behind her back when she saw Noreen looking at them.

'What doesn't make sense is the fact that less than twenty-four hours into your treatment for drug addiction, you think it's appropriate to ask me for drugs.' Noreen was still smiling.

'And what doesn't make sense to me is that you would expect me to do this without any support. It's cruel. Inhumane even.'

Noreen's smile slipped away at that point. 'You need to return your brain to its normal function, without the need to take chemicals to make it work. Until you do that, you won't be able to sleep.'

'But you don't understand. I cannot sleep without my pills. The only thing that gives me peace is the sleeping tablets. Everything else is messed up.'

'From what I've heard, the tablets didn't solve your insomnia. They just made life a whole lot worse.'

'I wouldn't say worse,' Greta countered, not liking how this conversation had turned.

'According to my notes, you almost killed yourself. I wouldn't call that fine. Was that your rock-bottom moment Greta? When you were pulled from the bath?'

Greta had no answer to that.

'You've forgotten how to look for the beauty in your life. It's there, hidden amid the chaos and mess. Can you let me help you find it again? At least be open to the possibility that rescue is possible. That you can get out of this?' Noreen asked.

Greta found herself nodding once. A silent, small gesture that maybe it was time to finally look for help. Noreen glided out of the room, leaving Greta and her shakes behind.

Chapter 8

Greta scrambled backwards across the single bed, screaming, as the man moved towards her. If he managed to reach her, there was no doubt in her mind that he would kill her. Her back slammed hard against the cold wall and he disappeared. She reached for the light and switched it on, her heart pounding so fast that she could feel the vibrations in her chest. Her pyjamas were wet through, her body drenched in a cold sweat. She'd had a variation of this same nightmare ever since she was a young child. Ever since the advert. The fear was sometimes paralysing and other times, like just now, she would scramble and claw her way backwards, to escape his gnarly hands, as they reached out to her.

Her body ached, not just from the emotional onslaught of terror but also from the hours of non-stop puking she'd endured the previous evening and night. Yesterday had been one of the worst days of her life. She suspected much worse was to come.

There was no way she could go back to sleep. She longed for her iPad or phone, wishing she could while away the hours until morning, scrolling through social media. But without either of them to distract her, that left her with only her thoughts. She was never comfortable with them, which left her in a right pickle. She'd had the same recurring nightmare, on and off, for as long as she could remember.

Some nights she didn't remember much about the nightmare, she just awoke knowing that she was terrified. Others, she could remember every moment in precise detail. The unknown hooded man trying to kill her was tall. He wore a long hooded black cloak. Yet, no matter how close he got to her, she never saw his face. It was always blank, as if someone had scrubbed his features away.

She decided to leave the light on and even though it took her an hour to fall back asleep, she eventually did.

Later, she managed to sit through Noreen's group session. This time it was about self-deception. Greta felt every word land uncomfortably in her gut. Did she lie? To herself? To others? She decided that if she did, they were only white lies, so they didn't matter. Or did they?

She thought too about when Noreen had asked Greta what she preferred to be called, G or Greta, after the first group therapy session. She had lied and said she didn't care. Greta hated the name G. She'd said as much to her family ages ago. She asked them to stop calling her Big G. But the very fact that she admitted she didn't like the name made her brothers cling to it even tighter. That's how they rolled in the Gale house. And her mother had thrown her eyes to the heavens muttering about notions again. Which was the worst offence any Irish person could commit, as far as her mam was concerned. When Aidan joined the local gym in an attempt to get a six-pack, he'd had notions. When Ciaran came home with chia seeds to sprinkle on top of his porridge each morning because some girl had told him to. Notions of the highest order. And when Greta had got headshots taken for her actress portfolio. She looked brilliant, with a bit of airbrushing and a soft filter. Notions eleven.

She figured it was easier to shut up and let the Gales continue to call her Big G. Was that self-deception? Greta didn't think she was very good at rehab. All she did was confuse herself.

Noreen's voice interrupted her thoughts, and she was pulled back to the group session again. 'Remember, there is a big difference between giving up and knowing when you have had enough.'

Should Greta give up her dream to be an actress? She'd now had nearly a quarter of a century of disappointments as she tried over and over to make her star shine once more. Were her moments over?

Big G

A has-been in da house.

Washed-up.

Literally.

Greta couldn't imagine doing anything else but acting. She'd had the bug ever since she was a little girl and wasn't sure she could give up now. She'd tried all the usual after-school activities as a kid. Soccer, piano, Irish dancing, gymnastics, GAA. But all they did was make her feel inadequate, because she never quite made the grade.

Greta remembered her teacher once saying to her parents, smiling, 'She's just not athletic, is she?' And although there was no malice in the comment, it hurt the seven-year-old Greta all the same. She felt like she was failing her family, her teacher. Herself. But then her mam sent her to drama club. Greta had shuffled in to class, expecting to fail. But instead she'd found her voice, her heart, her dream, *herself*. Her coach told her that she had *it*, whatever *it* was. That when Greta performed, she believed her. Greta had swelled with pride and she knew that this was what she wanted to do for the rest of her life. Nothing else mattered but acting. It was her everything.

Once the group session was over, everyone went to the gym for yoga. It was Greta's first experience and it wasn't a pleasant one. As she lay on a mat, all she could smell was feet around her. And she was sure Rory farted too, although he did a big job of waving his arms around, feigning innocence. Greta quickly discovered that she didn't have a flexible bone or muscle in her body. Her body spasmed about five minutes into the downward dog. And when the instructor pushed in her stomach, telling her to find her inner core, she very nearly puked again, all over her gym shoes. She felt Caroline's eyes on her, taking in everything, and when Greta left the room, Caroline followed her.

'I'm going to be sick,' Greta said, running into her bathroom. She begged Caroline to leave, embarrassed. But Caroline stayed and helped her to bed when her body had expelled everything left inside. She placed a cold compress on Greta's forehead and gently told her that she'd get through this. That better days were ahead.

Since she arrived at rehab, Greta had wished she had died in the bathtub on a few occasions. But never more so than right now. She couldn't get away from the voice in her head telling her over and over again how weak and useless she was. The voice that constantly relived her shame. She prayed for an end to her misery until finally her body was quiet, and she fell asleep. The hooded man from her dreams stayed in the shadows and somehow she managed to get through the night.

Halfway through her first week, a card was slipped under Greta's door. It was an appointment for her first one-on-one with Noreen. She felt like she was being called to the principal's office, which was a nice room as it happened, with a large mahogany desk sitting in front of a large bay window, overlooking the garden. It was pretty out there, with a twenty-foot weeping willow tree in the corner, a bench underneath it. Noreen stood up to welcome her then she motioned Greta to take a seat. It was a soft comfortable armchair, similar to theirs at home. Greta was relieved to see a large blush velvet cushion, which she placed on her lap. If a seat was missing a cushion, then she'd place her handbag on her lap. A well-rehearsed trick to hide her stomach when she sat down. She had accumulated a stockpile of ways to hide her body over the years.

Selfies, taken at the right angle, only of her head, never her body.

Sleeves. God forbid her wobbly arms might be on display.

Oversized jewellery to distract people from her over-sized body.

And she always stood behind someone or something in photographs. Hiding, Greta was very good at.

'Have you been out to the garden yet?' Noreen asked.

'I've gone for a short walk most mornings before group therapy. I've been feeling ill so I've not managed much more than that.'

'Now that you're feeling better, you should expand your horizon a little more. Follow the path to the end of the garden. You'll see a gate. Head out through that, and you'll end up at our beach, which is only accessible from this house, so it's totally private.'

'I've never really been the outdoorsy type, but I'll give it a go.'

'I'm interested to hear about what you feel is the event or defining moment that tipped you into addiction. Have you any thoughts on that?'

'I don't know,' Greta said, and she wasn't being difficult. She really *didn't* know. Events and timings were all muddled up in her head.

'In my experience, people don't start taking pills unless there's something else going on. We need to work out what that is for you. You said that you hadn't been sleeping well for nearly a year before you began taking them?'

'My mam says that I've never been a good sleeper. My brothers were never a bother for her, but me, I've always been difficult. So I think it's been an issue for me for most of my life. Obviously the past year or so it's gotten out of hand. It's always been the same, Big G, being different.'

'I can't imagine what that must be like. What do you do during those times when you can't sleep?'

'I watch TV. Catch up on social media. Play games on my iPad. Sometimes I cry.' Greta meant that as a joke, but it didn't land like one.

'I want you to be honest here and dig deeper. Is there any event or time that you think could have triggered the insomnia?'

'No. I can't think of anything.' She pushed away her hooded man.

Noreen looked disappointed. She wrote something else into her notebook. Greta had no idea what the woman wanted from her. 'What do you want me to say? That I had some big childhood trauma, which I can blame my problems on? My parents are nice. I come from an ordinary, sometimes pain-in-my-ass family. None of this is their fault.'

'So the fault is all yours?'

'Yep. Big G takes a bow. She managed to screw this up all on her own.'

Noreen scribbled something in her notebook at that, then looked up and said, 'Why do you do that? Call yourself Big G.'

'It's my nickname.'

'I understood your nickname was simply G. Short for Greta.'

'My brothers call me Big G.'

More scribbling in Noreen's notebook. 'And is that how you see yourself? As big?'

Greta looked down at her stomach that swelled over her leggings. She'd seen pregnant women who had smaller stomachs than she had. 'Well yes. Because that's what I am. You can hardly disagree with that. I'm grossly overweight.'

'I'm not sure I'd call you grossly overweight,' Noreen said. 'What I am sure of is that you are very hard on yourself.'

'I'm honest, there's a difference.'

'And how long have you struggled with your weight?'

'Since I was old enough to be aware of my size. So I guess for a long time.'

'And have you tried to do anything about it?'

'I've been on every diet that has ever been invented. From cabbage soup to no-carbs, only carbs, vegetarian, you name it. I've joined most of the slimming groups at some point over the years. I even joined the gym last year and signed up to a personal trainer.'

'And how did those diets go?'

Honestly, for a supposedly intelligent woman, Noreen asked the most ridiculous questions. Greta pointed to her large stomach and said, 'How do you think?'

'You are a harsh critic.'

Was she? She didn't know about that. 'I just say it like it is. Every time I started a diet, I thought, this time it will work, this time I'll get that bikini body.'

'Who says you don't already have one of those?'

'I'd be happy if I could just wear a pair of skinny jeans with a T-shirt tucked into the waistband. Rather than my usual frenzy to find a baggy swing T-shirt that can be worn without clinging to my tummy. Surprisingly hard, I might add.'

'So is it just about how you look? You want to lose weight to feel better about your appearance?'

'No. It's more than that. I want to be healthy too. I'd like to bend over without a stabbing pain in my ribs. And more than that, my size is affecting my profession. There are limited roles for fat women. Thin is in. Size zero is the hero. Fat is not all that.'

'I can only imagine how hard that must be in your job. For most of us, it's impossible to conform to societal standards of beauty. But when your job is in the public eye, it must be even harder.' She looked through her notes, then said, 'When you hear the word "fat", how does it make you feel?'

'The word fat has haunted me my whole life,' Greta sighed.

'What do you mean by that?'

'My brothers, my mam and dad, they are all thin. All of them. But as soon as adolescence hit, I piled on the pounds. And my dad hated that. He'd nag me. "You're getting chubby G. Don't eat that G, it'll make you fat." Blah, blah, blah. It's a shaming word.'

'That must feel like a lot of pressure.'

'Not really,' Greta lied.

'What's making you so sad right now?'

Greta shrugged. 'I hate talking about my weight. It makes me uncomfortable.'

'And do you talk about it often?'

'Unavoidable lately. It's a subject that comes up quite a bit at home. My dad runs. He's moved from park runs to half-marathons. And now my brothers and he are talking about training for a full marathon together. I'm waiting for Mam to sign up next. The family who run together stay together . . .' Greta trailed off.

'How does it feel living with a family of keep fit enthusiasts.'

'I feel like they are judging me all the time.' She whispered. 'I want to be like them. But I don't know how.'

'You don't have to be like anyone Greta. You just have to be *you*.'

'The problem is, Noreen, that I keep making a mess of that.'

'Maybe. But that's in the past. You're making changes now.'

'Am I?'

'The very fact that you are sitting here talking to me about how you feel is a change from the woman I met on your first day, when you tried to get me to give you pills.'

'Sorry about that. My bad.'

'Oh I've had all sorts of requests here. But the point is that you are changing, and that's good. I would like you to think about how you see yourself. I think that between the pressure you feel at home and the pressure you feel at work, you have developed low self-esteem. We need to work on that too. So to start off, no more putting yourself down.'

'I don't think I do that,' Greta said.

'Every label you put on yourself is a negative one.' Noreen reached over and touched Greta's hand. 'These labels do not determine who you are. You get to decide who you are; nobody else should have that power. And it's only when you work out who you are, that you will be able to find a way to move on.'

'I'm not sure I understand,' Greta said.

'It's quite simple. You need to find out who Greta Gale is.'

'I don't think I'm brave enough to do that. It's easier to be Big G.'

'I don't think Big G is the person you are supposed to be. Maybe it's time to find out who that is.'

'I don't think I'm supposed to be this person either.' Tears stung her eyes, and she wanted to run out the door, all the way home to Dublin. She'd throw her arms around her family and tell them how sorry she was for everything she'd put them through.

'I've been Big G my whole life. I don't know how to be anyone else.'

'Yes, you do. Try being Greta. The days of Big G are over.'

Chapter 9

'You're looking less like a walking dead extra today, G,' Sam said when Greta walked into the TV room.

'Always the charmer.'

'It's a gift, I won't lie.'

'Er, Sam . . . em . . . I'm trying something for a while with my name. Can you call me Greta?'

'Sure. Homework from Noreen?'

'Yeah! My head is spinning from all the questions I have to find answers to. She wants me to find myself. I don't know where to start.'

Sam laughed, 'This "getting clean" shit is hard! But seriously . . . Greta . . . you do look better.'

'I feel better. I slept for five hours in a row last night. Without a single pill inside of me.'

'And how did you feel when you woke up?'

'Surprised!' Greta joked, and they both smiled at that.

'For a while there, I wasn't sure I was going to make

it. And truthfully, I wasn't sure if I wanted to or not.' She pushed aside the image of the hooded man. He had come back again last night. She had woken up, gasping for air, crying for help. Greta had kept these nightmares a secret for so long. She found it impossible to open up about them. But perhaps it was time to mention them to Noreen at their next session.

'Any word from Maggie?' Greta asked.

Sam's wife had refused to take any of his calls since he arrived at the centre. And later this afternoon it was his turn for family therapy.

He shook his head and said, 'I can't say I blame her really. I don't think she'll ever forgive me for what I've done.'

'Do you think she'll turn up?' Greta asked.

'No idea. To be honest, I don't know what frightens me more. Her turning up, or her not caring enough to come.'

Greta could understand that. Her own family session was in the not-too-distant future. Since her arrival at the centre, she'd attended several of these. Some opted to keep theirs private, but most wanted the support of their fellow residents in the room with them. And Noreen said they were learning experiences for everyone. They were always held in the afternoons, and while each one was different, they were all raw, painful and highly emotive. Only yesterday Eileen had faced her estranged husband. She listened to him, took every verbal hit he threw at her for over twenty minutes. Then she begged his forgiveness – for her addiction, but most of all for allowing that addiction to let her have sex with a stranger. The room held its collective breath as he looked at her, willing him to offer his wife something to cling to, some hope for their future.

'I have no inclination to be married to a slut.' His words bounced around the hall, making them all wince. 'Are we done?' he asked Noreen. Then he stood up and walked out of the room.

Sometimes reality bites.

'Maybe it's better if Maggie doesn't come. At least that way I can hold on to hope that she'll forgive me one day. If she comes here and says it's over . . . then . . .' He couldn't finish the sentence. He didn't know what he'd do.

In the end, Maggie did turn up. But despite a long and harrowing session, where everything was left on the floor for all to see, Maggie couldn't forgive Sam. She refused to speak, sitting opposite her husband, her face pale, her eyes bright with unshed tears.

'I'll never forgive myself for what I've put you through,' Sam said to his wife.

Give him something, come on Maggie.

'I believe you mean that right now. And I love you too, Sam. But I don't think I can ever trust you again.'

They sat within inches of each other, but they might as well have been miles apart. And a horrifying thought crippled Greta. What if her family couldn't forgive her either . . . ?

Chapter 10

'Well, are we Greta or G today?' Noreen asked when Greta walked into her office.

'You can call me anything you want. I want to go home. I'll sign whatever bullshit release form I have to. I'm getting out of here.'

The smile on Noreen's face froze, and she motioned to the chair in front of her. 'Sit down, and we can talk about it.'

'I don't want to talk about it. I don't see why I can't just go home. I can continue this programme as an out-patient or something.' Greta paced around the office, feeling adrenalin pulsing throughout her body.

'It doesn't work like that, Greta. And, speaking of work, that's what you have to put in here before you can go anywhere. And you haven't even scratched the surface of that yet.'

'I've not had a pill in over a week!' Greta shouted.

'But are you ready to admit that you are an addict? Because until you do, you can't even begin to sort through the mess that is your life.'

'My life is just fine! You don't know anything about it.'

'No it's not, and don't pretend otherwise,' Noreen said. She pushed her phone towards Greta with force. 'Call your parents. Go on. No one is forcing you to be here. If you don't want to stay, then leave!'

Greta reached for the phone, held it in her hand and looked at the dial pad.

'What's keeping you? Go on, ring your mam and dad. I'll give you twenty-four hours before you are out looking for pills. If you haven't already got a stash hidden somewhere.'

Greta felt a stab of guilt. Because there was a pack of pills under a loose floorboard that was hidden under her bed. She used to hide Easter eggs there when she was a kid so that Aidan and Ciaran couldn't rob them from her.

'I'm right, aren't I? You've another stash hiding, waiting for your return home. Admit it.'

Greta folded her arms across her chest.

'Admit it!' Noreen said again.

'There's another stash hidden under my bed.' Greta whispered her admission.

Noreen sank back into her chair and sighed. They sat in silence for a moment, then she said, 'Do you think that's normal behaviour? Hiding pills? Greta, you are an addict, and it's time you owned up to that. Why is that so hard for you to do?'

'Well, I'm not shooting up. I'm not off my face on

heroin or whiskey. I only take sleeping pills to help me sleep. I don't think it's fair to put that label on me.'

'You and your labels. So quick to call yourself fat all the time. But so slow to admit a truth! Addicts come in all guises. While I was buying illegal drugs on the streets from dealers, I was teaching, parenting, being a friend. But make no mistake. I was and will always be an addict.'

'I never bought drugs on the street,' Greta said.

'So does that mean you are less of an addict than me? Because you had a credit card and did some online shopping on the black market?'

Greta didn't like how this conversation was going. Sweat began to trickle down her face.

'If you were diagnosed with stage four cancer, would you get treatment?' Noreen asked Greta.

'Of course.' The change in the direction of their conversation startled her.

'If you had been diagnosed with stage *one* cancer, in the early stages, would you get treatment to prevent it from getting worse? Or just leave it as it was, saying it's not too bad.'

There was no answer to that. Or at least, not one that helped Greta. All her excuses and lies that she had told herself began to run through her head. Could she be wrong and everyone else right?

Noreen pulled the heavy drape curtains closed behind her, switching off the lights until it was pitch dark in the room.

'What are you doing?' Greta asked in alarm. 'I don't like the dark.'

'I want you to say out loud that you are an addict. Maybe you can find the strength to do it in the dark.'

Greta clutched the phone in her hand, and she let her fingers touch the dial pad, getting a feel for where the numbers were. She could call her parents. Tell them that she was uncomfortable with the line of therapy that Noreen was pursuing. Her dad would hate this, seeing it as mumbo-jumbo nonsense.

Yet somehow, some way, her hand quietened and made no further move.

Every fibre in her body was calling out for help.

She had spent the past year trying to numb her pain, but it hadn't worked.

She needed help. Because . . . because . . . because goddamn it . . .

'I'm an addict.' A whisper. Followed by silence, save for the sound of her breathing as it quickened.

'Say it again,' Noreen commanded.

'I'm an addict.' Louder this time.

The silence gobbled up the words, greedily. Greta wiped the sweat from her face and took a steadying breath.

Then the lamp on Noreen's desk flicked on, casting shadows into the room. 'Repeat it.'

The shadows from the lamp moved towards her, laced with menace. 'I'm an addict. I'm addicted to sleeping pills.' Tears spilt down her cheeks, hot and furious.

And then Noreen stood up and pulled back the curtains, letting the sun back into the room. She didn't need to ask this time.

'I'm . . . An . . . Addict . . .' Greta sobbed as her truth was set free.

She felt arms around her, catching her from falling. Noreen held her close, rocking her back and forth as her body released years of pain. Until she was done.

Noreen gently uncurled Greta's fingers from the phone that she still held with a vice-like grip. She gently wiped the tears from Greta's face. 'I'm proud of you. I knew you were a fighter.'

Greta had not heard those words said to her in the longest time. When was it? 'I think the last time someone said they were proud of me was when I was in the Christmas advert.'

'Sometimes it's up to ourselves to be proud. And today is one of those days, Greta. Because admitting your addiction is the first step, of many, many steps to come. And each of these steps will get you through this pain and help to ease it. I promise you.'

'I'm scared that my family won't forgive me.'

'Remember this. It takes time to regain trust, but in my experience, our loved ones have patience. They love and forgive. You just need to have a little patience of your own. Continue doing what you've started here.'

She picked up the phone again and pushed it towards Greta. 'Would you like to ring your mam, just to say hello? I think it might be a good idea. It's been a big day for you. I'll have to stay here while you make the call, though.'

Greta's heart began to hammer at the thought of hearing her mother's voice. She'd missed her so much. She punched her mother's mobile number into the dial pad and held her breath as it connected.

'Hello . . . is Greta OK?' Emily's voice shook.

'Hello Mam.'

'Oh love, is it really you? I saw Hope Crossing's number come up on the screen. I nearly passed out, thinking all sorts.'

Greta began to cry. 'Mam, I'm so sorry for everything.'

'Oh love, I know you are. Are you being good? Are you doing what they tell you to do?'

'Mam, I'm not a child any more; you don't have to keep checking up on me,' Greta replied, then realized that maybe she did. She'd not been very good at adulting lately. 'Sorry. Yes, I'm being good.' She glanced at Noreen who smiled.

'Good girl.'

'Is everyone OK at home?'

'We are all grand. Wait till I tell your father you've called. He's at work at the moment.'

'Tell Aidan and Ciaran I'm sorry too. Especially about them having to see me naked. I'd say they're still scarred.'

Her mam giggled, and the sound made Greta ache for her arms once more. 'Mam, I've got to go, but before I do, can you get something from under my bed. There's a wonky floorboard, and if you push it down, it opens. I've got some tablets hidden there.'

'Greta Gale!'

'I know. I know. Just get rid of them for me, please.'

'You can count on that, young lady! And while I'm at it, I'll give your room a good top-to-bottom clean. You might as well tell me if more surprises are coming my way.'

'That's the only ones hidden. I promise. I've got to go, but Mam, thank you . . .'

'For what love?'

112

'For not leaving me.'

'Ah love, I could never do that. You're part of me. So that means we're connected to each other, no matter what happens.'

Greta felt something give inside of her and tears once again began to overcome her. 'Bye Mam.' She clicked to end the call.

Chapter 11

Greta's next phone call home didn't go quite so well. This time she was allowed to call her mother, without supervision. And it appeared that Emily and Greta had forgotten how to talk to each other.

'It's rained for two hours straight here.' That, from her mother.

'I'd say it's been more like four hours here.' That, from Greta.

And then they both fell silent. Greta figured that her mam, like her, couldn't bear to talk about the weather for one more moment. They had never been that kind of a family. They had, however, always been good at avoidance.

She had to break the silence to tell her about the forthcoming family session and ask her to attend.

'Who needs to be there?' Emily asked, her voice filled with panic.

'All of you. Dad, Ciaran, Aidan. Uncle Ray.'

'Should I ask Father McBride, do you think?'

'No!' *Good Jesus.*

'OK love. We'll all be there. We wouldn't miss it for the world.'

Emily made it sound like it was a day out to see Greta graduate or something.

'What should we wear?' Emily asked.

It took all of Greta's self-control not to tell her to stay at home. 'Just wear your everyday clothes, Mam.'

'I don't know. I think I'd better wear a good dress. The one I had for your cousin Lorna's wedding last year. Remember the olive-green one. Everyone said it looked lovely on me that day.'

Greta vaguely remembered the dress, which came with a large flowery hat and gloves. 'Don't wear the hat and gloves!'

'What do you take me for? Honestly, as if I'd do that. And I'll get your dad's grey suit dry-cleaned. I might buy him a new tie. Something festive, to cheer us all up. Oh, I'll have to buy a new shirt for the boys. Your Uncle Ray will be grand. He always has a nice clean shirt in his wardrobe for special occasions.'

'It's not a special occasion, Mam.'

'You know what I mean. Sure we can make a day of it. If we leave early, we can stop for lunch on the way to you. It wouldn't do to have any grumbling stomachs in the middle of the session.'

'Great, Mam. Gotta go. There's a queue for the phone.'

As is always the way when you want time to slow down, it galloped along, then came to a shuddering halt as Greta waited for her family to walk through the reception doors.

She'd not seen them in two weeks, but it felt like years. Greta was proud of her progress, though. She'd given up her pills. Harder than that, Greta had admitted she was an addict. She discovered that she had a problem with the Fat word and she said goodbye to Big G. Saying hello to Greta Gale was a little trickier. Despite her best efforts, she still had no clue how to find her. And Greta had finally told Noreen about her nightmares, which they were now working on in their one-to-one sessions. She just needed to get through this and then . . . That was the bit she was not sure about. She had no idea what would happen when she left the centre. Greta watched the clock tick-tock at a snail's pace and was convinced that someone had messed with it to send her over the edge. Then all of a sudden the door to reception opened and in they filed.

Her mam got to her first and pulled her into her arms.

'You wore the hat.' Greta shook her head in disbelief.

'It looked awful without it. The hat finishes it off,' Emily said.

Uncle Ray pulled Greta in for a hug next, and she breathed in his familiar smell of coffee and Lynx. 'It's been very quiet at home without you.'

'I've missed you,' she realized the truth of her words as she said them. Ray was always there for her, their bond glued together when she was born. 'Did you find the owners of that stray?' She'd thought about the little dog often over the past couple of weeks.

'I called into every house on the road, but nobody owned it. So I took it to the Dogs Trust. They'll find it a new home. Cute little fella.'

'That's good. Thanks,' Greta said.

116

She looked over to her dad, Ciaran and Aidan, but they remained a few feet from her, avoiding eye contact.

Caroline hustled them all towards a busy hall. Family therapy sessions were a bit like soap operas for the patients. Watching someone else's problems play out in front of you – well, it took you out of your own for a while. Sam gave Greta an encouraging thumbs-up when she walked in. Eileen all but had the popcorn out, sitting forward expectantly.

Greta took a seat beside Noreen, and the rest of her family sat in a semicircle around them. Her mam had been to the hairdresser's, she noted. Her hair was shiny and bouncy, in a curly blow-dry. Her family were as her mother had promised, all wearing their Sunday best. But they looked like they wished they were anywhere but here. Greta understood that feeling. Her dad tugged at his tie and his white shirt collar, the creases from the packet it had been pulled from earlier this afternoon still crisp. Ciaran and Aidan were also in their best shirts, worn loose, their shirt tails limp and redundant on their laps, stained from their dampened hands.

A memory jolted her like a needle. The boys begging her to iron their shirts, because their parents were away for the weekend. Her telling them that she wasn't their mammy, that she'd got better things to do than help them get their 'pulling' gear ready. And all of them realizing that – with that admonishment – she sounded exactly like their mammy. They'd laughed so much that day that Greta's side hurt. The memory, so at odds with the now, brought tears, sharp to her eyes. There was no messing or teasing from her brothers here. She couldn't remember the last time they'd had the craic like that.

Maybe the rest of her family carried on having fun, and it was just she who had stopped.

Greta tried to keep her eyes downward, but she couldn't help sneaking glances at them to see how they were reacting to it all. Her mum was nodding enthusiastically at everything Noreen said. Her dad was stone-faced, hard to read, but listening intently all the same.

Underneath their need to do the right thing in a situation that was so far removed from anything they'd ever been in before, she saw the pain on their faces. There was something else, too. She could see guilt in their eyes. Two weeks ago, when she'd arrived here, all she'd wanted was for them to feel pain like she had. But now, she wanted to run over to them to tell them that none of this was their fault and take away any guilt that they had on their shoulders. *I'm the screw-up, not you guys.*

Noreen said, 'I know that you have all tried many times to save Greta. But it's not your job to save her. It's up to Greta to save herself. And I'm pleased to say that she's been working so hard here.'

Eileen clapped and cheered at this pearl of wisdom. *The big lick.*

Emily cleared her throat, jumping straight in. 'I don't understand why you started to take the tablets? What on earth possessed you?'

'I was tired,' Greta replied.

'I'm tired too. I've hardly slept a wink in weeks. But I didn't start taking drugs.'

'I regularly missed days of sleep. And the nightmares were back.'

'What nightmares?' Stephen asked. 'This is the first I've heard about any nightmare.'

'Do you mean the bad dreams you had as a little girl?' Ray asked. 'I can remember when I babysat you, you would wake up in a pool of sweat, screaming the house down.'

Stephen looked at Ray with irritation. 'All kids have nightmares.'

'Yes, those nightmares Uncle Ray. I'll regret taking that first sleeping tablet for the rest of my life. But that night after I took it, I slept. For eight hours straight. It was the best night's sleep I'd ever had. I thought I'd found the cure for my insomnia.'

'Some cure,' Stephen spluttered.

'I know that now. But back then, the feeling I had the next day was something I hadn't experienced in years. I felt alive, energized, ready to take on anything life threw at me. I had an audition that day, and I was electric in that room. Even when they changed the lines at the last minute, I nailed it. The casting director said so.'

'You still didn't get the part though,' Stephen said.

'No, Dad. I didn't get the part.' Greta sighed.

'Have you had any of the nightmares since you've been in here, love?' Emily asked.

Greta nodded. 'A few.'

'Can you help her with those?' Emily asked Noreen. 'Is there a pill she can take . . .' Then she stopped, putting her hand over her mouth. 'I'm sorry. That was silly.'

Noreen shook her head. 'Not silly at all, Emily. We're

giving Greta some techniques to help her get to sleep. Yoga and meditation before bed every evening has been of real benefit.'

'I suggested we do yoga together, but you wouldn't come with me,' Emily said.

'That was then, Mam. I guess I wasn't in the right frame of mind. This yoga is different; it's about relaxation and meditation. It's helping.'

'Why don't you all share with Greta how her addiction affected you personally? Pick one incident and share how it made you feel. Who would like to go first?' Noreen's voice was gentle and kind as she looked at each of Greta's family, one by one.

Greta tried to make herself smaller in her chair, which was impossible because her arse still spilt out, leaving her with no wriggle-room. She tried to guess what incidents her family would mention. In fairness, they had quite a big arsenal of offences to quote.

Emily began to tell them all about Christmas Day just passed. 'Greta went to her room after lunch, saying she needed a nap. We were all in the living room, watching—'

'*Indiana Jones.*' Aidan obliged her by filling in the blank.

'That's right. I do like Harrison Ford. He's a real man. A man's man. I didn't much care for him in that *Six Days Seven Nights*. I can't quite work out whether I like Callista or not—'

'Mam.' Aidan gave Emily a nudge.

Greta smiled at her mam; she'd missed her long-winded answers.

'Oh yes, where was I?'

'Christmas Day.' Greta helped her out.

'Oh yes, well Greta walked in. As if in a trance. But yet she was awake. Weird to see, actually.'

'Of course, we now know she was off her head,' Aidan said.

'Aidan!' Emily hissed. 'As I was saying, Greta stood in front of the telly, totally blocking out Indy. Then she started to re-enact *The Wizard of Oz*. Every part. Now I'm partial to a "ding dong the witch is dead" singsong, while I'm watching the movie, but not while Indy is trying to escape from a group of Nazis!'

Greta could have sworn she heard Sam snigger here.

'Sorry, Mam,' Greta said.

'Well, you do have a lovely voice. And it was quite something when you got to "Somewhere Over the Rainbow".'

Once they began to talk, it was as if a dam had broken as they confessed all of Greta's sins for her.

Greta whispered apologies for each offence and hoped that they would run out of steam soon.

But then it was Aidan's turn, who gave her a look so filled with loathing that it made her shiver. 'Stop saying sorry, G! There's nothing you can say that will make this OK. We've not even begun to get to the good stuff. Like how about the time you did a Facebook live video while off your face, and how it went viral? That was fun in college, knowing that people were ripping the piss out of my big sister. Or how about all the times you nearly burned the house down, cos you decided to have a midnight feast but forgot to turn the grill off before you passed out. Leaving Ciaran and me to take the blame. But of course, god forbid any of us ever suggested that it was you who did it!'

121

Greta felt a flush sweep over her body, remembering the shove Aidan gave her in the hall a few weeks back, after the last grill incident. He'd known all along that it was her. Where was the sibling code now? What kind of a sister was she?

Ciaran reached over and touched his brother's arm lightly, 'Easy now.'

The room sparked with Aidan's anger. Emily began to cry. Then Ciaran spoke. 'You don't know what it was like for us, G. That Facebook video was messed up.'

Greta couldn't deny that. In fact that video was another thing that haunted her. She remembered the dread exploding into a million pieces in her stomach, her chest, her head, when her brothers showed her the video.

Seeing herself on the screen, in her pyjamas. She'd wanted to cry, she'd wanted to run, she'd wanted to be anywhere else than right there, watching the horror story unfold. The face on the screen was a version of Greta that she didn't know. One that she didn't want to see or think about. Everything around her faded, blurred, disappeared into nothing until all that there was in front of her was this thing on the screen.

And the thing was her.

Her pyjamas were too tight. And the top was bunched up over her stomach revealing a flash of white, dimpled flesh that hung over the waistband of her trousers.

She figured she must have hit the Live button by mistake. She was mortified about it, but she'd not really thought about how it must have affected her brothers.

'I'm sorry,' she said for the hundredth time. 'I know

you don't want me to say that, but I don't know what else to say.'

Ciaran whispered: 'We just want our big sister back. That's all.'

Greta looked at each of her family and tried to convey her deep sorrow at the pain she'd caused them. And that's when Greta realized something. Her father couldn't look her in the eye.

'Dad?' Greta asked.

He didn't respond.

Emily nudged him roughly in his side. 'Say something.'

He remained silent, and Greta felt a stab of anger. 'You always have something to say. Don't tell me you've finally got no pearls of wisdom for me.'

Stephen stood up. He walked over to his daughter and stood over her, 'You want me to speak? Well, how about this? I didn't want to come here today to talk about how messed up you are. But if you want me to join in, no problem. You nearly drowned, G. You were under the water when we found you. If your mother hadn't insisted that we break the door down, you would have died. Another minute and that would have been it.'

'I've always had a sixth sense when it comes to the children,' Emily said, forlornly.

'And there you were in the water, like a beached whale. I had to get the lads to help me haul you out. Have you any idea what that was like for us?' Stephen said. He walked back to his chair and sat down.

Greta pulled her top away from her tummy, feeling everyone's eyes on the beached whale in the room.

'Is it my fault?' Emily asked.

Greta shook her head.

'No one ever wakes up and thinks they want to be an addict. It creeps up on you,' Noreen said.

'You're not supposed to live your life this way. This is not the future we envisioned for you,' Emily said.

'Greta's self-image is wrapped up in her addiction. One feeds the other, and both have to be understood,' Noreen said.

'But you are remarkable. Beautiful. Expressive. Creative . . . You're my gorgeous girl,' Emily said.

'I don't feel gorgeous, Mam, that's part of the problem,' Greta admitted.

'You've got such a pretty face,' Emily said.

'Have you any idea what it's like to be the fat one in the family?' Greta looked at them, one by one. 'I feel like the outsider. The odd one out in a room full of beautiful, fit, thin people.'

'You're not the odd one out,' Stephen shouted. 'What a thing to say!'

'You're all out running together. Aidan and Ciaran are sporty, playing hurling and soccer every day. And I know how proud you are of them both.'

'I'm proud of you too,' Stephen said.

'I see how you look at me. You're disgusted by my size.' The hidden fault line that had existed between them for years threatened to split open wide.

'Are you ashamed of your daughter?' Noreen asked.

'Not in the least!'

'Yes you are, Dad,' Aidan said. 'You talk about it all the time. You make comments about everything G eats. Have done for years.'

Stephen said, 'That doesn't mean I'm ashamed of Greta, though.' He turned towards her and said, 'I've never been ashamed of you. I love you.'

'But you're ashamed of how I look. My size. Just admit it, Dad,' Greta replied. 'You called me a beached whale only a few moments ago.'

'He did!' Eileen shouted from the back of the room. 'Out of order!'

Silence filled the room as everyone turned to look at Stephen. Emily willed him to shout no, never, I don't care how she looks. But he didn't.

'If you insist on pushing me, I think you do not exert enough self-control. You don't try very hard to lose weight,' Stephen replied eventually.

'Stephen!' Emily was aghast. 'He doesn't mean that.'

'Yes, he does,' Greta replied. 'Dad, do you think I'm not aware of my size? Because I know how big I am. And more than anything else in the world, I wish I was thinner. Then maybe, just maybe, I would fit into your perfect world.'

'All I try to do is motivate you,' Stephen said. 'Encourage you to lose weight.'

'Do you know how hard it is to hear you constantly say things like I should go for a run with the lads? Or watch you move the food from me when Mam puts it on the dining-room table, so I can't reach it to go for seconds?'

'Isn't it better not to have temptation at arm's reach? And while they are training, you could run around the pitch – what's so bad about that suggestion?' Stephen said.

'It doesn't matter what size she is. We have a beautiful daughter,' Emily said to him.

'I love my daughter and I want her to live. Not end up on a slab in the morgue, because her heart can't take any more,' Stephen replied.

Greta felt his bitter disappointment in her and she didn't know how to fix it. There were only so many times she could apologize. But then he said something that she herself believed to be true. Something that she had never acknowledged out loud, but kept inside of her, buried deep.

'You had it all, G. You used to be the cutest person on this planet, and you blew it. We used to go out, and everyone would point and stare and say, that's the girl from the advert. But now, instead, they point and stare at the fatty.'

There was an audible gasp in the room.

Ray shouted, 'Enough!' to Stephen, as Emily turned to Greta and clasped her hands between her own. 'Oh love, I had no idea that you were this upset about how you looked. I wish you had talked to me. I would have liked to help. And I didn't know your father's comments bothered you so much. He's just trying to help, that's all. We all are.'

'I keep it all in and act like everything is OK, Mam. Every day I pretend that I don't notice the judgement. I see the looks you guys make to each other when I go to the fridge for something to eat. And that's not just Dad. It's all of you. I'm tired of being Big G. Just so very tired.' She wiped tears from her eyes with the back of her sweatshirt sleeve.

Aidan said. 'I don't care how you look.'

'Me either,' Ciaran added. 'Who gives a shit what size you are, G. I never cared about that. I just don't want you taking those pills any more. I want to go back to the way it used to be, with us three having a laugh together.'

'Big G in da house,' Greta whispered.

'Yes!' Ciaran replied, smiling.

'I hate that name,' Greta admitted.

'No you don't!' Stephen jumped in. 'You love it. Always have done. What has been going on here this past two weeks? All these things you're saying? Out of the blue! It's bloody ridiculous.'

'I haven't loved that nickname for a long time.'

'So because we've called you the wrong name, it's all our fault?' Stephen said. 'I was waiting for the blame game to begin. It's always the bloody parents' fault.'

'I don't think anyone is saying that,' Ray jumped in. He knew his brother, and he knew Stephen hated to be wrong. That was the problem when you spent most of your life being right. It was hard to ever accept the possibility of being wrong.

'Dad, I'm not blaming you. It's all on me,' Greta said.

'Sometimes I think you hate us all,' Stephen said.

'It's me I hate, Dad. Not you. Never you,' Greta whispered.

Emily sobbed and looked at each of her family, one by one, begging them to find the right words to say, to make this right again.

'Can I say something?' Ray asked. 'Ever since you could toddle your way into a room, you could light it up. Always smiling, quick to laugh. Bubbly. I think that's worth noting. This past year you might have changed, but it's not how you've always been. I don't think it's fair to say you're something that you're not.'

Uncle Ray was always on Greta's side, and she'd never felt more grateful for him.

He continued, 'Yes, you've put on weight over the past few years. But that doesn't define who you are. How you feel comes from inside of you, not from anything that is said from anyone else on the outside.'

'Thanks, Uncle Ray.'

'I think you've lost weight, love. Your face looks much thinner now,' Emily said. 'Doesn't it, Stephen?' She nudged him.

'Yes. Sure.'

'I really am sorry,' Greta said to them, one last time.

'We know love. And so are we,' Emily replied.

'No more Big G. Promise,' Aidan said. 'Was a stupid nickname anyhow.'

'I never meant to make you feel judged. You always made a joke about your weight, I thought you didn't care,' Stephen said.

'I do care, Dad. And for the record, I judge me more than enough for everyone in this room, including you.'

They spent an awkward ten minutes sipping tea. Emily's hat was askance, looking like it was about to topple off.

Noreen told her that it had gone well. Greta wasn't so sure. All she knew was that every bone in her body ached. And the last thing she thought, as she closed her eyes to sleep that night was, *it hurts to be me. It hurts so bad that sometimes I wish I could disappear.*

Every session Greta had with Noreen seemed to create further unanswered questions, and she wasn't sure she was any closer to finding herself.

Chapter 12

It was Sam and Eileen's turn to leave Hope Crossing Rehab Centre. She would miss them both, because they had each helped her get used to life here. She'd always be grateful for that.

They didn't make any pacts to see each other again in the future. Sam joked that if their time in rehab had been a Hollywood movie, they would have fallen in love, planning marriage and babies together. But the truth of the matter was that they helped each other out because neither of them had anybody else. They kept each other sane in the moments that threatened to break them.

'I know one thing for sure. I'm never coming back,' Sam vowed.

'Never,' Greta agreed.

'Give me one last uninspiring gem before I go,' Sam said as he hugged her goodbye.

'I've prepared one especially for you,' my friend.

Remember it's not just on a Monday, your whole life sucks twenty-four/seven.'

Laughing, he saluted Greta, then walked out the door.

In five more sleeps, it would be Greta's time to go home too. She had one more session with Noreen to face first.

'I thought you might be interested to hear about some of the things people do while under the influence of sleeping pills,' Noreen said, looking calmly at Greta. 'In 2008, a woman, a nice kind woman who was living a good life, drove her car unbeknownst to herself. That kind woman killed a mother of eleven children.'

Greta saw Mrs Oaks's rhododendrons. The car smashed against her wall. Blood trickling down her mother's face.

'That wasn't the first sleep-driving incident. There's also the flight attendant who ran over a mother and her two daughters. Then there's the lawyer who killed a man while he was changing a flat tyre. Shall I keep going, or is that enough examples of how dangerous sleeping pills are?'

'It's enough.' Greta's lungs pushed her chest out, and her ribcage ached. Then she gasped a long, anguished sigh.

'No, it's not enough, Greta. What happened in the bathtub?'

Greta paled as she remembered Emily's voice sobbing, while she cradled her in her arms. *Oh love, what did you do, oh my love.*

'I fell asleep when I needed to be awake. I nearly drowned.'

'Yes. But why did you fall asleep? Say it!'

'I took sleeping tablets.'

'Why?'

'Because I was tired,' Greta whispered.

'Why did you take them while in the bath? Why not wait till you were back in your bedroom and were safe in bed?'

'I don't know.'

'You told me that the embarrassment of falling asleep on the flight was crippling. You also said it scared you.'

'It did.'

'Then why did you risk taking a tablet while you were in the bath?'

'I don't know. I wasn't thinking straight.'

'Yes, you do. Stop lying to yourself.'

'Do you think I wanted my dad, my brothers to see my naked, fat body, sprawled across the bathroom floor. Do you think I wanted that?'

'No. But I don't think you'd even thought that far ahead. I think that while you lay in the bath popping pills, something else was going through your mind. And there can be no more hiding from it. Look it squarely in the eye, Greta.'

Greta closed her eyes and thought of the damn fly and the nursery rhyme that she had said over and over again. She opened her eyes and looked at Noreen straight on. 'I thought that perhaps I would die and that, if I did, it mightn't be such a bad thing.'

'And now?'

Greta thought about the hell on earth she'd been through since she arrived at Hope Crossing. And how she'd pleaded with God to let her die; anything than face this head-on. But she also thought about her family. And the joy she got from acting. Her friends . . . Dylan.

She looked into Noreen's eyes and said firmly, 'Now, I want to live.'

All you need is confidence in yourself. There is no living thing that is not afraid when it faces danger. The true courage is in facing danger when you are afraid.
The Wonderful Wizard of Oz, L. Frank Baum

Part Three

Part Three

Chapter 13

Greta looked at the house she'd toddled her first steps in.

'We have to go in now, don't we?'

'We do. Or your mam will send out a search party.' Ray moved closer and whispered, 'But remember that I've got you.'

'I know.' She reached over to hold his hand, for a moment, in thanks.

For every time her Uncle Ray walked behind her, ready to catch her if she faltered. And for collecting her from the centre today. Stephen was still smarting from the family therapy and Emily had all sorts of wardrobe dilemmas about what one should wear to collect a recovering addict. It was easier to let Uncle Ray do it.

'I'm scared.'

'Of what?'

'Of what's on the other side of that door. The expectation that I'm fixed now.'

'Your family love you and just want you to be OK,' Ray said.

'I know that. What I don't know is what happens next.'

'You can work that out as you go along. None of us have all the answers. For now, start with what you *do* know.'

'I know I don't want to go back to how things were before.'

'Well that's something. Concentrate on that. Think of the next few weeks as a holiday, a career break, a hiatus if you will. Give yourself some time to work out what does happen next.'

'Yeah, you're right, I suppose. But if I win the lottery, I'm off to Las Vegas to see Dr Gale.'

'If you win the lotto you'd better take me with you. I'll carry the cases!' Ray joked.

'Wouldn't go without you,' Greta replied, with a smile.

'Why do you love her so much? The doctor?' Ray asked.

'She's living her best life. It's comforting to know at least one Greta Gale in the world is! One day, I'd like to say I'm doing the same. She gives me hope, Uncle Ray. I know you all think I'm mad, loving her like I do. And it's hard to describe, but there's been times when I've felt like I'm in the dark, on my own. And Dr Gale is a light, a beacon, helping me see the road ahead.'

'We all need hope in our lives,' Ray said.

The ground felt shaky beneath Greta's feet as she walked through the front door. She was home.

The only thing was, it didn't feel like home any more. She felt out of place, awkward, as if she no longer belonged in their three-bedroom semi-detached red brick. Greta knew it was only her mind playing tricks, but it seemed smaller somehow. Then the whiff of bleach and Mr Sheen furniture polish hit her. A smell that unleashed uncountable memories from her childhood, of her mam cleaning down the counter tops, dusting the TV, picking up toys from the floor. And in an instant it felt like home again. The hum of chatter silenced as she walked into the kitchen.

Greta looked at the faces of her family. A mixture of expectation, hope and fear on each of them. And Greta felt her heart give a little. They didn't know what to expect from this homecoming, any more than she did.

'Hello.' She felt shy in the way you do when you've not seen someone for a while, and you know you've changed. Not just physically. But from the inside out.

'You look like the old Greta,' Emily whispered as she took in the changes in her daughter. Her hair, shiny and pulled back tight into a ponytail. Her face, without make-up, with skin bright and unblemished, eyes no longer bloodshot.

'Almost back to your old self,' Stephen agreed. 'I can't get over it. You've lost so much weight. Just brilliant.'

So much about this comment worried Greta. She wasn't sure that she wanted to be the old Greta any more. She wanted her dad to know that she was changed in more ways than just her waist size, which was still considerable.

Before she left the centre that morning, Greta had one last physical check-up.

'Jump on the scales again, good woman,' Caroline said. Greta did as she was told and once again turned her eyes away. 'I swear if you shout out that I'm an even 300 pounds now, I'll batter you to death with your stethoscope.'

'That's what I love about you, Greta Gale. That lovely placid manner of yours.' Caroline peered at the scales. 'So you want to know then?'

'Just tell me the number or you'll see my lovely placid manner in full force!' Greta said with a smile.

'You're 229 pounds. You've lost twenty-one pounds! One for each day here. How's that?'

Greta was staggered by the result. She'd never lost that much weight on any diet before.

In this very room, three weeks previously, Greta had pinched herself hard in order not to cry. She hadn't wanted to give Caroline the satisfaction of seeing her weak. But since then, she'd cried, she'd screamed, and occasionally she'd laughed. Caroline had seen her at her worst. Once again, tears filled her eyes, but this time it was different. These were good tears, the ones that showed how grateful she was for this experience, happy that she had somehow come out the other side.

'Greta?' Emily shouted.

Greta blinked away the memory and looked at her mam. 'Sorry, Mam, what did you say?'

'How do you feel, love?'

'I feel good, Mam. Really good.'

Emily blessed herself and rushed towards her daughter, pulling her into her embrace.

Greta sank into her arms and, as they held on to each other, cracks in their relationship began to knit together.

'Nice sign,' Greta said, looking over her mother's

shoulders. A banner hung over the mantelpiece that said, 'Welcome Home.'

'Hey G,' Aidan said. Ciaran punched him on his arm, making him yelp. 'Sorry! I meant to say Greta!'

'Hey, you two,' Greta replied.

They stepped closer towards her and made a half-effort attempt at hugging her.

'Are you not sick of putting those on for me yet?' she joked, pointing to the good shirts they were once again wearing.

'Mam made us. She wouldn't have made this much fuss if the queen were coming.'

'Change into your trackies. I'm certainly no queen.'

'Open the bubbly.' Emily pushed Stephen towards the fridge, as she wiped her eyes with a tea towel that always seemed to be in her hand whenever she was in the kitchen.

'It's the good stuff. I got it from the off-licence, not the supermarket,' Stephen said as he peeled the foil off the bottle. 'Not that there's anything wrong with the super-market stuff. As good as any. But your mother wanted you to have the best. We both did.'

'Thanks, Dad. That's really kind of you. But I'll just have a soft drink for now. Or maybe a cup of tea,' Greta said, as the cork popped and the sound of fizz filled the air.

'What did she say?' Emily mopped up the escaped bubbles with the tea towel.

'She said she wanted a cup of tea,' Stephen replied.

They both turned to look at their daughter in shock.

'I'm not going to drink for a while.' This declaration from Greta was met with stunned silence.

'But I thought it was the pills that were her problem. She's not an alcoholic too, is she?' Stephen asked Emily, puzzled.

'No, Dad. I'm not an alcoholic. But alcohol could be a trigger for me, so it's safer if I avoid it for a while. Just to make sure I don't go rushing for the pills again.'

'Put it away, put it away!' Emily screamed, as if the mere look of the bottle was going to send her daughter back to rehab. Then she blessed herself for good measure.

'Will I pour it down the sink?' Stephen asked.

'No!'

'Yes!'

Greta and Emily shouted conflicting instructions at the same time.

Greta repeated, 'There's no need to throw it out. I'd rather you all have a drink. Especially as it's the good stuff.' But her words fell on deaf ears as her parents began discussing what they should do next.

'We should have thought about this,' Emily hissed. 'But it wasn't in any of the leaflets I got down at Doctor Hanrahan's.'

Emily began to pull bottles of wine out of the wine rack that sat on top of the fridge. 'Help me,' she ordered Stephen. 'And Ciaran, get your beers from the fridge too while you're at it. Oh Lord above, I put a good slurp of sherry into the trifle I made for dessert. Will I throw that out too? It's a minefield.'

Greta looked at them both in horror. 'Would you stop! I'm not going to go on an alcoholic binge, for goodness' sake! I've never been a big drinker, and I'm not going to take it up now. I just want to avoid it for a bit, that's all.

But I insist that you all have one. Honestly, it doesn't bother me.'

'I'll make you a coffee.' Emily started to fill the kettle, 'I've got Nescafé Gold in.'

'I'd prefer water, Mam,' Greta said. 'I'm trying to avoid caffeine too.'

This news nearly threw her mother over the edge.

She looked over at Uncle Ray, pleading him with her eyes to step in. He took the bottle from his brother's hands. 'Let's not be drastic. Greta has said it's fine to drink the champagne, so I think that's what we should do. I for one could do with a strong drink.' He poured a small glass for each of them, then put some water into a glass for Greta.

'I think it's time you made that toast you've been planning,' Uncle Ray said to Stephen.

When he didn't speak straight away, Greta said, 'I'd like to hear it, Dad. Honestly.' In truth she would have quite liked to sit in front of the TV and have the pleasure of a much-missed Netflix and Amazon Prime binge.

'We are so happy to have you back home where you belong. The house has not been the same without you. It's when something disappears from your life that you truly appreciate it. We're glad you're back. Welcome home . . . G . . . that is, welcome home, Greta.'

One by one her family clinked glasses, chiming, 'Welcome home, Greta.'

Stephen looked at how pale his daughter was. She looked about fourteen again and so very fragile. When she was a little girl, and the chain fell off her bike, she ran to him, her daddy, to fix it for her. But something – a monster – had crept its way into their lives, into Greta's world and theirs, and it was fierce. He wasn't sure that the battle to chase it away was over yet. He prayed for the strength to fight for his family and for himself, to do the best for her. He knew he got it wrong by overdoing it on the lectures. He would do his best not to mention diets or running. His wish for Greta was simple – that she would find happiness.

Emily looked at Greta and thought about the night that lay ahead of them and every one after that. It was all very well when she was in the treatment centre. She had made progress, and had even reached the heady milestone of sleeping for six hours in a row straight. But what if there was a secret stash of pills somewhere that they hadn't found? And then what if Greta had a weak moment when she couldn't sleep? The four of them, Stephen, the boys and herself had gone through the house looking into every nook and cranny. They hadn't found anything, bar several pairs of Emily's own reading glasses, which she had a habit of putting down and misplacing. As Emily raised her glass, she wished that her eldest child would find peace, that the monsters in her head would stay away.

While Aidan was delighted his sister was home, he didn't want to spend the afternoon looking at her. He'd promised the lads he'd join them for a game of snooker down at the pub later on. But when he glanced at his mam, it was as if she could read his mind. She shook her head, as if to say, 'Don't even think about it.' So he wished for an escape route.

Ciaran smiled at Greta as he raised his glass to her. He

was sick of talking about nothing else but her addiction. The drama was relentless. They'd have to hope that she got on with living now. Then he let his head get back to the snog he'd had with Claire Brennan the previous night at the pub. And he wished that she'd be up for round two tonight.

Ray watched his niece and saw how overwhelmed she was by the situation. He tried to put himself in her shoes and figured this moment, returning home to see them all, must feel very strange. Greta was the daughter he'd never had. Maybe it was the fact that he'd been the first to hold her, maybe it was because they 'got' each other. He thought about the conversation they'd had outside the front door.

And he wished he could find a way to make her smile again.

Chapter 14

Days passed and became a week and Greta got used to being at home again. Her family began to relax around her. The car she had crashed in February was now fixed, thankfully not a write-off in the end. Next door's garden looked almost back to normal. Ciaran was in love, and most of his sentences included a reference to Claire, his new beloved. She was coming for Sunday lunch at the end of the month. Emily and Stephen couldn't wait to meet her. Emily had found a Yoga Nidra class locally. Greta and her attended it together, three times a week. And it wasn't tortured; in fact, it was kind of nice. Emily felt like she was doing something useful and Greta continued to sleep at least five or six hours every night – without the need for the pills.

There were several messages from Dylan. So she called him, holding her breath as the call connected. She wasn't sure if Dylan would answer. They'd always texted or

WhatsApped each other. But after what felt like an eternity, he answered.

'Hi Dylan.'

'Hhhello, Greta.'

Greta had been practising how to tell him about her addiction, but every speech she'd made in her head sounded wrong. Would he want to be friends with her now? Surely that would be the final nail in the coffin of their friendship? A friendship that was so important to her.

'I'm sorry I've missed work,' she said, sheepishly.

'It's fine.' Dylan wanted to say so much more, but he knew the words were likely to get mixed up. So he left them where they were. When he heard her take a deep breath, then sigh, he touched his cheek, as if her breath had transported its way through the phone waves to him.

Just tell him. If he's a friend he'll understand. Instead, Greta said, 'This virus I contracted, it's just taken a lot out of me.'

Dylan believed her lie, without question. He wanted to meet for coffee, but Greta was reluctant. She knew she had to have a face-to-face chat with him, but she just wasn't ready yet. He explained that the Murder Mystery Crew had taken on a new actress to cover her roles. But he promised that, as soon as a part opened up, she would be back on the crew again. This meant that she was now, officially, out of work. Her parents were not putting any pressure on her to find a job. They were just happy that she was in recovery. But that would change in time. She needed a plan.

Greta was struggling with the transition from the

regimental structure of the centre and life at home. She missed the camaraderie of the other patients. By the time she left, she'd grown to like many of them. She learned that while they had different stories and addictions, they were all facing the same struggle to make changes in their lives. She missed Caroline and Noreen too, which surprised her. When she surrendered control to them, she leaned on them. Greta wasn't sure she could lean on her parents or brothers.

It felt strange having so much time on her hands. When she was at the centre, the days were full. Greta thought, back then, that gaining control of the TV remote again would make her feel euphoric. But she couldn't seem to find a single thing to watch. Just before she left the centre, Caroline had handed Greta's contraband back to her. And Greta didn't know what to do with it. She'd dropped her phone into her bag as if she'd been electrocuted. It felt weird to hold it in her hand. Greta realized something before the end of the first week in rehab. She was stunned to discover that she no longer wanted to check into social media. More than that, Greta felt relieved that she wasn't doing so. Because, her relationship with her phone had become about checking up on what her peers were doing and comparing herself – unfavourably – to them. She watched fellow actors and actresses walking a red carpet at yet another premiere, sharing news of new parts on stage and onscreen. Each post was a reminder that not all people – on the internet at least – are equal.

She lasted almost twenty-four hours at home, before she switched her phone and iPad back on again. Her brothers were at college, her dad at work and her mam at her slimming class. The solitude, something she craved in the past, now frightened her. She was scared to be alone. So her digital detox ended and Greta reacquainted herself with Dr Greta Gale. Maybe in finding her namesake again she could find herself.

She looked at this morning's post.

Drgretagale I get so many messages from y'all who have been clearing out your cupboards! Isn't it wonderful how we outgrow things that we once thought we couldn't live without. Let life lead you where you need to go. Trust the process. Trust the journey. #selflove #whatsinyourcupboard #fallinloveagain #inspire #strength #drgretagale #faith #canigetahellyeah

---

Greta found herself nodding as she read Dr Gale's words outloud. She *had* outgrown many things. She no longer had any interest in playing games on her iPad, something that she could lose hours on in the past. She wasn't reading Dickens, but she was reading. But trust the process? Greta wasn't sure she could be that brave. She picked up her journal and wrote on the top of a new page, **Trust the process**? While in therapy she had gotten into the habit of teasing out things in writing. Her confessional.

'Penny for them . . .' Ray said.

'Oh hi, Uncle Ray. Didn't hear you arrive. Don't think my thoughts are worth even a cent these days.'

'I'd pay more than that for them,' Ray said.

'Damn it. One sec.' Greta closed her eyes and tried to think of something positive to say. 'I have pretty ankles.'

Ray looked down and nodded, 'Well, they look like ankles, that's for sure.'

'I'm not losing it. My therapist at the centre – Noreen – reckoned I say too many negative things about myself. So for every negative thought I have, or that I speak out loud, she challenged me to counteract it with a positive one.'

'I think that's an excellent idea.'

'You'd think. But I'm running out of nice things to say about myself. Tea?' She filled the kettle.

'That green stuff you've been drinking, or the real deal?'

'I'll make both! You know, on my first day at the centre when I found out that they didn't have any coffee, I nearly wept. In fact, I think I did! Funny how you can get used to things. I can't cope with the Gale brew any more.'

'Blasphemous! Your mam must be horrified. You know, I reckon the longest relationship I have ever had in my life is with my strong tea. We go back decades – don't think I could say goodbye to her,' Ray said with a wink. 'Does the green stuff help, do you think?'

'Well, I'm sleeping better, so I think caffeine and me are better off going our separate ways for good. I don't know if I'll ever be a straight-eight-hours kind of gal. But I'm in bed by eleven most nights, and it's not unusual for me to sleep through till five a.m.'

'I'm proud of you. You've worked hard.'

'Thanks, Uncle Ray.'

'So why were you frowning when I walked in? What's on your mind?'

'I was thinking about the future.'

'Highly overrated.'

'Yep. But I need to get a job.'

'Are you not going back to the Murder Mystery job?'

'Eventually. When someone else leaves, then the job is mine again.'

They both drank their tea in comfortable silence for a few minutes.

'I think I've let life pass me by,' Ray said.

Greta put her cup down in surprise. She'd never heard her uncle complain about *anything* ever before.

'I always thought I'd have a family of my own one day. I look at you all and I think I'm lonely but I'm not really sure what to do about it,' Ray continued.

'Why didn't you get married, Uncle Ray?'

'I never found the right woman to ask.'

'I used to wonder if you were gay,' Greta said.

He laughed at this and said, 'Did you? I suppose a few might have thought that over the years. I'm not gay. I'm just not very good at talking to women.'

'You need to go online. Get onto Tinder. There are more single women than single men in Ireland. I read that somewhere.'

'Are you on it?'

'God, no. I don't believe in all that bolloxology that there's someone for everyone out there. Some people just aren't going to find love.'

'Well, with that attitude, how can you fail?' Ray said, raising his mug in a silent toast. 'You're still young, though. Only starting out in your life. You've loads of time to meet someone special if that's what you want.'

'I suppose. Right now, love is the last thing in my mind. And you're not that ancient, by the way. The best years of your life are not quite over yet.'

'Cheeky.' He laughed in response. 'I think I had the best year of my life a long time ago. Something else I've been thinking about a lot lately.'

'What year was your best year?'

'Nineteen ninety-five,' Ray said.

'No way! That was the year I did the Christmas advert. And now that I think about it, my best year too. And it's all been downhill since then. What happened to you in 1995 that was so good? Apart from seeing me on TV, of course.'

'Well, you were cute in those pigtails. But aside from those, in 1995 I had the best holiday of my life. The jamboree in Holland with the boy scouts.'

'Jeepers, Uncle Ray, that's a bit sad.'

'Not for me. I was a bit of a loner when I was in school. I didn't seem to fit into any of the usual cliques. I wasn't like your dad, playing soccer and hurling, with loads of friends. Then a flyer came into school. The scouts were starting in the village hall every Tuesday evening. I knew from the very first meeting that I'd found my people.'

'Dyb dyb dyb,' Greta joked, quoting the old scouting campfire chant.

'Do your best,' Ray said. 'That's what that saying means. I don't think most people know that when they quote it. And then you should reply "Dob dob dob", which means "We'll do our best".'

'You're right, I didn't know that. You and your random facts.' She felt a rush of love and affection for her uncle.

He raised his mug and said, 'To both of us doing our best.'

'I'm trying so hard. And while we are at it, I think it's time that both of us find a new "best year of our lives".'

'I'm glad you said that. Because I've got something that might help us achieve that,' Ray said. He reached into the inside pocket of his jacket and pulled out an envelope. 'I've been thinking about the world you and I have created for ourselves. And I realized that we've both looked back for too long. It's time to look forward.' He tapped the brown envelope. 'Inside this is our flight details and two tickets to see Dr Gale at her seminar in Las Vegas.'

Had Uncle Ray just said that? The goofy smile on his face as he showed her the details in black and white made her gasp and tremble. She couldn't believe her eyes. Her hands shook as she held the tickets. 'Why on earth would you do this?'

'I think the question should be: why wouldn't I? You're not the only one who wishes they were something else, living a different life. Do you know I never use my holidays up each year? I've got sixty days' leave accumulated right now.'

'Jeepers. I should have joined the civil service, never mind this acting malarkey,' Greta said.

'You'd make a terrible civil servant.'

'True,' Greta agreed.

'Once a year, I feel obliged to go on holiday somewhere, because that's what people do. I like city breaks the best. Lots to see and do. Plenty of ways to get lost in a city, unnoticed as the man on his own.'

'You have friends you could go on holidays with, surely?' Greta asked.

'All my friends are married with kids now. So no. I don't. Not any more.'

'So what are you suggesting? That we just take off?'

'That's exactly what I'm suggesting. You are not needed with the Murder Mystery gang for a while. This is the ideal time for you to take off. Think of the trip as time to work out what happens next for Greta Gale.'

'How come the outbound tickets are Dublin to Kansas City?' Greta said, taking a closer look.

'We're going to hire a car and see roadside America. A road trip.'

'We are?' Greta wasn't sure about the road-trip part. 'Why can't we just go straight to Vegas?'

'What is your favourite movie of all time?' Ray asked.

'*The Wizard of Oz.*'

'What is our second name?'

'Gale.'

'And what is Dorothy's second name from the movie?'

'Gale.'

'And where is Dorothy from?'

Greta grinned as she replied, 'Kansas.'

'We can't not start there! So let's make a wish list of everything we want to see between Kansas and Las Vegas. There's a whole lot of America out there, just waiting for us to check it out.'

'Like where?'

'I've always loved reading about the attractions and oddities that roadside America has. For instance, the biggest bale of twine is in Kansas. In a place called Cawker City.'

Greta felt laughter bubble up inside of her. They were going to do this. And she dared to believe that her dream to meet her heroine, Dr Gale, could come true. Uncle Ray joked about gambling and winning jackpots on the Las

Vegas strip. Greta talked about the movies she'd seen from *Ocean's Eleven* to *Casino* and *The Hangover*. It was like all her Christmases and birthdays had come at once.

But then Emily came home from Tesco, and as they helped her unload the groceries and filled her in on the trip, she scoffed at them both for their daydreaming.

'Notions!' she cried.

Greta turned to Uncle Ray and said, 'Notions eleven!' And they laughed so hard, Greta thought she was going to pee herself. She'd not laughed like that in a long time.

'Enough of these shenanigans. You can't go,' Emily said. 'You're only home a wet weekend from therapy. It's out of the question Greta. I won't allow it. People like us don't just up and go off to the other side of the world on a whim. Trips like this need planning. And Ray, I'm surprised at you. You should know better than to fill her head with nonsense.'

Ray stood up and looked at Emily. 'You're right. The Gales are not the kind of family who do spontaneous things. I'm certainly not. But it's time for change, right here and right now. I'm going to Vegas, one way or the other. The only question left to answer is this: Are you coming with me, Greta?'

Greta looked at her mam and knew that Emily was right. The right thing to do was to stay at home, with her parents and brothers. Safe. The trip was a nice daydream. But that's all it was.

'Dyb Dyb Dyb,' Ray said.

Do your best. Greta stood up and walked over to her Uncle Ray, replying in the only way that made any sense. 'Dob Dob Dob.'

Chapter 15

Stephen was equally gobsmacked when he heard about the planned trip, Aidan and Ciaran more than a little bit jealous. They all looked at Ray like he was having a breakdown.

Stephen was the most put out about the news. 'It's irresponsible. It's crazy. It's . . . stupid, Ray.'

'If I had a euro for every time you've called me stupid . . . I thought it was time I started acting like it. And you know what? It feels good!' Ray said with a cryptic smile on his face.

Stephen didn't like this new side of his brother. He relied on Ray. His right-hand man. Whenever they needed help, whether it was babysitting the kids or pulling a car wreck from next door's garden, he was there, quietly helping them all. He was steady. And he was most certainly not the kind of guy who decided to go off on a stupid trip at the worst possible time. But no matter how much he protested, Ray just shrugged and continued on his own course.

'I still don't understand why you are driving from Kansas to Las Vegas. Why not fly directly into Vegas? You have to drive on the other side of the road, you know,' Stephen said.

'I know that,' Ray replied.

'But you've never driven over there before,' Stephen continued.

Ray just shrugged and said, 'Well, there's a first time for everything.'

Greta and Ray poured over maps online, reading travel books that Ray borrowed from the library. Their wish list began to take shape.

'I want to see the Rockies.'

'Monument Valley!'

'Look, there's an OZ Museum!'

'Pancakes in an American diner!'

Right up to the goodbyes at the departures gate in the airport, Emily and Stephen were both convinced they would come to their senses and cancel their plans. As Emily hugged Ray and Greta, she handed them a small bottle of holy water each.

'I'll look after him, Mam,' Greta told her.

'It's not Ray I'm worried about,' Emily replied. 'Throw some of that holy water on yourselves every day. And the car too.'

'We'll FaceTime you. Aidan and Ciaran will show you how,' Greta promised.

And while Greta was excited, she was also worried about the aeroplane. Not the actual trip itself, because seeing a new country and meeting Dr Gale or at least being in the same room as her – well, that was all brilliant. It was the flight itself. The last time Greta was on board an aeroplane it hadn't been her finest hour. There would be no pills this time. But the seatbelt issue was still unavoidable. The first stage of their flight was to Toronto with Air Canada, then they flew into Kansas. Greta Googled every airline forum she could find to see how likely it was that she would have to ask for a seatbelt extender. The likelihood was real. Fat forum after fat forum online shared horror stories of people not being able to fit into their seats. A few admitted that they had been asked to buy a second seat because the armrest didn't go down entirely and their blubber spilt into the seat next to them.

Every time Greta imagined that scenario happening, she felt a cold sweat flush over her.

She measured the dining-room chairs at home to check whether they were the same width as the seats on the flight. She'd carefully sat her arse on them, checking to see how much she spilt onto either side. And she figured that, in theory, she should be able to squeeze into them.

As they sat at the boarding gate, she played a fun game of people watching that she liked to call, 'Who is fatter, you or me?' There was a good mix of people, all different sizes. Greta reckoned she was the biggest woman, all the same. There were a couple of big lads too. She wondered if they were freaking out as much as she was and figured feeling shite about yourself wasn't the preserve of women alone.

There had to be a better way to live her life than

spending it obsessing about whether or not she could fit into an aeroplane seat.

Her phone beeped.

Dylan: I feel like you're avoiding me. You still owe me a coffee! Safe travels, Silver Lady. Send me some pics.

Greta snapped her phone cover closed. Dylan was right. She had been avoiding him. Because as long as she kept him at arm's length, she could keep *him*. When they sat face to face and talked about what happened that night and she confessed about her addiction, it would change them. She knew that. He'd look at her in a different way and she didn't want that. She liked being his Silver Lady. His friend. Greta knew all she was doing was delaying the inevitable. When she got back from Vegas they would have to talk. But until then, Greta decided to hold on to her friendship with Dylan for a few more weeks.

When it was time to board, Greta moved slowly through the aisle of the aircraft, careful not to bang into anyone who was already seated. She always felt like a bull in a china shop on an aeroplane. God she envied those people with delicate, petite bodies. While Uncle Ray put their hand luggage in the overhead lockers, she slid across into the window seat.

'Are you OK?' Ray asked. 'You seem a bit on edge.'

'Fine,' Greta snapped, wishing he was anywhere but by her side now, about to witness her shame. She picked up the seatbelt and pulled it across her abdomen, sucking in her stomach as much as she could. And, to her surprise, it clicked shut without any trouble.

'It closed!' she screamed when she clasped the buckle.

'I think that's the whole point,' Ray said, snapping his own shut. He watched her closely and worried once more if he was doing the right thing bringing her on this trip. Stephen had made no attempt to hide how pissed off he was with his brother before they left. He had laid it out quite plainly. 'That's my little girl you are taking to the other side of the world. She's vulnerable. She's not out of rehab even a month yet. I've never heard anything so stupid in my life as this wild-goose chase. And what if Greta relapses while you are over there? If she does, then it's all on you. I will hold you personally responsible.'

Stephen had never treated Ray like an equal. Ray had felt an undercurrent of contempt ripple his way every now and then from his brother over the years. And after that lecture, Ray very nearly cancelled the whole thing. But, while he didn't have all the answers, somehow, deep inside, he felt like this trip was in the best interests of his niece. She said she wanted to find herself. Live her best life. And maybe the way to do that was to take her out of her comfort zone at home. Give her life a little reboot. He promised Emily and Stephen that he would watch her closely all the time. And he intended to make good on that promise. He knew that Greta wasn't his daughter, but he couldn't have loved her more if she was his own. He'd thought about their relationship many times. He loved all his family, but with Greta he felt an immediate kinship, a connection to her that made him feel like he belonged. He always thought he'd have children of his own one day, but that wasn't on the cards any more. But somehow, Greta fulfilled that paternal pull for him. Like him, she wasn't perfect. She was temperamental at the best of times, very up and down, one minute smiling, the next looking like it was the end of the world. But perfect was the enemy of good. His plan for this trip was to give Greta reasons to smile a bit more. He had a few surprises up his sleeve to help with that.

'It's not too late for us to go home, Greta. They haven't closed the aircraft door yet.' He gave her one last chance to back out.

'Not a chance, Uncle Ray. I cannot wait to get to Kansas and to see Dr Gale. I feel like Dorothy off to see the wizard! The wonderful Wizard of Oz!' And for the first time in a long time, Ray saw his niece's face light up with a smile.

Chapter 16

Greta and Ray spent most of the first leg of the journey watching movies. Their transit through Toronto Airport was seamless. Their flight to Kansas City was only a few hours long and, not for the first time since they took off from Dublin, Greta realized how lucky she was to have this opportunity.

'Uncle Ray. Thank you. In case I don't think to say that every day, thank you.'

'You've thanked me lots, and besides, this trip is as much for me as it is you.'

Greta looked at her uncle and realized that while she knew she loved him and he her, she didn't know much about his life. He'd always been there in the background, taking care of all the Gales, in his quiet way, but she'd never really asked him any questions about his hopes and dreams. 'Tell me why. I want to know. Honestly.'

'Well, a few weeks ago I came to the conclusion that my life had become small,' Ray said.

'Woah!' Greta exclaimed. 'That's a big statement.'

'I suppose it is. But it's true. Maybe I got up on the wrong side of the bed, but a few weeks back I woke up irritated by every single boring moment of my small life. Every day my alarm goes off at seven a.m. I shower using the same brand of toiletries that I've used for over twenty years. I eat two Weetabix with a banana chopped up on top and low-fat milk, every single day. I see the same people on my commute to the office, but the most we ever do is nod at each other. I realized that I was stuck doing the same mundane things every day. And none of it mattered. It was quite the realization. And by the time lunchtime came, I was at the tipping point. Mary, that's the dinner lady in our staff canteen, well, she didn't even wait to see what I wanted. She just ladled soup into a bowl and said, 'Same again, Ray.' Not a question. A statement. It really annoyed me. Something inside me snapped.'

'What did you do?' Greta asked, her eyes wide in shock.

'I told her to take back the soup and give me the special of the day. I hadn't even looked to see what it was,' Ray said, shaking his head at Greta.

'You rebel!' Greta laughed.

'Well, to me it was a rebel moment. It was cottage pie, and of all the pies in the world, that's my least favourite.'

'That's funny. It's Dad's favourite.'

Ray sighed. 'I know. We had it every week when we were young because Stephen loved it so much. Sometimes we'd have it twice, because Stephen asked. Anyhow, I took the pie and, with each bite, I tried to pinpoint what was wrong with me. I thought that maybe I was coming down with a bug. But I knew that wasn't it. Twenty-four hours under a duvet wasn't going to cure whatever was wrong with me. On the way home, I watched the other commuters on the bus. Most had headphones on, swiping left and right on their mobile phones. One or two read books and others just stared ahead, blankly, waiting for their stop. But all of them looked as bored with their lives as I felt.'

Greta felt embarrassed that she had missed all of this. She had been so focused on her own issues, she hadn't noticed that someone she loved was also having a hard time. 'Oh Uncle Ray, I'm sorry you felt like that. I had no idea.'

He patted her hand lightly, then continued his story. 'There was a young man and a girl sitting close to me. I'd not seen them before. The girl was telling a story that involved a lot of hand movements to punctuate her every point. And her boyfriend was transfixed by whatever she was saying. I couldn't take my eyes off them. And I felt a stab of jealousy so sharp that it winded me. This life, the one I cultivated and protected for decades, felt mean-ingless. What was the point of anything?'

'That must have been some look the boy was giving to the girl,' Greta said.

'Yep it was. Adoration. Love. Isn't that what any of us really want, after all?'

Greta sighed in recognition of his words. She'd never felt that before. Maybe one day, when she lost some more weight, she could allow herself to dare to dream of a boyfriend.

'Do you know that song, "Pure Imagination"? The one Gene Wilder sings in *Charlie and the Chocolate Factory*.'

'I love that song!' Greta said.

'Me too. It's my humming song.'

'Your what?'

'The song I'm most likely to have fixated in my head, the one I hum along to when I'm on my own.'

'Oh right! My humming song is "Somewhere Over the Rainbow". I give it loads in the shower every morning.'

'That I knew,' Ray said. 'There's a bit in the song that talks about travelling in a world of your creation. I keep thinking about those words. This boring, small, insignificant life I lead is all my creation. I've been feeling quite pathetic and stupid, to be honest.'

'Oh Uncle Ray, I had no idea. You are anything but pathetic or stupid!' Greta said.

The problem was that Ray had grown up in the shadow of a much cleverer older brother. His parents told everyone who was willing to listen that Stephen had been nothing but a pleasure to rear, giving them non-stop proud, heart-bursting parental moments. But Ray was a different kettle of fish altogether.

'Night and day, my two boys,' his mother used to say. There was never any malice to her words. Ray knew that both his parents loved him and his brother equally. But there was an undeniable truth that he could not avoid. They found Stephen's company more interesting.

He remembered his mother saying – whenever she went to his parent teacher meetings – that Stephen made her feel ten feet tall. 'It's a sin to be so proud, but my boy, he's a wonder. Clever, he's got brains to burn, that's what his teacher said. And funny and kind too. He's got it all. Oh, our Stephen will go a long way.'

Unfortunately Ray didn't make his mam feel five feet tall, never mind ten. It wasn't that he was a bold kid; in fact he was the opposite. Quiet and introspective. But no matter how hard he applied himself, the net result was always the same. He was a steady C+ kind of guy. Average. After a while he gave up trying to compete with his straight-A older brother.

He passed his Leaving Certificate. He took the exams to enter the civil service when he was eighteen and was accepted. He started work as a clerical officer, grade four, and since then he'd slowly, methodically, worked his way up the ranks. Now he was a principal officer and had a team of four people reporting to him. They liked him, he was a fair boss, always with his door open, ready to listen, to guide, to support. He didn't say much and had the reputation as a bit of a loner.

He had more than most – his own home, a small, three-bedroom, semi-detached red-brick house, around the corner from his brother's family. His mortgage would be paid off within the next twelve months. He changed his car every three years, but he rarely drove it, preferring the bus. When he wasn't working, he spent time with his brother's family. He volunteered at a local homeless shelter, doing the soup-and-sandwich run once a week.

Ray looked at his niece and said, 'I'm not telling you this for sympathy, just to fill you in on where my head is at. I don't want this to be as good as it gets. I want more. And so should you! I'm middle-aged now, and my hair is going grey. But maybe it's not too late to stop life passing me by. And it's not too late for you.'

'Of course it's not too late,' Greta said.

'Promise me that you won't let yourself end up like me.'

Greta thought about her own life. It was as if she'd been asleep for years. And it was now time to wake up. She just wasn't sure how to do that. 'I can't promise that, Uncle Ray. If I were to end up like you, I'd be lucky.'

They sat in silence for a moment. Greta knew that she didn't want to get to Ray's age and be the same. She wanted to change, to evolve, to do better. But how to do that was the tricky bit.

'Just don't waste the pretty,' Ray said, breaking the silence.

'I'm not pretty,' Greta whispered.

'Are you crazy? Of course you are. You just don't see yourself as we all see you. And don't dismiss my compliments. It's rude.'

'OK. I'll try. Promise. But you have to tell me when you're sad, too. You have one of those faces, you know. Hard to read.'

'I'm not sad, at least not most of the time. But I'm not happy either, Greta. Something is missing in my life. I didn't know what to do about it. Until we started to talk about this trip to Vegas and then the seed of an idea formed in my head. I don't know if I have the guts to go through with it. But first I have to show you something.'

He pulled his wallet out and carefully extracted a photograph, torn and worn, folded in half and hidden behind his bus pass. As always, when he looked at the image, the overriding feeling was bittersweet. 'Remember I said to you that my best year was in 1995, at the scouting jamboree?'

'Yes.' Greta was peering over at the photo in his hands, trying to see it.

'Well, it was also the worst year of my life too. This is the reason why . . .'

Chapter 17

Greta hadn't seen many photographs of Uncle Ray at this age. He was wearing his scouting uniform. A blue shirt covered in badges, with a red and white scarf and toggle at his neck. His smile took over his whole face, and his hair was a little too long and messy. She realized that he was quite good looking. She'd never thought about him like that. 'You look like Aidan, I've never noticed that before.'

He had his arm around a woman who looked about the same age as him. Her uniform was a different colour, though. Khaki green with a purple and white scarf and toggle. She had the same broad smile as her uncle's.

They looked very much like a couple in love.

Ray ran a finger gently across the photograph. He knew every detail of it off by heart, from her brown hair escaping its plaits on either side of her face, to the freckles on her cheeks from the sun. But most of all, he knew her smile. 'She's the only woman I've ever loved.'

Greta had never heard her uncle talk about this or in fact any woman before. They hadn't even landed on American soil, and she had discovered so many new things about him.

'When she smiled like she's doing here, it made my head spin,' Ray continued.

'She's pretty,' Greta said. 'What was her name?'

'Billie Haley.'

'Like the comet,' Greta said.

'I hope not,' Ray said. 'That's only visible twice in anybody's lifetime. It's not due back here until 2061 . . . And anyway, it's Halley's Comet, not Haley's, discovered by the English astronomer Edmond Halley.'

'You are such a nerd.' Greta laughed. 'Her uniform is different from yours, so she wasn't in the same scouting group as you?'

'Correct. She's American. From the Midwest. The first time I ever laid eyes on her was at Schiphol Airport on the day we arrived for the jamboree. You should have seen the arrivals hall. There were thousands of scouts from all over the world. It was chaos as everyone waited for their luggage. It was my first jamboree, and also my first time out of Ireland. I thought I'd stepped into another world.'

'A "we're not in Kansas any more, Toto" moment?' Greta whispered.

'Exactly that. We were waiting for our bags to come out onto the conveyor belt and I was trying to keep an eye on the younger lads in our group. We had twenty kids ranging in age from twelve years old to eighteen years old. They were hyper, as you can imagine. And sure I wasn't that much older than them myself at twenty-four. Billie walked by me. It was actually her hat that caught my eye. A bright purple one. And it fell off her head and landed at my feet.'

'She literally set her cap at you, Uncle Ray,' Greta giggled.

'Not so sure about that. Dumb luck, I reckon, that it landed by me. She was laden down with a rucksack on her back with another bag on her front. Which was the norm for scouting trips, the lot of us were in the same boat. But because of that, she couldn't reach down to get it, so I picked it up for her. She smiled that smile you see right there in the photo, and I swear, Greta, I fell in love with her on the spot. I know that's not a cool thing to say, but it's true.'

'I don't think it's uncool to say you love someone. What happened next? Was it all toasted marshmallows around the campfire while you sang "Ging gang goolie goolie whatsit", to each other?'

'Funny girl. Nothing happened at first – she disappeared, following the rest of her scouting group out of the terminal. And, to be honest, I thought I'd never see her again. You've got to remember that there were hundreds of countries taking part. Plus I had a job to do too, with lots of prearranged activities for our own scouting group.'

'You should have ditched those kids and gone looking for her.'

'Life is not all Hollywood moments, you know.'

'Ain't that the truth.'

'We pitched our tents and I have to tell you it was a sight to behold. Every colour under the sun, in that big field. And there was huge excitement because Queen Beatrice was coming to visit too.'

'Fergie and Andrew's daughter?'

'No. She's only a princess. Or is she a duchess? She's not a queen anyhow. I mean the queen of Netherlands. Lovely woman.'

'Did you meet her?'

'No.' He shook his head. 'But she did give a rousing speech.'

'That does sound lame, Uncle Ray. If you're telling the story again, I'd skip that bit. Just saying.'

'Noted. But you did ask. Anyhow, once the opening ceremony started, I got lost in the parade and the music. Our crew were all singing, "Singing in the Rain".'

'A-ru-cha-cha, A-ru-cha-cha . . .' Greta sang softly.

'That's the one. We were belting it out. And I suppose Lady Serendipity wasn't done with us. Because, despite the tens of thousands of people in that field, I saw Billie again. I'll never forget that moment – these big walking tulips were going by. Don't ask. And there she was, looking right at me too. She remembered the airport and tipped her purple cap at me.'

'I told you she was setting her cap at you! Please tell me you went to speak to her then.'

Ray nodded. 'I've spent a lot of my life feeling stupid, regretting things that I've done or not done. But the single best decision I ever made was at that moment. I marched over to her and pretty much from that moment we spent every spare minute of the ten-day holiday together.'

'Smooching around the campfire, eh?'

Ray smiled, and Greta thought he looked just like the young man in his photo again.

'We had our first kiss under the stars,' Ray admitted. 'I can't look at the stars any more without thinking about that kiss.'

'Uncle Ray . . .' Greta had never thought about her uncle as a romantic, but he was making her all emotional as he recounted his tale. She had a lump in her throat listening to him.

'Your first-kiss story is so much better than mine. I can't even remember the name of the guy I snogged. Pretty awful kisser he was too, to be honest. A lot of clashing teeth and tongues.' She shuddered.

'Not sure I needed to hear that,' Ray said, shuddering himself.

'Sorry. Moving swiftly back to Billie.'

'While we didn't have a long time together, camp time is different to real time. One day is like a week. So we crammed a lot into our short holiday.'

'What happened afterwards?'

'She had to go back home, as did I. We both cried. We swore we'd stay in touch. And we did for a while, writing to each other every week. She said she was going to come to Ireland, as part of a big European trip. I looked into getting a career break to go with her. But then her letters slowed down, dwindling until they stopped completely. I carried on writing to her for a few months. But I'm not a complete eejit; eventually, I had to give up. She moved on, I suppose.'

'That's so sad.' Greta patted his hand. 'Long-distance relationships rarely work out.'

They sat in silence for a while, both looking at the photograph. Greta decided there and then that she would put all her efforts into finding him a girlfriend when they got back home. Whether he liked it or not, she was putting his picture up on Tinder.

Ray shifted in his seat, turning towards Greta. 'I need to tell you something else.'

'There's more? Jeepers, Uncle Ray, you're a dark horse!' Greta replied.

'You'll never guess where Billie lives . . .'

'Surprise me.'

'Kansas. In a town called Cawker City.'

'Shut the front door!' Then the penny dropped. 'That's on our wish list! You put that place on our wish list!'

'Ssh,' Ray said to Greta, who was shouting now and drawing looks from the other passengers.

Greta looked at her uncle with sympathy and said, 'You do know that it's probable that she's married, with kids. The chances are that when her letters stopped, it was because she met someone locally.'

Ray found it impossible to visualize an older version of Billie, with her own family. To him, she would always be that twenty-year-old he fell in love with. 'I need to find a way to move on from 1995. I feel like I've been stuck since then. Just going through the motions, but not really living.'

'Is that why you kept going to world jamborees every year? You were hoping to find her again?'

Ray flushed red. 'Yep. But in my defence, I do enjoy the festival too.'

'So this trip, it's not just about me meeting Dr Gale and getting away from it all. It's a quest to find your first love too.'

He shook his head. 'I don't know if it is yet. But it might be. I know it's stupid. But the closer we get to Kansas Airport, the more I believe that we've got to try to find her. Do you think I'm crazy?'

'Hell, yeah. Certifiable. But I also think you're a fecking legend Uncle Ray. Count me in. Let's go to the last address you have of hers and see what we can find out. If she's married with a gaggle of kids then—'

'Then we drive on,' Ray said.

'And at least you'll know. But . . . imagine this for a second . . . maybe she's been thinking about you all these years too. Wouldn't that be something?'

'It will be enough to see her again. See how her life has turned out. To know she's happy. But yes, that would be something quite wonderful.'

Chapter 18

The rest of their journey went by without a hitch. They transferred flights in Toronto and arrived in Kansas International Airport at four p.m. They got a bus to the car rental terminal to collect their hire car. Greta left Ray to it and sat down with their bags and her phone.

Dylan: Well have you landed?

To answer or not to answer. Greta closed her phone.
They grabbed their bags and discovered when they went outside that it had been snowing. Heavily. They walked carefully until they found their car, which was covered in snow.

'It's bigger than I thought it would be,' Ray said as he loaded their bags into the boot of the black Chevrolet Suburban he'd rented. 'So remind me, what side of the road do they drive on again?'

When Greta gasped, he winked at her. And without any issue, he got them out of the airport and on the right road. Snowploughs had been out, and the streets were gritted and clear. With every passing mile, Greta's respect for her uncle grew. There was a lot more to him than most thought.

'This was worth every extra cent.' Ray pointed to the satellite navigation system that was on the window. He knew his niece. She could get lost in a department store, so no way was he leaving the directions up to her. 'First things first, let's go into this gas station and fill this baby up.'

While Ray pumped the gas, Greta went into the shop to buy road-trip snacks. When she was in rehab, she'd discussed her emotional eating habits, which died hard, it seemed. She needed something from the old Greta right now, and this came in the form of crisps, chocolate bars, biscuits, peanuts and cans of soda. She felt guilt with every ping of the barcode scanner. When Ray raised his eyes in question, she replied, 'It doesn't matter how old we are, road-trip snacks should always look like they were bought by an eight-year-old. And my eight-year-old self likes sugar,' she joked, trying to hide her anxiety.

Greta waited for a think-of-your-waistline recrimination from him. But all he said was, 'I've always wondered what a Twinkie was.' He picked up the bar for closer inspection.

'No lecture about eating healthily?'

'You're an adult, Greta, and if you want a chocolate bar, you should eat one.'

'I'm not planning on eating them all now. We'll leave

them in the boot, and if the need hits us, then we're sorted.'

'Good plan.'

'You know, Dad would have had a field day chastising me for getting these sweets.'

'Well, first of all, I'm not your dad, so it's easy for me not to have to chastise you. And second of all, I don't think Stephen means to do that. It's just . . . he's spent his whole life being an over-achiever. And he had our parents on his back constantly telling him how they were relying on him to succeed. That's a lot of pressure. I don't think he's ever found a way to release that. Or maybe he has with his running. I'm not excusing him. I know he's been hard on you. I'm just trying to explain.'

'He's been OK since I got home. But it still feels awkward. Like we are both stepping on eggshells around each other.'

'That will get better. Give him a chance. You were very honest telling him how you felt at therapy. But that must have been hard for him to hear. He's been thinking of little else, if I know my big brother at all. And he's been beating himself up for upsetting you like that. He loves you. There's no doubt about that.'

Greta didn't want her dad to feel bad. They had all wasted too much time feeling guilty about things they couldn't change. Maybe, by the time she got back, things would be a little less tense. She'd make it her business to make it so.

They made their way into Kansas City, where Ray had booked a hotel for their first night. But other than that, they were going to wing it and stay wherever made sense each night. Ray had to drive at a snail's pace as they made their way to the Raphael Hotel. Trees covered in powdery white snow lined the Shawnee River, which ran across the road from the hotel. It was beginning to get dark, and Kansas City was bathed in an orange glow, from flickering fairy lights.

With the car parked, Greta looked up at the grand hotel in front of them. The Raphael Hotel was framed by two massive pillars, an archway of golden light between them. 'It's so pretty and looks so posh. I feel like I should have dressed up more.' She brushed some crumbs off her black tunic, remnants from the flight. No matter how hard she tried, she always managed to spill food down herself when she ate, thanks to her more-than-ample boobs getting in the way of the cutlery. She'd lost count of the times her brothers had teased her about this at meal times. And each time, Greta would Big G it up, and laugh along with them. Shovelling down her pain with a second helping of whatever was on offer.

'We can't get used to this type of luxury,' Ray said, smiling. 'It's a treat to start us off. But we'll have to stay in more modest motels for the rest of the road trip.'

'That's fine with me,' Greta said. 'I'm still a bit over-whelmed about all of this. I can't quite believe we are here.' She dropped her bags to her feet and threw herself into her uncle's arms, like she used to do as a little girl. He laughed as he returned the hug, and all of his doubts about the trip disappeared.

'I'm really grateful. I know this must be costing you a fortune. I'll pay you back every cent.'

'No you won't. I'm paying for this trip because I want

to. It's my pleasure to treat you. Sure what are uncles for? I can hardly believe that only a few days ago, at this time, I'd be about to get the bus home from work.' He stopped and looked at Greta. 'Let's just grab this holiday by the scruff of its neck and shake every bit of adventure we can from it. That's all the payment I need. Deal?'

'Deal.' Greta smiled, then stopped to take a photo of the hotel entrance for Instagram.

Her room was beautiful. Yellow gingham wallpaper framed the giant king-size bed, which had gorgeous bed linen, in greens and yellows and brilliant whites. She threw herself on the bed and sank into the soft pillow top mattress. Despite the long flight, Greta felt wide awake and alert. They had decided to go out straight away and find somewhere to eat. Kansas City was renowned for its BBQs and jazz, so they were going to look for that. As she lay on the bed, she felt a familiar pull of anxiety nip at her. What if she couldn't sleep over here? Maybe her mother was right, it was too soon for her to go away.

Before she left, she rang Noreen to tell her about the trip and promised her she'd find a NA meeting while on the road. She'd been supportive about the trip and told her not to worry about her sleeping patterns too much. Stress was counterproductive. Greta supposed that she could sleep in the car tomorrow if she struggled tonight. Ray had already said as much to her. And she could go to bed early tomorrow night.

She snapped a pic of the room, then sent it to the family WhatsApp group. Should she send it to Dylan? She still hadn't answered his last two messages. She decided against it. Posting a bedroom pic seemed a bit weird. She shivered as she thought about the night she slept in his bed. What had happened that night? She kept replaying it over in her head but came up blank. She knew what Noreen would say. She had to just ask him. But that was easier said than done. She couldn't find the words.

Ray was waiting for her when she went back down to the lobby. Her heart squeezed as she took him in, standing at the foot of the stairs, holding a black folder in his hand. In a world of constant change, he still looked like the altar boy he'd been as a child. She'd never really thought about how he looked before. He was just her uncle. But he was also lonely and wanted to meet someone. Could she help him tweak his style a bit? She knew better than most that first impressions mattered, and she wanted Billie to take the time to have a second glance. To see the man he was inside.

She would have to do something about his hair, which he'd smoothed into place with half a tub of gel. It needed to look . . . less perfect. And his clothes didn't help. There was nothing wrong with them – it was just that everything was too put together. Too square. Brown chinos, navy jumper, and the collar of a navy check shirt peeking out, with brown leather shoes.

After a slippery start to their search for a jazz restaurant, they decided to go back and eat in the hotel restaurant. Greta still felt like she was in a dream. She wasn't sure if it was the jet lag kicking in or the fact that this reality was such a stark contrast from where she had been only two weeks previously. The menu was so extensive, neither of them had the energy to make a decision on their own. They went for the waiter's recommendation in the end and ordered the prime beef rib.

'Don't tell Mam, but this is the best roast beef I've had,' Greta said as she cut into the tender and juicy meat.

'Emily would have your head on a plate for that comment!' Ray laughed.

'So are you going to show me what's in your folder?'

'I thought you'd never ask.' Ray opened the folder and pulled out a typed A4 sheet, titled 'Ray & Greta's Epic Road Trip Wish List'. He'd typed up all the places they'd discussed visiting. 'I think you should have first pick to tick off our first stop!'

Greta grabbed his pen and put a large tick into the box beside Kansas City.

'Tomorrow we're going to the OZ Museum in Wamego?' Greta asked.

'We sure are. It's about time the Kansas Gales said hello to the Dublin Gales.'

Ray's eyes locked on the next stop listed on their wish list – the largest ball of twine, in Cawker City. And he knew that there was only one wish he wanted to come true. But what about Billie? Had she thought about him too in the years since they had last seen each other?

Chapter 19

'I've been awake for hours!' Greta admitted when Ray knocked on her door at eight a.m. She quickly added, when she saw the look of worry that fell over her uncle's face, 'But I slept before that, though.'

The relief on his face was almost comical. 'Your mother has already been in the family WhatsApp group checking up to see how you slept. How are we going to keep a lid on her this trip?'

'Don't even try. And, speaking of which, I promised we'd video-call her now. They are waiting for us. Let's get it out of the way before we head out.'

Greta and Ray sat down at the small table in her room, then waited for her phone to connect to her mother's.

The video-call connected and suddenly she was looking at her mother again.

'Good morning from Ireland,' her mother shouted.

'Hi Mam. You don't need to yell. Why are you looking

so fancy?' Greta asked, peering closely at the screen. Her mam was wearing a pink dress and jacket combo, with her best pearls. And she'd had her hair done too.

'This old thing,' Emily said.

Ciaran's face appeared beside Emily's. 'Mam thinks she's on the telly. She's changed twice.'

Greta giggled. 'You look very nice, Mam.'

'Thank you.' Emily smoothed her curly blow-dry with her hand, watching herself in the small box on the screen.

Greta moved her phone around the room to show her mam.

'Oh that's lovely. I like that wallpaper. Stephen, wouldn't that be lovely in our bedroom? Take a photo and send it to me, Greta. Or, better still, ask the concierge if they have a sample they can give you to stick in your case.'

Greta crossed her fingers behind her back as she promised she'd do that. Sometimes it was easier to just agree with her mam. They chatted for a few minutes more, then said their goodbyes, promising to video-chat again soon.

'I felt quite scruffy compared to Emily,' Ray said.

'Me too. We better up our game the next time! Imagine what she'd be like if she ever was on TV!' Greta smiled. 'You know, I've been thinking, are you sure you don't want to skip the OZ Museum to go straight to Cawker City and find Billie?'

Ray shook his head. 'It's too far to drive all the way to Cawker City in one go. We need to break up the journey somehow; makes sense to do so in Wamego. And as it's so early, we've got time to have a drive around Kansas City before we leave too. Then we'll make our way to Wamego. I've waited this long to find Billie, one more day won't hurt.'

'Are you stalling?'

'One hundred per cent.'

'At least you're honest!'

They went for a walk, taking photographs on the bridge opposite the hotel. It was so cold at five below that they felt their breath freeze as it left their mouths. As it was Sunday, and also because of the snow, the city was quiet. They decided to check out, and took a drive down Ward Parkway. The boulevard was beautiful, with wide, tree-lined avenues flanking large colonial houses. Fountains and statues were covered in snow.

Hungry for breakfast, they made their way into the city centre when Greta spotted something. 'Stop the car! Look at that, Uncle Ray!' To their right was a row of brightly coloured mammoth book covers. They'd found the Kansas Public Library car park. The library was closed, but they stopped for a moment to take some photos of each other, standing underneath the children's classics books, which included L. Frank Baum's *The Wonderful Wizard of Oz*.

They found a diner a few blocks away. 'It's like a movie set, isn't it? It's got a Fifties vibe, as if time stood still,' Ray whispered as a woman dressed in a green check dress, with a white apron tied at the waist, led them to their booth.

'I'm half expecting John Travolta to come in singing "You're the One That I Want".' Their booth came complete with its own wall-mounted jukebox.

'Twenty-five cents for two picks,' Greta announced,

flicking through the choices, delighted when she found two *Grease* numbers.

'I've never had eggs and bacon with pancakes. Gotta try that,' Ray said, reading the breakfast options.

Greta wanted pancakes too, but for some reason, Caroline's face popped into her head. 'Nourish your body, and you'll nourish your mind.' She tried to tell Caroline to feck off, but when their waitress Sherilyn came to take their order, she found herself ordering the egg white omelette with baby spinach, avocado, tomato salsa and turkey bacon.

'How do you like your eggs cooked, honey?' Sherilyn asked Ray.

He looked panicked for a moment, then said with more authority than he felt: 'Sunny side up.' When she walked away, he grinned and said, 'I've always wanted to say that, but I doubted myself for a minute.'

'You do that a lot, Uncle Ray. Doubt yourself.'

'Do I? And so do you.'

'Yes, you do. And touché! But honestly, you should work on that. Because from where I'm sitting, you are one of the smartest guys I know.'

'When you grow up hearing people say that you're not the full shilling, you can't help but believe it.'

'I've never heard that,' Greta lied, thinking of all the times her father had made fun of Ray. He was fond of saying, 'The light's on but sometimes no one is home, with our Ray.' It always felt like banter, but – more than anyone – she knew how much that cut, no matter how light-hearted.

'Maybe you should tell Dad to stop next time he says that.'

'Maybe.'

Their waitress came back with drinks for them both, telling them she'd be back with their food shortly. 'Y'all holler if you need anything.'

'I could listen to her accent all day,' Ray declared, adding milk to his coffee.

'That's because it reminds you of Billie's voice, I bet,' Greta teased.

'She did used to say "y'all" a lot. But I can't remember what she sounds like any more. I used to let our conversations, our many, many conversations, dance around in my brain. They've gotten a bit fuzzy now with time, I suppose. I tried to hold on to them for as long as possible. But then one day I woke up and I couldn't find her in my head any more.'

'I think long-distance relationships are easier now, with WhatsApp and FaceTime, et cetera,' Greta said.

'I remember all sorts of silly things. Like, her favourite book was *Little Women*. And she had this weird fascination with anything zombie-related. Her favourite movie was *Dawn of the Dead*.'

'Don't you love that show *The Walking Dead*, too?' Greta asked. She couldn't watch it; the walkers reminded her too much of the hooded man from her nightmares.

'I never miss an episode. I often wonder if Billie is watching it too.'

'It is a big show over here, so I'd say yes. You nervous about seeing her?'

'I keep bouncing between hope and reality. I've left it too late. She's probably forgotten who I am by now.'

Greta knew that there was a strong possibility that

Billie hadn't given Ray a thought over the past twenty years. The mind has a habit of dumping memories of people who are no longer important to it. Greta couldn't remember most of the names of her old classmates any more. Their faces had blurred too. Yet she could remember every single cast mate she'd ever performed with, right back to her drama-club days as a kid. You keep the stuff that's important, she supposed. 'If it meant so much to you, it stands to reason that it meant as much to her.'

'Not enough to stay in touch with me, though. She walked away, not me. If I'm honest, Greta, I'm a bit worried about how I'll react when I see her. I might hit the floor.'

Greta thought about all the times that her uncle had been there for her, catching her when she fell. 'If you fall, I'll be your floor,' Greta promised.

'You might regret that. I'm heavy.'

'Not as heavy as me. And you've been my floor for years now.'

Ray reached over and touched his niece's hand. 'Thank you. And hey! You are not allowed to say negative stuff about yourself any more.'

'Oh shit, I didn't even notice that I did that! OK, well while I might be heavy, my skin is the skin of a woman at least ten years younger than I am.' Greta took a bow.

Any further discussion was halted by the arrival of their platters. 'Wowsers,' Ray said, looking at his plate, which held two eggs, two strips of crispy bacon, and a stack of pancakes.

Greta realized that if this was healthy eating, American style, she was more than happy. Her omelette was delicious

186

and filling. But she did scoff half of Ray's pancakes all the same. As he said, there was a law or something in America that you *had* to eat pancakes. And if there wasn't one, there should be. They were incredible.

'Uncle Ray, we need to talk about what you are going to wear tomorrow when we get to Cawker City. I know there's nothing worse than someone talking to you about your appearance – trust me. But the first time you see the love of your life deserves a killer outfit. And please don't hate me, but you've got to let me do something about your hair, too.'

'What's wrong with my hair? On the clothes front, I have that covered already. I've got a new shirt and jumper in my case. I bought it before we left.'

'Let me guess, a navy check shirt and a navy jumper.'

His lack of response was answer enough for Greta. 'Will you trust me on this? I don't want to change you. Just make a few tweaks.'

'I'm not spiking my hair up or anything silly like that.'

'I was thinking some blond highlights,' Greta said, then burst out laughing when she saw the horror on her uncle's face. 'I'm joking!'

After breakfast, the road trip officially began when they joined the I70, a road they would be spending a lot of time on over the next week. Either side of the interstate was covered in thick snow, so there was little to see in the terrain. They listened to the radio and sang along to some Eighties music. Then both squealed when they spotted a sign on the way into Wamego that said 'Road to Oz Highway'.

When Ray and Stephen were kids, their family, along

with millions of others around the globe, fell in love with all things Oz, when RTE played *The Wizard of Oz* one Christmas Day. Sharing the same surname as Dorothy, Aunty Em and Uncle Henry tethered them to the movie too, as they joked that they must be related somehow. Ray could remember how that movie made him feel as acutely today as it had done on that snowy afternoon, in front of an open fire in his childhood home. He watched the black and white opening sequence, with mild interest, while he played with his Lego. Then Dorothy was swept into a cyclone, which surprised him. But when she landed into the technicolour world of Munchkinland with a crash, he was hooked. He fell in love with the friendships made on that road trip along the yellow brick road to Oz. He cheered Dorothy, the Scarecrow, the Tin Man and the Cowardly Lion on, through every song and dance, until they all finally reached the Emerald City and got their hearts' desire.

That Christmas a tradition began for the Gale family that Stephen continued with his own kids too. Once the Gales had finished their last mouthful of turkey, they would all move to the living room to eat their trifle and Christmas pudding. Once, Ciaran had half-heartedly suggested they not watch it, but the pull to Oz was too strong. It was more than a movie to them, it was part of who they were. It was home. It was family. It was hope. It was as reassuring and comforting as a big, soft blanket draped over their knees.

So, seeing that sign, even though they knew it was a touristy gimmick, both Ray and Greta felt a little bit of Oz's magic was reaching out to them.

'There're lots of Oz-themed attractions in Kansas,' Ray said. 'But according to my research, there's no town with more Emerald City panache than this one.'

They drove into what looked like a ghost town. Everything was closed. Ray parked opposite the OZ Museum.

'It's not quite what I had in mind,' Ray admitted.

'Let's just watch out for flying monkeys,' Greta joked.

'You used to jump into my lap, burying your head under my chin whenever they were unleashed,' Ray said.

'They used to freak me out!'

'Want to know something stupid? When I was a kid, I used to wish a tornado would take me away to the land of Oz,' Ray admitted.

'Sometimes I still do. So if that makes you stupid, then there's two of us,' Greta replied. 'Look, over here!' Greta walked over to an emerald green statue of Toto that sat at the top of a yellow brick road.

They looked at each other and laughed, memories of every time they'd watched the movie as kids and adults making them giddy. Greta grabbed Ray's arm and said, 'Come on, Scarecrow. It's time to follow the yellow brick road.'

'If only I had a brain,' Ray said.

Together, they skipped down the yellow brick road for a moment, turning back when they realized it ended in a dead end.

'Well, there's no rainbow over here,' Greta said. They made their way across the street into the museum. They made their way around the artefacts, which had lots of information about the Oz books, the life of L. Frank

Baum and the subsequent movie. They sat and watched a documentary about the making of the film. When Victor Fleming admitted that he slapped the young Judy because she giggled during a scene with Bert Lahr who played the Cowardly Lion, they were both shocked and outraged on her behalf.

'Judy was such a contradiction – a triumphant and tragic figure all at once. But with such an extraordinary talent. There was no doubt she was destined to perform. You share that with her.'

'The industry doesn't seem to agree with you, Uncle Ray.'

'You have to keep the faith and your time will come. I know it. Your acting career is going to take off. If that's what you still want, of course.'

'I'm not sure most would call it a career,' Greta answered with a self-deprecating laugh.

'Why do you always use humour to deflect questions?'

'Why do you always counter my humour with more questions?'

'I can still remember seeing you in your first-ever drama-club show. You were Dorothy in their production of *The Wizard of Oz*.'

'I suspect that I was given the role because I was the only one who knew the words to the movie off by heart. Mam made my costume out of a gingham tablecloth she had. And I borrowed Mrs Oaks's dog from next door and stuffed it into a picnic basket.'

'When you sang "Somewhere Over the Rainbow", you could have heard a pin drop. It was magical.'

'I can remember taking the final bow, watching Mam,

Dad, Gran and you in the audience. They were on their feet, cheering. Mam was pregnant with Aidan, I think. Her bump was sticking out. But she stood up and cheered, tears in her eyes. I can remember thinking to myself that I wanted to make them proud like that over and over again.' She stopped and shook her head. 'Now, the only tears in their eyes are of pain and shame. Not pride.'

'They were both proud when you came home from therapy. Seeing how well you'd done. They may not have told you that, but I could see it.'

'I hope you're right. Judy died from an overdose of sleeping pills at forty-seven years old. We nearly had that in common too. I think about that a lot,' Greta said.

'Are you done with the pills now?' Ray asked gently.

'Truthfully, I can't imagine ever taking one again. Just the thought of going back to that . . . that mess, scares me more than any flying monkeys ever did.'

'That's my girl,' Ray said. 'I think for Judy, she paid a tragic price for her early fame. A child who never had a childhood. What kind of parents give their child pills in the first place, then allow the studio to mess with her diet the way they did? She didn't stand a chance. But that's not your story. You have a family who support you. If you gave it all up tomorrow, they would still support you.'

'Even Dad?' Greta thought about what he had said at the family therapy session. *You used to be the cutest person on this planet, and you blew it. We used to go out, and everyone would point and stare and say, that's the girl from the advert. But now, instead, they point and stare at the fatty.*

191

'He didn't meant that,' Ray said. 'He lashed out, because he felt cornered. He's always been the same. He's not without flaws, but he loves you. And he fought for you. Fought to save your life, any which way he could. Don't forget that.'

Uncle Ray was right. Maybe it was time to focus on that, rather than on the things he might have said in anger. And maybe it was also time for her to reach out to her dad, try to mend some bridges with him. She'd held him at arm's length since she got home. The more Greta thought about it, the more she realized that she had put a barrier up between them for a long time now. She made it her business not to be in his company on her own. He wasn't the only one at fault for their fractured relationship. And she wasn't a child any more. It wasn't his job to fix them. It was theirs.

She opened her phone and, rather than just sending a message to the family WhatsApp group, she messaged her father directly.

Greta: Hi Dad. Hope the training is going well for the marathon.

It wasn't much, but it was a start.

Chapter 20

They drove for a few hours, moving closer to Billie with each mile, eventually stopping in a town called Manhattan.

'If you tell me that you'd rather stay the way you are, that's fine. But if you let me, I'd love to help you change things up a bit,' Greta said, when they spotted a shopping centre.

'I don't want to look like a boy-band reject.'

'I give you my word that there will not be a single Boyzone vibe. The look we're going for is the dashing romantic hero.'

When he parked the car up outside the mall, Greta took that as a yes. Within an hour, she'd talked him into buying two pairs of jeans, three sweatshirts, four T-shirts, one shirt – not check – a pair of boots, trainers and a new jacket.

'I don't see what's wrong with the coat I'm wearing,' Ray moaned. 'It's in perfectly good condition.'

'It's ancient! You need to bin it. Trust me. You know the saying. The clothes maketh the man. You are a good-looking man. Show that off!'

'Go away out of that.'

'You are! And I'm not just saying that because I love you. It's true. All these clothes do is to add a bit of icing for the top of your cake.'

'Thanks Greta,' Ray said, chuffed with her compliment. 'But if I'm getting some icing, you need to get some too. Go treat yourself to something new. I'm going for a sit-down. I haven't been in a clothes shop this long . . . well, ever . . . it's tired me out.'

She left him to his own devices for a bit and went upstairs to the women's section. Maybe it was time she looked at mixing up her own wardrobe, following her own advice. She had got into the habit of wearing black a lot. And here, on this road trip, she didn't feel that black suited her any more. She needed to technicolour her life up. Adding a splash of colour into her wardrobe was the first step.

A smiling shop assistant walked over to her when she got to the top of the escalator. She looked Greta up and down, from her boots to her double chin, and landed her glance on Greta's tummy. 'Our plus-size range is up another level on three.'

Plus size. These two words held so much power that they seemed to strip every ounce of confidence from Greta in an instant. It felt like the shop assistant was saying that Greta was abnormal in some way. Because to be plus-sized didn't mean that you were simply bigger. It implied so much offence. Greta felt angry, then hurt, then angry again,

194

to have been labelled in this way. She knew she was fat. Fair enough. But that didn't mean she was a lesser person than someone who could fit into a size zero. Skinny, tall, fat, small – they were all descriptor words. But somehow only negativity surrounded the words plus size or fat, especially when matched with the look that the woman had given her as she uttered them. And in one second flat, they made her doubt herself all over again.

She was sick of it. She couldn't let all the work she'd done with Noreen disappear. Greta walked over to the shop assistant and flashed her an even bigger smile. 'You made a lot of assumptions just then. And I didn't like it. I didn't ask you where the plus-size clothing was. As it happens, that's exactly where I *was* heading. And your directions would have been helpful if they were not followed by a look of disgust. You might need to work on that in the future. Oh, and for the record, I have really nice boobs. They might be big, but they don't flop. So there.' And as she walked away, leaving the open-mouthed woman behind her, she felt a little better.

The good news was that the store had a fantastic range of clothes in all sizes. Their changing rooms were large and, for the first time in years, she enjoyed trying on different styles. It was particularly nice that the US sizing meant that she was a size smaller than at home in Ireland. And in the end, she left with several new tops, a pair of jeans and a dress. She found Ray sitting on a bench outside the store, his eyes closed. Jet lag had caught him up. She sat down beside him, feeling exhausted herself. She checked her phone and there was another message from Dylan. He didn't give up.

Dylan: Well Silver Lady, are you ever going to answer me? It's freezing over here. Grey and miserable. Depress me further and tell me where you are!

'Is that Dylan again?' Ray asked.

'Welcome back to the land of the living. And yes it is, as it happens. How did you know?'

'You always smile when you get a message from him. I think you like him.'

'I do not!' Greta said. 'That's ridiculous. We're just friends.'

'The lady doth protest too much.'

'Shut up.'

He pretended to zip his mouth.

'I've been ignoring him. Dylan,' Greta confessed. 'I don't know how to tell him about the whole drug addict thing. So things have been a bit weird.'

'I can see how that must be a hard thing for you to say to people. But the way I see it, if he's a good friend, he'll accept you as you are. The good, the bad and the ugly.'

'I'm scared.'

'Of what?'

'Everything. What if he loses all respect for me, when I tell him about rehab?'

'I think you are being unfair to your friend there. Dylan always struck me as a decent guy. He clearly thinks the world of you. But maybe there's more to you avoiding him than just that.'

Greta looked at her uncle in surprise. He missed very little. 'I did something stupid, really, really stupid, that I need to apologize to him about too.'

'Oh dear.'

'I'm not telling you what it is, because it's too embarrassing. So don't even try to get it out of me.' Waking up half naked in bed with her best friend, with no recollection of how she got there, or what she'd done, was not the kind of thing you told your uncle about.

'I don't want to know, unless you want to tell me. But it seems to me that you could lose a good friend, because you don't have the guts to have an honest conversation.'

Greta recognized the truth of his words, but she liked keeping her head in the sand.

'Listen, for what it's worth, I'm scared too. What if Billie takes one look at me and only sees a middle-aged man, unrecognizable from the one she loved all those years ago? But I'm not going to let that stop me. And neither should you.'

'You're the same inside. Even if you have a few extra wrinkles.'

'And you're the same inside too. Give Dylan a chance. If he walks away, then he wasn't a true friend after all. What did you buy?' He nodded to the bags at Greta's feet.

'Loads! We're so going over our baggage allowance on the way home! I have a present for you too. I bought it earlier today in the OZ Museum.' She pulled a package from her handbag and gave it to Ray. 'It's not much. But I thought of you when I saw it.'

He unwrapped the paper bag and inside was a figurine of the Scarecrow, standing with his arms pointing in two different directions.

'It's struck me that you've always been my Scarecrow, Uncle Ray.'

'A head full of straw.' Ray tapped his skull.

'But he was the wisest one of them all in the end,' Greta contradicted. 'You keep us all tethered. All these years, whenever there's been a crisis, we look to you for help and support. And you're always there. I'm not sure any of us really thanks you enough for that.'

Ray looked at the Scarecrow and felt tears sting his eyes. He'd never wanted or asked for thanks from his family. But hearing Greta's words touched him.

'I'll treasure this,' Ray said, placing the Scarecrow figurine in his shopping bags. 'Answer me this. If I'm the Scarecrow, who is the Tin Man and the Cowardly Lion?'

'I haven't worked that out yet,' Greta said, smiling. 'I'm Dorothy, obviously.'

'But of course.'

'It felt like a cyclone, back then. I was out of control and lost in that storm. And then I landed in rehab with a thud. I think that was my land of the Munchkins. And Noreen has to be Glinda, the good witch.'

'Who did you kill?' Ray asked.

Greta thought about it, 'The Wicked Witch of the East is my addiction to sleeping pills.'

'Well, she's dead now. You did it. And now we're on our yellow brick road to the Emerald City, better known as Las Vegas!'

'I hope we don't meet any flying monkeys on the way. Or the Wicked Witch of the West,' Greta said, with a grin.

'I'll protect you! And for the record, Dorothy, I'm

honoured to be your Scarecrow. I do believe he turned out to be the favourite. If you ever tell Aidan and Ciaran this, I'll deny it, but you are my favourite too!'

They leaned into each other for a moment, shoulder to shoulder, uncle and niece, happy to rest in the mall corridor for a moment, reflecting on their journey ahead.

'Let's go find a hotel for the night. Then tomorrow we can make our way to Cawker City,' Ray said after a few minutes, jumping to his feet. He was ready for sleep, because the next day was going to be a big day for him, whatever the outcome.

The great thing about road trips in the US was the large number of affordable hotels and motels every ten miles or so, located in the services. And there was always a chain of diners close by too. They had something to eat in a Denny's diner, then checked into The Quality Inn, agreeing to meet the next morning at eight a.m.

Greta flopped onto the bed, with her new clothes in piles around her, and decided to take her uncle's advice. No more hiding from her friend. She wasn't going to push him away; if he chose to go, then that would be on him.

Greta: Hi Dylan. Sorry it took me so long to answer. We're in Kansas still. We found Oz today and we're trying to dodge flying monkeys as we speak.
Dylan: Ha! It was the lollipop-wielding Munchkins that gave me the collywobbles when I was a kid.
Greta: The collywobbles? Is that even a word?

He responded with a screenshot of the Thesaurus of the word.

Collywobbles

1 intestinal cramps or other intestinal disturbances
2 a feeling of fear, apprehension, or nervousness

Laughing she answered with her own screenshot.

Weirdo

1 an odd, eccentric, or unconventional person
2 a psychopath, especially a dangerous or vicious one; psycho

As Greta lay in her queen-sized bed, she flicked through what felt like hundreds of channels. She found an episode of *Oprah* and couldn't believe her eyes when she saw the guest – it was Dr Gale. Complete with her trademark glossy, shiny hair and big Hollywood smile, she made Greta feel scruffy just looking at her. Dr Gale was talking about weight loss, a subject that she explored in her book, *What's In Your Cupboard?*

'My mind has always bullied my body. So I had to find a way to stop that.'

'You cleared out your cupboard,' Oprah said.

'Yes I did. I threw self-doubt, fear and regret in the trash. But that wasn't enough. I had to throw out low self-esteem too. And so can all of you.' She turned to the studio audience. 'I say it's time to give our cupboards a good clear out y'hear? Can I get a hell yeah?'

'Hell yeah,' Oprah and her audience shouted back.

Dr Gale took Oprah and her audience to church. Greta fell asleep and dreamed that she was in a gospel choir with both Dr Gale and Oprah. The three of them

Beyoncé'd the heck out of 'Oh Happy Day'. Then the dream got weird when a gang of zombies started chasing them. Oprah handled herself like a boss, taking out every zombie that came at them with the heel of her four-inch stilettos. Greta awoke drooling, half expecting to see her famous gospel choir lying in the bed beside her.

As she'd fallen asleep at seven p.m. she was now wide awake and it was only midnight. The curse of jet lag! She drank a slug of water, then picked up her phone which had been charging.

Stephen: When I got back from my run, I saw your message. Made my day. The house is very quiet without you. Hope you are having fun.

The bridge was a little sturdier.

She sent Dylan a message telling him about her weird gospel choir dream. She hoped he was awake and willed the phone to ping back a message. The phone obliged.

Dylan: And you call me a weirdo.
Greta: If the cap fits. You'll never guess what Uncle Ray told me?
Dylan: He confessed he's on the run from the Guards?
Greta: If so, what did he do?
Dylan: Armed robbery. The local Centra.
Greta: What did he take?
Dylan: Tiffin chocolate.
Greta: Well, there's no doubt Tiffin chocolate is all kinds of delicious. But this is even better than a Tiffin grab. He

confessed that he's been in love with someone since he was twenty-four. A woman called Billie.

Dylan: Whoah! Go, Uncle Ray.

Greta: And there's more. She lives in Kansas. As in Kansas of the US of A.

Dylan: Shut the front door.

Greta: I know! That's what I said. We're going to her house tomorrow.

Dylan: What?

Greta: I know!

Dylan: Does she know?

Greta: Not a clue.

Dylan: The Ultimate Romantic Gesture move. Nice. The stuff movies are made of.

Greta: He is my new hero. If she's married with a house full of kids, she'd better let him down gently. I think I dreamt about zombies because of Billie. Ray says she likes those kind of movies. What if she tells him to feck off?

Dylan: I keep telling you, he's pulled the URG. She has to be impressed. Wouldn't you be?

Greta: I'd be gobsmacked if anyone loved me that much!

Dylan: You might be surprised who cares about you.

Greta: You, my friend, are an eternal optimist. In fact, if we are to remain friends, I'll have to knock that out of you.

And when they said their goodbyes, leaving Greta to flick through hundreds of channels on her TV, she was smiling again.

Chapter 21

The drive to Cawker City took them off the interstate. The flat prairie land on either side of the long, straight road was covered in a thick blanket of snow.

'If I wanted to get lost in the world, this place would be a good choice,' Ray said. They had driven for miles without meeting a single car. Farmland stretched for miles, dotted – every now and then – with wooden farmhouses and big red barns.

'Did you see that billboard?' Greta asked in shock.

Jesus is alive. Call here for irrefutable proof.

'Sure did. Hope you wrote down that number.'

'I'm tempted to call it for the craic! I should give the number to Mam. She'd sort them out. Have you noticed how the sky is the same colour as the snow on the ground? It's like someone has tipped a bottle of talcum powder into the air,' Greta said.

'Yes, it does look a bit like that.'

Greta squealed, and Ray sucked in his breath when they saw a large water tower with the words 'Cawker City' written on it.

'We're here,' Greta said.

Ray drove down the main street, realizing that once again everything was shut. 'These smaller towns have been hit hard by recession. You know I timed that we didn't meet a single car for over ten miles. Strange, isn't it?'

'It looks like this place has been frozen in time,' Greta said as they passed a red and white petrol station, with 1950s pumps, covered in snow.

'Red Crown gasoline. It could be a movie set,' Ray agreed.

He pulled in to a car park. He pointed to what looked like a large bus shelter. 'Look, this is where the largest ball of twine in the world is!'

'It's not how I imagined it when you spoke about it! Another thing off our wish list,' Greta said.

'Twine was one of our things, Billie and mine. You had to be there, I suppose. We might as well pop in, seeing as we're here.'

'Diversion tactics again, Uncle Ray.'

'Absolutely,' Ray agreed, getting out of the car. 'Don't slip. It's wicked icy.'

The open-air gazebo had a snow-capped roof, but the ball of twine it encased was dry. And huge. A large sign outlined the World's Largest Ball of Sisal Twine's statistics. It was started in 1953 by Frank Stoeber and was now 20,078 pounds and 43 feet in circumference.

'Why on earth would anyone want to do this?' Greta asked, trying to fit the whole thing into a photo.

'The ultimate hoarder, with a saving-it-till-later mentality, right? I can remember Billie telling me that they hold a Twine-a-thon festival here every summer. Or at least they used to.'

'Stop. This is bat-shit crazy. You do know that?'

'I think it's kind of wonderful,' Ray said, putting his hand into his pocket, checking for something. *Yes, it was still there.*

'Throw your arms around it,' Greta said giggling as she took pics of Ray trying to cuddle a ball of twine.

'Your turn,' Ray said, taking his camera out.

'Portrait not landscape. No! Go back a bit. Take it from a higher angle. Not that high!' Greta shouted out instructions. 'Let's just do a selfie,' Greta said, deleting each of his photographs when he showed them to her.

'When we were kids, you just smiled for the camera. You took your chance that your heads were all in frame. I preferred it then,' Ray said.

'It's worth taking a minute to get a decent shot! Look, get in with me. See, just hold the phone slightly tilted, not too high, never from below which would be chin carnage, tilt your head – not that much, subtle. Better. Now smile, looking down a bit more. There!'

'I'm exhausted,' Ray grumbled.

'But look how good we look.'

'I look weird. And the most interesting thing about this place is missing. Where's the twine? Perfect photo op missed while we looked for the right angle! Go over and cuddle that bale of twine and you are not deleting the pic.'

'Bossy!' Greta complained, but she did as she was told,

giggling as Ray made a big deal out of getting the right angle.

'Now, we both look like eejits,' Ray said, laughing too.

'At least no one is watching us!' Greta looked up and down the main street and couldn't see a single person. It would be a miracle if Billie still lived in this town because it looked like most had bailed out years ago. They got back to the car, and Ray punched Billie's address into the sat nav. She lived about three miles east of Cawker City. The road to her house was no more than a dirt lane, surrounded by a green woodland. When they got to the end of the road they found a picture-postcard white wooden house, complete with a swing bench on the front veranda.

'Straight out of an episode of *The Waltons*. You could be swinging on that by tonight, with your true love. Just saying.'

'I'm no John-Boy,' Ray replied, frowning again. This was it for him. On the other side of that door were answers to questions he'd held on to for decades. And he was terrified to ask them.

'Remember what we practised. Just tell her what you told me and it will be fine. But wait one sec. You can't go in looking like that.'

'Like what?' Ray asked.

'Like you are about to serve mass with Father McBride.'

Ray looked at his niece and frowned. 'I'm wearing the new clothes you made me buy.'

Greta reached over and pulled his T-shirt out of his jeans. Then she reached up and messed his hair a little. 'No more gelling it into place. It makes you look like a serial killer.'

'A serial killer who serves mass? I thought you liked me.'

Greta stuck her tongue out, tweaking his hair until she was satisfied with how her uncle looked. 'Now you're ready, Romeo. Go get your girl.'

'This feels like the bloody green mile.' He grumbled, wishing he was on death row, rather than about to face his biggest regret and wish. 'Maybe we should just go. She's gonna think I'm a stalker.'

'No she won't. It will be a lovely surprise for her. She will be delighted to see you. Don't worry. And I'm here right beside you.'

'Y'all planning to knock or just stand out there chatting all day.' A woman's voice startled them from behind the door.

They both jumped, and Ray stumbled backwards, falling onto the ground with a bang.

Greta supposed she'd better knock, even if it was pointless when whoever was in there could obviously see them. The door opened to reveal the oddest-looking woman, with long grey wiry hair, worn loose. She wore a bright pink and green tea dress, teamed with converse runners in red. It was a cool combination. Whoever she was, she had style.

She whispered to Ray, 'Is that her?'

He made a face and she supposed that the woman in front of them *was* a bit old to be Billie.

'You all right down there?' the woman asked Ray.

Ray nodded as he picked himself up off the ground.

'I'm Greta, and Mr Clumsy over there is Ray. A friend of his used to live here and we're hoping to find her.'

'What's her name and I'll see if I can point you in the right direction.'

'Billie Haley.'

'Well, the good news is that your search has come to an end. This is Billie's house all right. She's out at the minute, but she won't be long. I'm Lucy. We're neighbours. I live over yonder trees.'

They both looked in the direction she nodded towards. 'I'm here to watch Susan. That's Billie's mother. She doesn't like to be on her own.'

'We'll come back another time,' Ray said, and he started to walk back towards the car.

'Not at all. Come on in y'all. You don't look much like serial killers.'

Greta had to stifle a laugh at that.

'I'll make us a pot of coffee,' Lucy said, walking into the house.

'Remember what you told me yesterday. No matter how scared you feel, you have to do this,' Greta hissed when Ray didn't move. She had to push him into the house.

They sat down around a long oak table in the open-plan kitchen and dining room. Greta looked around the cosy kitchen, hoping to see some photographs of Billie. But there were none.

'So how do you know Billie then?' Lucy asked. 'Judging by y'all accents you're not from around these parts. Scottish?'

'Irish. I met Billie years ago through the scouts,' Ray said.

'Well now, it's not today or yesterday that Billie was involved in the scouts.'

'Twenty-four years since we last saw each other. Give or take,' Ray said.

My Pear-Shaped Life

'We're from Dublin,' Greta added. 'We're on our way to Las Vegas. On a road trip. We thought as we were in the area . . .'

Lucy looked at them both as if they'd grown several heads. 'Driving from Kansas to Vegas. You could have flown.'

'We want to drive. See roadside America and all it has to offer. Ray likes things like your ball of twine,' Greta explained.

'Nowt so strange as folk, my mother used to say. But in truth, we get thousands every year coming to see that twine.' Lucy placed two cups of steaming coffee down in front of them.

They heard the rumble of a car engine approaching, and Ray's hand shook so much, it made his coffee spill.

'You're a nervous one,' Lucy said. 'Here's Billie now.'

Greta and Ray both turned towards the front door, each holding their breaths. The door swung open, and a tangerine woman walked in. There was no other word for it.

Greta spluttered and blinked, once, twice. *What the actual?* 'Someone's been Tangoed,' she whispered to Ray. 'Is that her?'

He ignored Greta, his eyes never leaving the woman.

'That's come up well. Third time is always a charm,' Lucy said to the woman. 'By the way, you've got visitors.'

Ray's eyes locked on the woman who walked towards them. There was no doubt that, while this version of Billie was very different from the one he'd last seen, it was her. She was broader, yet somehow leaner, more angular. The softness of her face and her body had disappeared.

She was wearing a tracksuit, but her face, her neck and her hands were as Greta said, bordering on the colour orange.

Greta kicked him under the table. He stood up. 'Hello, Billie.'

'Ray? Raymond Gale?'

She hadn't forgotten him. He felt his knees buckle with relief.

'What on earth are you doing here?' Billie asked.

'We were in the area. Thought we'd drop in.' Even to Ray's ears that sounded lame.

Billie looked over at Greta, who waved back at her. 'I'm Greta. Hello.'

Billie nodded her hello back, placing a gym bag on the ground, by her feet.

A voice called out from behind them, 'Is that you home, Billie?'

'Yes, Mama.'

'I need your help.'

'I have to go sort my mama out. One minute,' Billie said.

'I'll go,' Lucy offered, but Billie shook her head and walked down the hallway.

Ray had often dreamt of meeting Billie again. But in the many different versions of the reunion he'd imagined, this wasn't one of them. They all sat in silence, waiting for Billie's return. Five minutes passed, then ten, until it got awkward.

'Maybe we should go,' Ray whispered to Greta. 'We can visit another time. She could be hiding, waiting for us to leave.'

'She recognized you, Uncle Ray. That's a good sign.'

'I tell you what, I'll go see what's taking so long,' Lucy said, then she too disappeared down the hall.

'Was she always this orange?' Greta whispered. 'Show me that picture again.'

'No. Not in the least. In fact, I'd say Billie was quite pale back then.'

'She's either been hitting the sunbeds too much, or had one spray tan too many. I've eaten lollipops that colour,' Greta said.

'Maybe it's the fashion down here in Kansas?'

'I didn't see anyone that colour yesterday in the shopping mall. Do you think her mum is OK?'

'No idea. I think we should go,' Ray said again, just as Billie and Lucy re-emerged into the kitchen.

'Sorry about that,' Billie apologized. Her face was flushed and she did look sorry.

'I hope everything is OK?' Ray asked.

'Mama is bedridden. She just needed some assistance with . . . her personal needs.' Her voice trailed off, leaving Greta and Ray to their imaginations.

'How long are y'all in Kansas for?'

'We're on a bit of an adventure, to be honest. A road trip between Kansas and Vegas.' Greta told her about their evening in Kansas City and then their day in Wamego, looking for all things Oz.

'Funny, I've never been there. And it's not that far from here.'

'Ah sure, we're the same with the Guinness brewery. Never been either, even though it's only a few miles away,' Greta replied. She made a face at Ray, trying to convey to him that he was being too quiet. But if he understood, he chose to ignore her. Greta realized that this reunion would go nowhere if she left it to him. 'Ray was hoping you could come out for dinner with us this evening? Or a drink if you'd prefer – you choose.'

'I've got something on this evening,' Billie said.

Greta watched the disappointment flood her uncle's face and felt a flash of anger. Billie was being quite rude. 'Can't you change your plans? We've come a long way, and I know Ray was really hoping to at least have a conversation with you!'

'I'm not making up an excuse. But you've arrived on the eve of a big event for me. Tomorrow I'm taking part in the Kansas Women's Bodybuilding Contest.'

Greta looked at Ray in shock. That was unexpected.

'I'm not normally this colour. It's just for the competition. All the competitors tan up beforehand.'

'Thank feck for that,' Ray said uncharacteristically, then apologized quickly as Lucy bellowed laughter. 'No offence.'

'None taken. I'm sure you both must think I look very strange. If I'm honest, I'm not even sure what I'm doing. I don't have a cat in hell's chance of winning. I haven't taken any steroids to help me build muscle, so I'll be one of the smaller contestants. Even so, I'd love to get into the top three.'

'Are steroids allowed? Surely there's tests to check for them?' Greta was shocked by her admission.

'Unfortunately they are prevalent in this industry. But I've never been tempted. I want to do this my way, on my own, without any help from anyone or anything.'

'Do you have to lift weights in the competition?' Ray

asked. His only knowledge of bodybuilding competitions was from his childhood watching *The Strongest Man* on TV.

'It's more about my physique. Which I have developed from lifting weights. I'm in the Ms Bodybuilder category. The tan by the way helps to accentuate the muscle tone.'

'Ohhh,' Ray and Greta said together.

'She's been training so hard,' Lucy said. 'I'm in awe of her. Between that and taking care of Susan, she's a wonder.'

Billie smiled at her neighbour. 'We all do what we have to. I would love to spend some time with you too, Ray, but it's just bad timing. I've been in training for over a year now for this competition. I can't bail on that, even for you.'

'Nor would I expect you to,' Ray said.

Greta watched Ray watching Billie. And hoped that one day someone would look at her the same way . . . even when she was the colour of an Oompa Loompa. She had to do something to get them together again. Then she had a brainwave and said with a smile, 'I've always wanted to go to a bodybuilding competition. . .'

Chapter 22

If Greta could have listed a thousand things she would end up doing while on their road trip, attending a ladies' bodybuilding competition would not feature on it. There were five divisions as part of the competition, Bikini, Figure, Physique, Fitness_ and Bodybuilding. Billie was taking part in the Figure division.

'It says here that this is a blend of bodybuilding and fitness,' Greta said, reading the brochure. 'Judges will look at symmetry, presentation, skin tone. And looking at the room, Billie has got the skin tone right anyhow.'

There was a sea of bronzed faces everywhere. It was easy to see who were the competitors and who were supporters, like Ray and herself, who were pale and un-interesting in comparison. But she wasn't feeling rubbish; in fact she was feeling pretty damn fine. She had a new pair of jeans on, which fitted her perfectly. Normally when she wore jeans, the button cut into her belly button within five minutes and she'd have to open it. She'd had these on for over an hour and they were comfortable. In fact, she could run her fingers around the waistband and not risk cutting off a digit. She'd also put on a bright yellow batwing top that her mam had bought her last Christmas, but she'd never had the nerve to wear. Somehow it seemed fitting to wear it in a sea of orange bodies. She realized that she must have lost a little more weight since leaving Ireland. The walking and healthy choices for meals were paying dividends. She was still overweight but she felt less Big G and more Greta, with every mile she was taking towards Las Vegas.

Her phone beeped. Dylan sent her a picture of a cat wearing a bikini.

Greta: Cute. But she's way out of your league.
Dylan: I've only got eyes for one, Silver Lady.
Greta: Who? Spill!
Dylan: That would be telling.
Greta: Coward.
Dylan: Yep. Take pictures of the orange one for me.

Greta and Ray wandered around backstage trying to find Billie, as she'd told them to do the previous evening. There were several tanning booths in operation.

'Please say she's not going for a fourth layer!' Greta said when they found her hovering around a tanning booth. They nearly didn't recognize her. Her hair was now arranged into the biggest curly blow-dry Greta had ever seen. And she was wearing full make-up that wouldn't look out of place on *RuPaul's Drag Race*.

'They are some lashes you've on,' Greta said, taking in the long thick black false lashes that looked like caterpillars on Billie's eyes. At the end of each was a small diamanté.

'I might get another layer of tan. What do you think?' Billie said.

Greta looked around at her competition. Most were in or around the same shade as Billie, all with big hair too. 'I think you look perfect the way you are. Don't overdo it.'

'Really? OK. Maybe you're right.'

'You look beautiful,' Ray said. He much preferred her yesterday when she had no make-up on. Despite wearing the new T-shirt that Greta said made him look hip and cool, he felt like a fuddy-duddy beside Billie. He was beginning to suspect that he was no longer the type of guy Billie would go for. 'Can I get you a drink or something to eat?'

'No!' Billie said. 'Sorry, didn't mean to snap. But I can't eat anything until after the competition. And I'm also off drinks too. I need to dehydrate myself some more.'

'Come again?' Ray asked, baffled by her statement.

'I'm abstaining from drinking anything; it helps to reduce body fat and ensure maximal muscle exposure.'

Greta's stomach growled in response to the thought of fasting like that.

Billie replied, 'I'm in this to win it. So I'm ready to do everything I need to do to ensure I've the best possible chance. Even if that means wearing fake tan, dying my hair, calorie counting . . . this competition is important to me.'

Greta replied, 'Well, good for you then, Billie. I wish I had some of your resolve. Problem is, some of my best friends are carbs.'

To her relief, Billie laughed at the joke.

'What do you need to do now?' Ray asked.

'Wait for my turn to go on. Change into my costume. I think I'll practise my poses some more.' She went on to explain how there were several poses each contestant had to make on stage, to show off their various muscle zones. 'It's the part of the contest I'm least prepared for. I've never been one to put myself on a stage for anything.'

'Give me your hand,' Greta said.

When Billie didn't make a move to do so, Greta leaned in and took her right hand in hers. 'Acupressure is a great way to relieve tension. It balances the circulation or something. We learned the technique in an acting workshop I was in. Let me show you.'

'You are an actress?' Billie asked.

'She was a child star. In the number one Christmas advert in Ireland, voted for five years running,' Ray boasted.

'He's my number one fan. Bigging me up comes with the job description!' And while Greta was chuffed by her uncle's unfailing pride in her, it was also depressing to think that her finest moment had been when she was eight years old.

'That's what uncles do!' Ray said.

Billie was taken aback. 'You're her uncle?'

'Yeah. Who did you think I was?'

'Her husband.'

Greta gagged. 'Ewwww . . . stop grossing me out. He's

old enough to be my . . . well, my uncle! Did we not say that yesterday?'

Billie shook her head. And the look of relief on her face was impossible to miss. Greta watched her give Ray the side eye, looking at him as if for the first time.

'Our bad! Give me back your hand. Right, use your thumb and forefinger to massage the soft area between your thumb and index finger. See?' She demonstrated the technique.

'Oh, that feels lovely,' Billie said, smiling. And Greta saw a glimpse of the woman that Ray carried in the photograph.

'Even better if you have the right oil. Do this just before you go on stage. It should help.'

'Do you ever get stage fright?' Billie asked.

'Sometimes. But having performance anxiety is kind of a deal-breaker for an actress. Once I start, I always seem to get lost in the role and I'm grand. But I know that stage fright can feel like you are being heckled mercilessly. Just remember that the heckler is in your own mind. And the worst thing you can do is to start arguing with him, right? Rarely does a performer of any description come off well with that. You've got to suck it up and ignore it.'

'Suck it up on stage. Ignore the heckler in my head. Massage my hand. Got it,' Billie said.

'Immerse yourself in the poses. Truly and completely. Focus on the performance, not the anxiety. Oh and don't forget to breathe.'

'That's really helpful,' Billie said. 'I'm going to go find a quiet corner to practise. And once the competition is over, I'll come to find you. I'd like to take you up on the offer of dinner. Because trust me, I intend to basically eat a cow once we're finished, win, lose or draw!'

The grin of delight on Ray's face made both the ladies smile.

'She's intense,' Greta said as Billie walked away. 'But I like her. You on the other hand, Uncle Ray, need to start talking to her.'

'She scares me a bit. She's really different from how she was back then.'

'You're not the same person either. A lot of time has gone by.'

'I'm not so sure about that. I don't think I've changed much since then. Which is perhaps the problem,' Ray said. 'Come on, let's find some seats near the front.'

'You know her thinking you were my husband explains why she acted a bit weird yesterday.'

Ray was kicking himself. He should have made it clear that he was single from the get-go. No wonder Billie had been distant.

'This competition means a lot to her,' Ray said.

'Yep. I wonder why? I mean, she doesn't strike me as the overly competitive type.'

'No she isn't. Or at least, she wasn't when I knew her. Maybe that's changed.'

'Maybe. But I don't know . . . it just feels like there is more to this for her than just picking up a trophy.'

'You're quite perceptive, aren't you?'

'I watch people. I think all actors do that. We borrow things from people in our lives. A look. A gesture. A tell.'

'Well if you see any more looks on her face that show

she cares for me still, let me know. Thanks, by the way. For helping her out earlier with the heckler. That was kind of you. How's the heckler in your head?' Ray asked Greta.

She thought about this for a moment. She had managed to quieten the negative thoughts somewhat. Last night, she'd looked at the photographs they'd taken at the ball of twine. And what she noticed was how happy she looked. OK, afterwards she'd noticed her big thighs that had never seen daylight between them, but it wasn't the first thing. That was progress. 'Quieter,' she said to Ray. 'I'm good. Promise.'

They took their seats and both looked around the room and the stage with wide eyes. It was alight with multi-coloured lighting. There was a large banner across the stage that said, 'Every Body Is Beautiful'. And, for once, Greta didn't feel the need to redress the bullshit. She realized that she liked the idea of everybody feeling beautiful, no matter their size. Every woman backstage looked confident and happy. And utterly glorious. And wasn't that the most important thing? Feeling good about yourself, ignoring beauty standards and finding a look that works for you and nobody else. That's what these ladies had done.

'Can you feel that?' Ray said. 'The atmosphere feels thick with tension, doesn't it?'

He was right, Greta realized. Just as she had rehearsed for an audition, these contestants had done the same too. Suddenly music belted out over the intercom, and their MC for the event came out.

'Kinda broad at the shoulder, slim at the hips, no other

bottle is better equipped,' Greta whisper-sang the Domestos bleach advert jingle as a massive bodybuilder walked out.

'It's strong it's thick, it sure is mean, big Dom, big bad Dom . . .' Ray finished, and they both giggled.

'Welcome, ladies and gentlemen. I'm Brad, your host for today. We're going to kick off the event today with the Figure competition. You sure are in for a treat. These ladies have been working hard and their muscles even harder.' The room laughed in appreciation.

'That's Billie's category!' Greta said. She crossed her fingers for luck, as she used to when she was a kid. Ray sat up straighter and felt his heart begin to beat faster in anticipation. Brad then told the audience that the ladies would start with poses to highlight their V-taper and lat spread, full felt muscles and defined quads and glutes.

It sounded like a foreign language to Greta and Ray. Brad called out each contestant, one by one to the stage. Each of them came on wearing a tiny sequinned bikini, and when they reached the front of the stage, they began a series of poses. And the weird thing was, Greta cele- brated their bodies, as she cheered each one onto the stage. She would have bet her savings that being here would make her feel bad about herself. But somehow, seeing these women move gracefully across the stage, she felt stronger too, and felt herself sitting up straighter in her chair.

'I didn't realize Billie would be wearing one of those. I assumed costume meant some sort of a fancy dress,' Ray squeaked.

'I'm not sure any of them are actually technically wearing anything. Postage stamp springs to mind. Look at that one, it has rhinestones all over the bottoms,' Greta said. They both tilted their heads to one side to get a better look.

Every now and then someone from the audience shouted out in support of their friend on stage.

'You're killing it!'

'Look at that back!'

'We have to do that for Billie when she comes out,' Greta said.

Then Brad said, 'Welcome Billie Haley, from Cawker City!'

Time froze for Ray, and everything disappeared, except for Billie, who walked into the spotlight and glided to the front of the stage.

'Holy shit, Uncle Ray. You are seriously punching above your weight with her! Look at that figure!'

Ray didn't answer, because he couldn't take his eyes off the vision on stage. He didn't want to miss a moment of this. She was wearing a silver bikini that looked like a mermaid's fishtail. The bikini bottoms were held together with a string of pearls across each hip. And the straps of the bra top the same. Billie's hair had been taken out of its ponytail and now fell in loose curls over her shoulders.

'She doesn't look so orange now when you see the whole look together,' Greta said. 'Oh look, I really like her shoes.' She was wearing a pair of sparkling silver four-inch heels. 'And she doesn't look too nervous. She's smiling anyhow. Holy shit, those abs are rock hard.'

'Should we cheer?' Ray asked.

'I nearly forgot. Here goes. Look at the back on that!' Greta screamed.

'Yeah!' Ray shouted, then apologized when Greta shook her head. 'I couldn't think of anything to shout!'

Billie posed to the front, the side, and then turned around, pulling her hair to the side so she could showcase her back.

Finally, Ray found his voice, saying softly, 'She's magnificent.'

Greta said, 'That's what you need to shout.'

So he did, and Billie heard him, turning towards his voice.

Once every contestant was on the stage, they formed a line, and Brad called out, 'To be the best, you have to play with the rest. Let's see the best these ladies have.' He called out a series of poses to them that they performed in perfect harmony.

'Front double bicep, please.'

'Back double bicep. Push down.'

'Side tricep.'

'They are quite graceful,' Greta said. 'Synchronized. They must have put so much effort into training to get to this shape. I'm in awe. I wish I was a gym bunny. I'm just too lazy to ever do something like this.'

When the poses finished, the ladies all stood side by side, while Brad waited for the results.

'Holy shit, that was quick!' Greta said when Brad announced he had the winning names.

'Finishing in fifth place . . .' Ray felt Greta's hand on his arm again. His eyes were focused on Billie. Her eyes searched the crowd once more, and when she saw him, she smiled back.

Then Brad got to third place. 'It's number twenty-four,

Billie Haley, from Cawker City.' He placed a bronze statue at her feet.

Ray and Greta jumped to their feet and began to cheer. She'd done it! They made their way backstage to find Billie, who had put a silk robe on and was guzzling down a bottle of water.

'Congratulations!' Greta said.

'I didn't win.'

'You came third! That's incredible,' Ray said. 'And you looked beautiful up there.'

'I'm in awe,' Greta said. 'Truly.'

'I wanted it so bad. I put every ounce of everything I had into this. And now it's over. I feel a bit . . . deflated.'

'You can try again next year?' Ray said.

'No. This is me done. The judges went for bigger girls in the end. First and second had much greater muscle definition than me. I don't think I can ever compete with that.'

'I think this is the first time I've ever heard someone complain about losing to a bigger woman,' Greta said. 'If this helps, I reckon one of my thighs is bigger than your waist.'

As Greta hoped, her words made Billie laugh. Which turned to surprise when Ray gave Greta a dig who went on to say, 'Of course my thighs are in perfect proportion to the rest of my body, which isn't horrendous.'

'I'm not sure that's what Noreen had in mind,' Ray said to Greta. Then he turned to Billie and asked, 'I promised you dinner Billie, and I'd love to make good on that promise. Will you join us this evening? I'd very much like that,' Ray said.

'So would I, Ray. Lucy is with Mama now, but she's messaged me to say that she can't stay late. So it will have to be a quick bite.'

Ray felt crushed. It felt like brick walls were continually being placed between them. Fortune favoured the brave. It was time to go for it. 'I understand you need to get home. But rather than just grabbing a quick meal here, why don't we order a takeaway and eat at your house? If that's not an imposition. That way, we're in no rush and can have that catch-up. I really would like to hear how you've been. What your life is like.'

And when Billie agreed, Ray began to feel a sliver of hope take root inside of him. Could this finally be his time to eclipse 1995?

Chapter 23

Lucy hugged Billie, whooping with delight when she saw her trophy. She placed it over the fireplace in the dining room. 'You should be proud of yourself, honey. You worked hard for that. Susan has been asleep for about an hour now.' She turned to Greta and Ray and said, 'I'm sorry I have to dash. But I hope to see y'all again soon.'

Billie said, 'I want to wash this day away, so I'm going to take a quick shower. Top drawer under the sink you should find some menus for an Italian restaurant that deliver. Order plenty. I'm starving! And in the fridge, you'll find drinks. Help yourself.'

She closed the door to the kitchen and left them to it.

'What do you think is wrong with her mother?' Ray asked.

Greta shrugged. 'She's keeping her cards close to her six-pack.'

'Ha ha. Funny. Seriously, I've been trying to remember

everything she ever said about her mother to me. She always spoke about her so lovingly back then. It's a bit weird her being locked in her room all the time, isn't it?'

'She's hiding something all right. What's the game plan here, Uncle Ray?'

'Order food and eat. Talk. I don't know. I'm making it up as I go along.'

'Don't let her brush you off any more. You need to get her on her own and get her talking! I think you should try to bring Billie out for a drink. Surely her mama can manage for a few hours on her own. I'm happy to go back to our motel and watch the weather channels some more.'

He laughed at this. They'd both discovered that while there were hundreds of channels to watch, most of them seemed to heavily feature the weather. 'Really?'

'Really. Don't waste this chance. Billie has been giving you the goo-goo eye too. I reckon she's still got a thing for you.'

'I thought I was punching?'

'No doubt about it. But there's no sign of another guy on the scene. Maybe she likes nerdy old men from Ireland.'

He stuck his tongue out at her and started to look through the menu. 'What will I order?'

'She said she was hungry. So we'd better order loads. We can pick at it, buffet style. Get me some kind of salad too, will ya? And some roasted vegetables.'

Ray rang the restaurant and placed the order.

Billie came back, wearing jeans and a T-shirt. Without the make-up, with her hair tied back again, she looked ten years younger. 'You look pretty,' Greta said.

'Thank you.'

'Small issue. They said they couldn't deliver. So we have to collect from the restaurant,' Ray said. 'I'll go if you give me directions.'

'You'll never find it,' Billie said. 'I'd go, but I can't leave Mama.'

'Is she still asleep?' Greta asked. When Billie nodded, she said, 'Well, why don't you and Ray go to collect the food together? I'll stay here in case your mama wakes up. And if she does, I'll just tell her you'll be back soon. Sorted!'

'She'll fret if I'm not here when she wakes up,' Billie said.

'Have you told her about us visiting?' Greta asked.

'Yeah.'

'Then, it's all good. Go on, you'll be back in no time, she won't even know you're not here.' Greta shooed the two of them out the door, then began to hunt down plates and glasses. The dining-room table looked like it also worked as a dumping ground. Piles of newspapers and magazines were on one end, with unopened white and brown envelopes beside them. And a vase with flowers that looked like they had died a death weeks before. She began to clear and clean, then laid the table, ready for food when it arrived.

'Billie? Is that you? Billie?' The mama was awake.

'Billie's stepped out for a minute,' Greta shouted back. 'I'm Greta. Did she tell you about Uncle Ray and me? Do you need anything?'

'Fresh water. I'm thirsty. But I can wait until Billie returns.'

Greta poured a glass with water from the tap, then made her way towards the bedrooms. Curiosity might have killed the cat, but Greta didn't care. She assumed the only door closed belonged to Susan, so she knocked on it. 'I have that water for you.' She knocked again and, when there was no answer, felt a prickle of panic. What if something had happened to the woman? She was supposed to be watching out for her. She opened the door and looked in.

A huge bed took up most of the room, and in the centre of it, a face peered out from under the duvets. She was alive at least.

'I have your water. I'll just leave it here.' Greta walked over and placed it on the bedside locker. 'Can I get you anything else?'

Susan reached over and took the glass, drinking it down in one go.

'Wow, you were thirsty. Here, I'll go get you another.'

'Could you fill the jug please?'

'Sure.' Greta picked up the jug that sat on the locker. As she filled it in the kitchen, she inhaled a lung full of air. Greta waved her hands in front of her, in an effort to get rid of the clawing, sickly smell that hit her when she'd walked into Susan's bedroom. It reminded her of the smell of baby wipes that used to be in their house when Emily had done a spell of childminding a few years back.

'Are you hungry?' Greta asked Susan when she walked back in her room. 'We've ordered from an Italian restaurant. Uncle Ray and Billie are gone to get the food.'

'She said that some friends from her scouting days were

229

in town. Where are you from? Scotland?' This was followed by a wheeze, huuuu-hhhhhh, huuuu-hhhhh.

So it was her lungs. Asthma? 'That's what Lucy thought too. We're Irish through and through. Do you want to get up for a bit? Get some fresh air? I can help you.'

Susan patted the bed. 'No, I'm fine here. But sit down and visit for a while. Open the window for a bit, though. I know it's stifling in here.'

'It's been snowing outside, so it's cold,' Greta said. 'I'll just open it for a few minutes, I don't want to freeze you!'

'I don't feel the cold, honey. I've got my own thermal blanket. Open it wide and then tell me how your uncle Ray knows my Billie.'

'They met at the World Scout Jamboree a hundred years ago. And fell in love. They used to write to each other all the time,' Greta blurted out, then realized that she might have exposed a secret.

'She used to go around the house like a lovesick puppy waiting to hear from him. I remember. Why did he stop writing to her? Did he meet someone over in Ireland?'

It was good news that Susan knew about Ray. And even better that Billie did love him, but the wires had been crossed somewhere. Greta didn't know whether to say something, correct Susan, or leave it. Her gut told her that she should interfere. Ray needed her help and she was going to give it to him. 'It was Billie who stopped writing. She broke Uncle Ray's heart.'

Susan looked puzzled. 'I was sure she told me that he'd finished with her. But to be honest, back then things were a bit messed up.'

Greta saw something flash across Susan's face. Recognition of something. 'How so?'

Susan ignored the question. 'Oh, I do declare, where is my head at? I nearly forgot! Did she win the competition?'

'She came third.'

Susan beamed at this news. 'Good for her. I wish I could have seen her.'

'She was incredible. I've never seen anything like it. Why didn't you go?'

'I don't go out much any more.'

'Why not?'

'I could give you a long-winded answer, about my lymphoedema, my arthritis, my knee and hip pain, but the truth really is quite simple. I'm too fat to get about any more. Getting dressed is a bit like a workout for me. It's easier to just stay in bed.'

Greta took a beat before she answered. Susan's words shocked her. The raw honesty of her words. No dressing things up or down. She respected that. 'You don't look that fat.'

Susan laughed. 'I've a thin face, compared to the rest of me. But trust me. I'm fat.'

'I'm fat too.'

'Not a bit of it. You're a slip of a thing!' Susan said.

'I don't think anyone has ever called me that before. I'll take it! But let's just agree that if I'm not fat, I'm definitely not thin either. I'm at the point where you can tell that Tayto crisps have played a part in my life.'

Susan smiled then said, 'Well, I'm at a time in my life where I break beds for sport. This is the third one I've done in this year so far.'

'You need to buy one with stronger springs.'

'Hah! That I do.'

'I broke a deckchair once. We had a week last year in May that was glorious. I decided to sit out the back and try to get some colour on me. All I ended up doing was getting a red backside when I hit the ground!' Greta admitted. Aidan and Ciaran had laughed for a week about that. She remembered thinking, this is it. Rock bottom for me. No more excuses. And she started a diet that lasted a week or two at most.

'I like you,' Susan said.

'Kindred breaker of furniture spirits?' Greta joked and they both laughed.

She grabbed her phone from the back pocket of her jeans. 'Here, look at some photographs of Billie on stage.'

'I can't believe that's my girl.'

'I've never seen so many muscles on so many tiny women in my life. The dedication it must have taken to get to that point.'

'Oh honey, looking like Billie isn't sustainable for most. But there again, looking like me isn't either. I think the trick is to find the middle ground somewhere between us two extremes.'

Greta wondered if the reason for Billie's need for a lean, mean body was in response to her mama's bedridden body. Looking at Susan, she recognized something in the woman's face. Something she'd lived with for a long time. Resignation that this was as good as it gets. Acceptance that there was no turning back. But that wasn't true for Greta any more. She was changed. She wanted more for herself. 'I'm working on finding that middle ground,' Greta admitted. 'I'm trying to make better choices with my lifestyle. But it's hard.'

'Good for you, honey. Find a way to live your best life, that's what I say. Eat potato chips if that's what you want. Just not every day like I've done, though. What do they say? You've only one body and you've—'

'Already ruined it!' Greta interrupted her, and when she saw Susan frown, added, 'Joke!'

'Ah, you're the funny one,' Susan said.

'So I'm told.'

'And if you make fun of yourself first of all, then no one else can do it, right?' Susan asked.

'Busted,' Greta admitted. 'You don't miss much, do you? You know something? I'm so bored of the whole fat conversation I have going on in my head, with my mother . . . It's exhausting.'

'How long have you been having that conversation with yourself, honey?' Susan asked.

Greta remembered the moment it started as if it were yesterday. And when Susan reached over to clasp her hand as Greta relayed the story to her, it felt like the most natural thing in the world. Greta was ten years old, and her mam had bought all three of them a new Christmas jumper. Emily was bouncing with excitement, her camera already out, ready to snap a photograph. Aidan and Ciaran slipped into their new blue argyle knits in less than thirty seconds. But Greta couldn't get her jumper over her shoulders. She tugged it hard, but it wouldn't budge – stuck half on, half off. She was sure her mam had bought the wrong size. And so was Emily. But the size was correct. It was Greta who was wrong. After that, her mam started to buy larger clothes for her and, even though she never said anything, she could see her watching her, monitoring her food. And her dad began to make comments about the need to watch what she ate, almost every day.

'God, it breaks my heart that children as young as that worry about their size. But it happens. You know I read a report recently that 81 per cent of ten-year-old girls and boys are afraid of being fat. When did you go on your first diet?' Susan asked.

'When I was thirteen. Dad suggested we all give up treats. Aidan and Ciaran weren't impressed. I overheard Dad telling them that they had to do it for my sake, because I was getting too pudgy. I felt so guilty, that I had failed and it was impacting them now too. I think ever since then I've been on and off diets continuously.'

Greta thought back to all the trips she'd had to the Liffey Valley Shopping Centre with her mam as a kid. Each time, they would end up going up another size, until there were no more kid sizes to go up. When she was twelve, she ended up wearing adult clothes. And she remembered standing in front of a mirror in the changing rooms of Marks and Spencer, sucking in her stomach because it looked too big. For decades now she had wanted to be skinnier, better, than she was. Food became both her enemy and her best friend, in a messed-up, abusive relationship.

Susan said, 'Diets never work unless you've got your head in the right place.'

'My problem is that I have an addictive personality. Once I'm hooked on something, I find it hard to say no. I had help from a dietician recently to help me with that.

She's tough, but I don't know, she just seemed to work for me. She talks about balance a lot. She says that if I want a bag of Tayto crisps, then I should eat one. But I have to eat an apple to redress the balance. It kind of clicked with me. Maybe it's time for you to look for guidance? There must be someone who can help you get back on your feet,' Greta said.

'I think I've left it too late,' Susan replied sadly.

'It's never too late to change. But I'm going to shut up now, because I know there's nothing more irritating than someone talking to you about losing weight when you haven't got any inclination to do so yourself.'

'That's for sure. I've heard it all. My problem is up here.' She pointed to her head. 'I might be fat, but I'm not stupid. I know my head has sabotaged my body for years.'

Greta knew that feeling. How many times had she allowed her emotions to control what she put into her body?

'I think us women have made a big old mess of ourselves in this world,' Susan said.

'So what's the answer?'

'The way I see it is this – you've got this body and you can choose to take care of it, or you can abuse it. If you do that, one day it will give up on you. Take me as proof of that very point.'

'I always forget that part. I usually go straight for the second bag of Tayto. I never know when to say no,' Greta admitted.

Susan looked at the curtains that fluttered and flew into the room, as the wind from outside swept in through the open window. 'Before this – ' she waved at her body – 'I had a life. A good one. We went on holidays with the children, throughout America. The best times of my life, back then. When we were all together. Oh, the sights we saw. Some people prefer a glass lake, perfectly still and even, without a mark. Me, I prefer the ocean, with its ebbs and flows, different colours and swells. It's perfectly imperfect as far as I'm concerned.'

'So the answer is to be like the ocean?' Greta asked.

'It's one answer.'

'And maybe I need to surround myself with more people who like an imperfect ocean too.'

'Now you are getting it,' Susan said, patting her hand.

Greta thought about all the ways she put herself down. She looked down at her stomach, which gave her so much pain.

'You said you have an addictive personality, Greta. How about you make a new addiction to be kinder to yourself? Can you try that?'

Could she start to love her body, with all its imperfections? She thought about the waves on Curracloe beach, somewhere she'd holidayed as a child. She pictured them crashing to the shore, then receding back to the ocean, leaving a trace of foam behind.

Greta blinked tears away and nodded once. A promise to Susan and, more importantly, to herself. She was going to try just that.

Chapter 24

'Hey Mama,' Billie said, walking in. 'Is everything OK?'

'Everything is fine. I've been chatting with this lovely young woman. Congratulations. I hear you did real good. Come here and give me a kiss.' She wrapped her arms around Billie and stroked her hair.

'I got third. I'll go get the trophy.'

'Why don't you come out to eat with us, Susan? We've ordered enough food to feed an army.' Then Greta blushed and said, 'Sorry, not inferring you need that much food.'

Susan laughed. 'It's OK, honey. My ego has long since been that fragile.'

'I've laid the table and there's a spot just for you,' Greta said.

'It looks really nice out there. Thank you for that,' Billie said. 'But I'm sure Mama would rather a tray in here.'

Susan thought about it for a minute, then said, 'You go on out, Greta, and I'll follow on in a bit. Get me the wheelchair, Billie, I think I'll eat with our guests tonight.'

Ray was peeking into the hall when Greta walked out. She shooed him back to the kitchen.

'What's going on?'

'You're about to meet your future mother-in-law. So sort yourself out.'

'She's coming out here?'

'She is. Jeepers, that's a lot of food.'

'I might have over-ordered. The portion sizes are huge,' Ray admitted. 'What's she like?'

'Nice. She's in a wheelchair, so don't stare when she comes in.'

'Noted. What's wrong with her? Is it cancer or something?'

'She's fat.'

'That's a bit harsh!' Ray said, shocked. 'I'd expect better from you!'

Greta giggled. 'Her words, not mine. She doesn't get out of bed much any more, 'cos she is too fat to get about. She tells it like it is and I *love* her.'

All sorts of images flashed through Ray's mind, landing finally on Jabba the Hut in *Star Wars*. He felt quite ashamed of that as he shook the image from his head.

'Honestly, she's just wonderful. I thought Noreen was Glinda, but Susan is too. Can you have more than one Glinda, I wonder? We had the best chat. She's kinda wise in a non-preachy way.'

'I think there can never be too many Glindas in our

lives. In fact maybe we should all try to be a Glinda every time we get the opportunity.'

'I like that idea. You'll love Susan, Uncle Ray. Promise. And she said that Billie was in love with you back then. But she thought you had broken Billie's heart, not the other way around. There's something going on here, but I can't work out what. How did you get on with lover girl? Did she fill in any blanks for you?' Greta asked.

Ray shook his head in dismay and did the thumbs-down sign. It hadn't gone well at all. They'd had a stilted conversation about how mild the weather was. And how pretty the trees were on the avenue. He'd given pretty much monosyllabic answers to everything she said, and she wasn't much better. 'I can't seem to find a way to make a connection with her. She's polite with me, but reserved.'

'Just tell her about your life. Your job. That kind of thing. Actually, what is it that you do in work, Uncle Ray?' Greta realized she had no clue.

'Really? After all these years you still don't know?'

'No clue.'

They both jumped when they heard the door bang close down the hall. Ray stood to attention, looking like he was about to salute a sergeant major. 'Relax!' Greta hissed.

Billie wheeled in her mama and Greta felt her heart give a little. How was it possible that she felt she knew this woman and was understood by her in one conversation? But something had happened in that bedroom. A connection had been formed. Susan was wearing a dressing gown, in a pretty denim blue, with tiny yellow and pink flowers on it. And Greta noted that Susan looked as nervous as Ray did. A line of sweat had formed on her face, which she blotted away with a small cloth she clutched.

'I love your dressing gown! I'm a divil for wearing black all the time. I'm trying to add some colour into my wardrobe,' Greta said, pointing to her bright yellow top.

'It's from Walmart. Cheap as chips. And you should always wear sunshine colours. They suit you,' Susan said.

'I'm delighted you decided to get up and eat with us.' Greta turned to Ray, but he was rooted to the ground. Kicking him in the ankle, hard, he yelped, but he at least walked forward, albeit with a slight limp.

'Good evening, Mrs Haley. A pleasure to make your acquaintance.' His voice sounded more Downton Abbey than Dublin. Then he bowed.

What on earth was he doing? The big eejit. 'Come sit beside me,' Greta said to Susan. She pushed aside a dining chair so that her wheelchair could be moved into the spot. That left Ray to sit beside Billie.

As half of the group seemed unable to act like ordinary people, Greta and Susan found themselves doing much of the chitchat. Billie poured water for everyone, then began spooning out food onto everyone's plates. It was apparent Greta was going to have to get Billie and Ray on a trip down memory lane if they were going to have any chance at rekindling anything. Greta thought about all the conversations she'd had with Dylan about Ultimate Romantic Gestures. Her always scoffing and pulling them apart. Him defending their importance in the world. And, this time, she wanted Dylan to be right and her wrong. She wanted Uncle Ray's URG to work. He deserved happiness more than anyone else she knew. Because he was good. Through and through.

'So Billie, tell me about the first time you met my Uncle Ray!' Greta said.

Ray would have liked to kick Greta under the table; he owed her several for payback of the few she'd given him in the last forty-eight hours, but was afraid he'd get Susan, so he pulled back.

Billie smiled at the memory. 'In Schiphol Airport. I was with my friends Mary-Beth and Anna-May.'

'I remember them!' Ray said. 'You three were always together back then. How are they? Do they still live around here?'

Billie looked at her mama, and something passed between them. 'We lost touch.'

'It happens,' Ray said. 'I'm not in touch with any of my school friends any more.'

'Nor me, thank goodness. All of mine were mostly assholes,' Greta said.

'How come?' Susan asked.

'I was a fader for the first couple of years in school. As in I always faded into the background,' she explained. 'But then I got cast for an advert when I was eight.'

'On television,' Ray added.

'And it turns out that most of my school pals preferred me as a fader. They were not so keen on my fifteen minutes of fame.' It had been around this time that Greta had started to use food as an emotional crutch. Susan looked at her in understanding. She got it.

'They probably didn't even realize what they were doing. Most people want to see you do good, as long as it's not better than they do themselves. I'd love to see your advert,' Susan said.

Ray took out his phone. 'I can show you on YouTube.' He hit play and they watched the young Greta light up the small screen.

'You haven't changed a bit,' Billie said. 'That was very cute. And now I want one of those biscuits!'

'You are a special young woman. It shines through in this advert and it shines through you right now, sitting here beside me,' Susan said.

Greta felt a blush creep up on her cheeks. She felt shy and happy and proud all at once. And she liked the feeling.

'Are you still in touch with your school friends?' Ray asked Susan.

'I've not stayed in touch with anyone. Except for Lucy. She was a few years older than me, but we walked to school together most days. She's been a good friend.'

Greta was sure she saw tears glistening in Susan's eyes. She reached over and patted her hand as Susan had done to her in the bedroom earlier. 'I bet you've been a wonderful friend to her too. She's lucky to have someone so wise as you in her corner.'

She turned to Billie again. 'Now I think it's time we got these two back to when they met each other. What do you think Susan?'

'I think that's exactly what we need to do!' Susan agreed.

'I could barely walk I was weighed down so much with my rucksack and tent. I didn't have the muscles back then I have now.' Billie flexed her arms and grinned.

'Show off!' Greta said.

'My cap fell off and landed at the feet of your Uncle Ray. And when he put it on my head, he gave me this look. It was almost a question. I couldn't get him out of my head. So when I saw him at the parade later that day, I walked over to say hello.'

She looked at Ray, and he looked at her. And, like that, they were back twenty-four years. They'd found their selves again. And the floodgates opened.

'Do you remember when Tom went into the bushes to go to the loo and came back covered in briars, saying he'd been chased by a bear?' Ray said.

'And the bear came out a few minutes later. It was only a . . .' Billie said.

'Rabbit!' they both said at the same time.

And on and on the stories came, about fellow scouts and themselves. Susan and Greta were happy to listen. There was a lot of laughter around that table.

'So what made you come to Kansas after all this time?' Susan asked.

Ray looked at Billie and thought about saying that he was there because he was still in love with her daughter. But of course, he didn't. So instead he said, 'Billie told me years ago that Cawker City had the biggest ball of twine in the world. I like twine. So I thought I'd come to check it out.'

'That's a long way to come to see a ball of twine – no matter how big,' Susan said.

'He really likes twine,' Greta said. 'And we're going to see Dr Greta Gale too. She's giving a seminar in Las Vegas.'

'I was only watching her on *Oprah* yesterday!' Susan said.

'Me too!' Greta said. 'I love her.'

'You have the same name!' Billie said, shaking her head in surprise. 'I've just realized.'

Ray said, 'Greta is one of her biggest fans.'

'We all need a hero,' Susan said.

'I do love her. But I'm starting to realize she's not my hero. Uncle Ray is,' Greta said. 'I wouldn't be here if it wasn't for him.' And she didn't just mean sitting at this table. Then an idea hit her, a way to repay her many, many debts to him. She turned to Billie and said, 'Why don't you bring Uncle Ray to see the ball of twine now!'

'I'd love that,' Ray said. And he gave Greta a look that said, don't kick me, I know not to mention that we've already been to see it!

'But I can't leave Mama,' Billie said.

'Your mama's perfectly fine,' Susan said.

'If you fancy the company, I'll stay here with you Susan,' Greta said.

'I couldn't think of anything I'd rather. We can have another chat. That's that settled. Off you both go,' Susan said, waving Ray and Billie off.

'She likes him. I can tell,' Susan said when they closed the door behind them.

'Does she? I find her hard to read,' Greta admitted. 'She seems happy that he's here sometimes, then others, she's like stone.'

'She wasn't always like that. She used to be a free spirit, never at home, always running around the woods with her friends. And she had lots of them. People always gravitated to my Billie. Her smile used to light up the room.'

'Uncle Ray said that about her. And yesterday, at the competition, I saw a glimpse of it.'

'He knew her before . . . well, before things changed.'

'What happened?'

Susan sighed, then said, 'Life happened. And for some of us, it got hard. If you don't mind I won't say much more, because it's too difficult for me—'

'Of course,' Greta said. Life happened. She understood the devastating impact of those two words. The sleeping pills. Her failing acting career. Her weight. Her loneliness. How did all of that happen? Life. That's how. But that curiosity she'd had earlier was still piqued. She was desperate to know what had happened to the Haley family.

'But suffice to say that, afterwards, well, all of Billie's friends disappeared. Mine too. Except for Lucy. Piper, my youngest daughter, she ran away and hardly ever comes home to see us any more.'

'That's awful,' Greta said. She hoped Ray was getting the full story from Billie, so that he could fill her in later.

'Without Billie, I'd rot here on my own. She looks after me so well, and I feel her love every day. But she's not the Billie she once was. She's as hard as those abs she spends so much time on at the gym. Bitterness and hurt can do funny things to people if it's left to set in.'

Greta wasn't sure if Susan was talking about herself or Billie any more. And she thought about all of the negative feelings she'd been storing up inside of her for what felt like for ever. Like a cancer, they ate up all the goodness. If Greta didn't make a change would she end up housebound like Susan one day? Trapped in a body that could no longer support her.

'Is your uncle a good man?' Susan asked suddenly.

'The best one I know,' Greta said.

'Is he patient? Because he'll need to be, to get through to her. I watched Billie over the years. There's been plenty of men coming and going. Only natural, because she's a good-looking woman.'

'She's beautiful,' Greta agreed.

'But none of them stood a chance, because she's forgotten she has a heart. I saw one man stand here telling her he loved her. And she just turned on her heel and walked away, leaving him like a broken shell on the porch.'

'She'd better not hurt my uncle,' Greta said.

'Don't get me wrong. Billie is a good woman. Deep down she has a heart of gold. Look at how she takes care of me. But she's forgotten how to love anyone else or be loved herself. She's afraid of getting hurt. She doesn't want to lose control.'

'And that's what the bodybuilding is about too, I bet,' Greta said. 'She can control that, can't she?'

'Exactly,' Susan agreed.

'Ray still loves her, Susan. He's never stopped. And he's a good guy. He deserves to be loved back by someone.'

'Well, let's hope that she gives him a chance. I won't stand in their way. There's nothing that would make me happier. And what about you Greta? Do you have a special someone?'

Greta shook her head. But, for the first time in years, she thought about the possibility of having someone in her life. And the idea didn't scare her; in fact she realized that she would like that very much indeed.

Chapter 25

'Tell me about your life here,' Ray said as they drove.

'I'm a waitress in a diner.'

'Here in Cawker City?'

'No. There's not much call for a diner here any more. When I was a kid we were a busy community. But there's only five hundred or so living here now. Most have gone to bigger cities for work.'

'Ever tempted to leave yourself?'

'Every day. But Mama needs me. So I stay,' Billie said.

'You planned to travel the world,' Ray said.

'Plans change, Ray.'

'I suppose they do. Do you like waitressing?'

Billie shrugged. 'It's a job. It pays the bills. The tips are a godsend. Which I need, because I go through a lot of shoes.'

'You've lost me.'

'I'm on my feet all day. I can put up a hell of a lot of

miles each shift, hence I go through a lot of shoes. How about you? What do you work at?' Billie asked.

'I work for the government.'

'Ooh, very James Bond.'

'I could let you go on believing that, but I'm hoping you'll get to know me well enough to catch out that lie. I'm more of a civil servant than a spy.'

'Spies are totally overrated. And I bet you look better in a tux than Bond.'

'Yes, Ms Moneypenny,' he said in his best Sean Connery accent.

When she spluttered laughing, he said, 'Sorry, I don't know why I did that.'

'It was funny. So if you are not a government spy, what do you do for them?'

'I work in the Department of Justice. In the legislation side of things.'

'Do you like that?'

'I don't dislike it. But I'm not sure it's a job I would have dreamt about as a kid.'

'A detective,' Billie said. 'That's what you always wanted to be.'

'You remembered!' Ray was surprised.

'I remember everything about that summer,' Billie said. 'It was the happiest time of my life.'

'Mine too,' Ray said.

'Here we are.' Billie pulled the car up. 'I think a lot of people are disappointed by the reality of roadside America curiosities. I hope, after all this time, that's not the case for you.'

'It's everything I thought it would be,' Ray said, and

they both knew he wasn't talking about the twine any more. 'Confession time. Greta and I stopped by this yesterday.'

'Why didn't you say?' Billie said, getting out of the car.

'I wanted to spend time with you. I was worried if I said we'd already been, you'd suggest we went back to the hotel. Anyhow, it's worth a second visit. I mean, the time and effort it took to make this. It's impressive. Is he still alive, this Frank guy?'

'No. Not any more.'

They walked around the bale, inspecting every inch. Ray pulled out his phone, as thousands of tourists had done before them. Ray felt his heart thump when she stepped in close to him, her breath on his cheek, as he snapped some selfies.

'Why did you stop writing to me?' Ray blurted out, unable to wait any longer to find out.

Pain flashed over Billie's face, and he wanted to take her in his arms to make it go away.

'Life got difficult for us here . . . it's hard to talk about. So much has happened over the past twenty years.'

'I would have liked to have helped you with . . . well, with whatever hardships you had.'

'I'm not sure you could have, Ray.'

He found his courage and reached to clasp her hand between his. It had been over twenty-four years since he'd last done this, and yet it felt like it had only been minutes ago. It triggered so many memories. He longed to feel her touch, caressing him once again.

'I'm sorry I ghosted you. I think that's what the cool kids call it now. At the time I felt I had no choice,' Billie said.

'I thought about you often. Wondering if you were happy. Are you?'

Billie shrugged. 'I'm not unhappy.'

Ray shook his head in wonder; the similarity of her words to his own was remarkable. 'I said the same thing to Greta, word for word. She's been going through some stuff, but that's her story to tell, not mine. It's why I wanted to bring her on this road trip. Take her out of the life that she had created for herself and see if the journey helped her recreate something new, better.'

'You love her.'

'She's the daughter I always wanted to have.'

'I'm sorry,' Billie said.

'It's not your fault I don't have any children.'

'I think that somehow it is.'

Ray sighed as he looked at the woman before him. How had they ended up here? If they could go back to their younger selves and whisper in their ears, could they save themselves? 'Watching Greta go through so much pain left me unsettled. Reflective, I suppose. And I thought to myself, I'm not unhappy, but I'm not happy either. I'm somewhere lost in between.'

They looked at each other and saw their younger selves reflected in the eyes of the person in front of them.

'Maybe we could try to find our happy together,' Ray whispered.

Billie reached up and touched his cheek. It was as glorious as he remembered. *She was going to say yes*.

He was wrong.

'It's too late for us, Ray. My life is here with Mama.

Yours is in Ireland. We had our chance, and we lost it. We can't go back.'

'Why can't we?'

Her face changed, the softness disappeared. 'Look, it's great to see you again, Ray. But I'm not the same person you knew back then.'

'Do you ever think that – if we had stuck together – maybe it could have turned out differently for us?'

'Sometimes. But then I realize what-ifs are for fools.'

'You said earlier that you didn't know what you should do next, now the competition is over. I've been feeling like I'm at some kind of crossroads in my life too right now. I suppose that's why I'm standing here in front of you, asking for a second chance. That day at Schiphol Airport all those years ago, I chose the wrong road. My gut told me back then that I should go with you to the States. But instead, I went home to Ireland, back to my boring life. And I've let years pass me by. How stupid is that?'

'Sometimes we just have to do the best we can with the cards that life deals us,' Billie said.

'Do you remember this?' Ray pulled something from his pocket that he'd had with him since he left Ireland.

Billie looked at the piece of twine that lay in the palm of his hand. 'Oh Ray, that can't be the same piece of twine?'

He nodded. 'I kept it all these years. Do you remember what I said to you that night at the jamboree?'

'You said that you can fix anything with a piece of twine, that even a civil servant can become MacGyver. I've never forgotten that.'

251

'It was one of my better lines.'

'Can it fix me?'

'I think especially you,' Ray said.

Billie blinked back tears and said, 'I'm not sure I can be fixed.'

'Just tell me what part of you is broken and I'll do everything in my power to help make it better,' Ray said.

'All of me,' she whispered.

As he had done all those years ago, he wrapped the twine around one of her fingers, then looped it around his own, in a figure of eight. 'I told you once that this bound us together for ever. I need to make good on that promise.' He leaned in and kissed her and the years disappeared, and they were both twenty again, kissing for the first time, for the one-hundredth time.

'I never stopped loving you,' Ray whispered.

Billie said, 'I wish you weren't leaving tomorrow.'

'We can stay for a few more days.'

'You can't do that. You have a plan to drive to Vegas, to find this Dr Gale. You can't just change that. It would break Greta's heart.'

'Then you should come with us! You said yourself that you don't know what's next for you! You can figure that out on the road with us two. I'll book a returning flight for you, or you can keep our hire car and drive it back, if you prefer.'

She shook her head.

'I'll take care of all the costs,' Ray said, worried that a tight budget might be a factor in her decision.

'It's not about money. I have commitments here.'

'Surely you can take a few days' holiday from your job?'

'Yes, I can do that. But what about Mama?'

'Lucy can check in on her.'

'I can't ask her.'

'Why not?'

'Because . . . just because. Plus we can't just pretend that the past twenty-four years haven't passed without a word from either of us. For goodness' sake, Ray, I don't even know if you ever got married, anything . . .'

'That's why you have to come with us. In the car, you get to ask me anything. We'll have all the time to catch up then on our lost years. Please give me a chance to make you fall in love with me again. Please.'

He really thought she was going to say yes. She looked at the twine that was still wrapped around their fingers, then she yanked it off and handed it back to him.

'It's impossible. I'm sorry. We better get back home to Mama.' They drove back to Billie's house in silence.

'This one's a cheat,' Susan grumbled when they walked back in. 'She's managed to rob over twenty dollars from me in this card game. A good job you both came back when you did, or I'd have lost every last cent.'

'She lies,' Greta said, pointing to Billie and whispering, 'She's the cheat.'

Billie kissed her mama on the forehead, 'I'm glad you had fun. You know, I'm so tired, I think the excitement of the competition has caught up with me. I think I'll bring you back to your room now, if that's OK, Mama, and we can say goodbye to Ray and Greta.'

Greta tried to catch Ray's eye, but he kept his head lowered. She walked over to Susan and leaned in to give her a hug.

'Thanks for the lovely chat. Don't forget about the cupboard,' Greta said.

'I told you earlier, you're a special one. I know one when I see one. Beautiful inside and out. Hey, don't make that face when you get a compliment. Take it and say thank you,' Susan ordered.

'Thank you,' Greta pretended to salute her. 'It takes one to know one.'

'And I'll leave this little gem with you. If you hear something said about you that's untrue and you know that with one hundred per cent certainty, then let it go over your head. But if you know there is merit to the comment, then let it sit on your shoulders for a while. My mama gave me that advice, and it's never steered me wrong.'

'I'll remember.'

Greta gave Billie a hug next and whispered to her, 'He loves you. Just in case you wondered and he was too shy to tell you.'

'He told me. I hope you find what you're looking for in Vegas, Greta,' Billie said.

'Goodbye Ray,' Billie said.

Ray took the twine from his pocket and placed it in Billie's hand, 'I've held on to this for twenty-four years. It's your turn to take it now. And, for what it's worth, you're wrong. It's never too late. If you change your mind and decide to come with us to Vegas, we'll be at the ball of twine in the morning at ten a.m. waiting for you.'

Chapter 26

Ray and Greta arrived at the largest ball of twine ten minutes early. He parked their SUV, and they both walked over to wait for Billie.

'Jesus, it doesn't half smell here,' Greta said. She was tired and feeling a little irritable. The hooded man had been back last night for the first time in weeks. She'd only managed to sleep for a few hours. It scared her, his return, so she'd texted Noreen, who answered her within a few minutes.

Find a Narcotics Anonymous meeting. Go every day if you need to. You have my number, use it. I mean it. Call.

She thought about telling Uncle Ray about it, but he had enough on his plate, worrying about Billie.

Ray began to pace around the ball. Greta stretched her two arms out to see if she could get them around the bale. Not a hope. She took out her phone and snapped a selfie for Instagram. #ThingsBiggerThanMe.

There was a new Dr Gale post too. She had arrived in Las Vegas and had posted a photograph in front of the famous 'Welcome to Fabulous Las Vegas' sign.

Drgretagale Only a few more sleeps! I've arrived in fabulous Las Vegas ready for my talk on 11 April! Do you know what? If you believe in yourself, anything is possible. I dreamed that one day I would come to Las Vegas and here I am. I found my purpose and if you find yours, I know your dreams can come true too. Last few tickets remaining. Link in bio. Can I get a hell yeah? #wellness #drgretagale #whatsinyourcupboard #mindfulness #inspire #drgretagale #positivethoughts

---

'Dr Gale says we need to find our purpose,' Greta said. 'What does that mean, do you think?'

Ray gave her a look, then rechecked his watch. 'Billie isn't coming, is she?'

'Maybe using the backdrop of a ball of twine to ask her that life-changing question wasn't your best move, Uncle Ray.'

'It was significant to us,' Ray insisted.

'You said. Intertwining and bonds that tie them together. I think she's going to come. She cares about you. I just know it.' When she told Dylan about her uncle's question to Billie, he said it was very *Sleepless in Seattle*. Greta was not sure that a ball of twine had quite the same romantic appeal as the Empire State Building had in that movie. But different strokes for different folks and all that, and it was obvious that the twine meant something to them both.

Her phone beeped and, as if she conjured him up, there was a new message from him.

Dylan: Any sign?
Greta: Not yet. What will I do if she bails?
Dylan: Don't you mean bales?
Greta: That's so lame, it's funny.
Dylan: I keep telling you, I'm a funny guy. Keep me posted.

They waited, until both of their faces were red with the cold wind that whipped across them. 'I can't feel my toes,' Greta eventually admitted. She didn't want to give up, but it was now half past ten.

'She's not coming,' Ray said, and Greta felt her heart break for him. She didn't say anything because every single thought she had felt contrite. So she put her arm around him and led him back to the car.

'We could drive up to her house,' Greta said.

'What would be the point? She's made her decision. At least I tried, right?'

'You did. And you gave it everything. You really did.'

'Sorry I'm late.'

Billie!

Ray ran towards Billie, skidding on the icy ground and almost toppling into her. She steadied him, but when he tried to embrace her, she pushed him back.

'You asked me yesterday why I never got married. I couldn't sleep last night, thinking about that question. And I realized that the reason every guy I dated fell short, was because I was comparing them to you.'

'Billie . . .' Ray whispered.

She held her hand up to silence him. 'I closed my heart to this. It's just Mama and me. And that's how I like it. It's better that way.'

'It doesn't have to be the only way,' Ray said.

'Now that you're back, I can't stop thinking about you. But I don't know if it's real. I'm so confused. I have no clue as to what I'm doing. So much has happened, Ray, I keep telling you that I'm not the same person I was back then.'

'Neither am I. We've both changed. But that doesn't mean that we can't still find that love again.'

She reached into her jeans pocket and pulled out the twine. 'I can't take this.'

Greta watched Ray's face crumple up as she placed it back into his hands and she snapped. This woman might be scared. She got that. She knew how the other woman felt. But she was messing with her Uncle Ray's feelings. And it was cruel.

With adrenalin pumping, Greta ran over to Billie. 'When we saw you up on the stage in your bikini – looking fierce, I might add – I told Ray that he was punching above his weight with you. Well, how wrong was I? Because it's you who is punching, Billie. This man is worth ten of you. And you'll spend the rest of your life regretting it if you don't give him a chance.'

'I like her. She's feisty,' Billie said to Ray.

'Me too,' Ray said.

'As I was saying before Greta's impassioned plea on your behalf, I can't take your twine. Not yet anyhow. But I *will* go with you to Las Vegas. If only to make sure you don't crash into a Colorado mountain on the way.

I'm not sure you have any clue what kind of a drive you have coming up.'

Greta screamed with joy then ran around the ball of twine, punching her arm in the air. Then something struck her about Billie and her rock hard abs and guns made of steel, that made her laugh out loud. 'I've just worked it out. Billie is the Tin Man!'

Ray shushed her, as Billie continued: 'I'm not promising anything, Ray, you've got to understand that. I don't know if I want to be bound to you – or anyone, for that matter. If you're OK with that, then I'd love to come along. If nothing else, I've got a Dr Gale book for Mama that I want to get signed.'

'I'll take it,' Ray said.

'Right, that's that then. Greta, I call shotgun,' Billie said, walking over to their car where she'd left a bag a few minutes earlier.

'Hey! That's not fair,' Greta grumbled. But her grumbles fell away when she saw Ray's face as he got into the driver's seat. He looked younger. He looked happy. He looked like the best version of himself. The one he perhaps always should have been.

Greta took a pic of the two of them sitting side by side in the car and sent it to Dylan.

Greta: Our double act is now a trio!
Dylan: Another score for the URG! Have I convinced you of their powers yet?
Greta: If she's still with us in Vegas, maybe.
Dylan: Where to next?
Greta: Denver, Colorado.

Greta thought about Susan lying in bed, hiding from whatever pain she had encountered in her life. And she knew that she didn't want to hide any more. It was time to get honest with her best friend. He deserved that much.

Greta: Can we talk? I want to tell you something important. About why I was sick. I don't want to do it in a message.
Dylan: OK.
Greta: Will I call you later? When we check into a hotel.
Dylan: Just remember I'm not very good on the telephone. When we talk here, I'm as smooth as silk. If we speak on the phone, I'll be juddering left, right and centre.
Greta: Just for the record, I never really notice any juddering when we speak.
Dylan: That helps. Are you OK? Is anything else wrong?
Greta: I had a nightmare last night. I get them sometimes. Last night was a doozy. Hearing a friendly voice might help.
Dylan: I promise to answer if you call. Because Silver Lady, I really would love to speak to you in person. It's been too long since we did that properly.

Greta put her headphones on and closed her eyes, to give the lovebirds up front some privacy. And she thought about Dylan and that night in Grayson Castle. That wasn't a phone-call conversation. She needed to ask him face to face what had happened. When she got home to Ireland, there could be no more avoiding it. And then she drifted off to sleep thinking about Ultimate Romantic Gestures and lions and tigers and bears, oh my.

A heart is not judged by how much you love,
but by how much you are loved by others.
The Wonderful Wizard of Oz, L. Frank Baum

Part Four

Chapter 27

They decided to spend most of the day driving through Kansas State, with Ray and Billie sharing the six-hour drive between them. They planned to cross into Colorado by that evening. They stopped for fuel in Colby, and while Ray pumped gas, Billie got out of the car and moved towards the side of the building. Greta watched open-mouthed when Billie began to do jumping jacks. The woman was a machine. Once she'd done a dozen or so of those, she then started to make lunges, then finished up by dropping to the ground and doing a dozen or so push-ups. By the time Ray came back to the car, she'd also jogged on the spot and done a couple of dozen sit-ups. Billie strutted back to the car without even a sweat broken.

'Do you always exercise in petrol stations?' Greta asked.

'Normally I go to the gym. But I can't do that because I'm with you guys. So I'm improvising.'

'Don't you care that people were looking?'

'I gave up caring what people thought about me a long time ago,' Billie said, turning around in her seat to look at Greta, who was making a face. 'Oh. I get it.'

'You get what?'

'*You* care about what people think.'

'No I don't!' The free spirit in Greta was horrified by this implication, even though it was completely true. She'd given up her gym membership after one session, because she'd felt traumatized at being the fat one on the treadmill.

'Glad to hear that. You can join me the next time I do it,' Billie said.

The conversation had taken a turn into Scaryville for Greta. 'If I were to get up and exercise like that, it would be giving people a free freak show.'

'Why?'

'People stare at you for all the right reasons. Except when you were orange. That wasn't a good look for you.'

'Funny lady. Listen, you might enjoy it if you gave it a go. And so what if someone stares. You'll be long gone and won't have to look at their judgemental faces soon enough.'

'Maybe. But I'm not fit. I'd find it easier to walk the plank than do an actual plank.'

Ray sniggered at this.

Billie continued, 'You don't have to be fit to exercise. It should be fun. If it's not, then you should look to find something that *is* fun to get your heart racing.'

'If I do it – and that's a big if, – then Uncle Ray has to as well.' Payback for his snigger felt good.

'Thanks a lot, Greta. Way to pull me under the bus with you,' Ray said. 'Right, let's keep going. And remember, keep your eyes peeled for roadside curiosities.'

'And gas stations. 'Cos the next one we stop at, you two are officially in Billie's Gas Station Boot Camp.'

The further west they drove, the less snow there was, and they could see more of the prairie landscape on either side of them. And with just under two hundred miles of the I70 behind them, Greta saw a sign for a Giant Van Gogh painting in a small town called Goodland. Ray's excitement at this wasn't necessarily shared by the others, but as they all needed to stretch their legs, they voted yes to the stop. They parked the car and walked towards the unmissable large steel easel upon which stood a replica of Van Gogh's *Three Sunflowers in a Vase*.

'It says here that it's over eighty feet high,' Ray told them.

'Do you know, I must have passed this spot dozens of times over the years, but I never thought of stopping,' Billie said. 'Oh, look at that. The sun has just come out for us!'

'You've made this road trip before?' Ray asked.

'I've taken part in a few bodybuilding competitions in Colorado. And I've driven to Vegas a couple of times for the weekend.'

'With your mama?' Greta asked, giggling as she pictured Susan on the slot machines. She bet she'd love them.

'Nah. Mama never leaves home. Last time I made the trip was five years ago with my then boyfriend.'

'Ooh, tell me more,' Greta said, finding this far more interesting than the painting, which had already lost her.

'Nothing exciting to share, really. I date. And one or two of those over the years were serious enough that we went away for the weekend.'

Ray pretended he wasn't listening as he took photographs of the painting, but he inched closer to the ladies just the same.

'Were you ever tempted to get married?' Greta asked.

'I find it curious why people are so fascinated with that. One of the first things people always ask,' Billie snapped.

Greta held her hand up. Sometimes Billie scared her. She could look quite cross when she was annoyed about something. 'Sorry, I wasn't prying.'

'Yes, you were. In answer to your question, I've never been interested in getting married. I've had two proposals in my life, but I turned both down.'

'You didn't love either of them?'

'Not enough to say yes,' Billie admitted.

'I've never really dated anyone,' Greta said.

'You have lots of time to fall in love, to find the one.'

For some reason, Dylan's face popped into Greta's mind. She shook it off. He was her friend, and that was all.

'Let's get a selfie in front of the painting,' Greta said, and pulled Ray and Billie in beside her for the snap. She'd send it to Dylan later on. He'd get a kick out of it.

'You know, I always thought Van Gogh was overrated,' Billie said, squinting as she looked up at the painting.

'I love the randomness of it. Why a Van Gogh and not a Monet?' Ray asked.

'Kansas is the Sunflower State,' Billie said.

'D'oh!' Ray laughed. 'Van Gogh cut his ear off, you know. Delivered it wrapped up in a paper to a woman in a brothel he was fond of. And when he awoke the next day, he had no recollection whatsoever of doing it.'

'Maybe he was addicted to sleeping pills too,' Greta whispered. It seemed like the kind of dumb-ass thing she would have done in the not-too-distant past. Not that she had ever visited a brothel. Why the hell had the hooded man come back last night? She was doing well. She hadn't been tempted to take a pill, not even once. But this morning she had woken up again with that feeling that she'd done something wrong. Uneasy. Anxious.

Ray looked at his niece and realized that she looked tired. Dark circles that had disappeared were beginning to show themselves again. Damn it. He'd been so wrapped up in seeing Billie again, he'd taken his eye off her for a while. And that wasn't good enough. He moved closer to her, and whispered, 'How are you doing? Sleeping OK?'

'Well, I've managed to get a good eight hours' sleep . . . over the past two nights.' Greta attempted a feeble joke.

'Are the nightmares back?'

'Actually, yes. Last night I had quite a bad one. I just can't seem to switch off. I'm scared that some bad habits are coming back.'

'You need to call your counsellor.'

'I texted her earlier. And Noreen said I need to find a NA meeting.'

'Tell you what, let's go find a diner to get some lunch. Then we can look at possible locations for a meeting. I made an Excel spreadsheet with options before I left. I'll phone a few and see what works best for you.'

'Thanks, Uncle Ray, you thought of everything, didn't you?'

'That's the boy scout in me. Always prepared.' He

winked, then leaned in and kissed the top of her head. 'I'm sorry for not asking you how you were doing. That's my bad.'

'You had a lot going on. And while I appreciate your help, I should call the NA centres myself.'

Ray put his two hands on her shoulders and said, 'I know you can. But I'd like you to let me do this for you. You'll make me happy if you let me help. OK?'

Greta let herself lean on her Uncle Ray once again. And, having his support, his understanding, helped.

Ray said to Billie, 'We reckon it's time to find the next set of services, have something to eat. Other than Bill's Shooting Shop over there, I don't see a diner close by. Sound OK?'

'Fine by me.'

Within a few miles, they were seated in a booth waiting for their waitress to get their orders. Ray stepped outside to make a few phone calls.

'You've been quiet. Are you OK?' Billie asked.

'Did Ray tell you about what's been going on with me this past year?' Greta asked.

When Billie shook her head, she continued, 'You know Dr Gale's new book, *What's in Your Cupboard*?'

Billie nodded.

'Well, my cupboard overfloweth. I've been a bit of a mess for the last year or so. Maybe longer, if I'm honest. I came out of rehab a few weeks before we left for this trip. Sleeping pill addiction.'

'Oh, I'm sorry to hear things have been rough. How are you doing now?'

'Up and down. I've worked hard to clear my cupboard

out, as Dr Gale would say. And this trip has been great, but last night I had some issues sleeping again. I get night terrors and I thought they were gone, but just as I was getting complacent . . . Anyhow, I need to find a NA meeting. That's what Uncle Ray is doing out there now. Ringing a few that he thinks will work timewise, while we're in Denver.'

Billie looked outside, where Ray was scribbling something down into a notebook, his phone to his ear. 'He would have been a great daddy.'

'Yes, he would. Are you going to break his heart again?'

'You get straight to it, don't you. I'll try not to. But I never asked him to find me. And I tried to send him away. You can't hate me if I can't give him what he wants.'

'Because of what's in your cupboard?'

'Clever girl. Yeah, because of my cupboard.'

'Maybe it's time for you to do a clear-out too.'

'Maybe.' Billie jumped up. 'I'm going to ring Mama. If the food comes, tell them I'll be back in a minute.'

And then Greta was on her own. She looked around the small diner, similar to several others that she'd been in over the past couple of days. It didn't look as charming to her now. It seemed so far from home that a lump jumped into her throat. She picked up her phone and flicked through the contacts until she found her mam. She almost called her, but then she thought about her face, strained with worry. She couldn't keep calling her mam when she was having a bad day. It wasn't fair.

Then her phone beeped.

Dylan: Have you left Kansas or have the flying monkeys caught up with you?

Greta: Still in Kansas. But not for much longer.

Dylan: Any photos for me?

Greta sent him the Van Gogh painting.

Dylan: I LOVE roadside America.

Greta: I didn't think I'd like it. Too kitsch. But it's kind of charming. It makes sense when lots of stuff doesn't. Sound crazy?

Dylan: Not crazy at all. And seeing as today is a day of culture for you, what with your world's largest easel and all that, I offer you a *Titanic* URG! Jack paints Rose like one of his French girls. URG drops the mic. Boom!

Greta: In reality, Rose was lying there, trying to sit at an angle that hid her tummy. And no matter how good an artist Jack was, she was only looking at her wobbly bits when he showed her the painting. URG you need to pick up your mic again.

Dylan: Jeez, you're a tough nut to crack. I'll find a movie yet that converts you from a cynic to a romantic. Did you watch *The Graduate* as I suggested?

Greta: As it happens, I downloaded it last night and watched it when I couldn't get back to sleep. And guess what? Another fail!

Dylan: You are grumpy today. What's more romantic than a guy turning up to stop a wedding? He saved her from marrying the wrong guy!

Greta: He should have told her the day before. That way she didn't have to have the hassle of jumping on a bus in a big dress.

Dylan: You are missing the point! URGs are not meant

to be practical. My new mission in life: as god is my witness, I'll find a URG that you can't tear apart.

Greta: You are such a drama queen. My food has arrived. But Dylan . . . while you may have failed to prove the validity of URGs, you have cheered me up.

Dylan: Then my work here is done. Chow down, Silver Lady.

Greta: Are you ever gonna tell me why you call me that?

Dylan: I think I might. Soon.

Billie and Ray arrived back in together, smiling at a shared joke. 'You guys look good together,' Greta said. No harm giving them both a little nudge closer together, Greta figured. 'How's your mama?'

'She was full of chitchat. Asking for you both too. You've got a new fan there, Greta: she's quite taken with you. I know she's in good hands with Lucy but I also know she'll struggle without me.'

'Maybe it's a good thing then? You being away, giving her some time on her own,' Ray suggested.

Billie wasn't so sure about that.

'Either way, thank goodness for Lucy, then. She's a good friend to her,' Ray said.

'The best. And one of the few who stuck by us when things were . . . difficult.' She speared a piece of steamed broccoli and ate it.

Greta looked at Ray, who shrugged in response to her silent question. Billie was keeping her cards close to her.

'Do you ever just have a burger?' Greta asked. 'I miss burgers.'

Billie shuddered, 'Never! Look, the way I see it is

this – low-quality food equals low-quality thoughts, and that in turn equals a low-quality life.'

'I couldn't live without the odd burger,' Ray said.

'I bet your arteries could,' Billie said.

Greta reached over and grabbed a chip from Ray's plate and he edged his plate closer to her so she could steal some more.

'Did you find a class for me?' Greta asked, then added, 'I told Billie about the NA meeting.'

'Oh, good. Well, I reckon if we put the foot down, we can be in Denver by six. There're several NA meetings downtown, depending on whether you want to go this evening or tomorrow morning. I've rung each to double-check that you can go and all said you are welcome.'

They finished their food in silence, each thinking about the road ahead.

Chapter 28

There wasn't much to see between Goodlands and Denver. With a full tank of gas, they just kept driving. They passed Kanorado with a cheer, as it marked their transition from one state to another.

The terrain changed as they made their way into Colorado State. The rolling plains of Kansas made way for the Rockies. And once again they found themselves surrounded by snow. Billie insisted they stop for fuel before they tackled rush-hour traffic driving into Denver City. Once Ray had filled up, Billie demanded they all do a round of star jumps and lunges. And as people stared at them, Greta reminded herself that she'd never see them again. It didn't really help, she still felt like a right eejit.

Billie was right about the traffic too. As soon as they got close to the city, the highway became a car park. Inch by inch Ray negotiated his way across several lanes, as the satellite navigation directed them to their hotel. Greta was grateful for her back seat and the fact that nobody wanted her to drive. And she noticed Billie's hand brushing Ray's leg more than once. Things were looking more promising by the minute.

'That's one serious view,' Greta said, snapping a picture of the stunning Rocky Mountains that formed the backdrop to their hotel on the west of the city.

'Denver is nicknamed the Mile High City. Because it's exactly one mile above sea level. It's one of the highest cities in the US,' Ray said.

'Fascinating,' Greta said. 'Sorry. Don't mind me. I'm just a bit jittery today.'

'We can go with you, to your NA meeting. Give you a bit of company,' Ray said.

'Uncle Ray, I love you. But I need to do this on my own. You've booked us into a hotel that is central to lots of meetings. I'm going to go for a walk and see where I end up. It's all good. Have a drink with Billie while I'm gone. You both deserve it, after that long drive today. I'll find you in the bar when I'm done, and then we can grab dinner.'

It was the perfect evening for a stroll. The temperatures were slightly warmer than they'd experienced in Kansas. Even so, she needed her hat and scarf. The wide streets looked quite modern, despite the Victorian buildings that lined either side of it. And they sparkled from the strings of lights that hung overhead. She walked slowly, enjoying the time to herself. The shops were closed, as it was now six p.m., but there was still a buzz in the city, as people wandered in and out of restaurants and bars. And then Greta spotted a sign outside an old church on her left-hand side.

Narcotics Anonymous Meeting.

6.15 p.m.–7.15 p.m.

All Welcome

She stopped for a moment on the steps and took a deep breath, closing her eyes. And she brought herself back to Noreen's office, with the curtains closed, in the dark, when she admitted for the first time that she was an addict. Holding on to that thought, she opened her eyes and walked into the building.

She followed the signs and walked through double doors into a large room.

'Welcome.' A man with long dreadlocks greeted her, ushering her in.

'Is this meeting open to everyone . . . Mason?' Greta asked, reading his name badge.

'The only membership requirement is the desire to stop using,' Mason said.

'I'm not using anything,' Greta said quickly.

'Good.'

'But I am afraid I might be tempted.'

'Then you're in the right place. Take a seat. We'll get started in a few minutes. There's doughnuts if you feel peckish.'

Greta's stomach growled. She decided that even Caroline wouldn't want her to leave such caramel gooey loveliness behind her, so she took one and bit into it. *Damn that's good.*

Wiping her hands on a napkin, once she'd finished the doughnut, in record time, she made her way to the circle of chairs. She texted Ray to let him know that she would be back at the hotel in an hour.

275

Mason cleared his throat, then began to speak in a loud, clear voice. 'Welcome to Narcotics Anonymous. Let's open this meeting with a moment of silence for the addict who still suffers, followed by the Serenity Prayer.'

Greta bowed her head and as the group began to chant, 'God grant me the serenity to accept the things I cannot change', it was as if she was back in Hope Crossing once again. And her heartbeat slowed down. It felt good to be back.

Once they had finished the prayer, Mason asked, 'Is there anyone here attending their first NA meeting, or this meeting for the first time? If so, know that you are the most important people here!'

Then Mason invited people from the group to speak. And this group made Eileen from Hope Crossing seem like an introvert. They were all sharers. And as she listened to each person chat about their struggles and their successes or milestones reached, she gained strength. Because she'd had her own successes too. She slept most nights, she ate healthily – most of the time – and she felt content.

Then it was her turn. 'Hello everyone. I'm Greta and I'm an addict.'

'Hello Greta,' everyone chorused in return.

She looked around the group, smiling shyly in response to their bright, encouraging grins. 'I used to think that I was different. That was back home in Ireland. You probably got that from my accent.'

'It's a beautiful accent. Reminds me of my grandmother,' a woman with red hair said.

'Thank you. Well, I told myself that I was better than

the others, that my addiction was different. But it's funny, sitting here listening to you all, I've realized that it doesn't matter where we are from and what our individual stories are. We're all the same. We're in this together, aren't we? Trying to get through each day.'

'We are,' a black woman to her left said.

'I've been struggling to admit to people that I'm an addict. I've hidden it from my best friend,' Greta said.

'And I bet that makes you feel guilty,' Mason said.

Greta nodded.

'You know what the biggest triggers for relapse for us addicts are? Most of them are around emotions – Stress, Anger, Loneliness, Fatigue, Hunger. And Guilt.

'That's me fecked, 'cos I reckon that just about sums up how I feel every day,' Greta said, and they all laughed together. Then she realized that wasn't strictly true any more. She used to feel like that. But things were different now.

'I used to be a master at self-deception. All with one purpose – to prevent myself from feeling guilty,' Mason said.

Greta recognized that truth. All the times she'd lied to her family, deceit tripping from her tongue, covering up her addiction.

'It's time you stopped lying to yourself and to others. Tell your best friend,' Mason said.

'I'm going to ring him tonight. Thank you,' Greta said.

While Greta was at the meeting, Ray and Billie took a seat at the counter of a bar on the corner of the street where their hotel was.

Carmel Harrington

'What do you want to drink?' Ray asked.

'Beer. Please.'

'Two beers,' Ray asked Marvin the bartender.

They took a swig of their Coors Light, draining half the bottle each in one go. 'I needed that,' Ray said. 'That was a long drive today.'

'Me too,' Billie agreed, going back for another slug.

'Two more.' Ray motioned to their new friend, Marvin, who told them he'd set up a tab.

'You worried about Greta?' Billie asked.

'Impossible not to be. But she's doing brilliantly, all things considered.'

'She is. I like her a lot. I remember you telling me about how you delivered her. That made you close.'

'I don't think I could love her more if she were my own. Same for her brothers at home. Great guys too. I'm lucky to have them living so near to me. But I think with Greta it's always been a little different – we are kindred spirits. I get her and I think she gets me.'

'You would have liked children of your own.' This was a statement from Billie, not a question.

'I always thought I'd have a houseful. But, as you know, life doesn't always end up the way we planned.'

'Why didn't you get married, Ray? From what you've told me, you'd be a catch. Good job, car, house . . . guys like you would be snapped up around Cawker City.'

'Maybe I need to move there then,' Ray joked. 'I lost my way a bit. I've not been living my best life. I might not have locked myself into my bedroom like your mama, but I've made a prison of sorts for myself all the same

278

too. I've done more living in the past week on this trip than I've done for the past twenty years.'

'That's sad. You shouldn't admit that to anyone. Goodness, we're a right pair, aren't we?'

'I'm just an ordinary guy, living an ordinary life. Some people might call me boring. Some have.'

'I find *some* people to be idiots,' Billie said. 'And by the way, you're not ordinary. Don't let anyone ever tell you that.'

'Thank you. And not just because you said that, but there's something I need to say to you too. I think you're magnificent,' Ray said.

'Shut up.'

'I mean it. And I'm talking about this version of you, Billie. Not the version I remember from that summer in '95. Although that version was pretty magnificent, too. I'm in awe of you. Just so you know.'

Billie hadn't cried in years. She'd spent decades isolating herself from social situations and had no close friends. By choice, because she had to protect herself from the pain of her past. This came at a cost – it took something precious from her. It took her heart.

'I get so scared,' Billie said as Ray's face moved closer towards hers.

'Of what?' Ray whispered.

'I shut down my heart years ago. I don't know how to open it again.'

'Your heart is stronger than you think,' Ray said. 'I've seen how it loves your mama. And Lucy too. I've seen its kindness to Greta. To me . . .'

And for a moment Ray thought Billie was going to

kiss him again. She tilted her head to one side and moved a fraction more towards him. Then she blinked and stepped backwards, only an inch, but it might as well have been a mile.

'Please Billie, let me in.'

She picked up her bottle and took another swig. 'Drink up. Greta will be coming out of that meeting any minute. Then we can all go for dinner.'

'I'm not giving up,' Ray said. 'Fair warning.'

'I'm counting on that.' Then Billie made a split second decision. She reached into her handbag and pulled out her hotel key-card pack. 'I only need one of these.' She slid the second one to Ray. 'After dinner, come to my room.'

As soon as Greta saw Billie and Ray, she knew something had shifted for them. They couldn't take their eyes off each other. She didn't know what had happened while she was at her NA meeting, but the sexual tension between the two of them was now off the charts. So she told them she was tired and left them to eat dinner without her. She went back to her hotel room and ordered a sandwich from room service.

She video-messaged her mam, who was annoyed that she'd not had any warning to put her make-up on.

'No one can see you but me. Honestly,' Greta said.

Even so, Emily grabbed her sunglasses and put them on just to be sure.

'I went to a NA meeting.'

Emily's mouth formed a perfect 'O' of surprise. 'In America? Oh, I'd say that was something else. Were there drug lords there? Did someone try to sell you crystal meth? Sweet divine Jesus, we should never have let you out of the country. You'll end up in the red desert yet, in a black bag.' Emily and Stephen were halfway through the box-set of *Breaking Bad*.

'Well, there was this one guy who said he was on the run from a drug dealer. He had a distinct look of Jesse Pinkman,' Greta teased.

'Very funny. Just be on your guard. And for that matter, never leave your drink unattended. Someone might try to slip something into it.'

'No crystal meth. No Rohypnol. I promise. But I can tell you that the snacks were better over here. Not a single custard cream or fig roll.' She licked her lips thinking about the caramel doughnut she'd devoured.

Emily said, 'Never mind all that: swear you've not had any pills.'

Greta replied, 'I, Greta Gale, do solemnly swear that I have not taken any more pills. You can get the Bible out if you want.'

'That's my girl.'

They chatted about Ciaran's girlfriend Claire and Greta filled Emily in about the new turn of events with Billie and Ray. It was nice. When they said goodbye, the evening still stretched out ahead of her. While she was delighted for Ray and his new romance, it kind of left her out on her own. Here she was, cooped up in Denver. She'd not heard from Dylan much today, but she knew he was busy with work. She opened a YouTube link to a Yoga Nidra class that Noreen sent her earlier. She was just about to give it a go when her phone beeped.

Dylan: What's your hotel like?

Greta: Big! My ears popped in the lift on the way up to my room.

Dylan: I've a question for you. What're your thoughts on *Sleepless in Seattle*? URG win or fail?

Greta: I've always found Meg Ryan's character quite stalkery. I mean, she gets a private detective to find out about a guy she'd just heard on the radio. If a guy did that, he'd be arrested.

Dylan: Ouch.

Greta: And it's highly unlikely that either the Meg Ryan or Tom Hanks characters stayed together. I mean, they'd hardly spoken a word to each other until they met in the last five minutes of the movie. They didn't know each other. Not really. I reckon that by the time their lift brought them back down to the ground floor on the Empire State Building, it also brought them back to earth too.

Dylan: So cynical.

Greta: I like to think I'm more of a realist.

Dylan: I'll chat further about this with you later!

Greta switched on the TV and found the movie *Love Actually*. She always got agitated when she saw the guy telling his best friend's wife he loved her, with cards. Totally out of order! But when it got to the bit where the kid ran through Heathrow Airport to find his 'one', she had to admit that even her cynical body couldn't see a thing wrong with it.

Her room phone rang, making her jump. She answered it, assuming it was Uncle Ray or Billie checking up on her. Instead, it was reception, saying there was a package waiting for her at the front desk. She slipped her feet into her trainers then made her way down to find out what it was. Had her mother sent her something? She giggled as she pictured opening a cardboard box with a copy of the Bible inside. She wouldn't put it past her!

'Hey, you,' a voice said from behind her, as she stepped out of the lift.

Greta spun around in shock. It couldn't be.

Standing before her was Dylan.

'It's unfortunate yyyyou thought Mmeg was a stalker. Because I think I've just ddddone the same.'

Greta couldn't speak. What on earth was Dylan doing here? She looked him up and down, his curly hair more unruly than usual, his face white with tiredness.

'Say something,' Dylan said.

'I'm willing to concede a URG win for Liam Neeson's son in *Love Actually*. I was just watching it,' Greta said.

He looked amused. And that made Greta happy. She always enjoyed making Dylan smile. She gave him time to formulate his response. She knew he liked to choose his words, pick ones that he knew he could say without faltering.

Dylan grinned. 'Cccool kid. Brave.'

'Why are you here?' Greta asked.

'You know friends can do URGs too. III . . . thought you could do with a friend.'

Chapter 29

They had an awkward moment staring at each other, wondering if they should hug. They had never been tactile. And Greta couldn't abide the whole theatrical double-kiss darling bullshit. Thankfully neither could he.

But Greta had changed over the past two months. She was now a shadow of her former fierce self and prone to tears at the drop of a hello. So she found herself walking towards him and initiating a hug after all.

It took him a second to put his arms around her, and she only allowed herself to stay in them for a moment. But at that moment, Greta felt quite undone.

'You're not sleeping in my room,' she blurted out to cover up her confusion.

'I have my own rrroom.'

'How did you know the name of the hotel we were in?'

'You pppposted on Instagram.'

She'd forgotten that. 'Total stalker move, Dylan. It's a good job that I like you and we're friends. Come on, I'll buy you a drink.'

They took a seat at the bar, and she ordered a beer for him and water for herself. 'I still can't believe you are here!'

'URG fail or win?'

'I don't know yet,' she said.

'You said yyyyou wanted to ttalk in person.'

'I meant on the phone!' Greta said. 'Wait till Uncle Ray finds out. By the way, he and Billie have been giving each other the side eye all day. I think they might finally be back together.'

'That's good, right?'

'It's amazing. And I'm taking full credit.'

'So wwwhat did you want to talk about?' Dylan asked.

Time for a stall. 'Tell me about work. What's happening with the Murder Mystery Crew?'

'ShShShit,' he said.

'Things are shit? What's happened?'

'No, literally shshshit,' he said, breaking into a grin. The previous weekend, halfway through one of the sketches, things went very wrong. The count, played by Jimmy, had the runs and had to leg it to the bathroom. Dylan couldn't get him off the toilet to come back and murder his wife, the countess. So the countess, played by Donna, had to improvise and say that it was the count who was dead. Then whatever bug Jimmy had hit her too, and she had to run away as well.

'Well, good enough for her!' Greta said, delighted by the news. She was still sore about her taking her Ruby

Mae role. 'And it's no surprise she got whatever Jimmy has. Sure they were shagging left, right and centre last I heard.'

'By the time desserts were served, there was only one ccccast member left!'

'Who?'

'John.'

'Oh sure that's grand. He loves the sound of his own voice. Bet you couldn't shut him up.'

'He sang three songs from *Les Misérables*.'

'I'd say they were all fecking miserable by the end of that all right,' Greta said, and the two of them started to laugh. And once they started, they couldn't stop, even when people began to stare.

'Dylan,' Greta said when she finally calmed down. 'This friendship URG thing you did. Epic win. But I need to tell you something. When I disappeared I wasn't sick.'

Dylan nodded, remaining silent.

'I was in the Hope Crossing Rehab Centre in Tipperary.'

She heard him suck in his breath, and rattled on an explanation. 'Drugs. Not cocaine or anything. Although my mam thinks I'm about to go all *Breaking Bad* now that I'm in America. But it doesn't matter what drug it was, does it? 'Cos I'm still an addict. I've learned that. But for the record, because you are probably dying to know what, it's sleeping pills to be precise. So there you go, that's my news I wanted to tell you . . .'

She wiped her hands on her trousers and cursed her physiological response to stress, which always resulted in her body breaking out into pools of sweat.

Dylan took another sharp breath.

'Sorry. Must be a shock for you.'

'Yyes,' Dylan said. Yet somehow it wasn't for him, as niggles of confusion began to make sense. Pieces of Greta's life that he'd been witness to and not understood now slotted into a jigsaw. 'Are you OO . . . K?'

'I will be.' She stifled a sob. *Why was she getting upset?*

'What can I do to help?' Just like that. No judgement. No rubbernecking, or asking a hundred questions that Greta didn't want to answer; no looking for the gory details. A simple offer of help.

It got her. So much so that she had to stop for a moment, because she was overcome. 'You are helping, just being here. It means everything to have my best friend here with me. Thank you for not giving up on me.'

'Wwhen dddid it start?'

'Do you remember when Gran died?'

Dylan nodded. Greta had been very close to her grand-mother.

'When I was in rehab, there was this guy – Tim – who confessed in group therapy earlier that week about stealing drugs from his neighbour's bathroom cabinet. I felt so superior to him. But I was no better than him.' She swallowed a lump back down into her throat. She needed to tell Dylan everything. Not sugar-coat her addiction. No more secrets. 'If I had said no to Mam when she'd asked me to help her clear out Gran's house after the funeral, then maybe I wouldn't have found her prescription in the top drawer of her bedside locker. I stuffed the pack of pills into my jacket pocket. Mam was less than two feet from me, rifling through gran's knicker drawer.' Greta felt the heat of shame rush over her body.

Her gran had been prescribed the pills to help her sleep while dealing with her chemotherapy. Chemotherapy that didn't work in the end. All it did was tear her up inside, make her vomit until there was nothing left. After all the pain she went through, fighting to live, and she was dead less than a week after the last session ended.

'That night I took the tablets for the first time. They knocked me out cold for eight hours straight. Which is why I went back for more. That's just over a year ago now. But things had gotten out of control.'

She told Dylan about the things she'd done while under the influence of the pills. About the hooded man. About the bathtub. All of it. And he listened, without flinching or judgement.

'Did Noreen hhhhelp with the night terrors?'

'She gave me some coping mechanisms to help deal with the aftermath. Noreen figured that I'd developed a fear of sleeping because of the hooded man. When I look at the timeline of my life, there is no doubt that in times of stress the nightmares always return. When Gran got sick, the hooded man was in my dreams every night. By the time Gran died, I was just tired, scared and so bloody sad, that the pills seemed like my only escape. But of course, the pills only made everything much worse.'

Dylan reached over and held Greta's hand. 'When you came to my room, you were out of it. You had taken a pill?'

She nodded. 'What happened that night?'

'I ddon't wwwant to . . . embarrass you.'

'It's fine. I've been mortified more times in the past few months than I have been in my entire life. And that's saying something, because I've had a fair few embarrassing moments from day one, to be honest.'

'I thought yyyou were dddrunk.'

'I was – kind of. I'd had a few glasses of wine. Then I took a sleeping pill before I went to bed. That combination, I've learned, is a big no for me.'

'Yyyou came to my room.'

Greta had no recollection of this fact.

It took a while for him to finish the story. But it turned out that Greta had knocked on his door. He'd been drinking a glass of water and Greta had taken the glass from him, then kissed him.

'You ppppulled me to my bed.' Dylan flushed red at this. Greta felt something inside her die, just hearing him recount the night.

She had to push him to tell her what happened next, because he was clearly embarrassed. And all the while Greta had no recollection of a single moment that they'd shared.

'Did we have sex?' She had to whisper this part. Not so brazen then. In fact, she was terrified that she had let herself become the kind of person that could not remember if she'd had sex or not.

'No!' Dylan's voice was loud and firm. 'I wwwwould never do that. You wweren't yourself. I could see that. No!'

The relief was instant, followed by confusion. 'But I woke up the next morning with my clothes in a pile beside the bed.'

'You took off your clothes. And then you sstarted ttto cry.'

It took a while to get this part of the story out of

289

Dylan. He confessed that when he turned Greta down, she got upset. She'd mentioned her belly. Then mercifully she'd conked out. Dylan decided it was safer to let her stay in his room so he could keep an eye on her. He was afraid she'd puke on herself and choke. At some point he must have drifted off to sleep.

'I only tttook my shoes off. I slept in my clothes,' Dylan insisted.

And Greta was one hundred per cent sure that he was telling the truth.

Greta realized that she had been fortunate that she'd knocked on his door, and not on the door of one of the other cast members. One or two of the lads there might not have been so gentlemanly.

'What was it like in rehab?' Dylan broke the silence.

Greta told him about life in the centre. Dylan listened. He was a good listener, always had been. She told him as much.

'It's easier to listen.'

'Because of your stammer? Or should I call it a stutter? Sorry, I probably should know!'

'I prefer stutter,' he said. 'That's how it fffeels to get words out. A stut, stut, stut.'

Greta thought that there was something wrong that someone as lovely as Dylan spent the majority of his life fading into the background so that he didn't have to speak out loud.

'Is it a pain?' Greta asked. 'Living with the stutter?'

He shrugged. 'Sometimes. It's embarrassing when words get stuck. Ess . . . Essp . . . when people jump in to fffinish my words.'

'Oh that would drive me mad,' Greta agreed.

'You never do,' he said. 'And you never play charades with my sentences.'

She thought about this for a moment, then the penny dropped. 'You mean people are guessing what you mean to say instead of waiting for you to finish your sentence?'

'Exactly.'

'I've been getting a lot wrong lately. It's nice that I got that right.'

'I think you get more right than you realize. You can get through this. I believe in you.'

He didn't stammer. It was as clear a sentence as Greta had ever heard. And when she said goodnight to him, the thought that kept ringing through her head was, *Dylan believes in me. Maybe it's time I started to believe in myself too.*

Chapter 30

Breakfast should have been awkward the next morning. But somehow, Dylan's arrival and Billie and Ray's rekindled romance balanced each other out.

'Are you coming with us to Vegas?' Ray asked.

'If yyyou . . . if yyyou . . .'

Ray began to speak, but Greta shook her head to shut him up, letting Dylan finish.

'. . . dddon't mind.'

'More the merrier,' Ray answered.

'I'm a blow-in too,' Billie said, then blushed as Ray pulled her into his arms, showing that she was anything but.

'Ewwwww . . .' Greta groaned.

Billie insisted on taking the first stint of driving, telling them they'd thank her for it. Ray sat beside her as co-pilot with Greta and Dylan in the back. As soon as they left the city, the road began to climb.

'We're driving through the Colorado Rockies. That's another tick on our wish list,' Ray whispered. 'It feels like a dream.' His eyes scanned left, right, straight ahead as he took in every angle.

'I've never seen anything like this before,' Greta exclaimed. 'It's so different from the terrain we had in Kansas.' The road wound through the rugged and steep rocky, snow-capped mountains.

'This road can get busy at weekends when the skiers head to the mountain slopes. You'll see the resorts a bit further on,' Billie said. 'Buffalo Bill's grave is on top of Lookout Mountain. That's next on your list.'

The road up was steep, and at times so narrow, they had to pull in to let traffic pass them by. Billie parked the car in the visitors' parking lot. 'Careful, they haven't gritted the ground yet.'

They walked gingerly across the snow towards the lookout.

Ray said, 'I can understand why he wanted to be buried here.'

They took pictures of each other with the spectacular backdrop of the Great Plains and the Rockies. It was cold, four below freezing, and more snow was forecast later that day. They spent an hour looking around the museum and bought some souvenirs in the gift shop. And, finally, they made their way up the narrow track to Buffalo Bill's final resting place.

As they reached the top, the sun came out, making the white snow glisten on his grave. He was buried with his wife Louisa, overlooking the mountains and plains where he'd spent the happiest times of his life.

'He was from Wexford you know,' Ray said. 'Or at least his father was. A Cody from the Bullring.'

'I never knew that,' Billie said.

'Plenty of cowboys in Wexford all right,' Greta joked, making them all laugh.

'And he was a feminist. He's well known for advocating equal pay and voting rights for women. Annie Oakley was paid the same as the men in his Wild West shows,' Billie said.

'He's going on my fantasy dinner party list,' Greta said, tipping an imaginary cowboy hat to him. 'He had to reinvent himself so many times when things went wrong. But he never gave up. I like that about him.'

'To never giving up,' Billie whispered, and they each chanted the same refrain.

They continued their drive through the Rockies, slowly, taking in the beauty around them. Billie stopped to refuel again, even though the car still had half a tank. Dylan's face made them laugh hysterically when he found out that they all had to do a quick ten-minute exercise class with Billie.

'If you're on this road trip, you're automatically a member of Billie's Gas Station Boot Camp,' Greta told him.

And after her tenth jumping jack, Greta realized that she had stopped caring what anyone thought about her. Maybe that was something else she was throwing out of her cupboard.

Having someone with them who knew the area somewhat was a considerable benefit. Billie made a quick detour to Georgetown, a small mining town just off the I70, nestled in the shade of the Rockies.

'I'm sure I've seen a Hallmark Christmas movie filmed here,' Greta said. Street lamps and garlands hanging between the old buildings were covered in a powder of white snow.

'Look,' Dylan said to Greta. He handed her a brochure that outlined the history of the old mining town. Founded in 1859, Georgetown was also known as 'The Silver Queen of the Rockies' because silver had been discovered there instead of gold in the Pike's Peak Gold Rush. 'Silver Lady and the Silver Queen, together.' He snapped a few photos of her.

'You still haven't told me why you call me that. Is it because of my grey hairs?' She tried to twist her hair in front of her eyes to see if she'd sprouted more since she arrived in America.

He laughed but left her guessing.

They wandered down Main Street, which had an eclectic mix of gift shops, filled with paintings and crafts from local artists. Then they took a ride on the Georgetown Loop Railroad, which brought them on a tour of the town's back yard.

Ray sat beside Billie with his arm over her shoulder. 'Smile,' Greta said to them, taking a snap of them both as they looked over towards her. Greta looked at the photo she'd just taken and felt a lump in her throat growing. To her horror, she began to cry.

'What's wrong!' Ray said, leaning in towards her.

'Nothing. It's seeing you two like this, you look so happy. It's lovely. And then I thought to myself, I'm really happy too.'

'Oh love,' Ray said, reaching across the aisle to her.

'I haven't felt like this in such a long time,' Greta sobbed. She looked around her, at the stunning views they were passing in this old-fashioned steam train. At her friends and loved ones who were with her here, sharing this magical moment. She threw her arms in the air above her and cried, 'I'm alive. I'm so fecking happy to be alive.'

Ray threw his arms in the air and shouted, 'Me too! I'm so fecking happy to be alive!'

Dylan shrugged and decided one for all and all for one. So he swung his arms in the air too and shouted, 'Mmmeee three!'

Billie said, 'If y'all keep shouting like that, there'll be an avalanche, then none of us will be fecking alive!'

'Come on Billie. Throw out some of that stuff from your cupboard,' Greta cried. 'Admit it, you're happy to be alive.'

And to her surprise, Billie realized that – right now – that was true. She hadn't had as much fun as she'd had this week in years. Decades, even. So she joined in.

It was one of those moments in life that would stay with them for ever. When they recounted it in years to come, they could never convey the importance of it to anyone else. It would always be a you-had-to-be-there moment for the four of them. Unforgettable.

Chapter 31

They drove through the skiing resort in Vail, a small town at the base of Vail Mountain. They stopped for hot chocolate and watched the skiers swoosh down the mountainside, elegant, fast, leaving a dusty trail behind them. They continued on to Glenwood Springs where they stayed for the night. The receptionist in their hotel told them that a visit to the Glenwood Hot Springs Pool was a must, as it had fifteen minerals that would do anybody good. For Greta, going to the beach or the swimming pool always made her feel uncomfortable. The thought of putting on a swimsuit, even one with a skirt to cover up her fat thighs, beside Billie in her cute bikini, was hard. But she was trying out this whole new world of giving zero fucks. So she pulled a bathrobe around her never-used-before navy swimsuit and made her way with the others to the hot springs.

Ray, as usual, had a leaflet in his hand, ready to play

tour manager. 'The therapeutic spring waters are called Yampah – that's Native Indian, by the way, and it means Big Medicine.'

'Colorado is famous for its springs. People have been coming for pilgrimages to the area for years,' Billie said.

'We're pilgrims too,' Greta said. The pool sat at the base of the mountains. With twilight closing in, the lights of the hotel and surrounding the poolside flickered on the water. It was one of the most beautiful things she'd ever seen.

'How hot is it?' Greta asked, looking at the steam rising. She dipped her toe in. 'Oh, it's glorious.'

They removed their robes and sank themselves into the steamy pool. Nobody looked at Greta and judged her. And, for the first time in a long time, Greta stopped judging herself too. Amid the snow-dusted peaks, they let the mineral-rich springs rejuvenate them.

Dylan admitted that jet lag had caught up with him, so they all had an early night. Which meant that they could have an early start the next day. The road provided non-stop, stunning views. They had plenty more opportunities for roadside stops too. And soon the vista changed once more, as the rugged Rockies became the red rock of Utah. They found a ghost town called Cisco in Grand County and stopped to take some pictures in front of some of the remaining buildings.

'*Thelma and Louise* was filmed here,' Greta said, feeling excited to stand on the same ground as Susan Sarandon. She sent the pictures to her mam, who loved that movie, and always thought she'd a look of Susan Sarandon about her.

'If we drive for another hour or so, we can stop in Moab,' Ray suggested. 'That way we will arrive in Monument Valley nice and early.'

It was Dylan who noticed the first flakes of snow dropping onto the windscreen as they drove. Greta thought it was rain when he pointed to them. Within a few moments, there was no doubt though. To their horror the road disappeared under a blanket of snow.

'New plan,' Ray said, slowing down to twenty miles per hour. 'We find a hotel at the next exit.'

'On it,' Greta said, opening up her phone to search Google maps. 'That's weird. The next exit doesn't have any hotels listed. Maybe there's a small motel there that's not recorded.'

They travelled in silence, with Ray concentrating only on the road in front of him. He was behind two cars, who were also driving at a snail's pace. Then one of them pulled into the side of the road, waited until the two cars behind him passed by, before rejoining at the back.

'Tailgating. Clever thing to do,' Billie said.

'What happens if the car in front does the same?' Greta whispered to Dylan.

'Tttrouble,' Dylan said.

The next services sign had a big cross through it. As did the next two. And it became apparent that they were on the part of the interstate that had no services on them at all. The road was almost empty, except for the small convoy of cars they were travelling in.

'Surely they will send out snowploughs?' Greta asked. By this stage, there was at least four inches of snow on the ground. Ray focused on the tracks made by the car in front; there was little else to do.

'We turn off the interstate for Moab in about five miles,' Billie said.

'Not unless the car in front is doing the same,' Ray replied.

Every muscle in Ray's body was flexed as he concentrated on keeping the car on the road. If they veered off, he wasn't sure he'd get them back on track again. They could be stuck for goodness knows how long. And at the rate the snow was coming down, they might freeze to death before anyone found them.

'I'm scared,' Greta whispered to Dylan. She reached over and clasped his hand.

'It will be fine,' Dylan said. But he was worried too.

'Any sign of a hotel?' Ray asked.

'Nothing.' All three answered him, their eyes all individually looking through Google.

'The exit for Moab is about a mile up the road on the left,' Billie said.

'OK. If the car keeps going straight we follow. Agreed?' Ray said. 'Wherever he goes, we do too.'

'Agreed,' they all said. They all agreed with the logic behind this decision. None of them wanted to go down a road on their own, blind.

But as luck would have it, the car turned left too. 'About twenty miles to go to Moab. And it's the nearest town to us, so we just have to keep going,' Billie said.

It took them over an hour to drive those twenty miles, but finally they reached their hotel in Moab. They checked into their rooms in silence, each of them exhausted and depleted from the adrenalin and fear.

'Is there a bar nearby?' Ray asked the receptionist.

'There's one across the road.'

'That's where I'll be in five minutes,' he told the others.

'Go on without me,' Greta said. 'I'm going to take a shower first.'

By the time she got to the bar nearly an hour later, Ray, Billie and Dylan had downed several drinks each.

She watched from the door at the three of them sitting at the bar, with their backs to her. The barman said something, and they all roared with laughter. She recognized the sound. They were halfway to being drunk already.

'Here she is!' Ray said, waving Greta over. 'The last of our white-knuckle-ride quartet. What would you like to drink?'

'A Diet Coke please.'

'Brandon, a Diet Coke for my niece. Greta, you've got to meet this guy, he's hilarious. You won't believe the rules in Utah. You can't have more than one drink at once.'

Brandon gave her the benefit of his best-winning smile and said, 'Mormon laws.'

'One drink at a time is OK for me,' Greta said, and this seemed to send Ray, Billie and Dylan into hysterics. She tried her best to join in, but with every joke shared, every bout of laughter, she felt the black dog nipping at her heels. Today was the first day Greta had missed alcohol. And a dull ache in her head took root and grew by the second.

'You OK?' Dylan asked.

'I've got a headache, to be honest. Would you mind if I leave you to it?'

'I'll go back with you,' Dylan said.

'No, you're having fun. Stay, have a few drinks. I'll see you in the morning.'

'I'll walk you out.'

They stood outside the bar and looked at each other. 'I thought we were in real trouble back there,' Greta said.

'Me too . . . You pppromise you're OK?'

'I'm grand. Have fun with Ray and Billie. I'll sleep this headache off and tomorrow I'll be grand.'

Dylan grabbed her hand and held it between his own. Then he pulled her towards him and into his embrace. She sank into his arms and heard her sigh join his. His hands moved lower, gently tracing the contours of her back, finally resting on her waist. He whispered her name but Greta couldn't look him in the eye, all she could think about was the fact that his hands were touching her love handles. A part of her body that she always disguised with loosely draped clothing. She pulled away, before he realized how fat she was and felt the same disgust she did. 'Go back inside, Dylan. I'll see you in the morning. Go!'

He walked back into the bar leaving Greta standing on the path, the weight of her embarrassment making her feet heavy. She looked up and down the busy main street. There was a supermarket up ahead, so she decided to get some painkillers for her headache. Greta made her way around the aisles, picking up and then putting back a bag of crisps several times. Then she remembered Caroline's words. So she stuck an apple in too, to redress the balance. Then she made her way to the drugs aisle to get some paracetamol. She'd never seen so many over-the-counter medications in one place before. Every cure for an ache and pain, cough and cold, fever, allergy, skin disorder, heartburn and digestive issue was available in brightly coloured boxes.

Then she saw them. Four rows full of sleeping aids, all promising a blissful night of undisturbed sleep. Greta thought about Ray, Billie and Dylan at the bar, drinking beer to numb the stress from their earlier near-death drive. And she thought, what about me? What do I get to take, to help numb my stress? And she thought about Dylan's hand brushing her fat. It was too much. She needed an escape.

The red poppy fields of *The Wizard of Oz* filled her mind and she wished she could fall into their opiate pillow. If these tablets were addictive like the ones she had taken at home, they wouldn't be available over the counter. The thought snaked its way around her brain. *Stop it!* She moved away and searched the aisle for something for her headache. She threw a packet of Ibuprofen into her basket then ran to the tills.

'Anything else for you today?' The cashier said, smiling brightly.

'Actually yes. One moment.'

Chapter 32

Ten minutes later, Greta placed the box of sleeping aids in the middle of the bed and stared at them. Her heart played the drums in her chest. Sweat prickled her skin. And her head ached so much that she thought she might vomit. She picked up the painkillers and swallowed two whole, with a glug of water.

If she took the sleeping pills too, she could fall into oblivion. Sleep off the headache. What harm would it do?

The faces of her family and her friends, followed by Noreen, Caroline, Sam and Eileen, all formed a queue to shake their heads at her.

Her phone beeped, making her jump. It was Dylan checking up on her. She threw the duvet over the pills then shook her head at her stupidity. As if he could see what Greta was thinking about doing through the phone!

Dylan: I'm sorry if that was weird. Are you OK?
Greta: I'm fine! Enjoy your night. I'm going to sleep now. You're a good friend.

What would he think if he knew that she was contemplating taking a pill right now? A feeling she'd forgotten about stepped back to say hello. Shame. She could message Dylan. Tell him to come to her room, take the pills from her, talk her down from making a stupid mistake. She flicked on Instagram. What would Dr Gale do? *Come on, send me a sign.*

Dr Gale would eat a bowl of salad, it seemed. A colourful mix of greens and berries filled the screen, with a post talking about living a clean life.

Greta scrolled on. The next photo was a close-up of Dr Gale, looking into the camera, eyes brimming with unshed tears. She looked in so much pain. Greta's heart swelled in sympathy. Never had she identified more with Dr Gale. She was suffering right now, just like her.

Drgretagale Are negative thoughts in your cupboard today? I've had a bad day too. It doesn't matter why, but it's made old issues creep back into my cupboard, multiplying until they are spilling out into every part of my life. It's time for me to replace negativity with words of affirmation of love. I'm taking back the power. I am a good person and I am worthy of love. Tomorrow I am going to wake up stronger, surer. #wellness #drgretagale #whatsinyourcupboard #mindfulness #inspire #drgretagale #positivethoughts

---

She'd asked Instagram for a sign, and it appeared she had received one loud and clear.

Then a new photo appeared on her newsfeed. It was a photo of Greta in Georgetown.

@Dylan1234 Silver Lady and the Silver Queen – Georgetown – together. No filter. Natural beauty shines through every time.
#Nofilter #Georgetown #roadtrip #goodfriends

Was that really her? The woman in the photograph was laughing, eyes bright, nose pink, wrapped up in winter woollies. More than OK. She looked pretty. Maybe it *was* time to take back the power. She placed the sleeping pills back into her handbag, then fell into bed fully clothed. Dylan's post had said #goodfriends. And that's what they were. It was better that way. Anything more would be complicated. She was so damn tired, the thought of getting into her pyjamas felt like too much effort. She closed her eyes and let the dreams take her where they willed. And somehow she got through the night.

She awoke to her stomach grumbling angrily at her. She'd not eaten much the previous day, and food was calling her. Guessing the others would be sleeping off hangovers, she decided to go down for breakfast on her own.

Halfway through her muesli, Dylan walked in, his hair tousled. His shirt was buttoned up one button wrong all the way down. He always looked somewhat bedraggled, yet he got away with it.

'How's the head?' he asked.

'I was just about to ask you the same thing,' Greta replied.

'I'm grand. I stopped after the fourth pint. Your uncle and Billie were still going strong when I left, listening to Brandon telling them about how he gave up a corporate job to smoke weed and ski.'

Then, as if Dylan had conjured them up by mentioning their names, Billie and Ray walked into the breakfast room, both wearing sunglasses.

Greta picked up a phone and took a photo. 'This I'm sending to the family.'

'Stop speaking so loud,' Ray said, sitting down beside her. 'You OK? You slipped off last night before I knew it.'

'I'm grand,' Greta said, flushing red as she thought about the sleeping pills she'd bought. 'I hear you had a good night.'

'I could kill Brandon,' Billie said. 'He talked us into smoking a joint with him. I am way too old for this.'

'Uncle Ray!' Greta exclaimed.

'I told you not to say anything, Billie!' Ray said. 'Honestly Greta, I only had a drag.'

'Oh, that's what they all say. Slippery slope, Uncle Ray. You'll be at NA meetings with me next.'

'It was the first and last time. Seemed like a good idea at the time,' Ray said.

'A day in Monument Valley will put us right. Next stop on your wish list,' Billie said.

'I can't wait to see Forrest Gump Point,' Dylan said.

'And the Goulding's Lodge. It's where *The Searchers*

was filmed. And *Tie A Yellow Ribbon*. I loved John Wayne when I was a kid. I wanted to be a cowboy so bad,' Ray said.

'Dad loves those movies too,' Greta replied. 'Anything by John Ford and he's all in.'

'We used to play Cowboys and Indians together when we were kids,' Ray said, smiling at the memory. He'd forgotten that. Yes, there were times when he and Stephen didn't get on in their childhood, but they'd had fun when they were kids too.

They finished breakfast then checked out. Greta offered to drive, so Dylan sat up front beside her, leaving Ray and Billie to nod off in the back underneath their sunnies.

As they said goodbye to Moab, the sun came out and followed them all the way to Monument Valley. It was hard to believe that only the previous night they'd had a white-knuckle ride in a snow storm. Monument Valley, which sat within the Navajo Nation Reservation, was located on the Utah–Arizona border, so they added another state to their road trip too.

'Wow,' Dylan and Greta said at the same time.

Blue skies and white clouds floated about the red rock. And three massive monoliths seemed to erupt from the red clay, extending the landscape like a panoramic post-card until it touched the horizon. Greta pulled into a layby on the right and climbed out of the car, shouting at Ray and Billie to wake up.

'It's . . .' She tried to find the words.

'Majestic,' Dylan said, standing beside her.

'The place where God put the West,' Ray said, joining them. 'That's what John Wayne said about this place.'

'I feel humbled,' Greta said. 'I've never seen a place where the sky and the ground come together so perfectly. It looks like someone has painted the landscape, doesn't it?'

They stood side by side, awe at Mother Nature's handiwork rendering them silent. They drove on for another mile and then suddenly they were at Forrest Gump Point. A long stretch of black road ran towards the three red monoliths, which today wore a snowy cap. Greta pulled over once again, and they walked to the centre of the road, their eyes locked onto the vista before them.

'I keep expecting galloping cowboys and Indians to arrive,' Ray replied.

'For me, it's Forrest running up the road, with a gang of disciples following him,' Dylan said.

'If I was going to stop running, this is where I'd choose to do it too,' Billie said. 'It's damn near perfect.'

'It's as if we are the only people left on the planet,' Greta said. Not a single person or car was in sight. Which meant that they could take as many photographs as they wanted in the middle of the road, without fear of being run over. Reluctantly they moved on and found the road to Goulding's Lodge. Ray, their unofficial tour guide, told them that it was Harry Goulding and his wife Leone who brought Hollywood to the valley back in the 1930s. They ran a trading post, and things were tough for the Navajo Indians who were starving to death in the valley. Harry travelled to John Ford's office and waited three days to see him, eventually persuading him to visit their ranch, saying it was the perfect location for Westerns. And the rest was history, with hundreds of movies filmed on site because of his vision and determination.

They walked around the small museum in the ranch, which only accepted donations for payment. They took pictures of themselves with an old stagecoach and posed beside a large cardboard picture of John Wayne.

Then they walked up the steps to the ranch café and took a seat by the window. Greta wasn't sure if it was the panoramic views or the food, but her tuna sandwich was the most delicious thing she'd ever eaten.

As they sipped their drinks, none of them felt in any rush to leave. 'I've seen *The Searchers* at least a dozen times. I never thought I'd ever see the cinematic canvas John Ford immortalized, in person. I'm quite . . . overwhelmed,' Ray said.

'Overwhelmed is a good word,' Greta admitted. She knew she would struggle to share how much this place had affected her. Every part of the trip had changed her, but never more so than right now. 'We're just tiny specks in the universe, aren't we?' she said, pointing to the majestic red rock towers.

They all nodded in agreement, feeling the same awe-inspiring emotions as her. It was another moment in their lives that would bind the four of them together.

'I've not been living my best life. I want to do better,' Greta admitted.

'You *are* doing better,' Billie said. 'All you can do is keep putting one foot forward each day. You'll get to where you need to be.'

'I think sometimes I take one step forward and two backwards,' Greta admitted, her eyes on her handbag, which still held the sleeping pills. Why hadn't she thrown them away yet?

'If heaven exists, do you think it looks something like this?' Billie asked.

'I hope so. I'd happily end up here,' Ray said.

'Do you think if you do one bad thing in life, does it wipe out all the good things you've done?' Billie asked.

'It depends how bad that one thing is, I suppose,' Greta replied.

'How about if you killed somebody?'

Chapter 33

Maybe it was the Valley, maybe it was the company, or maybe it was just time. But Billie was ready to tell her friends about what had happened over twenty years before.

'My dad was a good man. He loved his girls as he called Mama, Piper and me. We were his whole world, that's what he used to say.' She closed her eyes and could see her father, Norm, standing behind the three of them, somehow managing to wrap his arms around each of them. Keeping them safe.

'What happened?' Ray asked.

'His Achilles heel was alcohol. If he succumbed to temptation and had even one drink, a physical change overcame him. And the net result was that he lost every shred of decency in his body. It was as if all his good sense drowned in the bubbles of the beer in front of him.'

Billie told them about the many incidents throughout

Norm's adult life that had illustrated how poor his judgement was when he had even the smallest amount of alcohol. He threw up in the mayor of Cawker City's garden on his prize petunias one summer evening. He was only eighteen at the time and had just had three drinks. He swore off beer for many years after that. But after the birth of Billie, his eldest child, he succumbed to the cheers of friends who wanted to wet the baby's head. He didn't remember the walk home that night. But the next day he was accosted by the school principal, who berated him for peeing in the town square on his way home. In the process, he had flashed a group of eighth graders who were on their way to the library. Parents were involved. His mortification at having caused such embarrassment and fear to children made him vow once more not to drink ever again.

'He kept his vow not to drink for over twenty years. But then he had a row with Mama about the stupidest of things – he forgot to unload the dishwasher. She said he went to his office Christmas party, to spite her. Several hours later, drunk and one hundred per cent not in any condition to drive, he jumped into his SUV and he headed home. I don't suppose we'll ever know what happened. And it doesn't matter in the end.' Billie sighed, wiping a tear that escaped. 'He ploughed his car into a bus shelter on the outskirts of Cawker City.'

Greta thought about Mrs Oaks's flowerbeds and the blood dripping down her mother's face. *Oh Norm.*

Billie took a sip of her coffee, steadied herself then continued, 'They cut him out and transferred him to Cawker City Clinic Medical Centre. But by the time they got there, he'd died.'

'Jesus,' Dylan said.

'There's more though, isn't there?' Ray said. 'You said that someone was murdered.'

'Dad didn't just kill himself that night. He killed my best friend Mary-Beth and her boyfriend who were sitting in the bus shelter. Probably having a sneaky kiss before they went home. So I didn't just lose my dad that night. I also lost my best friend and our family's good name. Norm Haley became the bogeyman, the slayer, the taker of young lives. The ripple effect tore us all apart.'

'That's why you stopped writing to me,' Ray said, and Billie nodded.

'My sister Piper left Cawker City and married the first man that asked her. I'm convinced it was purely to change her surname. The marriage didn't last more than six months. Since then Piper has added a further two marriages and divorces to her arsenal.'

'All your plans to spend a year travelling through Europe—' Ray said.

'Gone in a click of my fingers.' She snapped two digits to illustrate. 'Mama turned to food for comfort. Unfortunately, she's never been able to fill the gaping hole of loss inside of her with carbs or sugar. She'll die trying, all the same.'

There was nothing that any of them could say in response to this, so they didn't try to fill the silence with trite condolences. They merely reached over and laid their hands over Billie's, in one big pile of friendship. Most days Billie didn't allow herself to think about the life she could have lived, had her father not drunk that night. But every now and then, she wept. Every tear filled with bitter regret.

'Poor Susan,' Greta said. She understood the pain she'd witnessed in Susan's eyes now. How many times had she too tried to fill a void inside of her with food? But it never worked.

'You know, the last time Mama was hospitalized, they had to get a special ambulance to bring her in. She weighs over four hundred pounds, which earns her the tag "super-super obese",' Billie said with a hollow, mirthless laugh. 'Isn't that bull crap? It makes her sound like some kind of superhero.'

'Can the doctors not help? Gastro bands or something?' Ray asked.

'We've tried every kind of intervention. From doctors to psychologists. I even got the pastor in. Nothing worked.'

'She's an addict,' Greta said. 'You can't make her stop eating, no more than anyone could stop me. Pills or food.'

'But you managed to stop taking your pills,' Billie said. 'Why?'

'I wanted to live more than I wanted to die.'

'Shit,' Dylan said on a sob. He wiped his eyes furiously with the sleeve of his sweatshirt, but as quick as he stemmed the tears, more erupted.

Greta moved closer to him. She was seconds from the ugly cry herself. Their waitress walked towards them with the coffee pot, then about-turned sensing a scene was unfolding.

'Is that why you are so disciplined with your exercise and food?' Ray asked. 'Because of how your mama is?'

'Maybe. The gym became my therapy. I liked it when my body became firm. And I suppose that when I body-build, I do it for Mama. For Piper. For my friend

Mary-Beth too. And I do it for my papa who, despite being a good man most of the time, made wrong choices that had catastrophic consequences.'

'Tttears are not the only indicator of someone's pain and grief,' Dylan said.

'Amen to that,' Billie agreed.

'I wish you had told me back then. I would have flown over,' Ray said.

'I know you would have. But I wasn't in a place that could accept help from anyone. We each dealt with the aftermath of the accident in our own way. Piper slept with any guy who asked her. Mama ate. And for a while, I drank. Like father, like daughter. Things got dark for a while.'

'That must have been horrific for you,' Greta said.

'It wasn't fun, I'll give you that. But Lucy was great. And her late husband, too. If it wasn't for them, I don't think we'd have survived it.'

'Did you think about leaving Cawker City?' Greta asked.

'Often,' Billie admitted. 'But with Piper out of the picture, I couldn't leave Mama.'

She pointed to the remnants of the apple pie in front of Ray. 'One of those every day will have you fifty pounds up at the end of a year. Within a year, Mama was unrecognizable as the woman she used to be. Fast-forward ten years and she rarely left the house any more. Fast-forward twenty years and the bedroom became her self-inflicted prison.'

'What a waste,' Ray said.

'Sure is. But life has a way of messing with some folk

more than others. Us Haleys have gotten their fair share of pain. Piper and Mama are still paying a high price for my papa's sins.'

'I think you might be too,' Ray said.

'Maybe.' Billie shrugged. 'Greta honey, you said that you are not living your best life. I think you are doing a darn sight better than a lot of people. Don't forget that.'

Greta reached over again to clasp Billie's hand. 'So we just keep on taking a step forward, one at a time. Together.'

Ray placed his hand over Greta's and said, 'Together.'

Then Dylan placed his on top of the others' and repeated, 'Together.'

And while they didn't know it in that moment, their pact would stay intact for the four friends for the rest of their lives.

Chapter 34

They left Goulding's Lodge quieter than when they arrived. But stronger somehow, in the shared revelation from Billie.

'Pull over!' Billie shouted at Ray, who was behind the wheel again. 'Look!'

A giant billboard sat on the side of the road.

Welcome to Utah. Life Elevated.

'You want a picture with it?' Ray said, stopping the car beside it.

'No. It's time for another session of Billie's Boot Camp and I can't think of a better place to do it!'

A series of groans filled the car. 'We're not at a gas station,' Greta said.

'You can't say no to me. I've just bared my soul to you. You might throw me over the edge if you don't do what I say.'

'That's emotional blackmail,' Greta complained, getting out of the car.

'Sure is, now give me ten jumping jacks.'

'Sadist.' Greta stuck her tongue out at her.

'Oh great, we've not seen a car on the road all morning, but now there's a fecking convoy to share our shame,' Greta said.

The cars beeped their horns as they passed them by and Greta took a bow. Billie was right. Who cared what they thought. She was exercising in Monument Valley, USA. If – a month ago – you'd given her a million things to guess she might be doing today, this would not have been included. By the time they left Monument Valley, the four of them felt ready to take on the world. They moved a couple of hundred miles closer to Vegas, over-nighting in Hurricane, a town about two hours east of their final destination.

They made plans to leave early the next morning so that they could arrive in the Bellagio in time for Doctor Greta Gale's show at two p.m.

'One more sleep,' Ray said to his niece, then went to his room with Billie.

'Fancy a cuppa in my room?' Greta asked Dylan.

'Pppretty intense day,' he said, flopping onto her bed. 'I wanted to say more to Billie. Bbbbut the words got stuck.'

'You said enough.' She put the kettle on. 'You OK? You got pretty upset earlier.'

'Made me think of my father.'

'He didn't kill anyone, did he?' Greta said, handing him his tea.

He smiled, as she hoped he would. 'He helped me with my stutter. My dad said that nothing ccccould hold me

319

back from chasing my dreams if I wanted them badly enough.'

'He sounds like a wise man.'

'Yep. Dad loved movies. Did you know that Samuel L. Jackson had a stutter?' Dylan asked.

'I didn't!' Greta said in surprise.

'Dad always said, "If Samuel can ddddeliver that monologue in *Pulp Fiction*, word perfect, anything is possible for you, son."'

'I'd love to meet him,' Greta said, wishing her father would encourage her as much as Dylan's father did for him.

Pain flashed across Dylan's face.

'What?' Greta asked.

'Nnothing,' Dylan replied, taking a sip of his tea. He flicked on the TV, looking for something light to watch. He stopped on an episode of *Frasier*.

'You've never mentioned your father before,' Greta said, trying to get Dylan to open up. She didn't like being left in the dark. Was this what it was like for Dylan when she kept things to herself? Like the pills she had in her handbag? Why should he tell her everything when she clearly had her own secrets?

'What aren't you telling me?' Greta persisted.

He shrugged.

'You can tell me anything.' Greta said. 'Keeper of each other's secrets. OK?' She was just about to tell him about the pills when he spoke.

'Bbbrace yourself for another intense moment.'

'Go on.'

'When I sing, I don't stutter,' Dylan said.

'I've never knew you could sing!' Greta said. 'Are you any good?'

Dylan shrugged.

'You are! Sing something for me now,' Greta demanded, then stopped when she saw Dylan's face. 'Sorry. Go on.'

'I had to sing "O Holy Night" in our nativity. Dad said that I had to be a righteous man like Samuel L. Jackson when I sang. When I was with Dad, he made me believe in the impossible. Even if I was wearing one of Mam's brown tunics, with a tea towel on my head, tied with a belt from my dressing gown.'

Greta smiled, remembering all the nativity plays she'd been in as a child. 'I was a star in ours. There were several rolls of silver foil used in my costume.'

'I kept my eyes on Dad through every note and www . . . www . . . wwwhen I finished, Dad jumped up and screamed, "Yes, yes, yes", over and over.'

'Oh, Dylan. That's a great memory to have.'

'It was the most incredible moment of my life.' For a moment he considered not finishing the story. But he needed Greta to know him. Every part.

'One minute Dad was cheering, the next he ssss . . . slumped and fell head-first into the lap of my friend Billy Murphy's mam. Pppeople started to laugh until they heard my mam scream.'

Greta held her breath in horror. She didn't want Dylan to finish the story.

'He ddddd . . . he dddd . . . . Ddddied.'

'So much hidden pain,' Greta said, reaching over to grab Dylan's hand. She clasped it tightly in her own, as he explained that – ever since his father's death – he'd had a chronic fear of singing in public. Illogical and irrational but, despite many counselling sessions, he'd never been able to overcome it. The following year, at the school's nativity, he became the stagehand, working behind the scenes.

'When they buried your dad, they buried your courage too,' Greta realized. 'And now you've become a professional stagehand of sorts in the Murder Mystery Crew. You keep yourself out of the spotlight.'

'Yes. But if I hadn't chosen this path, I would nnnever have met you,' Dylan said.

Greta pulled Dylan into her arms and held him, as he cried for his hero, his father. Her plan to talk to Dylan about the pills was forgotten, because he was too upset to deal with her problems right now. So they lay side by side on the double bed and watched the old movie *Casablanca*. Dylan fell asleep halfway through it. He looked so peaceful she didn't have the heart to disturb him, so she left him where he was, covering him with the duvet. They'd come a long way since she'd crashed into his room two months earlier.

'You should have woken me,' he said the next morning, his hair wild around his face.

'I think this makes us even!' Greta said, winking. 'By the way, something struck me last night while you snored. Remember I told you about Oz and how I'm Dorothy. Ray is Scarecrow. Billie is the Tin Man. You're the Cowardly Lion. You've got the *mane* for it, anyhow.'

'Will I find my courage when we get to Oz?'

'Of course you will. We're almost at the end of our yellow brick road. And when we get to Vegas, which is so the Emerald City, you are going to sing.'

'I ddddon't think I can.'

'Course you can. You've got me. I'll help you.'

The four friends were on the road by eight a.m. and grew more excited with every sign that directed them closer to Vegas. When they passed the 'Welcome to Fabulous Las Vegas' sign, they cheered and beeped the horn on the car, making the tourists queuing to get their photo op cheer too.

'Just think, Dr Gale was here only a few days ago. In this exact spot.' Greta couldn't quite get her head around the fact that later today she would get to see her heroine in the flesh.

'I know we've said it about every place we've visited so far on this road trip, but honestly, Vegas really does feel like a movie set,' Ray said.

'Wait till you see the Bellagio,' Billie replied. 'I don't think I've ever got a rush anywhere else more than the one I get when I drive down the Strip and see the beautiful hotels lining each side.'

They passed the hotels that formed replicas of cities like Monte Carlo, Paris, New York, Venice, the French Riviera.

'Where else can you visit so many famous places in one road?' Ray said.

'I can't wait to check out the casinos. Mam wants me to put a bet on blackjack for her.' Greta felt her body pump with excitement. 'Oh my god. Look, we're here. It's just like it was in *Ocean's Eleven*!'

They used the valet parking at their hotel and then walked into the beautiful lobby, which was heaving with guests and tourists who were just calling in to see the magnificent glass floral displays in reception.

'We made it to Oz, Scarecrow,' Greta said, giving Ray a huge hug. 'You made all of this possible.'

'That we did, Dorothy, with not a flying monkey in sight.' He kissed her head in the way he'd done ever since the day he'd delivered her.

'Do you think we'll get a chance to speak to Dr Gale?' Greta asked.

'Not a hope,' Billie said. 'I've seen this kind of gig lots of times. She'll be on and off the stage in a flash, surrounded by her people and security. Unless she does a book signing, then maybe you can get a photo or something.'

They decided to go to their rooms to freshen up before going to the event. Ray grabbed Greta and asked her to hang back with him for a moment, telling Billie he'd follow her up.

'What's up?' Greta asked, taking a seat beside him in a small bar, at the entrance to the casino. Her eyes were on stalks, as she took in the hundreds of people on machines, gambling. 'God, I love it here!'

'How are you doing? Things have been quite intense the past few days. I wanted to check in with you on your own,' Ray said.

'I'm fine,' Greta said.

'I don't quite believe you.'

'I've had a few speed wobbles. But hearing Billie and Dylan talk about their fathers has clarified things for me. As Dr Gale often says, we're all damaged.'

'How are things with Dylan?'

'He's a good friend,' Greta said, a little too quickly.

'I think he's more than that. Billie said something to me earlier. She said that Dylan looks at you the same way that I look at her. If that's the case, then he's hook, line and sinker in love with you.'

'I don't think so. We fell into the friend zone ages ago.' She thought about how it felt the previous night, to lie beside him in bed, watching him sleep. It felt *right*.

'Well, I don't think he knows that. I've watched you today. You like him too. I can see it. Don't let fear hold you back, like I did for decades. If I'd only just jumped on a plane all those years ago, to see for myself why Billie had stopped writing to me. Don't wake up in twenty years' time with regrets like I did.'

'I'm trying,' Greta said. They took the elevator to the twenty-eighth floor, where their rooms were. 'Thanks, Uncle Ray.'

'Anytime,' he replied.

Greta had been given a fountain view room, which not only had a perfect vantage spot from which to watch the show but also had a gorgeous backdrop of the Strip. The room was decorated in vibrant shades of indigo and platinum. The bed was bigger than any she'd ever slept in before. Greta wasn't sure she'd ever be able to go back to her small bedroom in Lucan. She took a photo and sent it to Dylan.

Greta: Check this room out. Vegas baby!
He sent back a picture of his room which was identical.
Dylan: Everything is better in Vegas!
Greta: See you in a bit.

Greta hovered over the phone, wondering whether she should add a kiss before she hit send. She'd never done that before on any of their messages. Before she could change her mind, she typed X, hit send, then threw the phone on the bed, squealing.

And seconds later she had a response.

Dylan: XX

Two x's. Oh my.

Chapter 35

'We've come a long way to get here,' Ray said when they walked into the theatre.

'I can't believe you managed to get tickets for Billie and me too,' Dylan said.

Greta couldn't speak, she was so nervous and excited. On the other side of the curtains, on the stage, was Dr Greta Gale. Her namesake. The person she'd spent years daydreaming about. And any minute . . .

'Holy shit, Uncle Ray. We're about to see *The Wizard of Oz*!'

The lights went low and music bellowed out from the speakers, bright green lights filling the stage. Then a voice shouted out,

'Ladies and gentlemen, for one day only, it's Doctor Greta Gale!'

Greta jumped to her feet, clapping and cheering with everyone else as Dr Gale glided onto the stage in a fog of smoke. She was wearing a long cream coat over a black top and skinny black trousers with killer heels. Her long platinum hair fell in soft, glossy waves around her perfectly made-up face.

'She's beautiful,' Greta breathed.

'What's in your cupboard, y'all?' she shouted out to the audience. And they all went wild.

'We've all got something in that big old cupboard, don't we? Some of us have just the one thing; others have a great big bulging stockpile that's threatening to spill out into our lives any minute. Am I right?'

The room erupted once more. She held each and every one of them in the palm of her hand.

'Maybe it's addiction.

'Maybe it's heartbreak.

'Maybe it's fear.

'Maybe it's loneliness.

'Maybe it's loss.

'Maybe it's all of the above.

'But whatever it is today, we're gonna talk about it, y'all hear? And I'm gonna help you clear those cupboards out!'

Each of the four friends felt that Dr Gale was talking to them specifically. That was her magic, Greta realized. She had the power to make everyone feel special.

'Have you ever had an epiphany? Or, what I like to call, an "a-ha" moment?' Dr Gale asked.

Everyone nodded. Some waved their hands in the air, as she took them to church.

'I bet it made you stop dead in your tracks, it was so profound. Well, here's what I have learned over my thirty-two years on this beautiful planet. Epiphanies are only life-changing if you apply the lessons that you learned from them. And most of us forget to do that, don't we?'

'It's true, I do,' Ray whispered to Greta. 'Do you know something, up close like this, I swear she has a look of my mother. I bet we're related somewhere down the way.'

Two hours went by in a flash as Doctor Gale shared her wisdom with them all. And then, before she finished, she said, 'Hands up if any of you had an epiphany today while I spoke?'

Greta looked around and, by the looks of it, they had come in thick and fast today. Not one person had their hand down.

'Well, here's where the hard work starts. Because I want you all to make me a promise – hell no, I want you all to make *yourselves* a promise. You mustn't forget this "a-ha" moment. Can you give me a hell yeah?'

'Hell yeah!' thousands cried.

And then the music came back on and she glided off the stage, to rapturous applause.

'She'll come back, won't she?' Greta asked. But that was it. She was gone and, as they made their way out of the theatre, they were all a little shell-shocked by the event and deflated that it was over.

'Life changing,' Ray said.

'Hell yeah!' Dylan said, giving Ray a high-five.

'I never got to speak to her,' Greta said. The disappointment was crushing. 'All this way . . . I just wanted to tell her how much she means to me. How much she's helped me.'

'I thought that might be the case,' Billie said. 'I'm sorry Greta.' Then she stopped in her tracks. 'It's not over yet!'

Their eyes followed hers to the security guard who was standing by the entrance to backstage.

'Why does he look so familiar?' Greta asked, looking at the big guy with a headpiece and a badly fitted black suit.

'Isn't that . . . ?' Ray looked a little closer.

'Oh god, you're right . . . it's Big Bad Dom!' Greta squealed. She turned to Dylan and said, 'He was the MC at Billie's bodybuilding competition – and he's shaped like the Domestos bottle,' she added to explain his nickname.

'He *is* kinda bbbbroad at the shoulders and slim at the hips,' Dylan agreed.

'Right, here's the plan.' Billie said. 'I'll go and distract Brad, then you three sneak backstage and go find that doctor of yours.'

'We can't do that,' Ray said.

'Yes you bloody can. You said yourself that you'd come a long way to meet her. Well, fortune favours the brave. Can you give me a hell yeah?'

Before they had a chance to answer, she ran over to Brad and threw herself into his arms, spinning him around so his back was to them and the entrance.

Greta, Ray and Dylan ran through the double doors into a long corridor.

'Where to next?' Ray whispered.

'Down there,' Greta said, pointing to a door that stood at the end of the corridor. 'It's the only way.'

They half ran, half walked, all the while expecting someone to grab them by the scruff of their necks. Taking a deep breath, Ray pushed the door open and they walked in.

A woman turned towards them and Greta almost didn't recognize her. Because the woman in front of them had short brown hair, which was matted to her head. In her hand was a blonde wig.

Before anyone had a chance to speak, the door behind them swung open again.

'I'm sorry Doctor Gale,' Brad shouted. 'They snuck by me, while this one distracted me.'

Billie ran up to Greta, Ray and Dylan, who stood side by side, clinging on to each other. 'Sorry, couldn't keep him out any longer. He's strong.'

'I'll have you sacked for this!' Dr Gale shouted at Brad, running behind a curtain. She came back a moment later, with her wig back on, her face still furious.

'I'm sorry, Dr Gale. What do you want me to do? Shall I call the police?' Brad asked, giving Billie another dirty look.

'I don't know yet,' Dr Gale replied. 'Who do we have here?'

Ray pushed Greta forward. 'Say something.'

Greta walked forward and curtsied. 'Hello. Please don't be cross with Big Bad Dom. It's just we've come such a long way to meet you. We had to find a way to meet you in person.'

'Aren't you just darlin! And such a pretty little thing too. So did you enjoy the show?'

They all started to speak at once, enthusiastically telling her how amazing it was.

'Wow.'

'A-ha moments everywhere.'

'My cupboard is so full.'

'We're big fans.'

'Where's that accent from?' Dr Gale asked, clearly charmed by the praise they were laying on her.

'We're from Ireland,' Greta said. 'In fact, my name is Greta Gale. Like yours.'

'You're joshing me.'

'No, honestly, I'm not pretending. I really am called Greta Gale.'

'Well ain't that a hoot? Come here and give me a big squeeze, darlin'.'

Ray had to push Greta forward again, because all of a sudden she seemed to have lost the use of her legs.

'You've really come all this way from Ireland to see little old me?' Dr Gale asked, as she embraced Greta.

'Yes. I'm your number one fan. I bet people say that to you all the time.'

Dr Gale nodded, for it was true. She was beloved.

'Sometimes it's as if your Instagram posts speak to me. They've kind of saved my life more than once,' Greta added shyly.

'Oh darlin', that's so kind of you to say.'

'And I wouldn't be here at all if it wasn't for my Uncle Ray. He organized everything. He booked the tickets and here we are—'

'Well isn't your Uncle Ray a darlin' too.'

Now it was Billie's turn to push Ray forward. He stood in front of Dr Gale and gave a little bow, blushing bright red as he did.

'Gosh, I never knew the Irish were so formal with all

your bowing and curtsying. I thought that was just in England for the Queen!' Dr Gale glanced in Dylan's direction so he thought he'd better bow too.

Billie held her hand up. 'I'm from Kansas. So don't be expecting any of that from me.'

This made Dr Gale laugh and even Brad was smiling.

'Is there something you want to ask me?' Dr Gale asked.

'Are you happy? Or just Insta happy?' Greta asked.

'I am. Not every day. But most. I have a good life. I work hard and I try not to sweat the small stuff. I have to clean my cupboard out every now and then. But I told you that earlier in my show.'

'I'm glad you're happy,' Greta said.

'Thank you, darlin'. As for Instagram, you know that's all smoke and mirrors, right?' She pointed to her wig. 'It takes hours to get me show-ready. I'm not a natural beauty like you are.'

Had Dr Gale called her a natural beauty? Greta grabbed hold of Ray in shock.

'And what about you, Greta, are you happy?'

'I've had some stuff in my cupboard that fell out recently,' Greta admitted.

'We all have,' Ray said, and Billie and Dylan nodded in agreement.

'Well, you'd better take a seat and have a visit. Tell me everything. Brad, don't just stand there, go get us all a cold drink.'

Greta told her about the cyclone of addiction she'd been in, her stint in rehab, the hooded man who terrorized her nights and her quest to find herself. Ray told her that his life lacked colour in Ireland, because he'd been stupid enough to let opportunity and love pass him by. Billie told her that she was afraid to open her heart to love, because of the aftermath of her father's death. Dylan admitted that he was scared to follow his dream to be a singer and songwriter, letting his stutter hold him back, ever since his dad died. And between them, they told her about their epic road trip, across six states, which led them to her.

'Oh my,' Doctor Gale said. She stood up and began to pace the floor. 'You've all been on quite the adventure. But you know, the greatest adventure of our lives is finding out who we truly are, on the inside.'

She stopped in front of Dylan. 'I think when you travelled to the other side of the world to support your friend, it showed great courage. You are braver than you give yourself credit for. Yes, sometimes terrible things happen for no reason. But I have a suspicion that if you allow yourself to follow that dream of yours, if you find the courage to sing again, something wonderful might happen.'

'I'll tttry,' Dylan said.

'And you Billie. What a strong woman you are. Not just in those splendid muscles you have, but also here.' She tapped Billie's chest. 'You said you are afraid to open your heart again. It's already wide open, darlin'. Just look at how you take care of your mama and your friends here. You have nothing to fear from love. Embrace your vulnerability.'

'I'll try to,' Billie promised.

'And you sir,' Doctor Gale said. 'I think you are the cleverest of them all, aren't you? You know, I've met many learned people, with degrees and doctorates, but they don't have a single bit of common sense between them. Just listening to you share your story, and hearing what your friends and niece have to say, shows me that while you may not have gone to university, you are graduating life with top marks. I think you need to move past the fear of judgement you have. Get out of your own way and start believing in yourself. It's time to come out from the shadows into the sunshine.'

'I give you my word that I will,' Ray said.

'And now my Irish namesake. First and foremost, you need to stop being afraid of the darkness. If you wait long enough, the sunshine always comes. I think you know already that you don't need pills to help you sleep. As for working out who Greta Gale is? Well, darlin', you are on the right path to finding that out already. Stay true to your authentic self. Be kind to yourself. Follow your dreams. Surround yourself with people who love you. Know your own worth. Learn from your mistakes. And remember that you only have one precious life. Make it the very best version you can. From what you've told me, you've been doing just that over the past few weeks. You don't need my help, darlin'. You've had the power within yourself all along.'

Chapter 36

With books signed, photographs taken and promises of further meet-ups if Doctor Greta Gale was ever in Ireland, they said their goodbyes to their heroine. Then they went back to their rooms to get ready for dinner, each of them thinking about the doctor's advice.

Greta smiled all the way through her shower. She had the power herself. Just like Dorothy had.

But that wasn't true. Yet. She had to do something first of all.

With a bath towel wrapped around herself, she pulled out the box of sleeping aids from her handbag, placing the pills in the sink, one by one. Then she turned the tap on. It was time to melt her Wicked Witch of the West. She held her breath as the water dissolved them to nothing.

Ding Dong the witch was finally dead.

She had never felt so powerful in her whole life. Tonight

was going to be a celebration. She didn't need drugs or alcohol to have fun. She just needed her friends.

Greta decided to wear the dress she bought in Manhattan the previous week. It was silver grey midi tea-dress, with cap sleeves. There was a tiny dove print in white that almost looked like a polka dot. She hadn't had the courage to wear it up to now. She stood in front of the mirror and looked at herself, turning sideways and twisting around so she could see her bum.

She wasn't thin. She never would be. But having seen dozens of super-thin, sculpted women on stage at Billie's bodybuilding competition, she realized she didn't want to be like that either. On the other hand, she knew that she couldn't continue her self-sabotage of the previous year. As Susan said, she needed to find her middle ground between the two extremes of the Haley women. She wanted to live. And right now, she felt like that was possible.

She thought about Dylan. Did he like-like her, as Ray suspected? Or did he just like her? She wanted to find out. And if they were meant to be just friends, that was OK. Because she knew now that she was ready to let someone into her life. Every time someone showed any interest in her, she always pushed them away, letting cruel thoughts dictate.

He must only like me because he has a fetish for big girls.

He'll run for the hills if he sees me naked.

If we have sex, I'll probably squash him to death.

And then she saw it. A large green pear sitting at the top of a fruit bowl on the table by the window. Its skin was almost perfect. But it had a small brown blemish near the single stem on top. She touched it and realized that despite this imperfection, it was still quite beautiful. In fact this blemish gave it character. Only a few months ago she'd looked at another pear in a hotel room in London, feeling wretched, despondent, desperate. So much had changed since that day. Greta had learned on this yellow-brick road trip to *her,* that sometimes the best moments in life came when things had gone a bit pear-shaped. . .

Greta stood in front of the mirror and spoke in a loud, clear voice, slowly, letting the words bounce around the room. 'I can't put off loving myself until I reach the perfect size. Because that doesn't exist. But I exist. I'm here. And I promise to love all of me. Every perfectly imperfect pear-shaped bit of me. I am enough. Just as I am right now. I am worthy of love.'

And then she left the room. She was ready to meet Ray, Billie and Dylan. The days of hiding in hotel rooms, while the rest of the world partied, were over.

'Wow, you look fancy,' Billie said when Greta met them in reception.

'I felt fancy tonight,' Greta said with a smile. 'I even put on lip gloss.' She did a twirl.

'You look beautiful. Both of you do,' Ray said. 'I don't know how I managed to snare two of the prettiest ladies as dates . . .'

'Such a charmer,' Billie teased, but she gave him a kiss of appreciation.

'Where's Dylan?' Greta asked, looking at her watch. It wasn't like him to be late.

'He's around. He said we should meet him outside at the fountains,' Ray said.

'Oh, good idea. I can't wait to see the fountain show with all the lights of the Strip,' Greta said.

They walked outside and found a spot in between a group of tourists.

'The show happens every thirty minutes, so the next one should be soon,' Billie said.

'Make a wish,' Ray said, handing each of them a fifty-cent piece.

'How many people make wishes at this fountain, only to have them sink to the bottom of the concrete floor never to come true?' Greta asked.

'I think that for some, no matter how many coins they throw in the fountain, or how many fingers they cross, if it's not meant to be, it just won't happen,' Billie replied.

'Well on that cheery note . . .' Ray said. 'Actually, hang on a minute. Rather than think about the ones that don't come true, why don't we focus on the ones that do? Close your eyes and make a wish, both of you. Go on, give it a try. Goodness knows it's about time one of us had our turn.'

Greta closed her eyes and felt like a child once more, blowing out her candles or throwing coins into a wishing well. Ray was right. She flicked the coin into the water and wished that Dylan . . .

'Hhhhello.'

'Holy shit this fountain is good,' Greta whispered, opening her eyes and seeing him standing before her.

'You lllook beautiful, Silver Lady. Nice dress.'

She felt a blush go from her forehead down to her neck.

They inched closer.

Dylan took a deep breath and tried to steady his mind. He knew what he wanted to tell her. What he had travelled thousands of miles to say and practised in his head dozens of times. But wanting to say something didn't always result in him actually spitting it out.

He was in love with Greta Gale and had been for nearly two years. He was pretty sure she had no clue about this fact. He was good at keeping secrets. The moment he realized he loved her was during rehearsals for the Grayson Castle *Midsummer Murders* show. She was playing the part of the vicar's wife. And in the middle of a scene, she tripped and fell. Everyone went quiet, shocked. But Greta sat up, and she laughed with her whole being. Her eyes, her body, every part of her just filled with mirth, and it was infectious. Everyone in the room roared along with her until they all held their sides, they were bellowing so much. And Dylan thought to himself, I want to hear that laugh for the rest of my life.

Dylan had fantasized about telling her how he felt so many times. But something always kept him back. Someone like Greta would never go for someone like him. He was a tall skinny guy, with a nose that was too big for his face and a mop of curls that refused to be tamed. Whereas she was beautiful, bubbly and funny, and everyone liked being around her. She shone.

'I thought iiiit was time for an Ultimate Ro-ro-ro . . .'

Greta tried to convey in a smile that she was happy to wait as long as Dylan needed to say his words, without interruption.

'Ro-rromantic Gesture!' Dylan finished with a grin.

'If this is a Forrest Gump URG, like the time Jenny and he jumped into the lake in Washington, you can forget about it,' Greta said. 'Just to be clear, I'm not getting into that water.'

'Noted. Plus we might ggget arrested if we did.'

They took another step closer.

'Friends who are in love make the best Ultimate Romantic Gestures. It's a well-known fact,' Dylan said, without a single stutter.

'Friends who are in love?' Greta whispered.

'That's what he said,' Ray jumped in, trying to be helpful. Billie clutched his arm in delight. She was practically hopping up and down on the spot with excitement.

'So what's the big URG then?' Greta asked, her heart thumping so loudly she was sure everyone on the Strip must be listening.

'The fact that the boy flew halfway around the world to surprise you?' Billie said. 'Honestly, Greta, what more do you want?'

Dylan smiled and said, 'Yes. That. But there's more.' He pulled a guitar from behind his back.

'Where did you get that?' Greta asked.

'I borrowed it from Big Bad Dddom.'

'Are you going to sing?' she whispered.

He nodded. 'You keep asking me wwww . . . why I call you Silver Lady. Here's why.'

Dylan started to strum the guitar.

Things like this didn't happen to Greta Gale. Not the Irish one, at least, who hadn't had an interesting thing happen to her since 1995. She looked over to Ray and Billie, who were in each other's arms, swaying to the music.

'Can he sing?' Billie whispered to Ray.

'I've no idea, but I don't think it matters,' Ray replied.

Dylan wasn't sure he could do this. Even as he strummed the opening bars to the song, he was thinking about abandoning his last URG card. But then he looked at Greta in her silver dress, the lights of the Bellagio behind her, framing her face. She looked like an angel. And he thought about how brave she'd been over the past couple of months. He didn't want to be a coward any longer. He wanted to be fierce and fearless, someone Greta could see as something other than a friend. Someone that she might love.

He heard a "whoop whoop" from Billie. Then a deep bellow of laughter followed from Ray. This was it. He blew a curl from his face and started to sing 'Like a Bridge Over Troubled Water'.

'Bloody hell. He's good,' Ray said.

'He's more than good,' Billie said.

Dylan's eyes locked onto Greta's and, for them both, everyone else faded. It was only them and the words in the song. She'd heard it sung by many different artists, but she'd never really listened to the lyrics properly. And she realized with each line, the song was her story. And Dylan's too. He was on her side, drying her eyes whenever she was weary. With every word he sung, she knew he was making a promise to her.

In times of difficulty, he would bring her solace.

Then he stopped strumming the guitar, and he sang unaccompanied, his voice strong. The words of the next verse rang out into the night air, promising Greta that her dreams were about to come true. And then she heard

Dylan's name for her: *Silver Girl. It was from this song!* She brushed the tears away from her face. She was not going to miss this moment with blurred vision! He started to play the guitar again, and by this time the crowd that had gathered began to sing the chorus with him too. When he finished the last note, he took the final two steps towards her. The crowd around them erupted into thunderous applause, but both of them were oblivious to it, only seeing each other.

'Your voice . . . it's incredible,' Greta said.

He grinned. Then grabbed her hand, holding it between his. 'I love you.'

She looked at his tousled curly hair that had grown long and needed a trim, at the start of stubble that had appeared on his chin, and the shirt he wore that could do with an iron.

She felt a jolt. She might as well have been struck by lightning. Greta had been walking around in a trance for years, but at this moment, this perfectly crazy wonderful moment, she was ready to wake up.

'To make this Ultimate Romantic Gesture work, you need to do one more thing,' she whispered.

'What's that?'

'You have to kiss me.'

Chapter 37

The four of them spent the evening together. They ate, they gambled, winning and losing until they broke even. They sat together in the bar at the Bellagio, chatting and laughing, listening to the pianist who sang to them. There was magic in the air that night, and they all felt it.

And when Greta checked Instagram and saw Dr Gale's post, she squealed with excitement.

The photograph she had posted was of the five of them taken earlier, all together in her green room. The doc in the middle of Greta, Ray, Dylan and Billie.

> **drgretagale** Photo of the day. I found my Irish cousins and my namesake. There's a new Greta Gale in town, y'all! And she's quite delightful.
> #family #allthatmattersisfamily #strength #heart #courage #love #power #home #intelligence #positivethoughts #instaquotes #canIgetahellyeah #strong #mindfulness #inspire #quotestagram

That night Dylan stayed in Greta's room with her and this time he took off more than his shoes when he got into bed with her. And Greta was awake for every delicious moment. There were no nightmares that night. In fact, she slept in his arms without waking once until seven a.m. when their alarm went off.

Dylan's perfect execution of an Ultimate Romantic Gesture prompted Ray to grab some of the magic for himself. He'd shared a room with Billie for the past couple of nights and being by her side twenty-four/seven made him feel alive. Unlike any other time in his life. She seemed happy too. So he dared to believe that they had a future together. The only problem was, whenever he tried to discuss what might happen next with her, she shut him down.

But tonight Ray was determined to get her to talk to him. He'd waited years for this, and he wasn't going to let her go again. He suggested a drink, just the two of them, before Greta and Dylan joined them for dinner. He went down to the bar ahead of her while she finished getting ready. He'd ordered them both a martini cocktail, and with the pianist playing a few feet from them, it couldn't have been more perfect.

'Hello you,' Billie said, walking up to him.

'Wow.' He struggled to find words. Billie was wearing a blue dress, the colour of cornflowers. He was glad he'd worn the shirt Greta had talked him into at the beginning of the trip. A classic white that she said looked good on every man when worn with a pair of blue jeans and a jacket.

'Wow yourself.' And she smiled that beautiful smile of hers and made his heart hammer in time to the Billy Joel number being played on the piano.

'I wanted to talk to you—' Ray said.

But Billie's phone rang, cutting him off. 'It's Lucy. I've got to take this. Sorry.' She kissed his cheek and walked out of the bar.

When Billie didn't return in fifteen minutes, he went looking for her. She wasn't in the lobby, so he went upstairs to their room, feeling dread begin to prick at him. She wouldn't leave him on his own unless something were wrong.

As soon as he walked into their room and saw her packing her bag, her face hard once more, he knew he'd lost her.

'Mama is dead. While I was here with you, driving across the bloody I170, she had a massive heart attack. And she died on her own.'

'Oh my god, Billie, I'm so sorry.'

'Stop it. Don't you dare say you're sorry. If you hadn't arrived on my doorstep – something I never asked for – I would have been at home with her.' She pushed past him, her bag in hand. 'I'm going home.'

'Let me drive you. Just give me five minutes to get my things together,' Ray said.

'I'm on my way to the airport. I'll get the next flight out of here. It's over, whatever this was. Go home, Ray.'

'You can't mean that. Not after everything we've been through this week.'

'I mean every word. Don't follow me or I swear I won't be responsible for my actions.' She paused at the door for a moment, and her face softened. And for one moment he thought she was going to change her mind. 'Just promise me one thing. Don't go back to that world you created that was so small. Get out, have adventures. A guy like you is a catch. I keep telling you that. The right woman for you is out there somewhere. But know this for sure. It's never going to be me.'

And she walked out of his life for the second and final time.

Chapter 38

And so the duo, that became a trio, then a quartet, was back to being a trio again.

Greta called Billie and begged her to reconsider her decision. 'Let us help you bury your mama. That's what friends do. I liked her so much, I'd really like to be there, to say goodbye and to help you.'

But Billie was adamant that they should stay away, no matter how hard Greta tried to get through to her. Greta sobbed for Billie's loss. Not just her mama. But for Ray too.

Ray, Greta and Dylan had no choice but to fly home a few days later, each changed by their time on the road trip. Emily and Stephen were waiting in arrivals for them.

'Oh my goodness Stephen, look at our girl. She's smiling!' Emily shouted, waving frantically to her daughter. She ducked under the steel barrier and ran to Greta, pulling her into her arms.

'I've only been gone ten days!' Greta said, laughing, hugging her back hard.

'You look fantastic. There's a glow about you, isn't there Stephen?'

Greta looked at her dad, who was standing back, shuffling his feet. 'Hey, Dad.'

'Hello. Are you OK? You look OK. You look more than OK,' Stephen said.

'I'm really good. Honestly. Do I get a hug?'

'I wasn't sure you wanted one from me,' Stephen said. 'I've been too heavy-handed with you. I can see that now.'

Greta's reply was to move into his embrace and snuggle in close. 'I'm lucky to have you on my side, Dad. I haven't forgotten that.'

'So we're OK? You've forgiven me?' Stephen asked.

'There's nothing to forgive,' Greta said, and realized that this was true. She'd learnt a lot on the road trip from her friends. Not least of which was that Greta was lucky to have both her parents alive. When she thought about Billie and Dylan's pain at losing their fathers, it made her want to weep.

Stephen looked over his daughter's head to his brother Ray. 'Thank you.'

'For what?'

'For taking such good care of my girl.'

'My pleasure,' Ray said.

'Are you going to introduce us to this handsome man?' Emily said, looking Dylan up and down.

'Yes of course! Mam, Dad, this is my . . . my Dylan,' Greta said.

'Dylan, from work? Well now. You'd better come over

for Sunday lunch next week, we've got Ciaran's new girlfriend coming, we might as well have you too,' Emily said to him. 'Besides which, I feel like I know you, seeing as I've been looking at your picture for the past few days.'

Stephen jumped in to explain. 'Your mother has had that picture of you all with Dr Greta Gale blown up and framed.'

'Oh the excitement in my slimming class when I told them that my Greta and Ray were best friends with Dr Greta Gale. And when I told Amanda, she was green!'

'I'm not sure we're best friends,' Ray began, but was shushed by Emily.

'Tttthank you for the invite, Mrs Gale,' Dylan said.

'Oh, what a lovely polite young man,' Emily said, charmed. 'Maybe some of your manners will rub off on my two bowsies at home.'

'Oh I missed you, Mam,' Greta said, going in for another hug.

'See you tomorrow?' Dylan said to Greta, over Emily's shoulder.

'Absolutely.' And as she watched him walk away, her heart fluttered with happiness.

Later that evening, Dylan messaged her to tell her that Greta could have her slot back with the Murder Mystery Crew. While they'd been away, Donna had taken off on a cruise ship for the season, leaving a broken-hearted Jimmy behind. Greta knew that she'd let her cast mates down in the past couple of months. But she was ready to work hard. They all welcomed her back, with nothing but open arms – and a lot of slagging when they found out about the new romance between her and 'the boss'.

With Greta's encouragement, Dylan began to write his own songs. Now that he'd started to sing, he couldn't seem to stop. His mother told him that his father would be so proud of him. He was finally a righteous man in every sense, as his father always wanted for him.

And Greta found the courage to call her agent, Michelle. She hoped in this case her journey wasn't coming to an abrupt end. It took her a few attempts to get a word in edgeways with an irate Michelle, who was determined to have her say about Greta's absence. But once Greta explained about her addiction, her time in rehab and how strong she was feeling now, Michelle was surprisingly understanding.

'Do I have a future with you?' Greta asked. She wanted to know. No more hiding away from truths that she didn't like.

'Do you want to continue doing auditions, hoping for that break? Or is it time for a switch in direction?' Michelle asked.

'I don't want to quit the business. But maybe the business is quitting on me.'

'Here's what I think, for what it's worth. Maybe all this time, something has been holding you back. You've been numbing yourself with drugs. Even so, you've been good, nailing every audition. It's just been bad luck that you've not got your big break yet. Imagine what you can do now that you have your head straight. Maybe now that you are truly alive, you will start to see results. How's that for something to think about?'

Greta was astounded at Michelle's words. 'So you are not firing me then?'

'Of course not. I have faith in you. I keep telling you, Greta. We only need one casting director to say yes.'

She suggested that Greta take a break for a few more weeks, then they could have a chat about the future.

Days became weeks as each of them slotted back into their lives at home in Dublin. At first, Ray found it hard to settle down. He missed Billie, and he wasn't sure he would ever be able to forget her. He sent her a text message every day. But she never answered him. Both Greta and Dylan tried to get her too, but she had disappeared again.

Greta and Dylan spent a lot of time at Ray's house, watching movies with him and reminiscing about their trip. Both of them were worried about Ray. Their care and support kept him going. And he remembered the last thing that Billie had said to him before they said goodbye. *Don't go back to that world you created that was so small. Get out, have adventures.* He had every intention of doing just that.

Greta spoke to Noreen about her relationship with Dylan. There wasn't an express rule against dating in your first year of sobriety, contrary to popular understanding. It was suggested that it was better not to date, as it often took focus off recovery. Noreen told Greta that only she could decide whether it was the right time or not.

'Would you want to date *you* right now? Have you learned to love yourself yet? Because it is only then that you can truly love Dylan and be loved in return.' Noreen had asked.

Greta thought about that a lot. Recovery for her came

one day at a time. But she felt stronger, more sure of herself than she had in years. And being with Dylan made sense when a lot in her life didn't. Her relationship with Dylan was healthy and his support was endless. She felt safe when she was with him and she was her true self, with no smoke or mirrors. And as Uncle Ray said, love couldn't be penciled in at a specific time. When it called, you had to answer it or regret it for the rest of your life.

Greta continued going to NA meetings in the city once a week again, and afterwards she would call to meet Ray for lunch. Today, she had a plan. She was determined to get his profile up on Tinder. She wouldn't take no for an answer. As she walked down the quays towards his office, a man ran out of the local betting shop. He crashed into Greta, almost knocking her off her feet.

'Hey watch it,' Greta said, then froze when she realized who was standing there. 'Oh my god. Sam! Hi!'

Their eyes locked. He looked panicked then resigned.

'Are you OK?' Greta asked. She glanced upwards to the neon green betting shop sign. 'Oh, Sam.'

'You were right. It wasn't just Monday that sucked. It was every day.'

'Have you time for a coffee? We can catch up,' Greta suggested.

He shook his head. Then he pulled his collar up around his neck and walked at speed in the opposite direction. She wanted to cry for him.

'You OK?' Ray asked when she got to his office.

'Do you remember me talking about a guy called Sam from Hope Crossing?'

He nodded.

'He's back gambling. I just saw him come out of the betting shop up the road.'

'Ah, I'm sorry to hear that.'

'So am I. I liked him. I bet his wife didn't take him back. Or maybe she did, and he still gambled. Uncle Ray, don't ever let me relapse.'

'You don't need me to watch over you, Greta. You're doing just fine on your own. But I'll always have your back, of that you can be guaranteed.'

They walked to a nearby bar and ordered soup and sandwiches. 'It's a bit surreal being home, isn't it?' Greta said.

'It is.'

'How are you doing? I don't suppose you-know-who has answered your messages yet.'

'You can say her name. I won't fall to pieces. But I won't lie either. I've had better times. I miss her.'

'I know.' Greta reached over and squeezed his hand. 'I'm so sorry it didn't work out. I miss her too. I thought we were friends. All four of us.'

'I thought we had found our way back to each other . . . She kept telling me not to make it into something it wasn't, but . . .'

'You thought she'd change her mind? I did too, for what it's worth, Uncle Ray. You were good together.'

'It's time I accepted the fact that this wasn't meant to be. I gave it a good shot. At least I can always say that. Let's change the subject and talk about nicer things. Like, for example, how's lover boy?'

Greta beamed.

'That good?' Ray laughed. 'Being happy suits you.'

'He asked me to be his girlfriend. Formally. He said he didn't want any misunderstandings.'

'I take it you said yes.'

'Of course I said yes. I've never had a boyfriend before. I'll probably mess it up.'

'Probably,' Ray agreed laughing. 'Have you been sleeping OK?'

'I seem to be a solid six-hours-a-night gal these days. Who'd have thought it? And this morning Michelle called. My agent. Remember Louise, that casting director I auditioned for in London, just before I free-falled in spectacular fashion?'

'Yeah . . .'

'Well, she rang Michelle and specifically asked for me. There's a part she has in mind that I'm perfect for. She said, and I quote, it's mine to lose.'

'No pressure then.'

'I know! I'm meeting them both for a chat about it all tomorrow.'

Ray leaned over and kissed his niece on her forehead. 'You're creating a nice world for yourself. That makes me very proud.'

'Thank you. Oh and I called the Dogs Trust up, by the way.'

'To check up on your little stray black dog?'

'Yeah. Every time I walk down our street, I half expect to see him. I can't get him out of my head. Which is ridiculous because I barely knew him. So I thought, maybe I'll adopt him. Give him a home. I asked Mam and Dad; they said it was OK with them, as long as I was in charge of any poop situations. And Dad didn't even bang on about the exercise opportunities that walking a dog would give me. I could see him practically holding his hand across his mouth to hold in the lecture!'

'Poor Stephen! But that's great news!'

'Not really. Another couple have already fostered him, with a view to adopting last week. I should have called before we went away. I left it too late.'

'Ah, that's a pity. Will you get another dog, do you think?'

'Dunno. It was him I wanted. What about you, Uncle Ray? Have you been still eating the specials every day? Mixing it up a bit?'

'I had a Thai chicken curry yesterday, I'll have you know. Had heartburn for the night. But don't worry, I'm not going back to the way things were.'

Greta grabbed his phone and started to swipe through the apps. 'Well, first things first, I'm going to get you loaded onto Tinder.'

'That's never going to happen.' He grabbed his phone back. 'But I have a plan. One of the lads in work told me about this friendship club he's in. A place where singles can get together with other singles. They go to the cinema, or for a drink, do a table quiz, that kind of thing. You probably think it's lame.'

'I don't think it's lame at all. I actually think it's very cool. And if I were going onto a table quiz, I'd want you on my team every time. Nobody knows more useless information than you do. And that's surprisingly helpful in a table quiz.'

'Well, as it happens, I've agreed to go with him to a table quiz on Friday night. The way I see it, it's better than sitting in on my own.'

'Brilliant. Jeepers, look at the time. I'd better go. I'm meeting Dylan in a bit. He's got this idea for a song he wants to run by me.'

'My boyfriend is so talented, I really love him . . .' Ray teased. 'Go, live, love, have fun. I'll see you at the weekend.'

As Ray watched his niece run out the door of the pub, he could hardly recognize her from the woman she was only a few months ago. She was going to be OK, he was confident of it. He made his way back to the office and found himself humming 'Pure Imagination' once more. But this time, it didn't irritate him. He wasn't going to stop until he had created a world for himself that he wanted to live in.

And just when he stopped looking for her, she was there, standing outside his office. 'Billie.'

'I've been waiting for you.' She moved closer to him, and he breathed in her scent. He held her in his arms, and she clung to him.

'Thank you for your messages. And for the flowers you sent for Mama's funeral. I'm sorry I didn't answer sooner.'

'How did it go? Sorry, stupid question. I'm sure it was horrendous.'

'It was, as all funerals are, sad. Horrifically sad. She's back with Dad again now. Buried side by side.'

'Did Piper go to the funeral?'

'She did, and announced that she is getting married again.'

'Number four?'

'I think so. It's hard to keep track, to be honest.'

Despite the ordeal of the previous few weeks, Billie looked well. And Ray felt his heart flutter in the way it always did whenever he was near this woman. 'Why are you here, Billie?'

'To apologize for being so horrible to you.'

'You were in shock over your mama, so no apologies necessary.'

'Even so, you deserved better. I figured I owed you an explanation. I realized something after we lowered Mama into the ground. I lost you twenty-four years ago because I was lost myself. And when you came looking for me, I thought, this is it. A second chance. And you helped me navigate my way back. Our time together on that road trip was the best time of my life. It was life-changing.'

'For me too,' Ray said. 'For all of us.'

'I know that I kept saying to you that I wasn't the same girl you used to know. But over the week, I began to think that maybe we could go back to that time and find a new "us" again. But Ray, I'm so sorry, I love you, I really do, but I don't want to be with you.'

So she was here to say one more goodbye.

'And I want you to know this. I don't want to be with anyone. I know it's a cliché, but it really is a case of, it's not you, it's me,' Billie said.

Ray reached over and wiped away the tears that were falling down her cheeks with his thumb. 'Don't cry, my love. You've had too many tears in your life; there's no need for any more, not for me. You've made me so happy. I'll always be grateful for the times we've shared.'

'You deserve someone who can give you everything, Ray. Love, marriage, kids. But I know that's not me. I don't want that. Not any more.'

'What do you want?' Ray asked.

'I don't know. But I've decided it's time to find out. I've sold our house. And I'm going to finally do my tour of Europe. Maybe somewhere out there, I'll get inspiration.'

'I could go with you,' Ray said. It was worth one more shot, he figured.

'That wouldn't work,' Billie said, and he knew she was right. Their time as a couple was gone.

She kissed him one last time. 'Be happy Ray. Promise me that.'

Ray reached into his pocket and pulled out their piece of twine. He placed it into her hand and closed her fingers around it. 'I promise to be happy if you promise to keep this. I told you that this twine bound us together. That's an unbreakable bond. That still stands, but this time it's one of friendship.'

'You still want to be my friend?' Billie asked.

'Of course. For ever.'

There is no place like home.
The Wonderful Wizard of Oz, L. Frank Baum

EPILOGUE

Six months later

Quite a crowd had gathered into the Gale family's small sitting room.

Ciaran and Claire were showing photographs of their recent weekend break in Prague to an unenthusiastic Aidan. Emily and Stephen sat side by side on their sofa, sneaking looks at Ray and his new girlfriend Chloe. They'd been dating for a couple of months, but this was the first time he'd brought her to a family occasion.

'Look at the way she looks at him,' Emily whispered to Stephen. 'She's besotted. I'll have to get a hat before the end of the year, you mark my words.'

'SSsh . . . she'll hear you.' But Stephen had to agree that it did seem serious.

'OK?' Ray asked Chloe, worried that the noisy family get-together might be too much for her.

'It's fun,' she whispered back.

'Even Emily's not-too-subtle interrogation over dinner?'

'Oh, you mean the part where she asked me if I wanted kids or not? That I could have done without,' Chloe said.

'You never answered her,' Ray said, trying to sound nonchalant.

'No I didn't, because it's none of her business. But if you're asking me, then yes, I'd like kids one day. With the right man.'

Ray kissed her and felt a bubble of happiness. He'd been feeling a lot of those lately, ever since he met Chloe at the scouting jamboree that summer. As Greta said to him, when he stopped looking for Billie among the tents, he found something else.

The door opened, and Greta and Dylan walked in. They were inseparable now, rarely apart.

'Come on Judy Garland,' Greta called, and the little black stray she'd found and lost trotted in behind her. 'He' had turned out to be a 'she' in the end. To Greta's joy, fate had stepped in when the couple who'd fostered her changed their minds about keeping her. When the Dogs Trust called Greta to see if she was still interested in adopting, she didn't hesitate to say yes. A decision she never regretted. Now, she couldn't imagine her life without her little spitfire that was named after one of her heroes.

Greta had received her 'six months clean' chip a few weeks previously, and it was one of the proudest moments of her life. She felt strong in her mind and her body as she walked up to the front of the room to collect it. She had the odd nightmare, but the happier she became, the less they seemed to bother her.

The TV show in which Greta had been cast had not started filming yet, due to some internal conflict with the director and the studio. Greta wasn't sure if it would ever be resolved, but that was OK. She had an audition next week for a play, and if that didn't work out, something else would come along. She had faith.

Her phone beeped, and Greta picked it up. It was a message from Billie, sending love to them all.

Billie: Wish I was there with you all. I'm watching on the RTÉ player right now. Give Ray and Dylan my love. Hope Chloe is getting on ok with everyone. I bet they love her. I'll call tomorrow for all the gossip!

Billie had spent less than three months in Europe, then found herself in Durban, where she now volunteered in a monkey rehabilitation centre. Her heart had no limitations as she tirelessly worked to help protect the animals she'd grown to love in the wild.

'Sssh . . . it's time!' Emily squealed, making them all jump.

The nine o'clock news was over, and the adverts were about to start.

In a wonderful twist of fate, Greta had been asked to reprieve her role in the beloved biscuit advert, twenty-five years later. It had been Louise's idea actually, formed from something Greta had said at her audition for Clara all those months ago. She pitched an idea to the biscuit company, to reprieve the advert for its anniversary, and they called Greta's agent to book her almost immediately.

'This is it!' Stephen said. 'Whisht everyone!'

They all watched the scene unfold on the screen. Greta's character woke up in the middle of the night on Christmas Eve, just as she'd done all those years ago. But this time she walked into the kitchen in a pair of red silk pyjamas, her hair tousled.

'You look sexy as hell,' Dylan growled in her ear. And she felt it. She looked damn fine!

The woman on the screen poured a glass of milk for herself, then walked into the sitting room, where she found Santa eating a biscuit.

In a scene that mirrored the one she had done in 1995 when she was only eight years old, Greta said, with a perfect pout, as she placed a hand on her hip, 'I want one too, Santa!'

Then she snatched the biscuit from Santa's white-gloved hand, winking to the camera. Santa laughed his big ho, ho, ho and the advert ended with the caption:

Time moves on, but thankfully some things never change.

'I've never seen her look more adorable,' Emily said to Stephen. 'I think Greta looks very like me in this advert, doesn't she? Are you crying, Stephen?'

He wiped his eyes and said, 'I'm just so proud of her.'

The room filled with shouts and cheers as everyone congratulated Greta. Dylan attempted to pick her up, then decided to spin her around instead. She'd never be *that* thin. She looked at the crazy, madcap family that she loved so much, with Judy Garland running around them all in circles, excitedly yelping so she could join in with the noise.

Greta looked at the paused TV screen where her face was frozen, smiling at the camera. The woman looking back at her had a round face, that was true. And she had a body that came with love handles and back fat. But more than any of that, the woman also glowed with health, happiness and sheer joy.

It had taken the help of three special friends and an epic road trip, but she'd accomplished her goal.

She'd found Greta Gale.

She was loved and she loved with every perfectly imperfect pear-shaped part of herself.

And she was enough, just as she was.

Dear Reader,

When I started teasing out my idea about a woman who goes on a search to find her famous namesake, I had no idea where the story would bring me.

Body image, addiction and big balls of twine oh my . . .

In fact, wonderfully, my research brought me on the very journey you have been on. With Mr H by my side, we undertook an epic road trip of our own – driving through the prairie plains of Kansas, the snow-capped Colorado Rockies, the mighty red rocks of Utah, ending our trip at the bright lights of Las Vegas. It was one of the best holidays of my life.

One of the epigraphs I use in this book is from *The Road to Oz*, by L. Frank Baum. *It isn't what we are, but what folks think we are, that counts in this world.*

He was a wise one, wasn't he? I wonder, did Mr Baum realize how accurate this statement would still be one hundred years later? When I started to write Greta's story, one of my close friends said to me, 'You need to open a vein on this one.' And Catherine was right, because in order to do Greta's story justice I had to dig deep. Greta's character is overweight and struggles with her own self-worth. She's an aspiring actress, where thin is in and fat is not all that. Life is not easy for her, but she doesn't let the world know that. While Greta's life is very different to mine, we share one thing in common – that voice in our heads, the heckler, the naysayer who feels compelled to tell us that we are not *enough*.

Through the many drafts of this book, I realized that this writing experience was different to any other I've had to date. This time, it felt personal. I knew there could be no holding back. I had to open those veins and look at my own negative body image, to really understand Greta and her struggles. And as over used as the word often is, this book brought *me* as well as Greta on a journey.

Here's what I've learned. We know in our heads that we must love our bodies whatever shape and size they are, for good mental health. But the truth is that putting that knowledge into practice is difficult, sometimes impossible. Because we also know, thanks to images and articles on social media and in magazines, that life could be a whole lot better for us if we only had a thinner body, better hair, flawless skin, were taller, shorter, cleverer . . . the list goes on and on.

You know, I've been on a diet, on and off, for my entire adult life. In fact, the first diet I can remember going on was when I was twelve years old. Since then I've been super skinny and I've been fat and I've been everything in between. Greta's tricks to hide her weight are borrowed from me and I suspect many of you too use them. The cushion on my lap, sleeves to hide my wobbly arms, oversized jewellery to distract from my mum tum, hiding behind friends and family in photographs.

Like Greta, I've never been happy with the size I am.

Even when I was at my thinnest, I often didn't feel *enough*. Isn't that sad? Wouldn't it be great to go back and whisper some truths in our younger selves' ears? Tell us that we are smokin' hot just as we are. In fact, watch this space, I might just write about that very thing one day soon . . .

But here's the good news. As I've gotten older, I've also grown a little wiser and in the main, acceptance has come my way. I'm bored with the weight conversation that I've had for decades, with friends, family but most of all, with myself and that heckler in my head. I want to teach my children a new narrative, that doesn't include the self-loathing. I want them to understand that a lot of things we see on social media have been filtered and airbrushed. I want to pull back the curtain so to speak and show the truth of the Wizard, who has his own hangups. More than anything I want my children to grow up feeling *enough*.

I don't have all the answers, I'll have to work on my mental, emotional and health wellbeing for the rest of my life. We all do. But, I do know this. I'm perfectly imperfect as I am and so are *you*. My size does not change my worth. I am enough. *We are enough.*

Now the other thing that I wanted to mention about *My Pear-Shaped Life* is its connection to *The Wizard of Oz*!

I'm often asked about my love of all things *Oz*. And I especially love getting messages from my readers when they spot an *Ozism* in one of my books. The movie came first for me. I can't remember a childhood Christmas that didn't include a trip down the yellow brick road. But it was only when I was ten or eleven that I picked up a copy of the book from the library. And I realized that Baum's *Oz* was so much more than my beloved movie. Since then, I've read the complete collection of books (there are fourteen) and I've read, watched and loved all books and movies that have a connection to *Oz* too.

Somewhere Over The Rainbow sung by the irreplaceable Judy Garland, is one of the lullabies that I sing at bedtime to my children. It always calms them, making them feel loved and safe. I love *Oz* because it taught me that if I know myself, truly know my mind, my heart, my courage, then I'm always home.

When I explored plot lines and characters for this book I kept going back to one of the most iconic of all road trips – that of Dorothy and her friends on the yellow brick road. And I realized that our stories shared many themes – hidden inner strengths, the power of friends and finding our true selves as we make our way home. I hope readers had fun finding the *Oz* parallels that are scattered amongst this read. I should stress that *My Pear-Shaped Life* was never intended to be a fantasy read. It has its two feet firmly in the world that we all live in – one with many shades of grey, multi-technicolour and everything else in between. We need rain and sunshine to get those gorgeous rainbows, right?

Hopefully, even if you've never read or watched *The Wizard of Oz* you will have enjoyed reading Greta's story. But I think *Oz* lovers will enjoy the parallels and the imagery, from the obvious to the more subtle. I look forward to book club chats with readers where we can tease these out in person!

As with all my books, despite my many months

researching the issues in this novel, I'm sure that there are some errors. All mine! Please forgive me for any that jar.

Finally, to my lovely readers, I hope you've enjoyed meeting Greta and her friends. Some of you have been with me from the beginning, other readers I've picked up along the way. But all of you are in my heart. Every time you get in touch, reviewing a read on Amazon or Goodreads, find me on social media or via my website for a chat, come to see me in person at an author event, you give me a gift. You really do. I hope you enjoyed *My Pear-Shaped Life* and will take it into your hearts. For reading group questions about *My Pear-Shaped Life* visit my Facebook page or website.

Love,
Carmel

ACKNOWLEDGEMENTS

Writing a book is hard! But it's made considerably easier with the help of the many Glindas I have in my life. This comment will only make sense if you've read the book!

I've said it many times, because it's true – when I signed with my agent Rowan Lawton, my writing career began to make sense. We've had many adventures over the past couple of years and I know there are many more to come. Rowan, thank you for your enduring faith and support in me. You are a warrior, a dear friend and your editorial advice is always spot on. Every single suggestion you made during this process, helped to make Greta's story better. I would also like to thank the very lovely Eugenie Furniss who helped me tease out plot lines when Greta's world was just a seed of an idea, waiting to grow roots.

The entire team at HarperCollins will always have my gratitude. I've been with them from the beginning and over the years we've become friends as well as colleagues. Thank you Charlie Redmayne, Kate Elton, Kimberley Young, Lynne Drew, Ellie Wood, Elizabeth Dawson, Jaime Frost, Claire Ward, Adam Humphrey, Sarah Shea, Tony Purdue, Patricia McVeigh, Jacq Murphy, Ciara Swift and the many many people who work behind the scenes to make my words a finished novel. But most of all, thank you Charlotte Ledger, my editor. The best word I can use to describe Charlotte is extraordinary. Working with Charlotte is a joy and I trust her editorial judgement implicitly. When she pushes me to dig deeper, she's always right. So, special thanks to you Charlotte, for guiding me to find more lovely with each book we do together.

Hazel Gaynor and Catherine Ryan Howard, there are not enough words to thank you both. You keep me sane, you keep me entertained, you keep me in good stationary and French 75's, but most of all, you keep *me* in your tribe. Here's to a future filled with *corners* with you two by my side.

I would like to thank the clever book retailers, media, book bloggers and libraries who work tirelessly to find new ways to get books into the laps of readers. Your passionate love of all things literary helps authors like me, every day. As does the incredible team at Tyrone Guthrie. I've started my last four books at this incredible writing retreat. There's magic in that Monaghan air.

Thank you to the writing community that make me smile whenever we get together or chat on social media. Too many to mention, but there are a few that must have a special shout-out. Claudia Carroll, Debbie Johnson, Caroline Grace Cassidy, Alex Brown, Cecelia Ahern,

Marian Keyes, Paul Dunphy Esq, Vanessa O'Loughlin, Shane Dunphy, Fionnuala Kearney, Margaret Madden, Maria Nolan, Madeleine Keane and Andrea Carter.

Thank you to Valerie Whitford, Evelyn Moher and Jill Stratton who help with admin in *Carmel Harrington's Reading Room*, on Facebook. This group with monthly reading challenges and bookish chat, is so much fun to be a part of. New members are always welcome, so come find us!

To all at Virgin Media One on the *Elaine* show, but in particular Elaine Crowley, Sinead Dalton and Ruth Scott, thank you for letting me be part of your gang. I've had some hilarious moments with my fellow panelists on that show. And thank you to fellow panelists Eunice McMenamin and Caroline Grace Cassidy who answered my questions about life as an actress.

To my dear friends who make my day brighter every day – Ann & John Furlong, Margaret & Lisa Conway, Fiona & Philip Deering, Davnet & Kevin Murphy, Gillian & Ken Jones, Siobhan & Paul O'Brien, Sarah & John Kearney, Caroline & Shay Hodnett, Liz Bond, Siobhan Kirby and Maria Murtagh – thanks for all the laughter and support.

And now to my O'Grady and Harrington families who make me laugh almost every day in our various WhatsApp groups. You guys always have my back and I hope you know that I have yours too. So thank you Tina & Mike O'Grady, Fiona, Michael, Amy & Louis Gainfort, John, Fiona & Matilda O'Grady, Michelle & Anthony Mernagh, and Sheryl O'Grady, Ann & Nigel Payne, Michael Gates & Rita Timson, Evelyn Harrington, Adrienne Harrington

& George Whyte, Evelyn, Seamus & Patrick Moher, and Leah Harrington!

And now to my H's. George Bailey, our rescue dog and newest member of our family, you keep my feet and heart warm every day, while I write. Eva my clever step-daughter who makes all of our days more fun when she comes to visit. My children, sweet, thoughtful, artistic Amelia and funny, kind, Elvis-loving Nate, I know I tell you this every day, but let's go for it again – I love you both. So much. And last but never least, my husband Roger, Mr H, who has been my constant since the day we met. Thank you for being considerate and supportive of my crazy deadlines. And for making me a cup of tea every morning as soon as you wake up. But most of all, thank you for loving me.

My final thanks goes to you, the reader. I promise to keep writing books for you all for as long as you want to read them. I hope you enjoyed Greta's pear-shaped life. If you did, come find me for a chat and tell the world! Oh and one last thing – always remember that you are *enough,* just as you are.

Carmel